WHEN THE CARNIVAL CAME

WHEN THE CARNIVAL CAME

An Olivia Penn Mystery

THE OLIVIA PENN MYSTERY SERIES
BOOK IV

KATHLEEN BAILEY

First hardcover edition: November 2024
First paperback edition: November 2024

ISBN (hardcover): 978-1-956270-12-9
ISBN (paperback): 978-1-956270-11-2
ISBN (e-book): 978-1-956270-07-5
ISBN (audio): 978-1-956270-13-6

Editing by Serena Clarke at Free Bird Editing
Proofreading by LaVerne Clark at LaVerne Clark Editing
Cover design by Robin Vuchnich at My Custom Book Cover

Published by:
Rhino Publishing LLC

www.kathleenbaileyauthor.com

For Marcy
Thank You

Some things have to be believed to be seen.

— MADELEINE L'ENGLE

Olivia Penn stood at the foot of the dock, staring at the thirty yards of worn pine extending into Lake Crystal. The gentle spring breeze rustled through the lush forest, spreading the sweet scent of Virginia bluebells all the way to her. As a child, she'd run without hesitation onto the dock and jump into the water, never fazed by the creaks or wobbles of the knotted slats. Often, she thought only of outleaping her friend A.J., who frequently raced alongside her and playfully teased that she couldn't beat his perfected cannonball.

Now those memories felt like they belonged to a different person. With her focus fixed on the end of the dock, all she saw was the replay of the last time she'd been here. Six months ago in October, she'd made a desperate one-way dash onto the dock, chased by a man who then tried to drown her.

Processing the events from that night was still a work

in progress. She would occasionally bring her father's beagle puppy, Buddy, to the park to play fetch or go for walks, but she would always stay on the front side, nearest the entrance. She'd stare at the trail that cut through the forest and led to the lake, thinking it would be the day she set her eyes on the dock again. But there had always been some excuse not to. She was running late. It looked like rain. Buddy needed to be fed.

Today was different. Now she stood two feet from the dock, ready to let go of that moment from her past. Perhaps the passage of time had steeled her courage, allowing her to trust that she would be okay. Maybe, too, it had something to do with the strong, supportive hand wrapped around her fingers, fitting like a glove tailor-made for her.

The romance that had sparked between her and Preston Hills over Christmas felt different from any other she'd experienced. They'd grown close through a series of traumatic events, which gave them a true under-standing of each other even before their relationship began. He'd ignited more in her heart over the last five months than her previous boyfriend had in two years. That was both exhilarating and unsettling. She found everything about him attractive, and from the way he held her, she sensed he felt the same. She'd fallen hard and fast for him, but her prior relationship had left her hesitant. Now a simple walk on the dock didn't seem nearly as scary as did trusting in her heart for what she hoped was real.

"You don't have to do this," Preston said, caressing her wrist with his thumb.

She turned and looked up into his cognac-brown eyes. His chiseled jawline was even more pronounced under his freshly trimmed, short-stubble beard. "It's so silly."

Releasing her hand, he pulled her tightly against his chest. He tenderly stroked the back of her head, then glided his hand down the lengths of her blonde hair to where it ended a few inches below her shoulders. "It's not silly at all. Nobody would blame you for never wanting to step on the dock again."

She knew he was right, and this wasn't about proving something to herself or anyone else. After everything that had happened to her over the past year, she was confident that walking onto the dock wouldn't turn her into a puddle. Yet, she'd avoided doing so for six months, and that niggled at her.

She rested her hands on his broad shoulders, still feeling the rush of adrenaline from their close contact. Morning coffee lingered on his breath, but they'd passed the point of that mattering. "Thanks for coming with me."

His dimple popped as he gave her an extra-tight squeeze. "There's nothing else I'd rather be doing on a beautiful May day."

"Yeah, right," she jested, as they loosened their hold. "I'm sure escorting a damsel in distress onto a dock is your ideal Sunday afternoon."

"I'm glad you wanted me here."

These days she always wanted him near. Since their first date on New Year's Eve, they had talked daily and now got together several times a week. On Tuesdays, he was a regular for dinner at the home she shared with her father, William Penn. She'd usually spend Saturday or Sunday afternoons at his house. Sometimes they'd eat lunch outside on his picnic table. Sometimes they'd walk in the field behind his house. Sometimes they'd just talk, rocking on his front-porch swing.

Her father and Preston got along well. The last man she'd dated wasn't her father's favorite, but he generally stayed out of her love life and kept most of his opinions to himself. She'd always wondered whether he would've been more vocal with his reservations if she had gotten engaged to her former flame. Thankfully, it never had gone that far, but she hoped he wasn't holding back any similar concerns about Preston.

Preston's mother had championed the pairing from the get-go. Almost from the day Olivia came home to Apple Station to visit her father, just about a year ago, Bev had unapologetically encouraged a relationship between her and Preston. Olivia's first meeting with him wasn't under pleasant circumstances. The last thing she could have imagined back then was standing next to him feeling the way she did now. Since they'd become a couple, Bev had stopped meddling, happy to allow nature to take its course.

"Shall we do it?" Preston asked.

"Let's."

With two steps and a pounding heartbeat, she stood on the first dull gray board of the dock. The decking had seen better days, and many townsfolk advocated for its full restoration, but local budget constraints limited annual repairs to the replacement of only the weakest and wonkiest of the weathered wood slats. The straight, open platform had no railings or offshoots. A kayak lift and a ladder accessorized the far end, and visitors frequently used both on warm weekends. The last time she was here, an algae bloom had colored portions of the lake toxic green, but on this sunny day in early May, the water was sapphire blue.

She kept to the middle of the dock, trusting Preston wouldn't have an issue with skirting its edge. Her stomach tumbled before they got a quarter of the way out, and the muscles at the base of her skull tensed, making her head feel heavy and constricted. As she took a deep breath, he wrapped his arm around her shoulders and shifted closer. His hand slid down to where her T-shirt's short sleeve ended, comforting her like a weighted blanket.

She followed the smooth swimming of two mallards, trailed closely by six brown-feathered ducklings. The adults circled their shadowing brood, creating ripples that bobbed the babies and incited high-pitched quacking.

"Your dad is coming home tomorrow, right?" Preston asked.

"Yes. He drove up to Chantilly and parked at a

friend's house. His friend took him to the airport and is picking him up again. It saved my dad a boatload on parking fees at the terminal. I wanted to drive him there and then meet him when his plane arrived back, but he insisted on doing it this way."

Her father had been away for the past three weeks at a renowned baking school in Oregon. She'd splurged at Christmas, buying him a course of professional lessons as a gift. His enthusiasm for baking had sparked when he volunteered to help her with a special holiday feature for *The Apple Station Times*. Though gainfully employed as an advice columnist for a newspaper in D.C., she occasionally did freelance, unpaid work for the town's local paper. In December, her weekly hometown column had morphed into "The Twelve Bakes of Christmas," turning her father into a Paul Hollywood wannabe.

"I bet he's glad to be coming home," Preston said as they approached the halfway point.

A tiny splash caught her attention, and she glanced off to her side as a silvery fish jumped twice more above the water's surface. "He is. I talked to him this morning, and he already has plans for what he wants to bake when he gets back."

Two boys playfully screamed on the shore, and she jerked her head in their direction, checking that they were okay.

Preston pulled her closer and lightly massaged her arm. "I don't mind being a guinea pig if he needs taste testers."

As they neared the end of the dock, she leaned into him, wrapping her arms around his waist. "I think you're trying to distract me."

His guilty smile confirmed her suspicion. "Is it working?"

They stopped and turned to face each other. "Since we made it all the way out, and I'm still standing, I would say yes."

"How do you feel?"

She took an easy, deep breath and exhaled freely. "Okay. I don't know why I had such a mental hang-up about this."

He held her eyes for a moment, then leaned down and brushed her lips with a gentle kiss.

"And how do you feel now?" he whispered.

She tried to suppress a smile, but the butterflies in her stomach refused to let her play it cool. "Even better."

He matched her flirtatious grin and moved in for what she knew would be a fiery encore. Just as their lips met, his cell rang, suspending them in the intimate pose. They both laughed, jinxing each other, knowing what came next.

"To be continued," he said. Then he backed away, dug his phone out of his jeans pocket, and answered the call. "Detective Hills … Hi, Kevin … Yeah, I know. Hold on for a second." He lowered the phone, mouthing to her, "I'll just be a minute."

She nodded, looking out across the lake as he paced a few feet back along the dock. Such interruptions were par for the course. That was what happened when you became involved with a cop, especially in a small town with only a few full-time officers. He seemed to get called about every incident, whether minor or major, and she accepted that came with the territory.

The mallards and ducklings swam past her, gracefully gliding toward the shore. She and A.J. used to meet regularly at the park for picnics until the murder that occurred here in October. She glanced up at the bluebird sky and then at all that was blooming around her, thinking it was time they resumed their weekly get-togethers by the lake.

"Alright, Kevin, I'll see you soon." Preston ended the call and pocketed his phone. "Sorry about that."

"Was that Kevin Fields?"

"Yeah."

Kevin was Preston's good friend and a former park ranger. His parents owned Fields Farm just off the Snickersville Turnpike. They'd planned to sell the organic farm in the fall, but the buyers backed out after the family ran into legal troubles. Now Kevin was learning the business of running the farm from his parents and helping to manage its daily operations.

"How's he been?" she asked.

"He's good. He seems really taken with the farm, and his parents are thrilled to have him on board." He gently grasped her hand. "I'm sorry. I have to cut today short. Something's come up. I wanted to spend as much time here as you needed, but we'll come back. Maybe after work one day this week."

"No worries. I feel okay. Like I said, it was silly."

"Stop saying that. It's not silly."

They turned and strolled hand in hand back to the shore.

"I saw the flyers around town for the carnival they're having at the farm," she said.

"That's what Kevin was calling about. The entourage pulled in about an hour ago, and there's already trouble."

"What's going on?"

"Some in the crew are getting into it with the people who have shown up on-site looking for jobs. Carnivals attract a *unique* workforce."

"It's a hard job. A lot of physical work for very little pay. Carnival workers get a bad rap."

"Sometimes yes, sometimes no. Kevin's parents were on the fence about hosting the carnival, but they need the money. He said they're getting a good fee for leasing the land. They're even receiving a portion of the gate over a certain amount."

"Interesting. So how does this involve you?"

"Kevin asked if I could come by as a show of force, just to let the crew know that he'll call the police on them if they get out of line."

She playfully bumped his shoulder. "That sounds a little like intimidation."

"Nah, me?" he joked. "It's only a friendly meet and greet."

They were halfway along the hard-packed dirt trail leading back to the front side where Preston had parked his F-150 truck. Blooming mountain laurel thrived in the partial shade on both sides of the path. The delicate white petals looked like tiny bells, and their fragrance reminded her of a grape-flavored drink she used to enjoy as a child.

"We'll have to go to it," she said.

"To the carnival?"

"Yes. I've always loved carnivals, since I was a kid. Especially at night, when everything's all lit up."

"Okay. Maybe next weekend. But you're not getting me on any rides. I don't trust them one bit."

"Agreed. I'm with you on that."

When they got back to his truck, he opened the passenger door for her and closed it once she was settled. After getting behind the wheel, he pulled out of the lot and headed back to her house. They lowered the windows, allowing the refreshing air to flow through the cabin, and listened to country music on the twenty-minute drive home.

"What are you doing the rest of the day?" he asked.

"Probably some housework. I have to water Sam's plants too. In fact, you can drop me off at her place."

Sam was the Penns' neighbor and Olivia's good friend. She'd moved into A.J.'s childhood home a few years ago, but they weren't acquainted until last May. She was a former Marine who now worked as a security consultant. In December, Olivia had witnessed Sam's unique skill set during a life-and-death standoff, realizing there was more to her than met the eye. She frequently traveled for work, and Olivia always gathered her mail and watched her house when she was away.

After turning onto Olivia's lane, Preston slowed in approaching Sam's house, pulled into her driveway, and stopped near the top. As he shifted into park, Olivia unfastened her seatbelt, leaned across the center console, and met his lips for a parting kiss.

"To be continued," he said.

She nuzzled against his chest for a moment, managing a nod, then slipped back over to the passenger side. "To be continued." She opened the door, swung her legs out of the cab, and slid down off the seat. "Thanks again for this afternoon. Be careful."

"Will do."

Matching his smile, she closed the door then waved as he backed down the driveway. Once he was out of sight, she went up onto the porch and entered Sam's house through the front door. She proceeded to the kitchen and made quick work of watering two African violets in the sink. After they drained, she set them back on the windowsill, perfectly positioned to catch the afternoon sun. Then she went about doing her cursory checks, ensuring that all was secure. Although expecting nothing otherwise, she always did a walk-through regardless. That's what Sam would do if the roles were reversed, so she'd do the same.

After the first floor passed muster, she went upstairs

and did a look-see through all the opened rooms. A guest bedroom, an office, and a meditation nook all remained unsurprisingly undisturbed. Sam only ever kept one door shut, and Olivia knew from all the time she'd spent in the house as a child that this was the main bedroom. Though she'd been inside it when Sam was home, she never trespassed while doing her checks.

With nothing out of place, she was about to breeze past the bedroom when a muffled, distinctive ring from a cell phone sounded from inside. She froze for a beat, then turned, facing the door until the standard ringtone ended.

Huh. That's weird.

She stepped closer to the bedroom, put her ear up to the door, and listened. Sam would always give her a heads-up when she was coming home. That was her typical MO anyway, but she hadn't been in contact for several days. The cell rang again, and Olivia stood still, waiting until it stopped. Then, even before she could debate whether to go in, the ringing resumed. Whoever was calling expected or desperately wanted the phone to be answered. Sam's voicemail had probably picked up each call, which seemed to prompt the caller to redial.

Positioning her hand to knock, Olivia stopped short of making contact with the door.

Did Sam come home? Why wouldn't she have told me? She had to hear me downstairs. Maybe she's not alone.

As the phone rang once more, she pegged the probability that someone was in the room as low, but not impossible. In all the times she'd watched Sam's house, this had never happened before. She could have dismissed her curiosity about the oddity if she weren't concerned that there might be some sort of emergency. Surely, if Sam was inside, she would've answered the calls. While the ringtone played for the fifth time, she grabbed the shiny satin-nickel knob. Then, with a quarter turn and a little push, she cracked open the door.

CHAPTER 2

Filtered light from the two covered windows dimly lit the room, allowing Olivia to see the bed and the nightstand. Stilling her breath, she leaned closer to the gap and listened for shuffling or rustling. As a veteran of hide-and-seek in the house from when she was a child, she knew the best covers in A.J.'s old bedroom were in the closet and behind the bathroom door. The closet was always the best option, as she could huddle in its corners and remain undetected if he were too hasty with his search.

With her thoughts wildly wavering between silly over-reaction and slasher-film terror, she rifled through the worst-case scenarios. In theory, the external security cameras around the house should've alerted Sam to any breaking and entering. The camera feeds linked to an app on Sam's cell, which appeared to be in the bedroom without her. Surely, Olivia opening the door would've prompted a response if someone was inside. She rocked back on her heels, second-guessing not returning to the kitchen to grab the largest knife from the countertop block.

Getting a grip, she reached through the narrow gap, feeling for the wall plate about a hand's width from the doorframe. With bang-bang execution, she flipped the light switch up and swung open the door. Two white ceramic lamps on a six-drawer oak chest illuminated the room. Five unanswered calls, but no bogeyman or Sam in sight. The ringtone sounded again, seemingly from inside the top drawer of the nightstand. Figuring it was better to be safe than sorry, and to ease her nerves, she moved quickly to ensure no one was there.

She went straight to the closet and pulled open the louvered bi-fold doors. Facing her were a tidy array of hanging clothes, a stack of plastic storage drawers, and a shoe rack with more high heels on it than she would've guessed Sam owned. Instinctively, she pushed in the blouses toward the back, not expecting to poke someone and sure as sugar not knowing what would happen if she did. Then she checked both corners, finding them occupied with narrow shelving units that not even the tiniest of monsters could hide in.

She backed away from the closet as the cell silenced, crept past the oak dresser, and peeked into the open bathroom. *Great.* The shower liner was closed. Unpleasant memories flashed of her and A.J. watching *Psycho* in this very room, unbeknownst to their parents, when she was only ten. That ill-advised choice led to her lifelong habit of triple checking the bathroom door lock before showering. Now she wished she'd gone back for the knife. But surely, if someone was just a few feet from her, she'd sense it. *Right?* A rustle of clothes, a slight shift in stance, a hint of breathing.

Looking over her shoulder, she scanned the room for anything lying around that she could use to poke at the liner from a distance. The bedroom, like the rest of the house, was neat and sparse. She always thought of Sam's decor choices as Swedish death cleaning meets Special Forces. A hefty, hardcover novel within arm's reach on the dresser corner would do. She picked up the burly volume, kept behind the doorframe, and flung it toward the shower.

The white vinyl liner whooshed inward, and the book thunked in the tub. She relaxed her stance, freeing a held breath, as an automatic fragrance dispenser on the counter puffed out a shot of vanilla mist.

"I'm sure that's *exactly* what Sam would've done." She went over to the tub, ripped open the liner, and picked up the book. After a quick inspection to ensure the toss hadn't damaged the hardcover, she put it back where it belonged. *No harm, no foul, nobody ever needs to know.*

Now certain that she was alone, she stared at the nightstand, questioning whether to look inside the drawer. Why would anyone repeatedly call a cell not in Sam's possession? Sam was intentional about everything, so it was no accident she'd left it in the bedroom. Olivia had never seen her with multiple phones, but it made sense she'd have a dedicated one for work. Perhaps she normally didn't take her personal cell with her on a job. *Seems reasonable, but is it?*

A rattle and a muted buzz from inside the drawer suggested that the caller's strategy had shifted to texting. Curiosity and concern convinced her that Sam would want to know what was going on. If the situation was reversed, Sam wouldn't hesitate. She crossed the room to the nightstand, which looked much like her own. The narrow top drawer was about half the size of the bottom one. Separating them was a storage cubby containing a long-handled flashlight, a camp lantern, and a mini bat.

She slid the drawer open, finding two phones, a journal, and a large, sheathed knife. She tapped on the screens, and though both cells were locked, one displayed the preview of the text that had been sent by the caller less than a minute ago.

The lone word, "Answer," sounded too pressing to ignore, making her choice simple. She took her phone out of her jeans pocket, found Sam's number, and dialed. A second later, the other cell in the drawer lit up, displaying Olivia's name. *Super.* She hung up and switched tactics, sending Sam an e-mail asking for a callback ASAP.

She sat on the edge of the bed and eyed the sheathed knife, wondering if Sam had ever had to use it. This past Christmas, Olivia's father had gifted her a tactical pen, which she kept on her nightstand next to a notepad.

Though it was meant for self-defense, thus far she had found it more useful for recording random musings in the middle of the night. Leaning down toward the cubby, she grabbed the mini bat, guessing that it weighed about two pounds. She imagined a well-placed swing would inflict substantial soft tissue damage. Speculating on how many more weapons Sam had stashed in the room, she thought perhaps it was time to up her own home-defense cache.

She put the bat back and glanced at her cell, seeing a new message in her inbox. A tap revealed a standard out-of-office reply from Sam that lacked a return date or any additional numbers for help in her absence. Going zero for two, one option remained. Sam had given her an emergency number to use if she were ever in dire straits. This certainly didn't seem to rise to that level, and the last thing she wanted to do was raise a false flag. But what if the missed calls and text related to whatever Sam was involved in?

Not likely, but it's possible.

She closed the drawer, stood, and scrolled to the fake contact in her directory where she'd stored the emergency number. After a smidgen of debate, she went with her gut and dialed. Two rings, then three distinctive rising tones sounded, and an automated message played: "The number you have reached is no longer in service."

Wonderful. So much for getting in touch with you in an emergency.

Now both a stranger and Olivia were trying to get hold of Sam, but she appeared to be off-the-grid. There was nothing more Olivia could do, and none of this was her business anyway. She'd simply wanted to ensure everything was okay in the bedroom and that Sam knew someone had been attempting to reach her.

She went over to the closet and closed it, glancing at a framed photo on the dresser of Sam and her late husband, Aaron. The same picture in a different frame sat on the fireplace mantle in the living room. They'd been married for less than a year when he was killed in combat. Olivia never asked much about him, as Sam always insisted that she'd gotten past his death a long time ago. In the photo, they were on a beach in the Caribbean with the sunset blazing behind them. Aaron looked like a Top Gun pilot with a broad smile, a buzz cut, and sparkling blue eyes. Olivia always sensed a familiarity when looking at the picture, though she couldn't pinpoint why.

She crossed the room, turned the lights off, and shut the door. Hopefully, Sam would return soon, and all of this would end up being much ado about nothing. But for now, with no way of getting hold of Sam, all Olivia could do was wait and cross her fingers that this was something they'd laugh about later.

CHAPTER 3

When she returned home, three small shipping boxes sat stacked on the porch's top step, waiting to join the bevy of other parcels piled in the living room. Frequent deliveries had been the norm over the past two weeks, thanks to her father, who'd been ordering new baking wares to update their kitchen based on the school's recommendations.

She'd guessed that several thin rectangular boxes contained sheets, racks, or pans. In handling the soft mailers, she deduced that a pastry brush, a wire whisk, and an offset spatula would soon be added to the mishmash of utensils in their stoneware crock. A large, heavy box most likely contained a stand mixer, which would claim a permanent spot on the kitchen counter. Though their vintage chrome-finished mixer was a workhorse, it wobbled at higher speeds, and two of the beaters were bent. It had suited their needs until her father wanted one with a larger capacity. A replacement was long over-due, and she hoped he'd picked out a bright color that would pop in the kitchen.

She gathered the three small brown boxes, cradled them in her arm, and opened the front door. Buddy scampered down the steps with his collar tags jangling and came straight to her, barking an exuberant greeting.

"Hey there, little guy."

He circled her and sniffed at the packages as she closed the door.

"Sorry, not for you. I'm sure Dad gotcha something, somewhere in all this stuff."

He followed her as she placed the boxes among all the others. After giving him a few pets under his chin, she went over to the couch to check on their house guest, Willow. The white, short-hair cat had been living with them since the start of the new year. She and her father had agreed to watch Willow while her owner, June Warner, was visiting family in North Carolina. When Olivia's good friend Paige passed away last May, her mother June took Willow into her home. Olivia and Willow were buds from the time Paige had adopted her, so the arrangement was a natural fit. June had returned to Apple Station in April, but she and her sister were leaving to embark on an Alaskan cruise in two weeks. Rather than shuttle Willow back and forth, all were happy to have her remain in the Penns' home. She seemed well-adjusted, and Olivia secretly didn't want her to leave.

Willow lounged across the top of the sofa with her head turned slightly to one side and all her limbs hanging in harmony with gravity. Olivia stroked her back and brushed her cheek. Willow blinked, then narrowed her eyes and purred, sounding like a tiny motor.

After giving the cat a few scratches behind her ear, Olivia went into the kitchen, grabbed a diet soda from the refrigerator, and sat at the table. She popped the can's tab and glanced at the food and water bowls on the floor. As usual, Buddy had demolished his dry kibble, and puddles lay on the mat from his tsunamic lapping from his bowl. Willow, in contrast, was a petite eater who hardly ever finished her meal or displaced a single drop of water. True to form, the cat seemed to have cleaned up after herself.

Olivia leaned to one side, took her cell out of her pocket, and checked the time. At just past seven, the sun wouldn't set for another hour. Looking at her e-mail, she saw that Sam hadn't replied, but she wasn't expecting her to anyway. Slipping the phone back into her pocket, she considered a remote possibility—Sam's security cameras.

She wouldn't go away blind. I'm sure whatever phone she has can access the feed. I could write a note, "Call me ASAP," and hold it up to a camera. Maybe she'd see it. It's not a completely crazy idea.

Her stomach rumbled as she sipped her soda. She and Preston were supposed to have gone to dinner at the Apple Station Inn after their lake excursion, but his day-off pop-up duties had squelched their plans. With her blood sugar needing a boost, her scheme would have to wait. Last night, she'd finished all the chicken and pasta salad that she had prepared earlier in the week. Going back out for something seemed like a lot of effort, and tossing together a plain-Jane garden salad left her uninspired. Her stomach grumbled again, demanding she stick a fork in some food. She countered with a simple menu and a spoon.

"Cereal and soda it'll be. The dinner of champions." She pushed her chair back, stood up, and turned to grab a bowl from the cabinet when Buddy's sharp barking drew her attention to the living room.

"Buddy, are you bothering Willow in there? Leave her alone. She's a nice, quiet cat who doesn't spill her water everywhere."

When Willow first came to stay with them, she and Buddy had been wary of each other. There were a few days of mutual scampering, swatting, and hiding, but they quickly resolved their differences. Now Buddy seemed only displeased that Willow could leap onto Olivia's bed and nestle beside her at night. Though he'd try to follow, he could never jump higher than the box spring. The whimpers following his failed attempts always tugged at her heart. She'd end up hoisting him up and setting him next to Willow, relegating herself to the edge of the bed.

Now Buddy stood facing the front door as heavy knocking spooked Willow into abandoning her lookout perch atop the sofa. Olivia crossed the living room to collect what was probably a ceramic baking dish her father had ordered from Italy. He'd given her a heads-up that the delivery date was today, and she'd need to sign for it. Nearing the door, she scanned the floor, checking Willow's whereabouts. They'd managed thus far to keep the indoor kitty from escaping, but Olivia never lowered her guard. Telling June that Willow had returned to her wild roots wasn't a conversation she ever wanted to have.

Satisfied that Willow was more interested in inspecting the boxes yet again, she peeked through the peephole. A bouquet of yellow carnations blocked the tiny view. *Huh.* Preston had never sent her flowers before, but maybe it was to make up for having to cancel the rest of their date. She shooed Buddy back, turned the deadbolt, and opened the door.

When the bearer lowered the bouquet, her focus darted to the driveway. Instead of the rose-red minivan from Flora's Florist Gallery she'd expected, a black luxury sedan with dark-tinted windows sat parked behind her Expedition. The well-dressed deliveryman wore a charcoal-gray suit, a blue shirt, and a burgundy-and-white striped tie.

"Can I help you?" she said.

"Flower delivery," he replied in a New Jersey accent. As she opened the screen, he inserted his foot in the gap and planted his wing tip on the doorsill. "For Sam," he added, looking past her into the living room.

She shifted, preparing to block him from coming in. Glancing at the umbrella stand just to the right of the door, she eyed her high school softball bat, which her father always kept handy as a first-line home defense. It may not pack as much punch as Sam's weighted mini bat, but she still had a solid swing.

Standing tall, she steeped her tone with authority. "You've got the wrong house."

"Is Sam here?"

She reached for the knob and grasped it. "Like I said, you've got the wrong house."

His arm shot up, and he smacked his palm against the door, preventing her from shutting it.

"Hey, what do you think you're doing?" she snapped. "Back off, or I'll call the police."

He quickly lowered his hand and stepped back. "I'm sorry, miss. That was rude of me. I want to make sure Sam gets these flowers. You just came from her house. She isn't there?"

Thirty minutes ago, she'd chalked up the oddity of what happened in Sam's bedroom as fancies of an over-active imagination. Now she believed her gut feeling was right. The phone calls, the text, and this creepy guy who looked like an extra from *Goodfellas*—none of it was a coincidence. She'd lay odds he was the mysterious caller. If he'd wanted to come in, he could've done so. But his agenda seemed to involve Sam, not stirring up trouble with her none-the-wiser neighbor. She eased a bit, still cautious but curious about how far she could play this.

"Sam's away. I was watering her plants."

He stared at her as if waiting for her to say more. "Where'd she go?"

No idea. "To a conference. In Florida. I don't know when she'll be back."

His lips curled up in a thin smirk. "In *Florida*. Can you contact her?"

She subtly scanned him from head to toe, memorizing his features. He was a few inches shy of six feet tall and weighed an unathletic two hundred pounds. She'd describe his ice-blue eyes as lovely if he weren't so intimidating. A gaudy gold signet ring looked puny on his meaty hands, and his French cuffs extended beyond his suit sleeves, revealing round silver cufflinks.

"Sam doesn't like to be contacted when she's away unless it's an emergency," she said.

"What if it is an emergency? Say if something happened to her house."

She glanced at the piled boxes, both to give her a moment to think and to ensure Willow wasn't about to bolt for freedom.

"I tried calling her when I was over there to ask her a question, but I didn't get an answer. Her voicemail picked up. I guess she's busy. If you want to leave your name and number, if she gets back in touch, I can tell her you brought her flowers."

He scanned the living room again, then thrust the carnations at her. She had no choice but to grasp the bouquet as he released the craft-paper wrapped stems into her hands.

"Let Sam know she got a flower delivery. I'd appreciate it if you try to get back in touch with her today. Thank you." He backed away, turned, and thumped down the porch steps.

Lickety-split, she shut the screen door and flipped down the measly lock. "Who should I say the flowers are from?"

"The name is on the card," he called out over his shoulder.

She pivoted, tossed the bouquet onto a nearby end table, and pulled out her phone. She snapped several pictures of his back, one of his profile, and two of the car's license plate. Though the mesh screen would distort the images, and the numbers on the plate would probably be too small to make out, at least she'd have something to show Sam.

She closed the door and locked it as Willow weaved between her legs. Reaching down, she rewarded the cat with a few strokes to the top of her head. "You did a good job, little kitty. Thanks for not making a run for it when you had the chance."

The carnations were the color of butter and carried no scent. She couldn't keep them in the house even if the bearer hadn't been a mafioso lookalike. Before June left in January, she'd provided Olivia with a list of foods that were toxic to cats and a hyperlink to the ASPCA's database of poisonous plants. After scanning the webpage, Olivia had assumed almost everything could harm

Willow and subsequently banned all greenery from the house.

Knowing she'd probably hear from Sam in the next few days, she reached between the stems and plucked out the petite folded card. Certain that Sam would want to know who sent them, she opened the card and read, "Spring Hills, Nine."

CHAPTER 4

Olivia surmised that the message signified a time and location. Spring Hills was a decommissioned army base about twenty minutes northeast of town. Until five years ago, the large-acreage property was off-limits to the public and a source of wild rumors among locals. Officials had touted the out-of-the-way installation as a training school for military intelligence. Many had speculated, though, that the razor-wired fences guarded a top-secret facility.

When a real estate company purchased the property, the army removed the fencing and the guard towers but left the three main buildings intact. Delays in rezoning had stalled the construction of two housing developments, a commercial center, and a community park. While the red tape was unraveling itself, the land remained abandoned and largely unkept. The heavily wooded area attracted hikers, hunters, and curiosity seekers. Since the owners were absent, there was no on-site security personnel or perceived threat of being charged with trespassing.

On one of Olivia's visits home soon after the base's closure, she and her best friend, Sophia, had driven onto the property to look around. Their venture was anticlimactic as they saw no secret satellite dishes, radiation warning signs, or evidence of alien landings. Instead, they came across two horseback riders and a few people flying model airplanes using remote controls.

She read the card again, certain that Sam was supposed to meet someone, maybe her carnation-bearing admirer, at Spring Hills. But why and when exactly? The why was too broad for her to speculate. Perhaps it was personal, but given what she knew about Sam, she guessed it was related to her job. The unwelcome visitor didn't strike Olivia as Sam's colleague. Rather, he seemed to expect something of her. The urgency of his message combined with the missed calls suggested the *when* of the meeting could well be tonight.

Willow meowed and stood on her hind legs, eyeing the carnations.

"No-no. Not for you. Get down."

A rapid burst of light rapping on the door froze Willow with her ears perked and front paws dangling by her sides, looking like a prairie dog. Olivia craned her neck to get a view of the driveway through the bay window. No black sedan, no delivery truck, no other vehicle but her own. The knocking, backed by more oomph, started again. Willow lowered herself to the floor, scampered to the sofa, and squeezed under it.

Olivia allowed one more round of knocking before answering, and it came quicker and louder than the last. Buddy wandered over to her with his white-tipped tail sweeping from side to side.

"Come here. Sit. Stay."

He wasn't as intimidating as a German shepherd, but he had an on-command bark that could inspire a fright. With Willow safely under the couch, Olivia stepped closer to the door and peeked through the peephole, hoping to see Sam.

Could this day get any weirder?

A twenty-something-year-old man stood on the porch wearing dark slacks, a white short-sleeved dress shirt, and a yellow tie. A black name tag was pinned to his shirt pocket, and he carried a pack on his back.

She eased, thinking it was a shame that he hadn't shown up at the same time as her last visitor. *An advice columnist, a Mormon, and a gangster walk into a bar.* Sighing out an amused breath, she unlocked the door and opened it.

"Good evening, ma'am. My name is Mark, and I'm here today in your neighborhood sharing a brief message of hope."

Not wanting to be rude or discuss salvation as the sun was setting on a Sunday, she dialed up a smile, matching half of his broad grin. "Hi, Mark. I'm sorry, but I was just about to sit down to dinner."

He bobbed his head as if hearing that for the thousandth time today. "I don't mean to take you away from eating. Are you having a good day?"

"Ah, yeah. A little weird, but blessed all the same. Please excuse me, but I'm in the middle of something."

"I understand. I haven't eaten since breakfast."

If he was gunning for an invitation inside to grab a bite, he was out of his mind. She glanced down at Buddy, contemplating provoking a bark to help move him along.

"Can I leave this pamphlet with you?"

Relieved at not having to rile up Buddy, she unlocked the screen and opened it. "Sure."

He stepped forward and handed her the pamphlet, looking past her into the living room. "Pretty flowers. Are they from your husband?"

"No." She held up the open card as if providing proof. "They're for my neighbor."

His focused shifted to the card. "That makes sense. I was just over there, but no one answered. I know many don't open the door when they see me on the other side. Thank you for doing so. Aah, cute kitty. Girl or boy?"

She peeked over her shoulder at Willow, who had emerged from under the sofa and was watching them while lying in a perfect loaf position on the floor.

"Girl."

"I have a cat too. He's a ginger. Cheeto. My folks are taking care of him while I'm away on my mission."

If she wasn't so ravenous, she'd be less abrupt and offer a gentler goodbye. "Well, thanks for the pamphlet."

She grabbed the door as he scanned behind her again before he took a step back.

"Thank you for speaking with me today. If you'd like to talk further or need any help, my phone number is on the back. I'll be around the neighborhood for a while longer if you change your mind."

She flipped the pamphlet over and read his name and number, which were handwritten on a white sticker label.

"Thanks, Mark. Don't you usually travel in pairs? And on bikes?"

He grasped the shoulder straps of his backpack. "True. My companion and I split up. We wanted to cover as many houses as we could before it got dark. Okay, good night then." He spun, hurried down the steps, and hustled toward the end of the driveway.

Buddy had abandoned his guard position and now was lying on his back by the boxes. Willow was standing, rapidly scratching with both forepaws at the presumed mixer box. "You two, what a life. Thanks for being ready to pounce to protect your human."

After closing the door, she grabbed the bouquet from the end table, went into the kitchen, and binned it. She hated doing so to perfectly good flowers. It wasn't their fault they came laden with some serious sketch, but Sam wouldn't have given a second thought to tossing them.

Before considering what, if anything, to do, she needed to eat. She gathered her cereal, bowl, and spoon, and after adding a cup of milk to her mix, she dug in. None of what had happened over the past two hours sat right with her. Though Sam could take care of herself, it was worrisome that Olivia couldn't reach her. If she was supposed to be at Spring Hills in an hour, would she have been walking into something blind? Without evidence of imminent danger, the police would likely dismiss Olivia's concerns. Sam probably wouldn't even want them involved if this pertained to her work.

She nixed her plan to contact Sam through the security cameras. Tomorrow, during the day, maybe she'd go back over. The possibility that the mafioso was still watching the house was enough to keep her away for the night. She didn't want to raise any undue suspicion that Sam was hiding inside, considering his veiled threats.

After she finished dinner, she cleaned the bowl and the spoon in the sink while considering what to do. Spring Hills was an enormous property, but she had some familiarity with it. To her, it made the most sense for a meeting to take place near the three primary buildings. The parking lot had clear views, and the solar-powered security lights lit up the vicinity. The large headquarters was the nearest landmark on the base, and the access road provided a quick, easy exit.

I could take a drive out there. Stay back a distance. See if she's there. But then what?

The chances that she'd encounter anyone were slim. Though none of this was her business, she couldn't ignore the oddity of the last few hours. Five months ago, in December, Sam had backed her up in a tight situation without hesitating to ask questions. By doing so, Sam had probably saved her life. Olivia wouldn't charge in like Sam, but she had Preston, and thus the entire police department, on speed-dial if something seemed off.

"I'm not doing anything else tonight anyway. I'll just take a quick drive there. That's all."

She put the bowl and the spoon away, then threw out the soda can in the recycling bin. After checking on Willow and Buddy in the living room, she grabbed her zip-up hoodie and left for Spring Hills.

CHAPTER 5

A pair of white cement posts that had once anchored the base's main security gate marked the turnoff from Morrow Lane to Spring Hills. Olivia's last visit here was in October two years ago. She and A.J. had visited the area on a Saturday afternoon to take in the fall foliage while hiking along a hidden gem of a forest trail that skirted the backside of Fields Farm.

She passed a second set of smaller posts, where an auxiliary gate once stood, figuring she'd follow the first spur of the roundabout ahead. The road wound a short way to a small field overlooking the three main buildings. Not wanting to stumble across anyone in the parking lot, she avoided the middle lane for now. She'd only ever driven about a quarter mile down the third offshoot, which led farther out on the property. As surveillance was her aim, she'd stick to the high ground tonight and keep her distance.

Upon reaching the hilltop, she scanned the area, ensuring no one was around. The road paralleled the length of a flat, patchy dirt and grass field that was about fifty yards wide. The best vantage of the buildings and the lot was on the opposite side, but she wasn't keen on leaving her vehicle to set out on foot across the field. During her last visit, she'd seen several SUVs parked there, while a small gathering was having a tailgate party. Alone and at night, that precedent was enough for her to decide to drive across. Taking it slow, the Expedition barely blinked at the tame off-roading, and she got to the other side in no time.

She stopped near the edge of the hill and parked straight on, about thirty yards from the rear of the small lot. The old headquarters obstructed the view of the two buildings behind it, but this was as far as she planned to go. Her doubts had doubled on the drive out, nagging that this was a wild goose chase. But she'd made the trip and would stick to her plan to observe from a distance for the next thirty minutes, ready to call for help if needed. Satisfied with her position, she cut the engine, unfastened her seatbelt, and allowed the cabin to go dark.

According to an article she'd read years ago in *The Apple Station Times*, the three buildings below were the primary structures on the property. The headquarters, designed in the style of a Georgian mansion, stood in stark contrast to the utilitarian red-brick buildings behind it. The L-shaped barracks had housed base personnel, students, and visitors. Officially a storage site, the windowless third building was always shrouded in mystery. Rumors circulated that it had an underground level equipped as an ancillary bunker for cabinet officials in the event of a national emergency. A service road encircled the complex, with entry and exit points on opposite sides of the parking lot.

All was quiet around the headquarters. She tilted her phone up from the center console to check the time and noticed a missed call from Preston. With only one bar of reception now, she must've hit a dead zone somewhere along the way. He hadn't left a message, and she'd rather not call him back at the moment and risk having to explain what she was doing. She'd kept things from him in the past during touch-and-go situations when they were just casual acquaintances. Though he'd understood her motives, she didn't want to sidestep his trust again now that they were a couple.

After five minutes passed with only a lone bat swooping around the parking lot for company, she relaxed in the seat, rested her head back, and yawned. It was nearly nine o'clock, so she wouldn't be hanging out here for long. If no one showed by a quarter after, she'd chalk the venture up as a lark and conveniently omit it from Sam's debrief.

Her thoughts drifted to Tuesday's dinner menu. Last week, she'd made a pot roast with mashed potatoes, which always went over well, but perhaps it was too soon for an encore. Of course, she'd first have to see if Preston could come, but regardless, a grocery run sometime over the next few days would probably make her to-do list.

She leaned forward, resting her wrists on the leather-wrapped wheel, tapping a one-two-three waltz rhythm with her thumbs. A raccoon crossed the sidewalk in front of the headquarters and went out of sight around its near corner. Her cell buzzed, and she looked down at the screen, seeing a text from her father. She slowed her Viennese triple count and glanced up before opening his message, spotting the raccoon scurrying back into view. She followed its flight across the lot, then traced its line of retreat to its origin as someone peeked around the edge of the building.

She thrust back against the seat and slumped instinctively. With the dark backdrop of the field and the forest, her black SUV naturally blended in with the overlook. Still, she sat motionless, staring just over the dashboard at the partially obscured figure who was scanning the area. She placed her finger on the push-button start, preparing to press it for a quick exit. Even though she'd initially thought others might be here, she'd almost convinced herself not to expect it. With her pulse pumping high in her throat, she reached blindly for the lock button on the door panel and double-clicked it to be safe. Scooting forward a little, she watched as the person stepped around the corner and stood with their back to her.

She grabbed her cell, steadied it on the top of the steering wheel, and opened the camera. Despite the low lighting, the image wasn't half bad. Increasing the magnification turned everything blurry. She adjusted the settings and zoomed out to improve the resolution. Her eyes darted back and forth from the screen to the person, trying to meld both images into a more telling view.

Just as the lens achieved a happy medium, the person turned around and faced the lot. Olivia lowered the cell onto the center console, recognizing Sam. She eased a bit, then quickly refocused and scanned the area below to ensure no one was sneaking up on Sam. Calling or trying to signal her from where she was parked would be folly. Whatever was brewing didn't directly involve her, and for now, she'd wait to see how it played out.

Sam glanced left and right again, then went out of sight around the corner.

"Where are you going?" Olivia squeezed the wheel as if needing a full cup of juice from half a lemon. She'd come here wanting to be Sam's backup, but now, blinded by the building, she was of no use. Sam had to be parked elsewhere, which meant others could be too. She could be in trouble at any moment, and Olivia wouldn't know it.

After grabbing a flashlight from the storage cubby and switching off the cabin lights, she opened her door, slid down off the seat, and checked the time on her phone, shielding the screen's illumination with her body. Fifteen past nine. If someone was coming for a meeting with Sam, she thought they would've been here by now. She stood still by the hood for a moment, listening for anything unusual, then took a few steps back and silently closed the door.

She went to the top of the hill, squatted to lower her profile, and waited for another minute. With all still quiet, she stood up and started down the gentle, grassy slope. Upon reaching the parking lot, she jogged about twenty-five yards toward the headquarters for cover, keeping her head on a swivel and her steps light.

Now standing where Sam had been a few moments ago, she peeked around the corner and traced the dark length of the building. A soft glow from the security lighting in the back gave her an idea of how far she needed to go to reach the rear. She turned on the flashlight, directing the beam close to her feet, and maneuvered past a patch of groundcover juniper. Crunchy dead leaves lined the building's foundation, so she kept an arm's length away, not wanting her footsteps to announce her presence. Random trash lay scattered about, and halfway along she inadvertently kicked a can of spray paint lying on the ground under a boarded-up window. She froze as it rolled to a stop, thanks to a fallen tree branch that looked like a divining rod.

Waiting no longer than a few shallow breaths, she pressed forward until within five feet of the rear. She slowed, stepping lightly, and sidled closer to the building, following the tapering leaf line until it ended just before the corner. She turned off the flashlight, stashed it in her pocket, and crept to the edge. Then she lowered a bit and peeked around the back.

Sam was standing about twenty yards from her, facing away and looking at someone lying on their stomach by her feet. Olivia straightened and scanned the low-lit area. As they appeared to be alone, she rounded the corner and took a few steps forward.

"Psst. Sam."

She spun, then snapped in a hushed voice, "What are you doing here?"

Olivia inched forward but quickly picked up her pace upon realizing the man was unconscious. "Looking for you. What's going on? Is he okay? Does he need help?"

"You shouldn't be here."

Olivia squatted next to the man and reached out to give him a light shake, but Sam grabbed her arm.

"Don't touch him," she said. "He's dead."

After Sam let go, Olivia stood up and quickly glanced at her to see if she was injured.

"Are you alright? What happened? Did you …" She couldn't bring herself to finish the question, unsure if she wanted to hear the answer.

"No, I didn't. He was gone when I got here. I'm fine."

The man looked like he was sleeping, though his positioning prevented the telltale of his chest's lack of rise and fall. There wasn't much she could determine about him, other than that he was wearing jeans and a blue nylon windbreaker. He appeared to be in his late forties, but it was difficult to discern for sure with half of his face hidden.

"Are you okay?" Olivia asked again.

Sam nodded, looking all around. "We've got to get out of here." She stepped closer to the man and snapped several pictures with her phone.

"Who is he?" Olivia said.

"I don't know. He doesn't have a wallet on him."

"Is he the person you were supposed to meet?"

Sam gave her a side-glance. "You shouldn't have come."

"I was worried about you. I've been trying to get in touch with you since this afternoon. I was watering your plants and doing my walk through when I heard a phone ringing from inside your bedroom. I'm sorry, but I went in to check it out. You received six calls in rapid succession on a cell in your nightstand drawer. I didn't know if there was some sort of emergency or what. I tried to call and e-mail you. By the way, the super-secret number you gave me—not in service. Then, about twenty minutes later, this creepy dude showed up at my house with a bouquet of carnations for you."

Sam held her hand up. "Wait. Say more about him."

She elaborated with a mini character sketch and showed Sam the pictures she'd taken.

"Do you know him?" Olivia asked.

"Not by name, but I have an idea. Text me those."

She selected all the photos and sent them. "Done. But they went to the cell that's sitting in your nightstand drawer."

"Thanks. I'll get the forwarded message."

"Whoa. Hold on. So that must mean you knew I had tried to call you."

She nodded. "Sorry. I received both calls and your e-mail. Mark said everything looked okay. He hung around for a while to make sure, then he called me after you left. But obviously, neither of us thought you were coming here."

"Mark the Mormon? What?"

"Mark, not a Mormon, is a colleague of mine. I asked him to check in on you when you called the emergency number."

Olivia rubbed her forehead, needing a moment. "Of course. Because when you have a friend who is a *security consultant*, a Mormon is never just a Mormon." She let out a deep exhale, checked all around, and looked down at the man. "What about the calls to the other cell in your drawer?"

"That phone is a burner."

"What's this about? Where's your car? How is it you're even here? Have you called the police yet?"

"No. Mark read the card you showed him that came with the flowers. When I heard they were meant for me, I understood the gist of what had happened. I knew the meeting was supposed to be here, but thanks to you, I found out the time. I'm parked on a lane down past the barracks. It exits onto the turnpike. Our John Doe's car is on the other side of the storage building. The trunk is open, but it's empty." She glanced down at the man. "I partially rolled him when I got here. There's blood on his shirt, but without a closer look, I can't determine the cause. There're no signs of trauma or struggle. With no drag marks or tire tracks, it was likely close range, probably by someone he knew."

Sam's phone buzzed. She glanced at the screen and answered. "What do you have for me? ... When? ... Okay, thanks."

She ended the call and pocketed the cell. "We've gotta move now."

Sam gestured at the building and took off running. Olivia kept pace right behind her as they headed toward the front.

"What's happening?" Olivia said between quickened breaths.

"Where are you parked?"

"On the upper field."

As they neared the front of the headquarters, Sam held her arm out to slow Olivia until they both stopped short of the corner. Sam peeked first, then waved her forward until they were both on the sidewalk.

"Mark has been monitoring the police scanners. He picked up a transmission confirming that the police were on route, responding to a call from a state trooper who found a body here."

Olivia quickly looked around. "What? Where is he?"

"I think someone set me up. We both need to leave."

"Shouldn't we wait for the police? Tell them what happened?"

"No. I can't stay, which means you need to leave

immediately. You can't let anyone know you were here, or that you saw me tonight. You haven't heard from me in days. Do you understand?"

"Sam—"

"Liv, promise me you won't tell Preston."

Olivia's stomach sank, replaying the words in her head. "Whatever is happening, he can help."

"We don't have time to debate this." She gripped Olivia's forearm. "Promise me."

She owed Sam her life, but lying to Preston about anything involving a dead man was a gross breach of trust.

"Liv, promise me."

Sam had to leave, and Olivia was holding her back. She'd come here wanting to help Sam by calling the police if needed, but now she had to hide her from them. Though not privy to the big picture, she had to choose, as every second of indecision placed Sam at greater risk.

"Yeah, okay," she said.

Sam nodded. "Now, go. Run as fast as you can."

They both backpedaled in opposite directions.

"How can I get in touch with you?" Olivia called out.

Sam shook her head. "Don't try to." With that, she turned and dashed out of sight around the corner.

Seeing Sam bolt shook the last bit of hesitation out of her. She spun and sprinted through the parking lot, hitting the hill at full tilt. About halfway up, her foot slipped on a dirt patch, and she threw her hands forward, catching herself before her knees touched the ground.

She shuffled her feet, popped up, and pressed on until she was back in her car.

She fired up the engine, quickly reversed, and crossed the field much faster than she'd driven onto it. Once on the lane leading to the roundabout, she picked up the pace, then ramped it up even more on the main access road. Her eyes locked in on her exit, praying not to see headlights coming her way. Reasons and excuses spun in her head like a pinwheel in the wind, weaving a plausible web for why she was there.

I was just taking a drive. Nobody else was there. I didn't see anything unusual.

"Oh, jeez." She reached across her shoulder, grabbed the seatbelt, and slowed a bit until she fastened it. Then she sped up again until within twenty yards of the exit. Her eyes shifted left, looking for the earliest sign that her lane was clear. With no cars coming her way, she cut the corner short, taking the right turn at speed.

Relief eased her grip on the wheel now that she was off the property. She sped up, surpassing the legal limit in just seconds, wanting to put distance between herself and Spring Hills. With a quarter mile in her rearview, flashing red-and-blue lights appeared in front of her. She tapped the brakes, slowing down, and maneuvered onto the lane's shoulder.

Blaring sirens pierced the cabin's silence, and as the patrol cars neared, she came to a stop. The three cruisers whizzed by her, zip-zip-zip. A dark pickup truck with a flashing blue light on its dash followed behind them. She sank in the seat and held her breath until Preston passed by. Watching in the rearview mirror, she waited until the four vehicles turned into Spring Hills. Then, after checking for oncoming cars, she steered back onto the road, quickly revved up to speed, and didn't look back.

CHAPTER 6

Usually by nine on Monday mornings, Olivia would already be at work in her office, tending to e-mail or planning the week. But after a mostly sleepless night, she'd lingered under the covers, finally waking when Willow padded over her pillow to curl up next to Buddy. She'd held out hope into the wee hours that Sam would send a brief word, but no messages came through, and she knew it was pointless to reach out to her.

Now, sitting at the kitchen table with her rapidly cooling coffee and an untouched banana in front of her, she debated on how best to proceed with the day. Having never fled a crime scene, the protocols of acting normal when things were anything but were new to her. Maybe she'd approach the morning as usual: answer e-mail, write her columns, and schedule calls.

Wonder if I left any evidence behind that connects me to a dead man.

The only thing she could do to help Sam was keep her word about not telling Preston. There shouldn't be a need for him to know about either of them being at Spring Hills last night. He rarely discussed police business with her, and she knew better than to ask. If Sam had slipped away clean, there'd be no reason for him to suspect anything.

Willow wandered into the kitchen and greeted her with a meow yawn. She sauntered over, nuzzled Olivia's leg, and milled around her chair.

"I know. I'm late today. I'll get a move on."

By this time on weekdays, Willow normally would be asleep in Olivia's backyard office. Two weeks into Willow's stay with them, Olivia had added a cat tree, a litter box, and a water fountain to the one-room cottage for her comfort. She'd usually take Willow out with her for a few hours in the morning while she wrote her columns, then bring her back to the house at lunchtime.

She broke off a piece of the banana, popped it in her mouth, and reached for a package of cat treats on the counter. When Willow's big blue eyes spied the yellow bag, she licked her lips and sat at Olivia's feet. She picked out the bite-sized, freeze-dried chicken bits, one by one, and fed them to Willow by hand. As the cat chewed each one, Olivia polished off her breakfast and drank half of her lukewarm coffee. After they'd both had their fill, she resealed the bag and cleaned up while Willow went over to her water bowl and lapped up a healthy measure.

While she watched Willow groom herself for a few

minutes, Olivia's thoughts drifted to her to-do list for the week. With a murder investigation on Preston's plate, he probably wouldn't make it to dinner tomorrow. Perhaps she could skip the grocery run and make do with the freezer and the pantry stores until the weekend. They most likely wouldn't be seeing much of each other over the next few days, and that may be for the best.

She hated to keep anything from him, but there was a lot they didn't talk about. Sophia was still the only one she trusted with her deepest, darkest secrets. Preston had gotten to know Sam somewhat since her involvement in a police matter in December, but he never asked Olivia much about her except in casual terms. Maybe he knew more about her than he let on. Olivia had learned that selective sharing in a relationship cuts both ways.

Knocking on the front door froze Willow as she was licking her front paw. Her ears turned and twitched, trying to locate the source of the interruption. Olivia glanced at the wall clock, stood up, and pocketed her phone. Last night her father had texted to let her know that the delivery of his baking dish was delayed, and she could expect it to come today, right about now. She went to answer the door, peeking at the driveway through the bay window. As expected, a large brown delivery truck sat parked behind her Expedition. She wouldn't have minded had it been Mark instead, spreading his message of hope. At least then she could find out whether Sam had made it out okay. After signing for the package and placing it among all the others in the living room, she returned to the kitchen.

Willow had fallen asleep on the sofa, so Olivia let her be, electing to go to work solo this morning. She filled a thermos with water, locked the back door, and went out to her office. Once inside, she sat in her chair and booted up her laptop. Curious about whether the news from last night had hit the presses, she opened a browser and clicked on a bookmark for *The Apple Station Times*. Though she didn't expect a full article, there may be mention of it in a sidebar that displayed recent headlines right under the weather forecast. Sure enough, near the top of the sidebar, one sentence reported, "Body Found at Spring Hills on Sunday."

With the official word released, she'd have a legitimate reason to ask Preston about the murder without raising his suspicion. Her interest was less about who the victim was and more to ensure the police hadn't connected Sam to the scene.

She needed to call him back anyway. Enough time had passed since last night, and she didn't want him to feel ignored. She took her phone out of her pocket and dialed his number, waiting only two rings before he answered.

"Good morning, Liv."

"Hi. I'm sorry I didn't return your call yesterday. Something came up, then it got late."

"Don't worry about it. I was just calling to say good

night. I'd planned on trying again, but something came up for me too."

Let me guess. "Work related?"

"Yeah. There was an incident at Spring Hills."

"I saw on the paper's website that a body was found there."

"Uh-huh. News travels fast. It was late when I finished up at the scene, then I went to inform the family. I didn't get back home until after midnight, and I thought you'd already be sleeping."

She stood up and started pacing. The police had quickly determined who he was despite him not having a wallet. Maybe it was in his car, or maybe they used the vehicle's registration to identify him. She wondered and worried about what else, if anything, they'd discovered.

"Was it someone local?" she asked. "How was he killed?"

"Hold on a sec." His voice lowered as she could hear him speaking to Deputy Jayden Stone. Jayden had joined the department about a year ago and was the only female officer on the staff. In a short time, he came back on the line. "Sorry about that. He had a stab wound, which was likely the cause of death. He wasn't a local, but we didn't need to go far to find the next of kin."

She pivoted, heading back across the room. "Why is that?"

"Since we've already released the name, I can tell you he was the carnival's manager and the owners' son, Robert

Klein. He arrived in town yesterday with the rest of the entourage. I'm sorry, but I've gotta go. I think we have a lead. I'm out at Spring Hills, and Jayden just found something."

She stopped dead in the middle of the room, dying to ask him more, but she knew she couldn't, and he wouldn't answer anyway. At least he didn't mention Sam at all, and that had to be a good sign. Now, if the lead pointed to anyone but Sam, they might both be in the clear.

"Okay," she said. "We'll talk later. I know you'll be busy over the next few days, so don't worry about making it for dinner this week."

"Yeah, probably. I'm sure you and your dad will want to spend a lot of time catching up. I'll take a raincheck as soon as things settle."

"Sounds good. Be careful."

After they said their goodbyes and ended the call, she went back to her desk, sat, and put her phone down. She swiped her finger across her laptop's trackpad, waking the screen, and looked again at the paper's home page. There were no updates posted to the recent news, but since the police had released the victim's name, that would likely change soon. Her focus drifted to the local events section and she read the top headline, "Klein Amusements Opens Carnival on Wednesday." She hit the link and read the story, which detailed the general FAQs, including information about the rides, food, and hours of operation.

None of this made any sense to her. Why would Sam be meeting the manager of a carnival? And why would someone set her up to take the fall for his murder?

She opened a new tab and searched for Klein Amusements. The top result led straight to the company's homepage. On it, a video automatically played of a thrill ride whirling strapped-in passengers upside down.

"That's a no-go. I wouldn't ride that for a million dollars. Well, *maybe* for a mill."

Colorful banners with cheerful text filled the screen, highlighting the company's commitment to safe family fun. As a kid, she'd always enjoyed going to carnivals whenever they set up close to town. Later in life, she'd watched a documentary exposing the sometimes-shady side of the business. Afterward, her childhood memories of the rickety rides and no-win games took on a different vibe. To an impressionable child, carnivals were weekend wonders to behold in random fields or parking lots. Behind the allure, though, she'd learned the working conditions were rough and those in charge were often a tough lot.

She read through the history of Klein Amusements under the about section. Robert, aka Bobby, was the son of the owners, who'd started the business almost fifty years ago. Nicky Klein, Bobby's sister, joined him in managing the carnival's daily operations after their parents retired. A photo of the siblings standing together in front of a carousel was at the bottom of the page.

Below it was a caption that read, "We take pride in providing affordable entertainment." If pressed, she couldn't have positively identified Bobby as the man she saw at Spring Hills based on the website picture.

Wholesome family fun was their motto, except for last night. Within hours of arriving at Fields Farm, Bobby was killed somewhere, one would think, he had no reason to be. Wrong place, wrong time didn't seem to apply. Though it was a tragedy, she doubted the carnival would be canceled. They'd leased the land and were already on site. She knew carnivals often operated on a week-to-week basis, and losing that much revenue would be a major blow. The Kleins had lost a son, but pulling the plug on even a single booking could set the business back for the entire season.

She looked again at the paper's website and refreshed the browser. Other than the forecast changing from sunny to partly cloudy, the headlines remained the same. Betting that her friend Cassandra, the paper's senior staff writer, was already working on the story, she picked up her phone and called her at the office.

"*Apple Station Times*, Cassandra speaking."

"Hey, Cass. It's Liv. Got a minute?"

"If you have a story, I've got a minute."

"I assume you know about the body found at Spring Hills last night."

"Oh, yeah. Terrible. It's one of the carnival people, the head guy. How do you know about it?"

"I just talked to Preston."

"Anything you'd like to share with me? Off the record, *of course*."

"No. Do you have any details yet?"

"Only the victim's name. I'm leaving the office shortly and driving out to Fields Farm. The victim had a sister who helped him run the business. I'm going to try to speak with her."

"Alright. Can you keep me informed?"

"I *can*, but what's your interest in this?"

She hesitated, careful not to hint at her personal stake. She trusted Cassandra, who'd helped her in the past, but Olivia had no handle on the scope of Sam's involvement. "I can't say right now."

"Hmm. Interesting, Penn. Okay. I'll play along, but you keep me in the loop too. Your hush-hush has a history of paying off big. Hey, while I have you on the phone, I talked to Marco last night." Marco Esposito worked as a reporter at Olivia's paper in D.C. In January, he and Cassandra had collaborated on a story about the capture of a legendary jewel thief. "He said there's an opening on your staff, and he encouraged me to apply."

"In what department? Management has been laying off people left and right."

"He didn't go into specifics, but I'm thinking about it. It would be a step up, a big one. You like it there, don't you?"

Yes, and no. Her opinion of her job had gone from

great to just fine. The pros were solid: stability, salary, and satisfaction. But she had no desire to live in the city again. The traffic, the noise, the busyness—good riddance. Despite this, her thoughts about leaving had little to do with the position itself. Over the past year, she'd changed and now wanted something different for her life.

"Yeah, I think you should go for it. I'll ask my editor about it and give her your name along with a glowing recommendation. She knows everyone there."

"Thanks, Liv. That would mean a lot."

"You deserve it. I hope it pans out."

After agreeing to keep each other posted, they ended the call. Olivia wrote a quick e-mail on her phone to her editor, Angela, letting her know she wanted to talk sometime about the job opening for Cassandra. Now there was nothing more she could do about last night, other than wait for Sam to return, for an arrest to be made, and for her to put the incident in her rearview.

She slid the laptop closer and squared her chair up to the desk. Needing to get her mind off things, she switched gears and got down to business. She opened the weekly list of reader questions Angela had sent, deciding to answer all those that were pre-selected as suggestions. Over the next two hours, she penned three columns, dealing with conflicts between friends, in-laws, and co-workers. Because she'd often fielded similar queries, she didn't need to do much research. She added her standard disclaimer about her opinions not being used as legal advice as needed.

After finishing the third column, she stood up, stretched, and checked her e-mail on her phone. At the top of her inbox was a message from Angela, asking her to call when she had a chance. She scrolled right away to Angela's number and dialed.

"Angela Forte."

"Hi, Angela. Olivia here. I saw your e-mail."

"Yes, thanks for calling me back. I saw yours too. It's hard to believe the paper is hiring newbies while laying off senior staff. Younger and cheaper, that's how it goes. But I want to talk to you about something. Are you sitting?"

This can't be good. "If this is about live streaming the weekly chats, you already have my answer."

"I still don't understand why you're being so stubborn about that. You'd be a natural on camera. Sort of. But this is not about that. Do you know the name Evelyn Walters?"

"Can't say that I do."

"She's the editor-in-chief of *Modern Mosaic Magazine* and a friend of mine from college. I visited her this weekend in Manhattan, and she's looking for an editorial assistant. Someone who is smart, reliable, and determined. Guess who I thought would be perfect for the job?"

"You?"

Angela grunted. "No, Einstein. You."

"Angela—"

"Wait. Don't say anything yet. Hear me out. This is a tremendous opportunity. You'd be working with some of the top talent in the industry in the heart of New York's publishing mecca. Think of the connections you could make. You still want to write fiction, *right?* We both know you can't earn a living doing that these days, but if you had a job up there, it would take a lot of pressure off the writing. We're talking the big time, not to mention a huge salary boost."

She didn't disagree with Angela's assessment of the publishing industry. She'd put her manuscript in a drawer months ago and had given little thought to it since.

"I don't know the first thing about working on a magazine. *Modern Mosaic.* That's about entrepreneurs, right? Small businesses and start-ups."

"Yes, but not your mom-and-pops. It has international reach. I told Evelyn about your background, and she said it's not a problem. You'd be working side by side with her. She just wants someone who comes as a trusted recommendation, and she's eager to speak with you."

Olivia's gut reaction was no, not interested. But it piqued her curiosity. It wasn't so much the job as it was the opportunity to do something new. She picked up a turquoise fountain pen Preston had gifted her at Christmas and drew random squiggles on a notepad.

"I really appreciate you going to bat for me, but I'll have to pass."

"Why?"

"I'm living here now, and I don't want to leave."

"Are you saying you're not even the least bit intrigued?"

"Of course I'm intrigued. It's a very attractive offer. Maybe six months ago, I would've considered it, but not anymore."

"What's changed?"

She took a deep breath and slowly exhaled. A lot had changed. She didn't want to be that far from her father, and she enjoyed spending time with her friends. And there was Preston. "My life is here now."

"You don't want to write an advice column forever, do you?"

"Well, no. I am thinking of doing something different."

"Here it is then, lined up on a silver—no, platinum platter for you."

"I like my life where I am."

After a moment of tense silence, Angela continued, "What's holding you back? A year ago, you were on your way to New York."

"Things have changed."

"Things or people? Is this about the guy you've been seeing?"

Though she and Angela weren't PJ pals, Olivia had told her about Preston. She couldn't keep anything from her anyway. Like a top-notch editor, Angela would push until she got answers, and once again, she'd accurately sussed out the story behind the story.

"So, you would forego this great opportunity for a man that you've known for how long?"

"I met him last year, and we've been dating for five months, but—"

"Oh, Olivia. With two ex-husband skeletons in my closet, I'm telling you right now, think of yourself first. You've got to take care of you."

"It's not just about him."

"*Uh-huh.* But it's a lot about him."

She hated that Angela was usually spot-on about everything.

"Olivia, you know you're dear to me. But as a friend, this needs to be said. Look what happened with your last relationship. I'm sorry, but it's the truth. No man is worth sacrificing your own goals over."

"That was harsh, and it's not like that."

"What is it like then? Are you going to pass on every opportunity that comes your way because the guy you're with may be the one?"

She shook her head. "That's not fair. And that's not how I think."

"What does he do for a living?"

"You know what he does."

Angela groaned out a sigh. "You're going to be a cop's wife. That's what you've dreamed of since you were a little girl?"

Her defensiveness reared as she retorted, "We're not

even close to marriage. The thought hasn't crossed my mind." But it had hypothetically, more than once.

"You better think long and hard about this. You know I only want what's best for you, right?"

Olivia nodded, taking a moment to calm her tone. "Yes. You're like my tough-love, truth-telling fairy godmother."

"You forgot to add, who looks fabulous for being almost sixty. I remember the first day you walked into my office. You were this young, gung ho, bright-eyed girl from a small town. I thought you'd last two months, at most."

"You never told me that. And you do look at least ten years younger."

"Thank you, and you proved me wrong. You're like my fledgling. I won't be here forever. The truth is, I'm thinking of moving on myself. Tell me, is writing this column what you want to be doing for the rest of your life, or even for the next five years?"

"No, and no."

"Okay, then. It's time to make a change. I don't want you to be stuck here if it's not what you want. You need to move when the opportunity arises, which it's doing now. Promise me you'll at least think about it."

She'd been sure staying in Apple Station was for the long-term, but Angela made excellent points. Her father could live by himself. He'd done so for over ten years, and he would never want to be the reason that she didn't pursue her dreams. Maybe her head was too clouded about Preston. Maybe she'd fallen too fast. Maybe she was a little scared to trust her heart.

To satisfy Angela, and without entirely lying, she promised, "I'll think about it."

"Thank you, Olivia. That's all I'm asking. Remember, if you always do what you've always done, you'll always get what you always got."

CHAPTER 7

At only half past noon, Olivia was more miffed than hangry. Despite the call ending on a positive note, she was upset with herself for getting defensive about Angela's honest opinion. Her take on Preston's role in Olivia's semi-rejection of the job at *Modern Mosaic* was bang on. Long-term thinking at this stage in their relationship was on the back burner. Slow and steady was her mantra, as she felt no rush to get that serious with him so quickly. Not shutting Angela down on the matter, though, spoke volumes about her own hesitancy.

She closed her laptop without bothering to log out and shut down properly. Needing a break and a hit of comforting carbs, she stood and left the office. After locking up, she crossed the yard, hoping lunch would help clear her mind and reset her day.

Entering the kitchen through the back door, she

heard Buddy's friendly bark and Willow's claws scampering across the floor in the living room, hinting that he was chasing her around the sofa. Buddy always seemed to think it was a game, but she wasn't certain Willow took it that way. She looked in on them, making sure all was in fun. Whenever one stopped, so would the other until they mutually started up again. Besides, if Willow ever really felt threatened, she could outrun and out-hide everyone in the house.

As Willow gained a half-sofa lead over Buddy, a heavy thud from a closing car door stopped both in their tracks. Happy-go-lucky Buddy barked and lolloped to the door, eager to greet their guest. The wary Willow hid under the coffee table, watching Olivia's reaction as she stepped closer to the window for a view of the driveway.

Her sixth sense slowed her steps upon seeing Preston's truck. Normally, she'd welcome a surprise visit, but he was supposed to be following up on a lead in a murder investigation. Now that he was here, panic popped the question: Did the evidence at Spring Hills point to her or Sam?

She went out onto the porch, waited by the railing, and greeted him with a hammed-up grin. "Hey there, stranger. This is a delightful surprise."

He returned half of her smile as he came up the steps. "Sorry I didn't call ahead." He leaned down, giving her a perfunctory kiss on the cheek. "I need to speak with you about something."

His all-business game face heightened her suspicions about the timing of his visit. "Okay. This sounds official. Do you want to go inside?"

"No. I can't stay long." He paused, glancing at the far end of the porch for a moment before locking eyes with her. "When did you last speak with Sam?"

She didn't have to act startled. Had he called instead and asked the same question, she would've had more time to think. She could've put him off by pretending Buddy was up to something naughty and she needed to get off the phone right away. But hiding her microexpressions and acting normal while face-to-face with him was a delicate dance.

"She's been away for about a week. Why do you ask?"

"Have you heard from her since she left?"

Her thoughts were racing. The question required a simple yes or no, but she parsed her words, avoiding the either-or choice. "I tried to call her yesterday, but I couldn't get hold of her. Is there something wrong?"

He pulled his cell out of his jeans pocket. "What I'm about to show you needs to stay strictly between us."

She swallowed hard, reflexively nodding while her stomach tumbled over keeping a secret from Sam.

"I want you to look at this," he said, swiping the screen until he found what he was searching for. Then he turned the phone toward her. "Do you recognize this person?"

The black-and-white nighttime photo showed a ghostly figure in a forest standing about fifteen feet from the camera. Even with the facial features blurred, Olivia didn't have to look twice to recognize Sam. She drew in closer to the screen and narrowed her eyes, buying time and trying to act convincing.

"I have no idea."

"Take another look."

She gave him the best quizzical expression she could improvise, raising her eyebrows and wrinkling her nose. After a second look, she shook her head and shrugged. "I really don't know."

He swiped to the next shot of Sam. Thankfully, this one was less telling as she stood in profile, but Olivia still could identify her from what she'd been wearing.

"That doesn't look like Sam to you?" he asked.

She popped her eyes wide open. "Sam? Where were these taken?"

He lowered the phone and slid it into his pocket. "Last night, a trail camera took those pictures in a section of forest at Spring Hills nearby the old barracks. This morning, when we expanded the search perimeter around where we found Klein, Jayden came across the cam. The owner's name was on it, and we located him at his home, not too far from the site. He said he'd heard word of a bear sighting in the woods there and wanted to gather evidence as a public service. More likely, he's been hunting on the property. Given the choice to face a warrant for all his cameras or just show us what was on the one, he obliged."

"But Sam's away," she said.

"That looks like Sam to me, but I thought you'd be a better judge. We both know the nature of what she does. I know she's your friend, but I think that's her in the photos."

She placed her hands on the small of her back and shuffled her feet. "Are you suggesting she had something to do with what happened there last night?"

"I don't know. I don't want to believe so, but I need to speak with her sooner rather than later. If you hear from her, call me. But you can't tell her what I showed you."

She felt like a fresh bloom withered and died inside of her. All she could do was nod, as if blindly signing a contract without reading it.

He placed his hands on her arms, just below her shoulders. "Thanks." He leaned down, brushing her lips with a kiss, but she barely responded. "Are you okay?"

She took a step back and glanced toward Sam's house. "Yeah. This has just thrown me a little."

"I'm sure there's an explanation, and the sooner we can clarify matters, the better it'll be for Sam."

"Who else knows about this?"

"For now, just us. I can't sit on this for too long if we don't find some other evidence. I want to give her the benefit of the doubt. I owe her at least that much after what she did to help capture Mason Andrews. Who knows what would've happened to you at the storage facility had she not been there."

"Yeah, we both owe her."

He kissed her cheek. "I need to get back to work. I'll call you later."

"Okay. Be careful."

She watched as he returned to his truck, got in, and reversed down the driveway. She stared past the front yard at the wildflower field across the road. The forecasted clouds had thickened, obscuring the sunlight that had shone so brightly this morning. She tilted her head to one side, eliciting several cracks in her neck, which always happened when she tensed her shoulders under stress.

She couldn't pretend anymore that this was a normal day. Preston had connected Sam to the crime scene, and it may be only a matter of time before he discovered she had been there as well. Remaining passive and hoping for the best was no longer a viable plan. Someday there would be a reckoning for what had just happened between them. She was under no illusion that her role would remain anonymous, but her resolve to protect Sam had doubled.

Sam needed to be warned ASAP, but likely, any attempts to contact her would go unanswered. There was no time to play games by calling her and hoping Mark would show up again. She had two numbers that redirected incoming calls to a cell in Sam's possession. But she didn't know how to locate that active phone. Using back channels to find someone who didn't want to be found wasn't in her skill set. However, she had an acquaintance with one person who may have the ability.

She turned and went inside, hustling to grab her keys, wallet, and a cereal bar from the pantry. After checking on Buddy and Willow and finding them both napping, she left the house, got into her car, and went to call on Dylan Carter.

CHAPTER 8

The last time Olivia visited Dylan's neighborhood, he wasn't living there yet. In December, she'd come here to speak with his mother, Stacey, about her ex-husband's past dealings with Preston's deceased father. Though her first meeting with Dylan was under difficult circumstances, they'd since become casual friends. She'd see him in town occasionally, mostly while waiting in line at Jillian's Cafe for an afternoon coffee. During one such run-in, she learned that he'd bought a house in his mother's subdivision. That didn't surprise her, as he adored his sister Darcy's five-year-old daughter, and she and Darcy both lived with Stacey.

Their small development featured tightly packed split-level homes with white siding and modest front porches. Chain-link fences separated the tiny yards, and all the residential parking was streetside. She'd never been to his house, but she knew he worked from home as an IT consultant. Formerly a hacker, he had changed his ways, now working to prevent others from doing what he used to. She had his phone number and thought about calling ahead, but her business with him was delicate and best addressed face-to-face from the get-go.

She'd planned to stop and ask Stacey for his address, but when she drove up to Stacey's house, Dylan and Kaitlyn were in the yard playing soccer. He was crouched in front of a folding net set up near the fence. Kaitlyn dribbled the ball left and right, then wound up and boomed a kick that he let pass by. She jumped up and down like a kangaroo, celebrating her score.

Olivia pulled along the curb, stopped, and turned off the engine. As she got out and shut the door, Dylan stood tall, grinning a warm welcome when he saw her. A Jack Russell terrier inside their fenced yard charged across the lawn, fiercely barking as she stepped onto the sidewalk and waited by the gate. The neighbor's tiny terror, who she well remembered from her last visit with Stacey, surprised her by being on the Carters' side of the fence.

"Max, pipe down," Dylan said as he came over to greet her. He patted the wiry white dog's head, spun him around, and gave him a little tush-push back toward the house. "Hi. This is a surprise."

She returned his greeting as Kaitlyn skipped over to the gate and pointed at her.

"I know you!" Kaitlyn exclaimed.

Olivia kept a straight face. "No. I don't think you do. We've never met before. Do you live here?"

Kaitlyn grinned, showing off a missing front tooth. "You're lying! You came and talked with Grandma and Uncle in the house."

She scrunched her eyes. "You caught me. You have a super memory."

"I knew you were lying." Kaitlyn unlatched the gate and swung it partially open.

Dylan shot his arm forward, stopping her from opening it farther. "Hold on, pumpkin." He peeked over his shoulder. "Be careful. We have to watch so Max doesn't get out."

"He won't get out."

"We just need to pay attention to where he is."

She pointed toward the soccer net. "He's there."

"Okay. You can let our friend in."

Kaitlyn opened the gate a little more, allowing Olivia to step into the yard.

"I thought Max was your neighbor's dog," she said.

"He is," Dylan replied as he closed the latch. "We were always concerned for Kaitlyn's sake whenever he was outside. He used to run back and forth along the fence, barking like mad. We were worried he might be dangerous. But I think he just wanted to get on this side and have fun with her."

Kaitlyn grabbed Olivia's hand. "He's my friend. Did you come to play soccer with us? Look, I lost a tooth."

Olivia acted shocked. "Did you find it?"

"No! I didn't *lose* it. It fell out. And then I put it under my pillow and got ten dollars from the tooth fairy."

"*Wow*," she said. "Business must be good for the tooth fairy these days. I used to only get a dollar."

Kaitlyn released her hand, ran over to the soccer ball, and picked it up. Then she hurried back over, holding the ball out toward Olivia. "Do you want to play? You can be on my team."

Olivia squatted, getting closer to Kaitlyn's eye level. "Why aren't you in school?"

"Teacher workday," Dylan said.

"I see. I'd love to play with you because I think we'd beat your uncle, but I can't stay too long. Some other time, okay? I was hoping your uncle had a few minutes to talk."

"I sure do. It must be important for you to have come all the way out here. What's on your mind?"

She stood, glancing down at Kaitlyn. "It's grown-up stuff."

He nodded and placed his hands on Kaitlyn's shoulders. "Hey, pumpkin. Go inside and start lunch. There are some peanut butter and jelly sandwiches in the fridge that your mommy made this morning. I'll join you in a little while."

"Can we play more after?"

"Yes, but you have to let me win at least once."

"Never!" she gleefully shouted. "Bye." She spun, dropped the ball, and ran to the front door with Max yapping on her heels.

"Bye," Olivia replied, waving at her back. "She seems well."

"The new medication has made all the difference. She's so happy that she gets to go to school with her friends now. Since starting the medication, she hasn't had a single respiratory illness. Her pulmonologist was so impressed that she appealed to the insurance company on Kaitlyn's behalf. Last week, they reversed their decision and are now going to cover the cost of the drug. We owe Henry so much."

Henry Zimmerman, a retired widower, had generously paid for the expensive, experimental medication after bonding with the family during Christmas.

"How's he doing?" she asked. "I was thinking of visiting him one of these days. It's been a few months since I've seen him."

"You should. He'd enjoy that. He's become like Kaitlyn's grandfather. He comes over for dinner about once a month, and Kaitlyn absolutely adores him. It doesn't hurt that he's always giving her gifts." Dylan rubbed his hands together. "So, what's this grown-up business you want to talk about?"

"I need some tech help." She pursed her lips for a moment, then took a deep breath. "Is there a way you can pinpoint the location of a phone that calls are being forwarded to?"

He narrowed his eyes as if attempting to understand the question. "Technically, maybe. Are you trying to find a phone, or do you think someone is trying to find you?"

"I want to do the finding. I need to contact a friend,

and the only numbers I have for her are being sent to a cell that she has in her possession."

"Why don't you just leave a message or text her, since she's getting the calls?"

"It's complicated. I have to get in touch with her, warn her about something, but she doesn't exactly want me to do that. I wouldn't be here asking if this weren't serious. She helped me with what happened at Christmas involving your father, and I think she's in trouble."

He nodded. "I see. Do you share any location apps on your phone with her?"

"No."

"Hmm. Then locating her becomes tricky." He rubbed his Van Dyke beard several times, then glanced back at his mother's house. "Let's take a walk over to my place. It's just across the street, a few houses down. My mom is inside, so Kaitlyn will be okay."

He opened the gate, and after they were both out of the yard, he secured the latch. They crossed the street, talking as they walked.

"When's the last time you tried to contact your friend?"

"By phone, yesterday afternoon. I saw her later in the day, and that's how I know she'd received the forwarded calls on another cell."

"Call forwarding happens at the level of the network, not the phone. This is my place here."

He unlatched the gate, and she followed him on the walkway and into his house. His interior décor contrasted with that of his mother's home. Soothing, muted gray tones dominated the walls and the modern furniture. A large white desk with two monitors fronted the window, providing a view of the yard and the street. Stacey's home had more of a lived-in feel, with well-worn furnishings and Kaitlyn's toys scattered about.

He turned on a lamp and booted up his desktop computer. "Please have a seat."

She sat on the edge of a firm, pebble-gray sofa.

"You can't legally track a phone unless the person has consented," he said. "People don't realize they've agreed to be tracked by not turning off location settings in certain mapping and social apps."

"I don't want you to do anything illegal."

"There are means by which law enforcement can actively locate the general area of a cell, but it relies on that phone making a call or sending a text."

"You're talking about a cell site simulator?"

He raised his brow. "Exactly. That's not everyday knowledge. Have you had experience with them?"

While unraveling a blackmail scheme involving Preston's mother, Sam had introduced her to the technology. "It's a long story."

"It seems you keep interesting company. Without an incoming call, another way to determine a general location would be to comb through the carrier network data. The accuracy would depend on several factors. Do you have your friend's number on your cell?"

"I do." She took out her phone, opened the directory, and scrolled to Sam's contact information.

He held out his hand, and she gave the cell to him.

"Does your friend have the same carrier as you?"

"She does."

He tapped the phone against his palm several times. "Okay. Give me a few minutes."

"Dylan, I don't want you to do anything that you could get in trouble for."

He flashed a boyish grin. "I understand. Let me see what I can find." He turned, went into the hallway, and shut a door.

She was almost certain that whatever he had in mind wasn't kosher. Sam had warned Olivia not to contact her, but here she was, teetering on a slippery slope, trying to do just that. Technically, Olivia hadn't yet done anything illegal. The deeper she fell down the rabbit hole, though, the harder it would be to explain her actions if she got caught.

After about fifteen minutes, she heard the door in the hallway open. He returned to the room, holding her phone and a piece of paper.

"I have good news and bad news," he said, handing the cell back to her. "I called the number, and as expected, there was no answer. That call got forwarded to your friend's other cell, and luckily, it was on."

"How do you know that?"

"When our phones are on, they're constantly transmitting, and towers are always trying to receive the signals from the cells within their range." He flipped the piece of paper around, revealing a set of numbers. "The carrier showed the call was forwarded to a cell near these coordinates."

"Digging into network data doesn't sound legal."

He shook his head. "This is only between you, me, and one individual from my past who is happy he no longer owes me a favor." He went to his desk and sat in his chair.

She stood up and followed him over. "What's the bad news?"

"The first call I placed pinged a cell close to this location. When I called again to see if she was on the move, the cell wasn't transmitting."

"What does that mean?"

He typed on the keyboard and opened a mapping website.

"That means your friend is on to you. She must've gotten the first call, then switched her cell off."

"No more signal."

"Correct. Not until she turns it back on."

"But in the last fifteen minutes, she was someplace near those coordinates."

"That's a fair conclusion. Let's see what we got here."

He input the numbers, and a map popped up, showing only unmarked, undeveloped land. He expanded the view several times, looking for roads, landmarks, or towns.

"This looks like all forest here," he said, scrolling and

moving the map around. "The cell could be a mile or more in radius from this tower, which seems to be in the middle of nowhere. There's nothing much here—just a little lake. The nearest town is Gore. That's about thirty minutes from here, which I guess is reasonable if she wants to stay close by, but hidden, for whatever reason. Wait, what's this?" He zoomed in. "Here's something. That's the closest designated waypoint. Our Lady of Grace Monastery. Is your friend a nun?"

CHAPTER 9

After Olivia entered the monastery's address into her car's GPS, she drove twenty-five miles northwest to Gore. Before she left, she and Dylan had promised to keep the methods he'd used to obtain the information between themselves. She had to trust him as much as he trusted her. All three people involved only stood to lose if any of them spoke out of turn. No one else was in her need-to-know camp on this. If pressed, she could testify truthfully that she didn't know who pulled the data. She hadn't asked Dylan to call in any favors, but now, with the location in hand, she'd follow the trail for Sam's sake.

A community of Benedictine sisters lived on the monastery's pastoral grounds. Though the sprawling property was open to the public during daylight hours, she'd never visited the area. The sisters were regular attendees at all of Apple Station's town festivals, selling their homemade baked goods, jams, and hot sauces to support local charities. One year when she and A.J. went together to the Spring Fling Festival, she bought him a bottle of their award-winning Hotter than Hell Habanero Hot Sauce. He boasted he could withstand anything on the Scoville Scale, and she dared him to test his bravado with the sisters' specialty. Two days after eating a plate of buffalo wings drenched in the sauce, he was still suffering from a sour stomach and intestinal woes.

She might've missed the unassuming L-shaped hanging sign that marked the monastery's entrance if not for the GPS's instruction to turn. Once on Ministry Lane, she drove a short distance, passing a much larger, hand-crafted wooden sign fastened to a white cast-iron bench. On the sign was the engraved greeting "All Are Welcome." About fifty yards ahead, the property opened up, revealing the community buildings and the parking lot. Two older women wearing matching pink jogging suits were power walking beside the road. As Olivia came up behind them, they slowed, stepped farther onto the grass, and waved as she went by.

She placed the odds of finding Sam here as fifty-iffy. Upon seeing only a smattering of cars in the lot, her doubts doubled. Coming across Sam hiding out among the community seemed unlikely, but this was her only lead. If she couldn't contact Sam soon, she'd have to tell Preston what she knew, trusting he'd believe her. She didn't want the police to waste time and resources searching for Sam when they should be focused on identifying Bobby Klein's killer.

After parking and getting out of the car, she scanned the area without a solid plan in mind. The sizable complex appeared self-contained, with wings and additions that were all interconnected. Beige siding wrapped the facility's facade, and abundant, white-framed windows provided plenty of natural light. An extended covered portico led from the front sidewalk to a glass door. Figuring this to be a main entrance, Olivia decided it seemed like a good place to start. She wasn't expecting to come upon Sam praying by one of the many statues on the grounds. Rather, she'd show Sam's picture to anyone around on the chance they'd seen her.

A few happy sunbeams shone through the thin cloud cover, brightening the tidy, mulched flowerbeds lining the walkway. A robin hopped amid the phlox, petunias, and snapdragons, poking around the loose ground for worms. The door led into a lobby, with a main office visible just inside the entrance. She grabbed the long pull handle and tugged, but the door was locked. Looking for a bell, she glanced to her side and spotted a button on a steel plate mounted to the wall. Pressing it prompted a brief, high-pitched buzz. When no one came, she tried again and stepped closer for a better view inside.

"Excuse me, miss," a woman behind her said.

She turned and faced an older woman wearing a white cardigan over a blue-and-green flower-printed dress.

"You can go right around the side," the woman added, pointing in the opposite direction from where she was going.

Olivia's eyes followed the sidewalk where it traced the contour of the building. "Okay. Thanks." Before she could pull out her phone to show Sam's picture, the woman had already continued on her way. The pink-clad power walkers she'd passed earlier went through an opened gate about twenty yards from her. She hustled after them, hoping to catch up and ask if they'd seen Sam during their brisk tour of the grounds.

A staked sign simply stating "Blooms" stood beside a six-foot tall lattice steel gate that led to an open court-yard. She passed through the entrance, stepping straight into a charming botanical garden. Rustic terra-cotta-red flagstone formed crisscrossing walkways between numerous raised plant beds. Many of the plots contained only dirt, but a few boasted spring flowers and young vegetable plants.

The walkers had proceeded at a quick clip and were already on the other side of the garden by the time she spotted them. Two other women were working among the elevated planters. One was tending to tulips four rows over. The other was closer, kneeling in front of a freshly tilled bed and digging in the dirt with a hand trowel. A dozen or more seedlings in square plastic containers sat on the walk, waiting to be planted. As Olivia approached, the woman, who appeared to be in her mid-fifties, rocked back on her heels and looked up at her.

"You look like you're a little lost," the woman said.

Olivia greeted her with a friendly smile. *You have no idea.* "I'm looking for someone."

"The Lord?"

Olivia shook her head slightly. "Um, no. I'm not here for spiritual guidance."

The woman's cheeks raised, rounding her face into a perfect heart shape as she cackled. "I'm playing with you. You should've seen your expression. Priceless. I'm Sister Anne, but just Anne is fine."

Dressed in olive overalls and a white T-shirt, she looked more like a worker for a landscaping company than a nun.

"You were probably expecting a habit," Anne said. "Visitors always find it surprising we don't wear them here." She removed her gloves, placed them by a long-handled shovel, and stood up. "Is it one of our sisters you're looking for?"

Olivia took out her phone, opened her photos, and turned the screen around. "No, her."

Anne studied Sam's photo. "She doesn't look familiar. We have a lot of ground here, and visitors come and go during the day. I've been out here working since early this morning, and I *definitely* haven't seen her. Is she discerning?"

"As in, to become a sister?"

Anne nodded. "She'd make a fine one."

"I highly doubt it."

"Too bad. What about you?"

"Me? Do *I* want to be a sister? No. I mean, I respect the vocation, but I … ah … that's just not … I don't feel called."

Anne sighed. "Oh well. I had to try. We always need new, young recruits for the army of the Lord." She picked up her flower-patterned gardening gloves off the ground and put them back on. "Stay as long as you like. Enjoy the grounds and be sure to stop by the lobby before you go. Take one of our pamphlets on vocations in case you change your mind. It's never too late."

Olivia thanked Anne, then let her get back to planting. Between the size of the property and the word of a sister who seemed to be in the know, her hopes of finding Sam were running low. She strolled through the garden and checked the time on her phone. At just after three, she figured Preston may be at work for a few more hours, depending on whether the police had come up with any leads. She didn't want the day to end without telling him about Sam, risking further ill will by keeping the matter from him longer than necessary.

Another sister had joined the woman tending to the tulips, and they stood together talking as Olivia approached.

"Good afternoon, Sisters. Those are beautiful flowers."

The taller sister spoke first. "Mary Ellen here did all the hard work, planting the bulbs in November."

Mary Ellen waved her hand, brushing off the compliment. "But Louise, you've been taking care of them since they bloomed, and we've never had a prettier bed. You don't look familiar, my dear. Have you visited with us before?"

"No." Olivia looked back at Anne, who was watching them, and decided to change her tactics. "I'm meeting a friend here, but the grounds are so spread out, and I can't find her. She's not answering her cell." She opened Sam's picture on her phone and showed it to them. "Have you seen her around?"

They both leaned in toward the screen. Louise shook her head, while Mary Ellen tilted the phone in Olivia's hand for a better view.

"Yes, by the guest cottages," Mary Ellen said.

"Guest cottages? Where are those?"

Louise pointed as she spoke. "If you follow this sidewalk, go through the brown door, cross the hallway inside, and keep going straight to exit through the gray door. That's a shortcut, so you don't have to walk around the front. Head down the hill, go past the meditation grotto, and you'll come right to the cottages. You can't miss them."

"Thank you. When did you see her there?"

"This morning, quite early, just after six," Mary Ellen said. "I was leaving the grotto after my rosary when I noticed her and another woman talking by the angel on the quad."

"Okay, great. Thanks again."

They exchanged parting pleasantries, and Olivia took

off, following Louise's directions. The confirmation that Sam had been here, at least in the morning, quickened her pace, and she reached the cottages in no time. The four units looked like microhomes, not much larger than her backyard office. A grassy lawn about thirty feet across separated the two-by-two arrangement. The front of each cottage faced the others, and they all had two windows, providing a view of the small quad and a statue of a praying angel.

One potato, two potatoes, three potatoes, four. I think you're hiding behind one of these doors.

Drawn curtains covered three of the four cottages' front windows, so she went with the low-hanging fruit. Stepping to the front of the unit nearest her, she peeked through the window at the dark interior, seeing everything neatly arranged as if awaiting the next guest. With the first one down, she moved over to its neighbor and knocked on the door. When there was no answer, she tried again, and the door swung open almost immediately.

A woman about her age stood in the entrance and removed a pair of earbuds. "Hello."

Olivia held up a hand, offering a wave of apology. "I'm so sorry to bother you. I have the wrong cottage."

The woman just smiled, put her earbuds back in, and closed the door.

She turned to face the cottage across the quad, and had started toward it when the curtain in the fourth unit moved. Breaking her stride, she altered her course to see who was behind the window. Once at the front door, she knocked with the side of her fist.

"Sam." There was no answer, and she waited only a few seconds before banging on the door again. "Sam! If you're in there, open up!"

"She's not here," Anne said from behind her.

She spun as Anne moved in, placing the blade of her long shovel between Olivia and the door.

"Whoa, Sister. Anne. I'm just looking for my friend."

She raised the shovel higher. "Don't think I won't use this. 'For thou hast smitten all mine enemies upon the cheekbone, thou hast broken the teeth of the wicked.'"

CHAPTER 10

The guest cottage's white wooden door swung open, and Sam stepped out, holding her hand up between the muddy blade and Olivia. "It's okay, Anne. She's with me."

Anne lowered the shovel, clinking the business end of her impromptu weapon on the concrete walk. She pushed her red-framed glasses up off the tip of her nose, swapping her tough-as-nails demeanor for that of a honey-hearted sister.

"Right, then," she said as she hoisted the shovel, holding it horizontally. "Sorry about the misunderstanding. Vespers are at six if you'd like to join us. We're having a special dinner tonight—Thanksgiving in May. That's not really a thing, but we got a good deal on turkeys from a local farmer in November, and we need to get them out of the freezer. Louise and Mary Ellen, who you met in the garden, baked all kinds of goodies yesterday. It promises to be a scrumptious feast. I'll let you catch up. Tallyho." With that, she turned and strolled away.

"Come inside," Sam said.

After Olivia entered, Sam shut and locked the door. The cottage was more spacious than she'd estimated. A twin two-post bed, a small pine desk with a matching chair, and a sienna-brown sofa furnished the simple guest room. The microwave, the mini fridge, and the wardrobe all were white, and a cross on the wall by the window was the sole adornment.

"How did you find me?" Sam asked.

"I think the better question is, 'Do you come here often?' Is this one of your safe houses, or are you discerning?"

"The former, sort of."

Olivia jabbed her thumb indistinctly behind her. "What's the deal with Anne? Is she an actual sister, or is she a *sister* like Mark is a *Mormon*?"

"Real sister. She's helped me in the past. You didn't answer my question. How did you find me?"

"I had help from someone I trust."

Two light knocks on the door kept Sam from pushing for a name, which Olivia wouldn't divulge to anyone under almost any circumstances. Sam slightly parted the curtains, peeked through the window, and let her visitor in.

A well-dressed woman entered wearing camel linen pants and a matching blazer over a cream silk blouse. The perfect auburn highlights in her sleekly styled brunette hair surely weren't from a DIY kit. Her high cheekbones and thin, angular jaw would make any photographer smile. With barely a line showing on her expressionless face, her age was hard to pinpoint. Sunspots and slight discolorations on her pale skin hinted she may be in her mid-sixties.

Sam shut the door as the woman scanned Olivia from head to toe.

"Sam, I was unaware you were entertaining guests," the woman said in a posh British accent that didn't feel welcoming.

"This is Olivia Penn. Liv, this is Carolyn Shaw."

Carolyn stood with perfect posture, reminding her of a ballerina. She stared at Olivia without blinking, twitching a muscle, or noticeably breathing. "Ms. Penn, how is it you located Sam?"

Her authoritative tone suggested that she was used to asking questions and getting answers.

Olivia shifted her stance, glancing at Sam before answering. "Trade secret."

Carolyn cracked the thinnest of smiles, then went over to the sofa and sat down. She crossed one leg over the other, casually elegant, and stretched her arm across the sofa's back. Olivia imagined she'd look equally graceful lounging in a beanbag chair.

"I've heard a lot about you, Ms. Penn."

The power dynamic was clear, but she wasn't about to kowtow to someone she didn't know. "It's not mutual."

Carolyn slowly nodded. "I'm sure that'll change, but not today. As much as it would be polite to chat about what you're making for dinner, I don't have the time for civil small talk." She looked at Sam. "We have a problem."

"What's going on here?" Olivia said, eyeing Sam. "A forest trail camera took several photos of you at Spring Hills last night. Preston showed me the pictures this morning. He wasn't positive it was you, so he came to ask me what I thought. I covered for you the best I could. He's sitting on the evidence for now, but he wants to question you."

"Who is Preston?" Carolyn asked.

"A detective in the Apple Station Police Department," Olivia replied.

"And her boyfriend," Sam added.

"Ms. Penn, you keep an interesting social circle."

"Just Olivia is fine. I don't know who you are, but Sam is in trouble."

"Indeed, she is." Carolyn shifted her focus back to Sam. "I can't risk losing you. You'll have to stay out of sight. We'll have to find another way."

"To do what?" Olivia asked. "If I can help, I will. I'm already involved. I was at Spring Hills last night, and I know Bobby Klein was the co-manager of the carnival that set up at Fields Farm yesterday."

Sam settled on the other end of the sofa. "We can trust her."

Carolyn sighed and rubbed her forehead, revealing a tiny chink in her armor. "Desperate times call for desperate measures. You might as well have a seat. You're not in the principal's office."

Olivia moved the desk chair closer to them and sat.

"Do you know what Sam does?" Carolyn asked.

"She works as a security consultant," Olivia answered. She knew there was a lot more to it but kept to the basics, hoping Carolyn would start from the beginning to give her a broader scope of what was happening.

"I head a shadow organization funded by the government's black budget. We conduct covert intelligence operations, details of which are only shared within specific security circles."

Olivia had heard of the black budget, although she'd never speculated too deeply about it. But with that revelation, so much about Sam suddenly made sense. "I didn't know if that was an actual thing or just fodder to fuel conspiracy-theory podcasts."

"It's very real," Carolyn replied. "That's how we exist. Through non-disclosure, we avoid standard rules with our operational tactics. What law enforcement can't do legally, we can. If all goes well, nobody ever hears about what we do. Something, in this case, hasn't gone well."

"We've been tracking a criminal organization operating along the East Coast who are heavy hitters in the illegal animal trade," Sam said. "They deal mostly in selling exotic and endangered animals. Monkeys, tigers, lemurs, sugar gliders—to name a few. They buy and resell to individuals from New England to Florida. They're part of a multibillion-dollar criminal industry that offers high profits with low risks. Laws are in place to protect the animals, but there's not enough personnel to enforce them. Those who get caught often receive only fines. They pay them, then continue trafficking. This group we've been following has been a step ahead of us. We haven't been able to catch them conducting a transaction, so we changed our tactics."

"How?" Olivia asked.

"We used an informant who helped set up a cover for me," Sam said. "With a falsified background in place, I became a low-level driver for the organization. My job was to pick up the merchandise last night at Spring Hills, call my contact, and deliver the goods to the designated location."

"Was Bobby Klein the supplier?" Olivia asked.

"We believe so," Carolyn said. "This was the closest we've come to identifying those involved on both ends. I can't stand to see animals harmed. I want to deliver those responsible to their cells myself."

Olivia looked at Sam. "You believe someone set you up. Do you think the man who came looking for you with the carnations killed Klein?"

"Tommy Grasso," Carolyn said. "He has known connections in organized crime. The yellow carnations are a calling card. They signal disappointment." She crossed her arms, keeping a flat affect. "I know because that's what I gave my first husband on our second anniversary."

"It makes little sense for Grasso to have killed Klein," Sam said.

"Why kill your supplier?" Olivia asked rhetorically. "That's not a sound business practice. I'm assuming it was Grasso calling the cell in your room. Why was he trying to reach you on a phone you didn't even have?"

"His calls were forwarded to my primary. He was the only person in the organization I ever had contact with. All arrangements were handled over the phone. Drivers don't reach out to their contact until they're ready to deliver the goods. Once I had the shipment secured, our plan was to disengage, so there was no need to call the contact any point. I don't carry multiple phones for security reasons."

"You mentioned Klein's trunk was empty," Olivia said. "If he was the source, then someone probably took whatever you were supposed to pick up."

Carolyn uncrossed her arms and legs, then slid to the edge of the sofa. "Now that Sam hasn't delivered the goods, she'll have a target on her back. The buyers will think she stole the merchandise."

"Do you think Grasso will come after you? And why was he looking for you at your house?"

"He should've never found out where she lived," Carolyn replied. "We take great pains to keep our people safe. Therein lies the second problem. The timing of Grasso's visit points to a mole."

"We believe someone on our team leaked my identity," Sam added. "It's probable Grasso knew I was undercover, and he may have wanted to ensure I would go through with the pickup. I'd gone dark on him for a few days, and he was probably antsy to get me the details of the meeting."

"I don't understand," Olivia said. "If he knew who you really were, why would he still want you to take part in the transaction?"

"This organization doesn't handle the exchanges personally," Carolyn said. "They hire low level, but highly vetted drivers to pick up and deliver the merchandise. If something goes wrong, and the driver gets caught, then they can't implicate anyone. The drivers have never met their contacts or been told any real names. With only hours to go before the transaction, it's unlikely they could get someone to replace her, so they played along. We assume that once Sam made the pickup and received the drop-off location, their plan was to intercept her en route, retrieve the goods, and do away with her."

"They would ambush you before you could ambush them," Olivia said. "So, the yellow carnations were a poetic acknowledgment of the double cross."

"Indeed," Carolyn replied. "Had it not targeted one of my own, I would've said, well played."

Two loud voices outside the cottage caused them all

to fall silent. Sam stood, stepped over to the window, and parted the curtains for a peek. "It's okay."

Olivia shifted in the unforgiving seat, grateful for her own comfy desk chair with variable lumbar support. "If they'd risk your involvement in the transaction, whatever you were picking up must've been important. Do you know what was in the shipment?"

"Thirty parrot eggs," Sam replied.

"Hyacinth macaws," Carolyn added.

"Just eggs?"

"The hyacinth macaw is the world's largest flying parrot," Carolyn said. "They are magnificent birds with brilliant cobalt blue bodies. A large population lives in the wetlands of the Pantanal across parts of Brazil, Paraguay, and Bolivia. Fires and deforestation have reduced their habitat, and even though they are a protected species, their numbers are decreasing. They're highly coveted as pets, and a criminal industry of egg smuggling has sprung up to supply the need, particularly in Europe."

"How do you smuggle eggs?" Olivia asked. "How much are they worth?"

Sam leaned her back against the door. "Transport is tricky. Some will strap them to their bodies to keep them warm, turning themselves into human incubators. We don't know how these eggs got into the country. Each hatchling could fetch fifteen thousand dollars or more. If all the birds live, we're looking at a deal in the ballpark of half a million."

"Fifteen thousand for one bird?" Olivia repeated, mostly to herself, to let the number sink in.

"They're difficult to breed in captivity," Carolyn said. "They can be legally owned if purchased from a breeder. Wild-caught macaws and eggs poached from their natural habitats are illegal to trade. We're on the clock with this shipment. We believe poachers harvested these eggs from Brazil. Their breeding season ends in late April, and the incubation period is twenty-seven days. We don't know when they'll hatch. It could be any day. Without the proper care, they don't stand much of a chance."

"If whoever killed Klein took the eggs, don't you think they're probably long gone by now?" Olivia asked.

"That's possible," Carolyn said. "But we believe that Klein had partners and one of his associates may have killed him. The eggs would have to be kept in temperature-controlled incubators. Whoever has them would need to have care in place for them after they hatch. The buyers wouldn't pay for the eggs alone. The hatchlings would have to be viable. With the eggs so close to hatching, it's likely they're still in the area."

"Then you don't think the deal has happened yet?" Olivia asked, looking at Carolyn. "Klein isn't from around here. If he had a partner who killed him, it would make sense that it could be someone who came into town at the same time he did. Maybe someone else involved with the carnival."

"Indeed," Carolyn replied, glancing at Sam. "We

need to get someone on the inside. You're out of the picture. Unfortunately, we don't have anyone in the area."

"What about your guy, Mark?"

Carolyn stared at Olivia for a long minute. By the silence, Olivia was unsure whether she'd said something sound or foolish.

"He's logistics, not tactical," Sam offered, putting that suggestion to rest.

"Unless we have an alternate option," Carolyn said.

Olivia leaned in, eager to learn more about the other members of Sam's team.

"Say a reporter from the local paper who is writing a story about carnival life," Carolyn added.

The room went quiet as a cemetery at midnight. Olivia was unsure where Carolyn was going with this.

"That could work," Sam said.

Olivia's hand shot up. "Wait. What could work?"

"A vetted staff writer wouldn't raise any red flags," Sam said.

"Are you talking about somebody on *The Times* staff?" Olivia asked.

Carolyn glanced at Sam as Olivia looked back and forth between them.

"Or *me*? You're talking about me. Crucial fact—I'm not employed there. And what is it you think I could even accomplish?"

"You have ties to it," Carolyn said. "I hear you once worked as a journalist. It would be like riding a bike. Ask questions. Find out who is who. Determine if Klein had any enemies or was especially close to anyone. Probe rumors of his illegal activities."

She followed Carolyn's logic, though her mind was lining up reasons she wasn't the best candidate.

"Yes, I have connections to the paper. But I can't just show up on the carnival grounds saying that I'm writing a story when I'm not. They could fact-check that with one call."

Carolyn stood up and pulled her jacket sleeves down to cover her blouse cuffs. "Then make it happen with the powers that be. I hear you can be persuasive, or is that estimation of you too high?"

Olivia rose, triggered by the challenge and feeling like a commoner talked down to by royalty.

"I don't have all day," Carolyn continued. "Is Sam's life being in danger a good enough reason for you to play a reporter for a few days?"

When Carolyn put it like that, Olivia couldn't argue. Agreeing would mean losing her clinging grip on the slippery slope she was already halfway down. But the scenario intrigued her. If she could get Ellen on board, the logistics weren't unreasonable. Her own life wouldn't be at risk by simply asking questions under the guise of a cover story. She'd have to keep Preston in the dark a little while longer. Carolyn and the police were working toward related goals, but for now, Olivia conceded their methods were best left independent of each other.

"I'll have to talk to Ellen McCarthy, the paper's

editor, and tell her at least some of what's behind the ask. I'll keep your names and your black-budget team out of it."

"Agreed," Carolyn said, heading for the door.

"I'll do this for Sam, not you," Olivia said.

Carolyn stopped, half turned, and fashioned a faint smile. "Duly noted. I like you. You remind me of myself at your age." She pointed to Sam. "You stay here until we root out the mole who put us in this situation." Then she pivoted, opened the door, and left the cottage.

Olivia lowered herself onto the sofa, wrapping her head around what she was getting herself into. Masquerading as a reporter wouldn't be difficult, as that had been her actual job for years before starting her column. In a short time, she'd have to speak with Ellen and also devise a plan that included avoiding Preston for the next few days. Lost in her thoughts and with her focus fixed on the floor by her feet, she didn't even notice that Sam had closed the door and was now sitting in the desk chair.

"Liv, if you're not okay with doing this, we'll find another way."

She rubbed her hand over her forehead, feeling tension developing at the base of her skull. "No. I want to help and do whatever I can to get the target off your back. Your boss is quite intimidating. I can't imagine what working every day with her would be like."

Sam nodded, raising her brow. "Especially if she's your mother-in-law."

Olivia gasped, opening her eyes and mouth in equal measure. "No!"

"Yes."

"Carolyn is Aaron's mother?"

"She is."

"Wow. Your holiday gatherings must be *intense*."

CHAPTER 11

At half past five, the hustle and bustle around town was waning as the late afternoon shoppers headed home for their evening activities. Many of the stores closed at six, though those that sold food and drinks stayed open at least until nine. The threatening gray clouds didn't deter a group of teens from playing touch football on the town square's manicured lawn. Some were in shorts and tees, while others sported hoodies and sweats. The mix was typical of early spring, when days warmed into the seventies while nights turned cooler, often prompting Olivia to wear a light jacket.

On the drive in, she'd strategized various approaches to her task. Ellen would see through anything less than the true motivation behind the unusual proposal. Ellen could persuade anyone to do just about anything, but in this case, Olivia would refuse to share details regarding

Sam. If Ellen wouldn't come on board, Carolyn would have to devise an alternative plan.

After parking in front of Carol's Comforts, she lingered in her vehicle for a minute. Two young mothers, each pushing a baby buggy, strolled along the sidewalk toward her. They entered the boutique gift shop, each taking turns to hold the door for the other. She looked in the side mirror, then down to the corner of Cider Lane. All the lamppost lights flickered on at once, triggered by timers rather than by need.

Though it was a long shot, running into Preston while she was here wasn't entirely out of the question, and she'd prefer to avoid that for the time being. The police headquarters was several blocks away at the opposite end of town, but the Apple Station Inn was nearby the newspaper office. He visited his mother daily at the inn, which she owned and operated. Sometimes he and Olivia would meet there for a quick bite after he did minor, random repair work for his mother on his lunch break.

She still felt uneasy about keeping anything from him, but it didn't bother her as much now as it had earlier. The stakes had been raised. Sam needed protection from the police and those in Grasso's camp. That was enough of a reason for her to justify withholding what she knew from him for a while longer.

After another scan up and down the sidewalk, she got out, hit the lock on her key fob, and headed for the newspaper suite. Staffing typically fluctuated during the day as reporters were always in and out, working on their stories. By six, usually only Cooper, Cassandra, and Ellen remained.

When she entered, though, the buzz of the bustling workroom masked the faint jingle of the bells hanging on the doorknob. Cooper glanced over at her from where he stood by the copy machine just outside of Ellen's office. All the other reporters seemed busy, as if it were midday. Jeremy and Brad were talking in the back near the wall-mounted white board. Amanda had a phone secured between her ear and shoulder while she typed on a laptop at her desk. Cassandra was rifling through the file cabinet while Rachel shredded some paper.

Cooper checked the copier's paper tray, then came over, greeting her with a stretched smile. Even at the end of the day, he kept the top button of his blue Oxford fastened and his red satin tie tight. He'd recently gotten a haircut, trading his tousled locks for a polished, close-cropped style. "Great news. I got my letter of acceptance from Shenandoah University."

"Congratulations on another acceptance! Now that you have the choice between George Washington and Shenandoah, which way are you leaning?"

"I never thought I'd get into GW, so I really didn't think about everything that would be involved, especially the cost. The programs are a little different. GW is hard-core journalism, whereas Shenandoah is more broad-based media and communications. They both would be good. After I get my degree, I plan to work here at the paper for my mom until I've built solid skills and gained experience."

"You're already doing that."

"I guess. You've been a big part of that, as was Paige."

"She'd be so proud of you, as am I."

"Thanks. That means a lot. D.C. seems a long way from home, and I'm not sure that I want to leave this area. If I go to Shenandoah, that's practically right up the road. I wouldn't even have to move, and I'd save a lot of money."

"GW is close to where I used to live in Georgetown. It's not that far from Apple Station. I came back all the time on the weekends when I lived there. And you'll always have a home here."

"Just like you."

"Hey, Coop," Brad shouted from where he was sitting on Jeremy's desk. "Stop talking to your girlfriend on company time. We need your help."

Cooper smirked, shaking his head at the joke. The three men were good friends, but as the youngest, he bore the brunt of their teasing. "You're just jealous because she likes me more than you two clowns," he yelled back.

She gave him a fist bump. "You tell them, Coop."

"I better go before they break something. The last time they put their half brains together, they crashed the network."

As he turned and headed for Brad's desk, Cassandra popped up from her chair and came over to Olivia.

"Do you have news to share?" Cassandra asked.

"Not yet. What about you?"

"Zip. Nicky Klein gave me a no-comment. It was a wasted trip. Ellen has everyone working different angles on this. Spring Hills was already a hotbed of rumors. Now, with a suspicious death there—a carnival worker, no less— it's like the perfect storm of weirdness. I got a call today from a man saying he knows for a fact that a UFO landed there twenty years ago. He firmly believes someone killed the unfortunate Mr. Klein to conceal the truth."

"I take it you're not following up on that?"

"I gave him your name and number in case he has anything else to share," Cassandra joked. "If not for the extraterrestrial, then why are you here?"

"I need to speak with Ellen."

"Something involving Klein?"

She nodded. "I'll let you know if it pans out. By the way, I brought you up to my editor. She's going to ask around and keep your name circulating in the right ears."

"Cool. Thanks. See, there's some benefit to knowing you after all."

Olivia feigned her best shock-horror face. "I feel a little insulted."

"Kidding, Penn. You also bring in some good leads." She spun and returned to her desk.

Olivia gave a facetious thumbs-up to Cassandra's back as Ellen bustled out of her office and scanned the room until she found her target.

"Cooper, where did you put the number for the retired general?" Ellen asked.

"It's on your monitor," he replied.

Rachel passed by Olivia, heading for the door. "Hi, Liv. Bye, Liv. Love to stay and chat, but I've got a hot date."

"Say hi to Sean for me and be home by eleven. It's a work night."

"Yes, mother," Rachel jested, defiantly showing she'd crossed her fingers.

"Olivia, what are you doing here?" Ellen asked. "We'll be closing up shop soon."

"I need to speak with you. Do you have a minute?"

She waved Olivia toward her office. "Come in." Once they were both inside, she shut the door and plopped down in her high-back executive leather chair. "It's been a long day."

Olivia sat in the seat across from the desk.

Ellen reached forward and plucked an orange sticky note off the base of her monitor. "It was right in front of me. Cooper found the name of a general who'd worked at Spring Hills near the time of its closure. I don't know if we'll get anything useful from him, but I'm sure we can spin some headline." She stuck the note onto an over-sized coffee mug inscribed with the words "Editing:

Because Writers Need Heroes Too." "Okay, what's on your mind?"

Given the hectic vibe of the office, Olivia went with her rehearsed Plan A: Don't beat around the bush. "I'm fully aware I'm not an employee here, and this loose arrangement we've had for the local advice column has been unofficial."

Ellen nodded. "You want out. I knew this day would come."

"No. It's not that at all. This is about something completely different. It's about the carnival." She paused, trying to remember how she'd worded it best on the drive to town.

"And? Are you joining it?"

"Not exactly. I have a favor to ask. I want to see if you'd be willing to vet me as a staff reporter who's writing a story about carnival life."

Ellen pinned her elbows on the chair armrests, steepled her hands, and swiveled the seat back and forth for half a minute before speaking. "That was quite an article Cassandra and Marco Esposito collaborated on for your paper. Two reporters uncover exclusives about one of the most famed jewel thieves of this century, relying heavily on the account of an unnamed witness."

Olivia had shared details of her role in the takedown to Cassandra, provided she remain anonymous. She wasn't keen on dealing with the media attention that could come from the day's true-crime headline.

"Tell me more about your sudden interest in the carnival," Ellen said.

"Highly placed sources believe Bobby Klein was on the supplier side of an animal trafficking operation." She went on, providing the details to make her case.

When she finished, Ellen stilled her chair and rolled it closer to the desk. "Your source believes Klein's murder is directly related to this criminal organization?"

"Yes. If we can get eyes and ears among the crew under a legitimate guise, we may identify who else is in play. With the carnival leaving on Sunday, we don't have time to be leisurely about it."

"What makes you think anyone there would talk to you? Carnival workers are notorious for being a tight-knit bunch. Is this something that your boyfriend has asked you to do?"

She had to be truthful to underlie the gravity of the ask. "He doesn't know, and I want to keep it that way for now."

Ellen raised her eyebrows. "He'll find out eventually, and I imagine that'll be an uncomfortable conversation. What you're suggesting is quite a story. How credible is your source?"

She imagined Ellen and Carolyn going toe-to-toe, each refusing to bend. "One hundred percent."

"I take it you won't tell me how you came across this information, or who has asked you to do this."

"I'm sorry, but I can't."

"What exactly is it you want me to do?"

"Construct a cover for me to get in. Tell them you're running a feel-good story about the family business. Convince them it would be great press for them, and all I'd be doing is hanging out on the grounds, speaking with the crew about their travels and lifestyle."

"I won't agree to anything that'll put you in danger."

"There's no threat to me. It's just fact-finding to figure out who is who."

Ellen picked up her glasses, put them on, and slid the keyboard closer to her. "First, I need to look more into Klein Amusements." She started typing, then stopped and eyed Olivia. "If I can make this happen, I want you to keep Cassandra posted. If Klein's death is connected to animal trafficking, I want that story, with or without your name in it."

Olivia pushed up from the chair. "I understand. Thank you."

"I'll call or text you later and let you know."

As Olivia left the office, Cassandra sprung up from her seat and intercepted her before she got halfway to the door.

"What was that about?" Cassandra asked.

"It could be nothing, or we may be teaming up again. It depends on how convincing Ellen can be. If I get the green light, we'll be talking soon."

CHAPTER 12

Once Olivia had exchanged goodbyes with those in the office, she returned straight away to her Expedition, not wanting to tarry around town any longer. She wouldn't have minded a late-day pick-me-up coffee from the cafe, but it was close to six, and her father was due back home. The conversation with Ellen had gone better than expected, as she'd anticipated more prodding to reveal her source. Now, if Ellen could work her magic, Olivia may be helpful to Sam in some small way.

After a twenty-minute drive, she turned onto the lane leading to her home, spotting her father's red Escape parked at the top of the driveway. Even with Buddy and Willow keeping her company, the house had seemed too quiet without him there. He'd had a grand time at the cooking school, and she considered the hefty price tag as the best money she'd ever spent. Still, she'd missed him dearly, and seeing his car back where it belonged made all seem right with the world for the moment.

Passing Sam's house, she thought of the two plants sitting on the kitchen windowsill. Having had African violets when she lived in Georgetown, she knew they'd be fine on their own for another day or two. After parking behind her father's SUV and getting out, she hustled onto the porch and entered the house just as he was sitting down on the living room sofa.

He sprung right back up. "Hi there, stranger."

She closed the door, went over to the couch, and wrapped him in a tight hug. "I missed you. How long have you been home?"

"It's good to see you too. I got in about fifteen minutes ago." After they released each other, he sat back down on the sofa. "I may have gone overboard with the ordering. It looks like a UPS depot in here. I hope we have room for everything."

She perched on the arm of the sofa as Willow wandered over from the nearest brown box and brushed by her leg. "I'll do some rearranging. If we end up with any gently used doubles, we can donate them. Are you going to be hungry for dinner, or did you eat on the plane?"

"They fed us lunch, but that was around noon Pacific time. I'll be hungry if you're planning on making something. You really spoiled me with first class. They served us roasted chicken with small red potatoes and broccoli.

You'd be proud of me. I ate all the broccoli once I got butter to put on it."

She stood and patted his shoulder, glancing at the packages. "I'm very proud of you. When do I get to see what you bought?"

Willow jumped onto the sofa and sat next to him, sniffing his shirtsleeve.

"How about later? I want to relax for a while and have a beer. How's our house guest been?"

"She's loving the boxes. She'll be in seventh heaven when they're all opened and she gets to explore them. Otherwise, no issues." Her cell buzzed, and she pulled it from her pocket, expecting a text from Ellen. Instead, she sighed while reading a message from Preston asking how she was doing. "It's Preston."

"Now would be a good time to get that beer," her dad said, pushing up from the sofa. He gave Willow a few pets, then went into the kitchen.

"I'll be right in."

She stared at the screen for a moment, carefully choosing her words, then replied, "Okay, you?"

His follow-up was immediate. "Long day at the station. Is your dad back?"

A softball question she could hit out of the park. "Yes. Arrived a short while ago."

Maybe he won't ask. Then she read, "Say hi for me. Did you hear from Sam?"

Or maybe he will. Her thumbs hovered over the keys,

twitching to type, lest her hesitation raise any suspicion. "She hasn't called."

Crossing her fingers, she didn't blink until he replied, "Okay. Call you later tonight."

She ended the thread with an emoji blowing a kiss, as was her style. She felt like she'd sidestepped a boomerang rather than dodged a bullet, knowing the repercussions would eventually come back around. Willow meowed at her, and she brushed the cat's fluffy cheek a few times. After another distinctive meow, backed by more gusto, Olivia knew exactly what Willow wanted.

"Are you telling me it's treat time?" At the mention of the magic word, Willow intensified her ask until Olivia scooped her up and carried her into the kitchen. She set her down on the braided rug by the door and grabbed a packet of Willow's favorite salmon-flavored snack from the refrigerator.

"Is Preston coming over tonight?"

She shook her head, placed her cell on the table, and ripped off the end of the squishy tube. "No. He's busy." Kneeling on the floor, she squeezed out the puree until Willow had licked up every bit. "Are you happy, little kitty?"

"I hope I didn't ruin any plans you had," her father said.

Willow swept her tongue around her mouth and teeth, willing to have a second helping, as Olivia stood up. "No. He's working on a case. That's it for now, cutie." She binned the empty packet, grabbed a diet soda from the refrigerator, and sat opposite him at the table. "There was a murder at Spring Hills last night."

"What happened?"

She took a sip of soda, then turned the can round and round in front of her. She wasn't planning on hiding what had happened, or her potential involvement, from him. For better or worse, he'd assisted her in unraveling the blackmail scheme against Bev in December. She'd kept troublesome matters from him in the past so as not to worry him, but honesty had proved the best policy. Their teaming had led to a reversal in his opinion about her sleuthing. He had gone from lecturing her for investigating Paige's murder to proposing they open their own detective agency, wanting to be a Watson to her Holmes.

"I'm not sure yet."

"*You're* not sure, or the *police* aren't sure?"

"Both. We have a problem. Sam is in trouble."

She recounted everything that had happened since yesterday afternoon, excluding none of the dicey details. When finished, she leaned forward, resting her forearms on the table. "What do you think?"

"I think I need another beer." He swiveled in his seat, grabbed a can out of the refrigerator, and squared back up to the table. After popping the tab, he set the can down without taking a swig. "I'm not thrilled you went to Spring Hills by yourself. But if you hadn't, you wouldn't be able to help Sam. If this involves you just asking questions, I don't see the harm in that. I could go with you. No one at the carnival would suspect who I am. I could tell everyone that my daughter dropped me off for a day out. Then I could ask whatever intrusive questions you want to know. Old people like me can get away with that."

"Let's dial that back and consider it Plan B. I'm not sure Ellen can talk my way in. Bobby's murder makes it a delicate situation. I'm sure the family is reeling, and the police will be there investigating. They might not want a distraction like a reporter hanging around. Ellen is persuasive, but this one may be a tough sell, even for her."

"What about Preston? Eventually, he'll find out."

"Probably."

"Not probably. He will. Have you thought about how he'll react?"

She nodded. "A lot. But Sam is the priority. Right now, she needs to stay out of sight, out of town, and out of the police investigation."

"I agree. What is it that Sam's boss is hoping you can learn by doing this fake story for the paper?"

"It's possible Bobby Klein had a partner associated with the carnival. She wants me to ask around about him, get a sense of who his friends and enemies were."

He crossed his arms over his chest. "I can't believe a bird could be worth that much."

She picked up her phone, opened a browser, and searched for a photo of a hyacinth macaw. Several came up immediately, and she turned the screen toward him.

"That's a pretty parrot," he said. "A big one too. I bet

they take a lot of care. If this Bobby was the supplier and the eggs were in his trunk, the incubators they're in must not be that large. Are you sure the police can't place you there?"

"I can't be positive, but I parked on the field that overlooks the headquarters. I've seen cars up there before, so there are probably tire tracks all over it. I'm not worried about being identified by the tire treads. As far as I know, nobody saw me. I trust Sam. If Carolyn thinks this is a viable plan, then I want to help. She doesn't strike me as someone who wings anything."

"I trust Sam too, and if the police question her, they might arrest her."

Her cell buzzed, and she turned it back around, reading a text from Ellen.

"Okay," she said. "I'm in. Tomorrow, Bobby's sister is expecting me, and she's agreed to let me hang out on the grounds and interview the workers for the story."

She wrote a thank-you to Ellen, and just as she hit send, a message popped up from Cassandra.

She read, "Ellen told me the news. I knew you were cooking up something. May the force be with you. Keep me posted. Don't run away with the carnival. You make life too interesting."

Olivia replied with a smiling-face emoji and a four-leaf clover, then set the cell down.

"I guess it's a good thing Preston isn't coming over then," her dad said.

She stood up. "Unfortunately, I think you're right. I should get supper started. Is spaghetti okay?"

"Sounds perfect. I'll watch the news while you're getting things ready."

"There's something else I wanted to bring up with you. I think we should put up security cameras around the house and the office."

He nodded. "That's a good idea. If that guy shows up again looking for Sam, I'll tell him where he can go."

She opened a low cabinet, took out two pots, and set them on the counter. "I don't think he will. Even if he does, we need to maintain the appearance of being innocent neighbors."

"While you're making dinner, I'll call A.J. I'm sure he could install them."

A.J. owned and ran a general contracting business in town a few suites down from Sophia's physical therapy clinic on Blossom Avenue. He had become the local go-to handyman since hanging out his shingle about a year ago.

Her father stood up, threw away his empty beer can, and took the other one into the living room. While preparing dinner, she heard him speaking on the phone with A.J. Then, as they ate, he filled her in on the details of the conversation. Tonight, A.J. would buy everything online that he needed for the installation. He'd pick up the order from the home-improvement store in the morning, then come over and set up the monitoring system, boosting their security and peace of mind by nightfall.

After they finished dinner and cleaned up, they went into the living room, where he told her about his triumphs and misadventures in Oregon. The day's troubles faded into the background as his animated stories kept her thoughts off Sam and Preston. With the aroma of dinner still wafting in the air and Buddy and Willow lounging nearby, the house felt like home again. When Willow seemed tired of waiting, she padded over to the parcels and jumped onto the box that Olivia presumed held a mixer. Taking it as a hint, they got down to business. After Olivia grabbed a utility knife from the catch-all drawer in the kitchen, they set about unveiling all their new wares.

CHAPTER 13

By the time Olivia and her father had finished unpacking the parcels last night, they were tired and ready for bed. He'd purchased pans, utensils, and small appliances, as well as gourmet spices, extracts, and three varieties of cocoa powder. The heavy box she'd guessed contained a stand mixer was the showstopper, thanks to his color choice of an eye-popping candy-apple red. Never mind that it only matched his apron, oven mitts, and a set of spatulas in their kitchen. She sensed a new color scheme emerging, which was fine by her, as she wasn't in the least bit picky about such things.

Before going to bed, she placed the wares on the kitchen counters, where they would remain until she could make room in the cabinets and drawers. She tossed most of the flattened boxes into the recycling bin outside but kept a few in the living room for Willow to enjoy over the next few days. Just before turning in, she called

Preston, and they talked for a few minutes, mainly about her evening with her father.

This morning, after showering, she put on jeans and a black denim shirt, then came downstairs, perking up at the smell of freshly brewed coffee. The front door stood open, and as she stepped over to the screen to look outside, Buddy barked at her from where he was sitting on the porch. Seeing her father and A.J. chatting by the patio table, she went out and joined them. She kissed her father on the cheek and welcomed A.J. with a hug.

"An eight a.m. house call," she said, eyeing the table covered with boxes and bags. "That's priority service. I hope we didn't mess up your plans today."

"Not at all," A.J. replied as they released each other. "I didn't have anything scheduled for this morning."

"Do you want coffee or breakfast?" she asked.

"No, I'm good. I picked up all this stuff when the store opened at six, but I figured that was too early to come over. I stopped in town and ate at Jillian's to kill some time. I was just talking to your dad about how the cameras work. Some will be hardwired, but on the sides of the house and out back, I'll install the ones with rechargeable batteries. Since you're here, let me show you where I think they should be mounted."

They walked around the yard and out to the office as A.J. explained his plans. Neither Olivia nor her father had anything to add, trusting that A.J. knew best. After finishing their tour, they wound up back on the porch.

"I'll unpack all the equipment first, then start with the front door fixture," A.J. said.

"Sounds good," her father replied. "While you're doing that, I'm going to have a cup of coffee. Let me know when you're ready, and I'll help." He opened the screen door and went inside as Buddy followed close behind him.

A.J. picked up a utility knife from the table and started opening the boxes. "Are you sticking around and lending a hand too?" he teased.

"That would be too many cooks in the kitchen."

"If you're not up for tool talk today, what are your plans? As if there could be anything more interesting or fulfilling than home improvement."

She leaned with her back against the front porch railing and glanced toward Sam's house. "I have an online chat for work this afternoon. I want to go into town and return some leftover containers to the clinic. I was there for dinner two weeks ago. When Soph's mom heard my dad was away, she sent me home with a ton of food so that I didn't have to cook for a few days. I've been meaning to take them back, but I keep forgetting."

When Sophia had leased her suite in town, A.J. redesigned the interior of the former bakery to suit the needs of her practice. He built new rooms, including offices and a treatment gym, but kept a portion of the commercial-sized kitchen intact. Almost every week, Sophia's mother, Maria, and grandmother, Josefina, hosted a dinner for family and friends, inviting as many as could fit around the table.

A.J. pulled a wad of bubble wrap out of a box. "I'm going there after I'm done here. I can take the stuff back to save you a trip."

"Thanks, but I want to drop in and say hi. I haven't seen them since last week. Are you doing work there?"

"There's a leaky faucet in the kitchen."

"You're a jack-of-all-trades."

"And a master of none," he added, setting the empty box on the ground near three others.

"You said it, not me."

He pointed the fixture in his hand at her. "But that's what you were thinking."

She shrugged with a mischievous smile. "Maybe."

"So, you have your chat thing, then you're seeing Soph and her fam. Sounds like a pretty thin day."

She stepped forward, picked up one of the empty camera boxes, and tossed it at him in jest.

He adroitly deflected it with the back of his hand. "Wax on, wax off."

She leaned down, grabbed the box, and set it back next to the other empties. "I can never win with you, Karate Kid. You're incorrigible."

"You know our rule, Liv. You're not allowed to use words I can't spell."

She picked up a camera from the table and turned it around in her hands. "You'll be happy to learn there's more to my day. I'm also going to Fields Farm to inter-

view some of the carnival workers for the paper."
Sort of.

He stopped midway through cutting the tape of another box. "Come again."

"This has a rechargeable battery in it? How long does it last before it needs recharging?"

He grabbed the camera from her and set it on the table. Then they stared at each other, like they did when they were kids, seeing who'd blink first.

"Liv?"

"Yes?"

"Why are you, an advice columnist who doesn't work for our charming hometown paper, writing an article about a carnival? Your dad told me that an extra from *Goodfellas* who showed up at the house looking for Sam spurred this security shopping spree. Now, it just so happens that you're going to interview a bunch of carnies the day after one of them ends up dead?"

"I don't think they appreciate being referred to as such. How much do we owe you for all this?"

"Nope, Olivia Rose Penn. You're not smoking and mirroring your way out of this."

"Wow. I've never heard it put like that before. And the formal moniker. Pulling out all the stops. Look, I didn't say I was writing an article. It's not what you think."

"What is it then?"

She let out a deep breath, dropping her shoulders a bit. "Okay, maybe it's a *little* of what you think."

He shook his head, holding his hand up in front of him. "Don't tell me you're looking into this guy's death? Why?"

"No. I'm just asking some questions. That's what I do."

"No, it's not. You *answer* questions from the safety of a desk in an office."

She took a few steps back and leaned against the porch railing again, glancing at a wren that landed on the bird feeder in front of the azalea bushes. "I can't go into it, but it involves Sam."

"I thought she was away."

"She is—sort of. I'm doing this for her."

"What *exactly* are you doing?"

"Sorry, I can't say. But I'll be out in the open. There'll be lots of people around. I've got a cover story."

He picked up some bubble wrap and jammed it into an empty box. "You've got a cover story. That's wonderful. Are you going there looking like that, or will you be in disguise? Liv, Liv, Liv. Sometimes I think it would've been better and safer if you'd moved to New York as planned."

"Come on now. You don't mean that."

"Yes, I do. How long do you plan on keeping up this charade, and do you want me to go with you?"

"No, on the latter. Not sure about the former. Maybe a couple of days. The carnival is only in town until Sunday, and it opens tomorrow afternoon, so it depends on whether I can learn anything useful."

"What's your boyfriend think about this?"

She pursed her lips, glancing at the ground.

"Oh, I see," he said. "Preston doesn't know."

"It's temporary and necessary."

He smirked. "Welcome to the world of Liv Penn. Truthfully, I feel sorry for the dude."

She launched forward and playfully whacked his arm. "Moron."

"Now I really need to get these cameras installed ASAP." He grabbed the last unopened box, sliced through the tape, and removed the camera. "Just be careful around all those carnies. Excuse me, entertainment professionals?"

She picked up one of the empty boxes and stuffed some of the packing material inside. "It's a tough life for not much pay and, often, little respect."

"There's a reason for that. You can call them what you want, but they're a rough bunch."

"Maybe some, but certainly not all."

"I agree that it's a hard life. I'm not cut out for it. I was out at the farm on Sunday, putting up temporary parking gates for Kevin. When I finished, I walked around the grounds as the crew was setting up. I thought I recognized someone working there."

"How would you know anyone working for a carnival?"

"One of the crew looked like a guy I went to high school with. We weren't friends, but we knew each other casually. I said hi to him, but he didn't recognize me at all. I could've been mistaken because back in the day, he was a prep. Now, he's all tatted up and thinned out with long hair and a mountain-man beard. Still, I'm almost positive it was him."

The screen door opened, and her father came out onto the porch. "Are you ready for me yet?"

"Perfect timing, Dad. I'll let you two do your manly things with power tools while I tend to other matters." She gave A.J. a hug and a peck on the cheek. "Have fun. I'll be out back for a bit, then I'm going into town."

"Liv, remember what I said about being careful."

After giving A.J. a salute, she headed inside, stopping in the kitchen to grab two containers of yogurt and an apple. Armed with breakfast, she went out to her office to research Klein Amusements and prepare for what may be her toughest interviews ever.

CHAPTER 14

The Ferris wheel's white spokes and colorful cars loomed large in the distance as Olivia neared the entrance to Fields Farm. Her last visit here was six months ago during the organic farm's annual fall festival. Though a few carnivals would always travel through the area from spring to autumn, none had ever set up so close to town. If the week went well for both the Fields and the Kleins, she imagined and hoped it would become a regular stop on the carnival's circuit.

The designated parking lot was the same rutty parcel used for all the events held there. Agritainment had become a staple supplement of many local farms' budgets, and Kevin's family had joined the bandwagon, hosting seasonal festivals throughout the year. The pocked, grassy field hid a minefield of craters and mounds that stressed the struts of compact cars. Her burly Expedition jostled about as she crawled along, unable to avoid the close-packed hazards that had petrified through the years. She pulled up to the front row and parked among a few scattered cars and a white van.

Even though the rides weren't running yet, the view of the midway sparked fond memories of her childhood. Ever since she was a kid, she'd always looked forward to when her parents would take her to the carnival. If there were a carousel, she'd ride it twice, and playing the games until winning a prize was nonnegotiable. She used to sample all the festive food fare: popcorn, pizza, and funnel cakes. Now older and wiser, she'd simply soak in the atmosphere without indulging in such delicacies, thereby avoiding an upset stomach the next day.

The midway was about a fifty-yard walk from the lot, but the mechanical clink-clank of machinery reverberated clear up to where she'd parked. Step one of her two-part plan was finding Nicky Klein. After that, she'd wing it, speaking with anyone who'd give her a few minutes of their time.

While eating breakfast, she'd learned that Bobby's parents had started the business with only three rides. Now the carnival traveled along the East Coast from February to November. A confusing reference to two women involved in the company at different times gave Olivia the impression that Bobby and Nicky may not have the same mother.

Diving deep, she'd read through a thread of disgruntled posts from a year ago in a forum called *Carny Talk*, written by a former employee using the screen name

Mad Dawg. In his profane ramblings, he accused management of cheating him by withholding his pay. Further, he denounced the deplorable living conditions and treatment of the workers. Though he didn't name Bobby directly, the timeline coincided with when he'd already taken charge after his parents' retirement. She took the grumblings with a grain of salt as others responded to Mad Dawg's posts with praise for how the Kleins took care of their employees.

Now she got out of the car and locked up, glancing at the nearby marketplace barn that housed the farm's festival shop. The Fields sold homemade jams, pies, and breads, along with merchandise from local crafters, at all the special events. Just as she was about to take off for the midway, Kevin stepped out of the barn's double-wide entrance, spotted her, and came down the slight slope toward the lot.

She waved, waiting until he was closer to speak. "Hi, Kevin. That's quite a production going on over there."

He shook his head. "I don't know if it was dumb or wise to host a carnival here."

"I think you'll get large crowds this weekend."

"I hope so. We're getting a portion of the gate if the attendance is good."

Looking past her, his face lit up with a soft smile. She glanced over her shoulder, seeing Melissa Barns strolling along the path from the midway to the lot. Olivia had become acquainted with Melissa during a police investigation in October involving her son, Mikey. Since then, they'd formed a friendship, and she would sometimes see Melissa and Mikey at Sophia's clinic, where he received therapy.

Melissa joined them, and after they'd greeted each other, Olivia asked, "Is Mikey with you?"

"Kev's mom recruited him as her kitchen assistant for making cookies. When I left them, he was helping mainly by eating the chocolate chips. I'm trying to keep him away from all the noise while they're setting up. I just spoke with some of the crew, and they suggested bringing him by tomorrow before they open. They'll let him play whatever games he wants. They were very nice about it."

"That sounds like fun," Olivia said.

"I think he'll enjoy it. I hate to run out on you, Kev, but I need to collect Mikey from your mom's house and get back to work."

"Tell him I'll see him in the morning," Kevin said. "Be careful driving home."

Melissa exchanged goodbyes with them both, then walked away.

"Have you set a date for the wedding?" Olivia asked.

"No, but it'll be in August. We're flying in Melissa's grandmother, and there are some logistics involved with that. Be on the lookout for your invitation. I told Preston he's not getting his own because I figure he'll be your plus one."

She secretly smiled every time someone thought of them as a couple. "He better behave himself then, if he wants to enjoy the party."

"I'll remind him of that." Kevin buried his fingertips in his jeans pockets. "What brings you out here today anyway? If you can drive a tractor, I have a field waiting for you."

"Neither licensed nor insured for that, though it looks like it would be fun for about an hour." Shifting her stance, she glanced toward the midway. "I'm interviewing Nicky Klein and hopefully some of the crew for the paper."

Doubt furrowed his brow. "Good luck with that."

"I heard you had some problems when they arrived on Sunday."

"Yeah. It was like ants at a picnic. As soon as the trucks rolled in, all these people showed up here in the lot. I thought they were with the carnival, but it turns out they were looking for jobs. I assumed they'd already have a full crew, but somebody told me this happens whenever and wherever carnivals set up. There's an online job board that continually updates information about who's needed and where. Some of those who came with the carnival got into it with those looking for work. I called Preston, and he came by with a couple of deputies. He threw his weight around and said he'd be conducting background checks on anyone who gave him a reason to. That shut them up in a hurry, then they all went their separate ways. Now, with Bobby's death, the trouble has gotten much worse than a few guys almost coming to blows."

"I can understand that it must be worrisome with

your parents' house being within a ten-minute walk of the midway. Where's everyone staying?"

He pointed behind her. "They have all their bunkhouses and RVs parked down past the main setup. It's going to make a mess of that field, but we're getting good money for leasing it. I'll straighten it up before we plant there next spring."

"Unless this becomes an annual event."

He shot her a thin smile. "That's to be determined. Anyway, I don't want to keep you from your mission impossible. It was nice to see you."

"You too, Kevin."

They parted, and she took off for the midway. The layout of the grounds opened up as she neared. All the thrill rides were on her left, with the carousel and kiddie games set up in the middle near the food stands. Game trailers aligned end to end on her right, and the Ferris wheel anchored the rear of the lot. A prominent, golden-colored tent sat near the entrance with a sign in front that read "Tarot Readings."

Several members of a small crew were arguing at the base of an attraction named The Scrambler. By the looks of it, the ride, which resembled a yellow octopus, whirled seated passengers around while its arms moved up and down. As she scanned the midway, searching for someone to point her toward Nicky, a catcall whistle cut through the raised voices.

"Who are you looking for, sweetheart?" a man shouted from near the base of The Scrambler.

She turned, eyeing a lanky crew member wearing a purple polo and navy pants. A cigarette precariously dangled from his upper lip, which was topped by a handlebar mustache.

Before she could answer, a brawny guy with Popeye arms, sporting a blue T-shirt and black shorts, stretched his hands out toward her. "She's looking for me, and here I am. Just like in your dreams, honey."

A few of the crew behind him laughed. "You couldn't handle her, Slammer," one of them jeered.

"Do you want a job or a boyfriend?" added another. "Either way, my wife won't mind."

This may have been a bad idea.

"Hey, knuckleheads!" a woman yelled, marching toward them. "Get to work, or I'll find somebody in a heartbeat to replace your sorry selves." All the workers immediately turned their attention back to the ride as the stranger came over to Olivia. "You don't look like you belong here."

"I kind of feel that way. I'm looking for Nicky Klein."

The woman extended her hand, and Olivia reflexively did the same. "You found her," Nicky said as they shook.

Her firm grasp squished Olivia's fingers. Wearing a company-branded polo and cut-off jean shorts, she could've been mistaken for one of the crew. But with her long brown hair pulled into a tight ponytail and heavy mascara complementing pronounced eyeliner, she had the air of a boss lady.

"I'm Olivia Penn from *The Apple Station Times*. Ellen McCarthy said you'd be expecting me."

She nodded. "Yes, right. The article. Things have been chaotic around here. That's normal during setup, but with what happened to Bobby, it'll be a miracle if we're ready to open tomorrow. Come on. We can talk for a few minutes in my RV. It's quieter there."

"I'm sorry about your brother," Olivia said, walking alongside her as they made their way across the midway and toward the rear of the lot.

"Thanks. Half-brother. You probably think it's strange that we didn't cancel after what happened to him."

"I know carnival budgets are tight and missing one week could financially derail your season. I understand the show must go on, even under such tragic circumstances."

As they passed the Ferris wheel, the crew quarters came into view. Three bunkhouses, resembling trailers from a big rig, were aligned in rows with a wide lane between them. An assortment of RVs, campers, and cars sat parked around the units, making for an eclectic camp.

"You're exactly right," Nicky said. "People think carnivals are huge money makers and that we're rolling in dough, but many weeks it's hard to even make payroll. This is my place."

Nicky opened the passenger door of a large, crimson-colored RV, and Olivia entered, climbing up three steps. The luxury of the interior wowed her immediately. A sleek cream leather sofa sat across the aisle from a table with bench seating for four. The living space stretched farther back than she'd estimated from outside. In the middle, counters, an induction stove, and a sink faced a stainless-steel refrigerator that looked larger than the one in her kitchen.

Nicky followed her inside and closed the door. A clean-shaven man wearing rimless glasses, a white dress shirt, and dark slacks looked up from where he was sitting at the table with a laptop in front of him. Though he seemed to be only in his forties, male pattern baldness had taken full effect.

"I didn't know you were still here," Nicky said. "This is our accountant, Jeffrey Rollins. This is Olivia Penn. She's the reporter from the paper."

"Nice to meet you," he said, shutting his laptop. "I'll get out of your way. We'll go over the budget later, but there's no money for new hires."

Nicky holstered her hands on her hips and let out a frustrated sigh. "You're a ray of sunshine."

He placed his computer in a briefcase along with some files, then scooted to the end of the bench and stood. "Don't shoot the messenger. I'll be at the inn when you have time to go over the numbers."

"Are you staying at the Apple Station Inn?" Olivia asked.

"Yes. It's very comfortable and small-town quaint."

"If you haven't tried the restaurant yet, the food is exceptional," Olivia said.

"Thanks for the tip. That'll be dinner tonight." After a brief goodbye, he left through the same door they'd used to enter.

"Please have a seat," Nicky said.

She sat on the sofa and pulled out her phone as Nicky settled on the bench across the aisle.

"I'll just be jotting some notes for my research on my phone," Olivia said, trying to make her cover story appear more authentic. "This is quite a place you have."

"It's new for the season, but now I'm not sure what I'll do with it. Bobby had his own RV, just like this one, but we can't afford payments on both."

"Does everyone in the crew stay here on the grounds?"

Nicky nodded. "Mostly. If there are any cheap hotels nearby, some will book rooms there. But otherwise, if you don't have your own camper or vehicle, you're in the bunkhouses."

"I take it those are the white trailers."

"Yes. They aren't five-star suites, that's for sure. It's a place to sleep and to store your things. For the price, few complain."

"Does your accountant travel with you?"

"No. Jeffrey lives in Florida, but we have regular meetings throughout the season to review the books."

A muted cell rang, and Olivia looked toward the drawer under the countertop next to her, where the tone seemed to emanate from. "I can step outside if you need to get that."

Nicky slid off the bench, stepped across the aisle, and opened the drawer. She reached under a bunch of folders and grabbed the phone. After viewing the screen, she declined the call and tossed the cell back into the drawer, snapping it shut with a hip shove.

"A vendor, no doubt, wondering where their payment is from our last show," Nicky said, sitting back on the bench in a huff.

Olivia glanced at the satin-finished refrigerator, where a magnetic frame displayed a photo of Bobby and Nicky. "That's a lovely picture of you two."

Nicky reached to her side, plucked the frame off the door, and handed it to her. "From better days."

In the picture, the half-siblings were standing on a marina's dock in front of a cabin cruiser named *The Cod Father*. "Cute name for a boat," Olivia said, handing the frame back to her.

Nicky slapped it back onto the refrigerator door near the handle. "I always thought it was silly."

Olivia leaned forward. "I don't want to keep you for too long. I know how busy you are, taking over for Bobby."

"We were a team. He worked the contacts and the contracts, but I handled the nuts and bolts of the setup and the slough."

"Slough?"

"The carnival teardown. That's probably the hardest part of the job. Often, we have to do it at night, in the rain. Everyone is tired, but once the show closes, we're on the clock to get to our next location."

"You seem to run a tight ship, but it's apparent your crew respects you."

Nicky undid her ponytail, allowing her hair to fall on her shoulders, and tossed the black elastic band onto the table. "I respect them. This is a hard life for little pay. Some join us because they have no place else to go. For others, we're their only family. Many are looking for second or third chances to get their lives on track. We have good workers who probably have never had any run-ins with the law. We also have some with criminal records. As long as you show up, do your work, and don't cause trouble, we'll treat you fairly."

That piqued Olivia's curiosity, given the complaints Mad Dawg had leveled at the Kleins. Leaning into that angle, she pressed further. "I read a post in a forum from a former employee who grumbled about not receiving back pay, and what he described as a less-than-ideal working environment."

"I don't doubt the complaint, and I can't speak about money owed. My brother handled the payroll. Sometimes we need to let crew go, then they have an axe to grind. The work here is difficult and dangerous. You have to keep your head up and rely on the person next to you not to drop their side of the load. People are always getting hurt, and almost nobody has health insurance. I'm right in there with them, helping to set up the rides and the games, and I've had my share of injuries too."

She rubbed a bruise on her forearm. "I treat my employees fairly. It's true that some can get rowdy when we close at night. I don't take issue with them drinking and carrying on. But if they're not ready for the job come the following day, I have no qualms about firing anyone. The problem was that Bobby liked to blow off steam with them."

Olivia wasn't surprised that his public and private personas were vastly different. His after-hours camaraderie with the crew supported the theory that he could've had one or more partners connected to the carnival. With no love lost between him and some of his employees, the question was whether a business partner ultimately would've been his friend or foe.

"How did everyone take Bobby's death?"

"We had a meeting Monday morning. Some expressed condolences, but most were concerned about their jobs. They were worried we would cancel this week."

"It sounds like you've been the one running the carnival all along."

A knock on the passenger door prompted Nicky to stand and head toward the front of the RV. "Well, I am now. Bobby left the books in a mess, and we're opening tomorrow. I don't even have a full crew. As soon as we close on Sunday, we have a quick turnaround to set up for a fair in Maryland next week. Excuse me." She went down the steps and opened the door. "What do you need, Angel?"

"Slammer and Stash are about to fight."

Nicky grunted. "Okay. Run back over there and tell them I'm coming."

Olivia stood up and made her way to leave. "It sounds like you have a fire to put out."

"I have to stop them from putting each other in the hospital. I can't afford to lose two workers, especially Slammer. I told everyone today during our morning meeting that you'll be hanging around for a couple of days, gathering information for your article. If anyone gives you trouble, tell me. While everything's being set up, stay clear of the work for your safety."

They left the RV, then Nicky closed and locked the door.

"Thanks for speaking with me," Olivia said.

"I agreed to allow you here because I was told you would write a favorable piece. With Bobby's murder, we're likely to receive bad press. I'm certain more former employees will surface to slander him. It's true that sometimes all my brother saw was dollar signs, but that's not how I run things. When we pull into towns, we often get harassed by the locals and the police. Everybody thinks we're a bunch of dirty carnies. But the people who work here are family. We all endure hard conditions for next-to-nothing pay for one reason—to bring smiles to kids' faces. Whatever you write about my family's business, make sure that also gets included in your story."

CHAPTER 15

Nicky stormed off toward the midway, leaving Olivia standing by the door of the tricked-out RV. She had no doubt that Slammer and Stash would quickly settle their dispute if they wished to keep their jobs. Bobby may have been the figurehead of the operation, but Nicky appeared to have command of the crew. Though she ran a tight ship, there seemed to be a mutual respect between her and the workers.

Whether Nicky could be trusted remained in question. She had a vested interest in presenting the family business in the best light. In the two photos Olivia had seen of the half-siblings, they were all smiles, posing side by side. They could've been managing partners in more than just Klein Amusements. But if one or both were involved in the lucrative illegal animal trade, then why was the carnival facing dire financial straits? Bobby seemed to be the type who'd likely made quite a few enemies along the way. Could his murder be unrelated to the missing parrot eggs? Could someone seeking revenge for another matter have set him up?

She scanned the mostly empty camp. A few of the crew were busy in their bunkrooms, and the lone idle worker sat slumped in a webbed lawn chair, staring straight at her. Needing to start somewhere, she took two steps in his direction before he stood up, stuck his cigarette in a small can, and went inside a pop-up camper. Nicky's guarded willingness to talk may have belied the cooperation Olivia would receive. She'd heard that keeping business in-house was part of the carny code, and so far, she felt like an uninvited guest.

Steeling her game face for what could be an uphill and unproductive venture, she headed back toward the midway. Maybe Carolyn was right, and everyone had overestimated her power of persuasion. She'd conducted tough interviews in the past, learning that people are more willing to talk when they feel heard. When her former editor proposed she start her advice column, he cited her skills in listening and withholding judgment as key qualifications. Now she would need to lean into those talents to get a tight-lipped crew to reveal any behind-the-scenes dirt that may prove helpful to Sam.

The heavy machinery's mechanical clanking and sharp beeping had quieted by the time she returned to the midway, though everyone seemed in motion. Some workers were hanging stuffed animal prizes in the game stands' overhead spaces. Others were cleaning the rides, while two men were applying a fresh coat of red paint to the carousel platform.

The crew that had been working on The Scrambler was now gathered around an amusement fittingly named Blackbeard's Revenge. The ride featured an open gondola resembling a pirate ship, mounted on a central axle supported by four legs. She'd seen similar attractions many times before, and knew that the ride would swing back and forth, almost inverting the passengers.

Six men and two women stood in a semicircle around Nicky near the base of the gondola as she talked, gesturing at the ride and pointing at various crew members. She stopped abruptly when a man in his late thirties, dressed in all black, interrupted the meeting. After handshakes and hugs, all gathered around him. Some bowed their heads while others removed their hats. He held his hand up, spoke briefly, and blessed them, tracing a large sign of the cross in the air. Then he removed a small bottle from his back pocket and sprinkled the workers, the ride, and the ground with what Olivia assumed to be holy water. When he finished, some set about their tasks, while a few, including Nicky, lingered, speaking with him for a while longer.

Olivia looked around the midway, trying to find a friendly face for a chat. She spotted a woman in her sixties sitting on a metal folding chair near the deep-fried candy stand. A lap desk sat balanced on her thighs, and two rectangular plastic containers were on the ground by her feet.

The stranger caught her eye and called over, "Are you the reporter?"

Olivia closed the distance between them, not wanting to shout across the way. "How did you guess?"

The woman pointed to the Klein Amusements logo on her royal-blue polo. "You're not in uniform," she said with a toothy grin.

Olivia nodded, glancing down at her black denim blouse. "Indeed. I'm Olivia Penn with *The Apple Station Times*."

"Beatrice Podder, for real. Like the author but just a different spelling. My mom was a fan of hers. But everyone calls me Aunt Bea, so you might as well too."

Khaki shorts complemented her company garb, and her black sneakers were the yin to her white crew socks yang. With her shoulder-length gray hair and cheerful, round face, she reminded Olivia of her grandmother. A prominent vertical scar over her knee was a telltale sign of a joint replacement. One container by her feet held embroidery floss, while the other was half full of friendship bracelets.

Aunt Bea set her lap desk on the ground, stood up slowly, and hobbled a short distance to the deep-fried candy stand. With each step, she lurched onto her right side, suggesting a hip replacement could be down the road. She grabbed another folding chair, brought it back over, and opened it next to hers. Then she sat down and patted the empty seat a few times.

Olivia accepted the invitation, settling beside her. She

decided against making a show of using her phone to take notes, thinking it might trigger the crew to clam up. "How long have you worked for the carnival?"

"For the Kleins, about ten years. But I've been all over the country, working on and off in the business for almost thirty years."

"You must enjoy what you do."

"Best job I ever had. I started when my husband died, to support my kids. Now I do it to help my grand-babies. I'm not suited for office work. I've had desk jobs, but I'd rather be doing this. No offense, but you probably spend most of your day looking at a computer. Most people here couldn't and wouldn't want to do that."

Olivia pointed to the bracelets. "What are you working on?"

"I give these away to the kids, the crew, or anyone who asks." She bent forward, picked out a blue one from the container, and handed it to Olivia.

"Thank you. That's kind of you. Blue is my favorite color."

"I thought as much with those eyes of yours. Every year, the same kids come back to the carnival, and they call me the bracelet lady. I put all the bracelets in a big bucket, and I make the kids close their eyes before they reach in. No peeking allowed. They'll wish for a certain color, and even if they don't get the one they wanted, they still go away with a smile."

"It sounds like you make their day. That must feel good."

She nodded. "It does, and I count my blessings for having a job that makes the young ones happy. I run the kiddie ring toss and the duck pond, but I help wherever I can. I always ensure all the kids take home a prize, even if they didn't really win the game."

Olivia leaned in a little toward her. "I was talking to Nicky earlier, and she said most workers are here for that reason—to make children smile."

"Yep. She's right. I treat every kid that comes by as my own. For some of them, especially in those areas where times aren't good, coming to the carnival is their only vacation. I never forget that."

Olivia glanced around as a few of the crew near Blackbeard's Revenge appeared to be testing the ride. Nicky stood a short distance from it, still speaking with the young priest.

"If you've spent ten years working for the Kleins, you must feel they've treated you fairly."

Aunt Bea picked up an uncapped bottle of water from the ground and took a sip before answering. "Nicky and Bobby are—I guess now *were*—different. If we have problems, we always go to her. It's too bad he's gone, for his parents' sake. Rumor is somebody killed him. I don't know where the truth is in all that. I'm not one to speak ill of the dead, but he was heavy-handed. Do things his way or else he'd leave you at a gas station as the rest of the carnival pulled out of town. I saw it happen more than once, even to the ones he was carrying on with."

"What do you mean, carrying on with?"

"What other people do is their own business. I don't judge."

Sounds like a prince. "Was he involved with anyone currently?"

An unamused chuckle accompanied her smirk. "Bobby wasn't *involved* with any of them, but he'd entertain a few every season. It was usually the new girls, looking for favors or privileges. Some were no better than him, but some …" She turned her head, glancing toward the water-gun game stand across the way. A petite woman wearing an oversized Klein purple polo stood on a stepladder, hanging prizes in the stand's overhead space. "Some just believed his lies and are too green to know up from down."

Olivia looked at the young woman, figuring she was in her mid-twenties. Her hair was pulled back in a ponytail, and she was wearing sunglasses despite the thickening clouds. She appeared to be singing, though Olivia couldn't hear her or any music playing.

The suggestion that Bobby was a womanizer wasn't surprising. But it posed an alternative motive for murder: payback or jealousy by a present or former love interest. Could he have been with one of his flings at Spring Hills? Could she possibly be involved in his death or connected to the missing parrot eggs?

To fatally stab someone, you would need to be somewhat strong and have either a violent inclination or a fight-or-flight response when confronted with mortal danger. She looked back across the midway at Blackbeard's Revenge as Slammer watched the gondola whoosh through its stomach-dropping arc.

"Are there many problems among the workers?" Olivia asked.

"There're always disputes, but we handle things in-house. If people fight, they get it out of their system, then it's over. Nobody has privacy here. Everyone knows each other's business. The ride jocks and jointees argue, and the jointees constantly bicker with each other."

"I take it the ride jocks run the rides and the jointees are …"

"They're in charge of the games."

"What are the disputes about?"

"What most arguments come down to—money. Ride jocks receive flat pay, but the jointees are on commission. Those whose games are played the most get paid the most. It comes down to placement. The most profitable stands are set up in the front on the right because that's how most people enter the carnival. The jointees stuck in the back of the lot are always grumbling about not getting traffic down their end." She leaned down, picked up a bracelet off the lap desk, and dropped it into the container with the others. "We're all family here. We have to get along, otherwise it's a long season."

Olivia glanced again at Nicky. "Does that priest travel with you?"

Aunt Bea shook her head. "No. That's Father Alfonso Silva. He's from around here someplace. Last year when we were in Leesburg, he came there too. He blesses the rides and says mass sometimes. A couple of years ago, he married two young ones that had been with us for a few months. I heard they're no longer together." Her attention shifted as she pointed at the man who'd earlier identified himself as Olivia's soulmate. He was strutting toward them with a swagger and a mile-wide grin. "You better watch yourself, Slammer, or Nicky will send you packing."

"Come on, Aunt Bea. You know she loves me. She'd never let me go." He winked at Olivia, then turned back to Aunt Bea. "Are you selling us out, telling her all our dirty secrets?"

"What secrets?" Aunt Bea replied. "I hear you snoring clear down the other end of the bunkhouse. You talk in your sleep too."

"It's only when I have sweet dreams of you, Aunt Bea."

Aunt Bea cackled as Slammer went over to a cooler by the corn dog stand and grabbed a bottle of water. He chugged it all, crushed the plastic bottle with his hands, and tossed it into a recycling bin by the food trailer's counter. Then he stepped closer to Olivia, removed a yellow bandana from his back pocket, and wiped the sweat from his brow. "Can I ask you a question?"

I'd rather you not. "Sure."

"Is there a store in town that sells lightbulb grease? I just ran out, and I'll be in a real fix if I can't find some more."

She was a wee bit thrown, unsure of whether that

was euphemistic for something. Her confusion must've looked desperate, as Aunt Bea interjected for her.

"Don't you be messing with her. That's a joke they like to pull on the newbies. There's no such thing as light-bulb grease. You be kind to our guest."

He held his hand over his heart for a moment and bowed. "Sorry, Aunt Bea."

"What were you and Stash carrying on about?"

This time Olivia stepped in, spying an opportunity to get a real ID. "Stash? Is that a first or last name?"

Aunt Bea pointed at the lanky fellow with the handlebar mustache whom Olivia had already met from a distance. He was standing by the supporting legs of Blackbeard's Revenge, watching the pirate ship as it was slowing to a stop.

"Ahh, as in moustache," Olivia said.

Aunt Bea nodded. "Everybody goes by a nickname. I don't know the real names of half the people here." She pointed over toward the gondola, identifying no one specifically. "There's Steady Eddie, because he never misses a day of work. Next to him is Houdini."

"Because he disappears when we slough in the rain," Slammer added.

Aunt Bea bobbed her head. "That's true. Over there are Squirrel, Sizzle, and Ranger Joe. I'd avoid talking to Joe if I were you. Sometimes, he's not quite right."

"Don't stand beside Sizzle when there's lightning around," Slammer said. "He's been struck twice."

Olivia glanced up at him, not needing much imagination to guess the origin of his nickname.

Without being asked, he answered. "I've done time and paid for my crimes. But I'm reformed. See, me and Jesus had a talk while I was in the joint, and we're good now. I'm a crusader. I help those who can't defend themselves."

"What were you and Stash arguing about?" Aunt Bea said.

"We all know that Bobby was paying him on the side for running his personal errands. He was Bobby's little gopher. I learned gophers are rodents. That makes him a rat too. How many times when we set up, Stash is nowhere around. I talked to Bobby when we got here on Sunday. I told him I wanted a piece of that action, but he just blew me off. You know, he owed me money."

Aunt Bea waved a hand at him. "How much longer are you going to carp on about that?"

Slammer straightened as Stash and another worker carried a wooden bench toward the nearby carousel. "Bobby cheated me, not paying what I earned when we jumped to Luray last year."

"Maybe if you did more work instead of running your yap like a schoolgirl all day, he would've," Stash yelled over.

Slammer squared up to Stash, who lowered his end of the bench, not backing down from the challenge.

Aunt Bea scooted forward and planted a hand on her thigh, readying to stand if they forced the issue. "You two stop it. Get going the both of you. It's a long season, and neither of you will find another spot as good as this if Nicky fires you."

Slammer shook his head at Stash in disgust. "You ain't getting any more favors now that Bobby is dead."

"And you're not getting your money."

"He still owes me, and I'll get what's mine."

Stash smirked as he turned and started back toward Blackbeard's Revenge.

"Best of luck, brother," he shouted over his shoulder. "Let me know how it works out for you."

CHAPTER 16

Still steamed, Slammer trudged toward Blackbeard's Revenge, muttering to himself about getting the money Bobby owed him. Expecting a train wreck, Olivia eyed where his path put him on a collision course with Stash at the gondola's base. Two fighters entering the same corner at the end of a round were a recipe for trouble. When Slammer got back to the ride, though, he didn't even glance Stash's way. He resumed his work positioning steel barricades, unfazed by the co-worker that he'd appeared ready to pummel just a few minutes ago.

She imagined that seasoned, gruff men with big egos and matching bravado being at odds with each other was common in their line of work. Stash seemed to have had a special arrangement with Bobby, which apparently was no secret among the crew. More than one probably wanted a piece of the pie. Animosity and jealousy would likely be rampant. And if everyone was in each other's business, someone may know about Bobby's trafficking. Maybe, too, they'd have the scoop on whether Stash played a role in the lucrative business. Could Slammer be that insider? Both he and Aunt Bea corroborated Nicky's assertion that Bobby was motivated by money. Was Slammer's insistence that he'd get what he was owed connected to the half a million dollars' worth of missing parrot eggs? All of this would be more helpful to Sam's team if Olivia could learn both men's real names. But she wasn't holding her breath hoping for a sit-down, friendly chat with either.

"Are those two going to be okay working so close to each other?" Olivia asked.

"For now," Aunt Bea replied, glancing up at the blanketing, gray clouds. "It's going to rain. They know the job comes first. Whatever happens after hours is between them. Nicky may have a talk—" She abruptly stopped, shifting her attention behind Olivia. "Now we got *real* trouble."

Olivia looked over her shoulder, following Aunt Bea's focus, then whipped her head back around and hunched slightly in the chair. Preston was walking with Jayden past the Ferris wheel toward the heart of the midway. They must've been down in the campground, probably going through Bobby's RV or questioning the crew. This wasn't the venue or the time to have her come-clean heart-to-heart with him. Staged out in the open and without a graceful exit strategy, she might as well have been one of the sitting ducks in the kiddie pond. Scurrying behind the corn dog stand while maintaining her cover story seemed like a shoddy strategy. Maybe he wouldn't see her. Maybe she blended in. She and Aunt Bea, just two carnies shooting the breeze. She swiveled, chancing a second glance, and his eyes met hers as he was talking to Jayden.

"I wouldn't want to mess with that cop," Aunt Bea said. "He looks like a proper, mean one. I bet he doesn't take juice."

"What?"

"Bribes," she clarified. "Not saying anyone here does that, but it happens."

Olivia watched as Jayden took off toward the crew around Blackbeard's Revenge. Then Preston turned, heading for her and Aunt Bea. She stood up, needing to intercept him before he did anything that would blow her cover.

"I'm going to see what the police are doing here," Olivia said. "Thanks for speaking with me and for the bracelet."

"Anytime. It was nice talking to you."

"You too."

Hustling toward Preston, she pocketed the bracelet and met him in front of the carousel, out of earshot of those working nearby. She stopped a few feet shy of him, not wanting anyone to think they were friendly enough to be in each other's personal space.

"Before you say anything," she said, keeping her voice low.

He was in full detective mode, with squared shoulders, steely eyes, and a tight jaw. "What are you doing here?"

So much for giving her a moment to explain. She glanced around, noticing several workers by the teacup ride watching them. "I'm doing research for an article about carnival life."

"No, you're not."

Of course she wasn't. His lack of hesitation in calling her out didn't bode well for settling this someplace more private. "Okay. I'm pretending to write a story about the carnival."

"Why would you be doing that?"

She felt guilty as sin for keeping what she knew about Sam from him. But what she'd learned thus far lent support to Carolyn's theory that Bobby could've had a partner associated with the carnival. They were on to something, and she was in a prime position to investigate the angle without putting herself at risk. If she could keep her cover intact, she may piece together more of the behind-the-scenes of Klein Amusements.

"This involves Sam, doesn't it?" he said before she could reply.

"You'll have to trust me."

He planted his hands on his hips. "I hope whatever you're really doing here isn't related to Klein's death. For Sam's sake and for yours."

It's a bit late for that. "Sam wasn't involved in his murder."

"How would you know that?"

Because I was at the crime scene. "Please, just trust me."

"Where's Sam?"

"You wouldn't believe me if I told you."

He clenched his jaw. "Try me."

She looked around again and saw that they were attracting more attention. A cop and a reporter canoodling was a bad look. "You're blowing my cover."

He subtly shook his head. "Your cover?"

"I promise I'll explain everything later. Right now, the workers are watching us, and they'll refuse to talk to me if they think we're on the same team. Yell something at me about staying out of the investigation. Wave your hands around. Try to be dramatic."

He looked at her as if she'd lost her mind. "I'm not doing that."

"The crew will just shut down when you question them. I've already identified one, maybe two, workers who had a motive to kill Bobby. They know you won't take the juice."

He closed his eyes for a moment, as if struck by a sudden migraine. "You're talking carny now?"

"Please," she said through gritted teeth.

"This is far from over." He blew out a full breath, then pointed at her. "And stay out of my way!" he shouted in an apathetic, robotic voice.

She bit back a grin, as it was the least authoritative tone she'd ever heard him use.

He brushed by her, heading toward the exit. "I expect a call later."

"Thank you," she whispered.

As she turned to watch him walk away, the first rain-drops fell. One here, another there, missing her by comfortable margins. The rain's pattering picked up, then the clouds opened, letting loose all they contained. She scrambled, looking for the closest cover, but the barricades around the carousel would mean having to leg up over a nearly four-foot height. Those who'd been quicker to seek shelter already occupied the skimpy spaces under the food trailers' awnings.

"Over here," a man yelled.

She turned and ran toward the stranger, who was waving at her from a game stand near the entrance of the midway, close to the tarot tent. He held open the counter's swing door, and she ducked under cover, relatively unscathed by the spring shower. The breeze accompanying the pop-up storm bobbed the multicolored balloons arranged on the board behind her. Several plastic mesh buckets containing darts rested on a narrow ledge under the balloons, and prizes lined the perimeter of the dartboard. The crew member who'd saved her from a soaking wore a yellow T-shirt and khaki shorts. Atop his head sat a camel-colored western-style hat with a matching felt band and a silver buckle.

"Thanks," she said. "You saved me from getting drenched."

He tipped his hat in an aw-shucks kind of way. "Cowboy."

She pondered that for a moment. "Your nickname—because of the hat."

He beamed a smile wide as a prairie. "That's right." He removed the stylish hat, admiring it from all angles. "She's a beauty. I won her in a game of Texas Hold'em last year off a rookie ride jock. Not my fault he was drunk as a skunk. His unfortunate loss, my fortuitous gain. But where are my manners?" He donned his hat and hustled to the end of the counter. Then he returned with two worn wooden stools that looked as if scavengers had plucked them from the garbage pile of a run-down dive bar.

"Please have a seat. I don't think this rain will last too long. You know what spring showers can be like around here."

She sat on the wobbly stool, shifting back and forth until three of the four legs were level. Curious, she couldn't quite place his mild southern drawl. "Are you from the area?"

He waved his hand as if drawing a rainbow. "I'm from all over."

Alrighty then. She was glad, at least, to be out of the rain. She could've dashed to her car, but she would've gotten soaked, and besides, she was hoping to speak with more of the crew.

"And what's your nickname?" he asked.

"Olivia Penn."

"That's unique. I haven't heard that before, but I like how it rolls off the tongue."

She bet he had a bevy of barstool pickup lines at the ready. "I'm with *The Apple Station Times*."

He nodded. "I figured you were the reporter when I saw you talking to Aunt Bea and Slammer. What do you think of them?"

That was an odd turn of the tables. "They both seemed nice."

He burst out laughing. "Slammer, nice? That's a first."

Taking advantage of her cover story, she flipped the script. "So, you're a jointee, and by the positioning of your stand, you must be a profitable one."

"I'm not too humble to admit I have a flair for charming our fine guests." He leaned closer to her. "How am I doing with you?"

She grinned, looking at the balloons behind her. "The verdict is still out. You'd think it would be easy to pop a balloon with a sharp object, but I hardly ever won this game when I played it as a kid."

"I'll let you in on a secret, but you've got to swear not to tell anyone that I told you."

She nodded, anticipating another newbie prank.

He picked out a red dart from the closest bucket and showed her the tip. "See that. They're all dull—on purpose." Reaching behind, he hit a wobbly, sadly stretched balloon. "All the targets are underinflated. The art is to arc your throw so that the dart lands coming down on the balloon." He demonstrated the trajectory with his hand. "That's your best chance, anyway. There're never any guarantees."

"You don't consider that to be rigging the game?"

He shook his head. "Not at all, and besides, I'm following orders. I didn't buy these darts, and Bobby was the one who told me not to fully inflate the balloons. I know people think all carnivals rig their games, but it's not true. There's a system for winning, or at least tactics that better your odds. Our games are fair, but I can't speak for every carnival."

"Why would he tell you to underinflate the balloons?"

"Dinero. If too many pop, too many prizes leave the gate. He threatened to move me to the back of the lot if I kept cutting into his bottom line. It didn't bother me to follow orders. The more people play, the more I'm paid. When someone doesn't win the first time, you goad them on to try again. The couples are an easy mark. Some guys get all riled up when I challenge their manhood by their ineptitude in bursting a balloon. They end up trying five, six times—chucking the dart harder and harder, thinking that's how it's done. What about you, Olivia Penn? Do you have anyone special in your life who would go to such lengths to prove himself to you?"

She ignored the question but pressed on since Cowboy seemed to lack a filter. "Did you like working for Bobby?"

His smile flatlined as he reached toward the mesh bucket on the counter and dropped the dart inside. "As much as any boss. I saw you talking to the cop. What's the topic of the day?"

The flip of the inquiry was swift, bold, and observant. *Give a little, take a little.* "He didn't appreciate having a reporter hanging around. He thinks my presence is interfering with the police investigation."

"What are you doing here?"

Now she was fully on guard, as he seemed to be the one fishing for information from her. "I'm writing an article about carnival life. You've got some interesting co-workers."

That appeared to satisfy him. "True. You met two of the most colorful, Slammer and Stash. But there're a lot of solid folks here too."

"Like Aunt Bea."

"She's sweet." He pointed across the way at a man standing under the awning of the popcorn stand. "Over there is Steady Eddie. His real name is Luis Garcia, and he and many of the crew hail from a town called Tlapacoyan in Mexico. He's putting both of his kids through college. His son is studying to be a software engineer, and his daughter is going to be a prosthetist." Then he gestured down the row of game stands. "The old-timer down there in the blue hat, that's Art. He's worked in the industry his whole life—from the time he was fifteen. Now at seventy-two, he still won't retire. Says he's got nothing else to do."

The rain was letting up as the sun peeked through a break in the clouds.

"So, Cowboy, why did you join the carnival?"

He tipped his hat back a bit and folded his hands in his lap. "The adventure, the outdoor lifestyle, traveling all around the country, camaraderie with like-minded free-wheeling souls."

As the rain stopped, the workers who had been under cover emerged. A young man with shoulder-length hair and a long, scraggly beard strutted by the stand. Tattoos colored his arms, and he looked roughed up by a life on the road.

"Hey, some of us are going into town tonight for a drink," Cowboy called out to him. "You wanna come?"

"No, dude. Maybe some other time."

Cowboy leaned toward her and whispered, "That means never."

Although she was certain the man's haggard appearance wasn't unique among the crew, he bore a resemblance to A.J.'s description of his former classmate. "Who is he?"

"That's Lone Wolf. He keeps to himself. He runs the basketball toss, but he's not much of a barker. You've gotta work to drive business to that game because it's hard to win. Oval hoops, overinflated balls, springy backboards. He just sits around and never tries to attract players."

"That seems strange since his pay is based on commission."

"He's an odd one."

"Do you know his real name?"

"No. Never thought to ask, and I don't think he would tell me."

Her cell buzzed in her pocket but she let it go for the moment, guessing it could be Preston texting, impatient about her follow-up call. "Have you ever had any problems with your co-workers?"

He folded his arms over his chest and crossed his feet. "Not really. I get along with most everyone. As long as you do your job and lend a hand when you can, others will respect you."

She aimed to be more direct. "What about Slammer? He said Bobby owed him money from last season. Do you know anything about that?"

He looked off to his side, and she followed his focus as Slammer entered the tarot tent. "He's a talker. I wouldn't trust much of what he says. He goes on and on about his beef with Bobby, especially after he has a few shots of whiskey in him. I think just about everyone here feels like they've been cheated somehow at some point."

"But he had no problems with Nicky or—" She cut off her question when Slammer exited the tent followed by Tommy Grasso. They shook hands then went their separate ways, Slammer back to the ride side of the midway and Grasso toward the parking lot. "That man who just came out of the tent—does he work here?"

Cowboy stood up to get a better view of Grasso's diminishing profile. "I don't recognize him. He doesn't look like a carny to me."

"I thought you disliked being called carnies," she said

absently, knowing she'd just witnessed something significant but having no idea what it meant.

"Some don't. Some prefer showmen." He winked at her. "I couldn't care less, just as long as you call me."

She stood up, offering a polite smile. "With that kind of charm, you'll have no problem attracting players to your stand this week." She opened the gate and stepped out from behind the counter.

He tipped his hat. "I never do."

"Thank you for speaking with me."

"Anytime, Olivia Penn of *The Apple Station Times*. When Nicky told us a local reporter was going to be hanging around, asking questions for a feel-good piece about carnival life, I thought that was strange. You show up two days after Bobby got himself killed. Coincidence?"

"Unfortunate timing, that's all," she said, turning to walk away.

"One more thing you should know," he called out. After she faced him, he leaned over the counter and lowered his voice. "Nicky also told us this morning, in no uncertain terms, that we were not to say a word to you about Bobby."

CHAPTER 17

As she walked away from Cowboy's stand, Olivia's thoughts whirled around the unsolicited revelation. Keeping business in-house wasn't a surprising order, but it would make her attempts at gaining trust harder. She dug her cell out of her jeans pocket and checked the missed text, expecting it to be from Preston asking her to call him. For all she knew, he might be waiting for her in the parking lot, which would give her five minutes to come up with an explanation. In viewing the screen, she eased, reading a text from Cassandra that proposed a two o'clock brainstorming session at the inn. Thumbing a quick reply, she agreed to catch her in the lobby.

With her meeting in less than an hour and her online chat at three, she headed back toward her car, already planning to return tomorrow. Maybe she'd find a few more of the crew with some downtime in the morning who'd be willing to air dirty laundry.

Three workers were washing the gondola of Black-beard's Revenge, while Nicky was talking to a larger group gathered near the base of the Zero Gravity ride. Olivia frequently saw the attraction at the carnivals she went to. The ride spun at nauseating speeds, pinning standing passengers to its inner wall. Passing the tarot tent, she peered toward the lot, trying to spot Preston's black F-150. The coast was clear, so she quickened her pace. She couldn't tell if Grasso was in any of the vehicles, but even if he was, she doubted he'd recognize her. His presence there wasn't a coincidence, and his chummy handshake with Slammer raised a red flag.

After getting into her car, she reversed out of her spot and slowly drove across the bumpy field to the exit. Though far from discovering a gold mine of information, she'd gathered a few potential pieces of the puzzle. Stash was a gopher for Bobby, and Slammer felt cheated by the Kleins. Nicky, who'd initially appeared cooperative, had instructed her crew to uphold the carny code by not talking about her brother. She simply may have wanted to prevent bad press, or disgruntled employees from smearing the family business. She might also want to keep Bobby's shady dealings from coming to light.

His reputation as a player suggested another angle unrelated to any illegal activity. Could a scorned girlfriend or a jealous boyfriend have sought revenge? Olivia had spoken with three workers who'd painted unflattering pictures of him, with little prompting. She'd bet more had grievances, and that they'd be willing to talk, but not with Nicky around.

She arrived in town at one thirty, giving her just enough time to stop by the clinic and return Maria's containers. The morning's gray clouds had given way to a cerulean sky, and the dry sidewalks suggested the brunt of the storm had skirted the area. She parallel parked in front of a vacant suite, about half a block from Sophia's clinic. After waiting for several cars to pass, she grabbed a shopping bag off the passenger seat, got out, and locked up.

The empty shop she'd parked in front of was once a hardware store owned by Charlie Brewer. He was a kind, grandfatherly type who knew what you would need to fix anything. She would always remember coming here once to have an extra set of house keys made. When he finished cutting the keys, he handed them to her with a smile, advising, "Make sure you try them before you depend on them." She never forgot that lesson, knowing that it applied to more than just locks.

What he couldn't fix was the decline in business when a large home-improvement chain store opened about ten miles from town. His regulars remained loyal, but the loss of revenue forced him to retire and close the shop. The last she'd heard, he'd moved to Florida to live closer to his daughter and her family. The unit had been unoccupied for years, which always puzzled her. Jillian's, a block away, bustled with patrons from morning to evening. Though the cafe offered light breakfast and lunch fare, the community had lacked a bakery ever since Sophia took over her suite from its former tenants. Apple Station had everything else a cozy, small town could want except for a go-to local bakeshop selling pastries and sweets.

The faded red "For Lease" sign hung crookedly on the inside of the window, as if hoping the abandoned store someday would open for business again. Right above the door handle, someone had taped a carnival flyer. She'd seen the ads all around town over the past week, never reading beyond the headline. Today, she looked closer, noting the hours. The carnival opened at five tomorrow and closed at six on Sunday. That didn't leave long for Sam's black-budget team to identify the supplier and the buyer of the parrot eggs, or to locate them before they hatched.

After a short walk, she entered the clinic, finding Sophia and their good friend Tori Wellington kneeling on the foyer's carpeted floor, about four feet apart. Tyler, Tori's almost three-year-old son with Down Syndrome, was standing next to Sophia, holding onto her hand.

"Liv, you have both great and lousy timing," Tori said.

"Come on, Ty," Sophia urged. "You can do it."

He pointed at Olivia and giggled. "Auntie Wiv, Auntie Wiv!" He bounced, bending his knees, then dropped to his bottom.

Sophia picked him up and set him back on his feet, facing Tori.

He rubbed his face with his hand and blew raspberries. "Auntie Wiv."

"Liv, you're distracting him," Sophia said.

"Oh, I'm sorry. I didn't mean to interrupt."

"You just missed your boyfriend," Tori said.

"Preston?"

"Duh, do you have more than one?" Tori replied. "Good on you if you do. There are no rules these days."

"What did he want?"

"*Distracting*," Sophia repeated.

"Right," Olivia said. "Sorry. Should I go?"

Sophia pointed off to the side, halfway between herself and Tori. "You, here."

She set the bag down, hurried over as instructed, and knelt, knowing it was unwise to mess with Sophia when she was in therapist mode.

"He came to speak with me," Sophia said. "I told him not during a session. Sorry, but even being your boo doesn't earn him that."

"He probably wanted to see if you've heard from Sam," Olivia said.

"Why would he do that?" Tori asked. "Isn't she out of town? I thought that's why she couldn't make girls' night out last weekend."

"Ladies, please," Sophia chirped. "Gab on your own time."

That quieted them both in a hurry.

"Here we go, Ty," Sophia instructed. "Mommy, a little encouragement."

Tory drummed her hands on her thighs. "Come on, Ty. You can do it."

"Liv, do you have your phone on you?" Sophia said.

She whipped out her cell, displaying it as proof. "Yes."

"Start recording a video," Sophia ordered.

She opened her photo app and did as she was told.

"Okay, Ty," Sophia said. "Go to mommy."

Still holding Sophia's hand, he took a step, then another.

"Come on, Ty-Ty," Tori encouraged.

He stepped again, then Sophia removed her support. His arms remained raised at his shoulder level, but he was standing on his own. He shifted his weight left, then lunged forward onto his right foot. He beamed a broad smile and shrieked. After another wide, lateral step, he quickened his pace. Step-step-step, straight into Tori's arms.

She picked him up off the ground, holding him tight in a swinging bear hug. "You did it! You did it! You took your first steps!"

Sophia popped up off the floor, went over to them, and pried Tyler away. "Good job, Ty! Let's do it again." She carried him back over as he laughed and rapidly kicked his dangling legs like he was swimming freestyle. After she set him down on his feet, she knelt beside him, helping him balance. "One more time, Ty. Walk to mommy."

"Come here, baby," Tori said while still on her knees.

Sophia released his hand, and he took a step. Then, two, three, four, five steps straight into Tori's arms.

Tears streamed down Tori's cheeks as she held him close. "You're a big boy now. I'm so proud of you."

Sophia looked at Olivia. "Did you get all that?"

She nodded, dabbing the corner of her eye. "Uh-huh."

"Congratulations, mommy," Sophia said. "Ty is a walker."

At that, Tori sobbed, holding a giggling, wriggling Tyler tight in her arms. She opened her mouth to say something, but no words came. Olivia gave Sophia a high-five and grinned at the miraculous timing of this afternoon. A delay of a minute here or there may have led her to some other moment than this witnessing of two firsts: Tyler walking and Tori speechless.

CHAPTER 18

Tuckered out by his first big-boy steps, Tyler zonked out in Tori's lap soon after his momentous achievement. When he showed no signs of stirring, Sophia stood up, crossed the foyer, and rolled his adaptive stroller back over to them.

"Here, give him to me," Sophia said. She lifted him out of Tori's arms and placed him in the contoured seat. Then she secured his safety harness and wrapped his arm around his favorite stuffed koala-bear toy.

Tori stood up with her cheeks still blooming and hugged Sophia. "Thank you. I wasn't sure this day would ever come."

"I knew it would," she replied as they separated. "Now he knows he can walk, and he's going to want to, all the time. I expect that he'll become independent soon, at least on flat surfaces."

"Liv, will you send me the video?" Tori asked.

Olivia looked up from her phone screen. "I just did."

Tori grabbed her purse from the basket under the stroller seat and dug out her cell. They watched the playback, sharing a round of hugs and a few more happy tears.

"You better get him home, mommy," Sophia said. "I think you both need rest."

"You're right," Tori replied. "This weekend we have to celebrate. I'll call you both with the deets. Hopefully, Sam can come too. And your dad, Liv. And your mom and grandmother, Soph. A.J., too. Sorry, Liv. Absolutely bring Preston. I didn't mean to leave him out."

Sophia held up a hand and laughed. "Okay, we get it. Just let us know whenever. Take your little champ home."

Tori inhaled deeply, exhaling in double time. "Yes, ma'am. I'm so over the moon." She pulled Olivia and Sophia in for a group hug. "I hope someday you both feel as happy as I do right now." She released them, then peeked to check that Tyler was still fast asleep. "Okay, we're off," she whispered. "Ty and mommy are quietly leaving the building."

Olivia went over to the door and held it open as Tori pushed the stroller out of the clinic.

"Wow, that was amazing," Olivia said. "I'm so happy I was here to see his first steps."

Sophia plopped down on the sofa. "Tori has been through so much with him. Illnesses, surgeries, hospitalizations. He's just so resilient. I'm glad you were here too, *Auntie Wiv, Auntie Wiv.*"

Olivia chuckled at the spot-on impersonation as she picked up the shopping bag and crossed the foyer. "I brought back your mom's leftover containers."

"You didn't have to do that. We have so many."

She set the bag on the floor and settled into the sofa. "I always feel guilty if I don't, especially the good ones. I never know what to do. Some people expect it, others couldn't care less. There's no standard protocol."

"Unless stated otherwise, consider all future leftover containers from here as yours to keep." She glanced at her watch. "A.J. is coming by soon. We're going out for lunch. Why don't you join us?"

She shook her head. "I'd be a third wheel, and besides, I'm meeting Cassandra at two, then I have a work thing at three. A.J. was at my house this morning, and he said you have a leaky faucet."

"Yes, in the kitchen. It's driving my grandmother crazy."

"Is she here?"

"She and my mom are in the back, baking Mexican wedding cookies."

Olivia raised her eyebrows. "Hmm. Who's the lucky guy? Anyone I know?"

In a flash, Sophia grabbed one of the sofa's decorative pillows and flung it at her.

Olivia snatched the pillow from where it had landed in her lap. "First, this is mine now. Second, there's no need for such an outburst."

"They're for Melissa. My grandmother went nuts when she told her about getting engaged."

"I saw Kevin today. They haven't set a date for the wedding yet, but it'll be in August."

"The cookies are part congratulatory and part an audition. I think my grandmother wants to be the official cake maker and all-around baker for the reception. She said since I appear content never to get married, at least she'll have the chance to make someone's wedding cake before she dies. It was all very dramatic."

"Guilt trip, huh? I'll be sure to bring up Melissa's name when I say hi before I leave."

"At your peril, may I add, ringless maiden. You better be careful if you're on a time crunch. It's been over a week since they've seen you. You'll receive a grilling. Goodness knows how *your life* can change in seven days."

You have no idea.

"Did your dad get back from Oregon?"

"Yes. Yesterday. You wouldn't believe how much new kitchen stuff he bought. We had the grand unboxing last night. It'll take me the better part of an afternoon to reorganize the cabinets to find a place for everything."

"I assume A.J. wasn't there to help with that."

Olivia set the pillow off to her side. "No. He was installing security cameras around the house and the office."

"Was that at Preston's insistence?"

"No. In fact, he doesn't even know about it."

Sophia wrinkled her brow. "What finally prompted

this? As if three near-death experiences weren't enough to make your home more of a fortress. And why did he come here to ask me about Sam?"

Olivia removed her cell from her pocket, opened a picture of Grasso, and showed Sophia the screen. "On Sunday, this thug showed up at my front door, looking for her." She continued to relate the highlights of what she'd been up to over the past two days. Sophia was aware of Sam's work as a security consultant, though not in the detail which Olivia now knew. They could trust Sophia, and Sam may need her help before all of this was through.

When Olivia finished, Sophia grabbed the throw pillow and placed it behind her back. "So much about Sam now makes sense. Are you sure this guy can't connect you to her?"

"I don't think so. He seemed to buy into my innocent neighbor act."

"Is she safe at the convent? Truthfully, did you expect her to be incognito in a full habit?"

"Technically, it's a monastery. She seems to think the location is off-the-grid enough. Apparently, she has an understanding with Anne, the ninja nun. I wish she would've been in disguise. I'd never let her live that down."

"Is there anything I can do?"

"The only thing I would say is that if anyone comes asking about her whereabouts—you know nothing."

Sophia snickered under her breath. "That won't be

too hard to fake. If she needs a new safe house, she's welcome to stay with me. When are you going to tell Preston about all this?"

Olivia leaned her head against the sofa's high back. "I'm unsure, but hopefully before he decides to come back here and question you. I'll pass on your offer to her. I need to talk to her first before I speak with him. The police may not be aware of the connection between Bobby's murder and the trafficking. I'm fuzzy on how much Sam's boss would want me to share, if anything, with him. Theoretically, everyone is on the same team, but it's complicated."

Sophia nodded. "I get that. And I know how you two feel about each other." She paused with a question queued up on her brow. "Where do you see this going?"

Olivia shrugged. "My role is tiny, and I'm not sure how useful I can be."

"I meant you and Preston."

"I expect he'll be upset, but Sam's life could be in danger. Neither of us has done anything illegal. If both sides are working, whether together or in parallel, to bring down this criminal ring and solve Bobby's murder, it's a win-win."

"No, I was thinking more about you and him long term."

Oh. She glanced toward the entrance as a postal worker opened the door and stepped inside.

"Good afternoon," he said.

"Hi, Minh," Sophia replied as she stood.

He flipped the satchel on his shoulder around and rifled through its contents.

Where did she see this going? She'd not thought about marriage beyond casually pondering the what-ifs. Maybe one day, down the road. Preston may have a different view, especially after learning about her activities on Sunday night. Having lied about her contact with Sam wouldn't help matters. She'd placed her faith in his understanding, but would he consider her actions a breach of personal and professional trust? Her intent was to protect Sam, but would he feel her friends would always come first? If the roles were reversed, concern would weigh on her mind as well.

Minh handed Sophia a stack of mail. "Have a good one," he said, turning to leave.

"You too," Sophia replied. After placing the pile on the foyer's activity table, she came back over and sat on the arm of the sofa.

Olivia gave it a moment, hoping the interruption had distracted Sophia enough to get her off the hook from answering.

"Well?" Sophia asked.

Foiled by Sophia's steel-trap memory, she folded her arms, aiming for nonchalant. "I don't know. I haven't given it much thought. We're dating, as people do."

"But everything's good, perhaps even great, right?"

"Yeah."

"And it's been five months."

"So?"

"Do you two ever talk about something less loosey-goosey? Could you see yourself marrying him?"

What's with the twenty questions? Maybe I should ask you about A.J.

Just then, Josefina entered the foyer from the hallway. "Mi nieta, you're getting married? Felicidades!" She rushed over with her arms extended.

Olivia stood up, shaking her head as Josefina embraced her.

Maria joined them in the front, carrying a round tin. "Hola, Olivia. What's going on?"

"She's getting married!" Josefina exclaimed, releasing Olivia.

"Wow, what wonderful news!" Maria said.

Olivia held up her hands, cutting everyone off at the pass. "No, I'm not."

"Yes, you are," Sophia retorted.

"No, *I'm not*," Olivia snapped back.

Sophia stood. "I'm saying someday. That's all."

Olivia groaned, reaching down for the pillow on the sofa. Sophia seized it first, knowing exactly what Olivia was planning to do with it.

"Ay, caramba," Josefina said. "You two should be like Melissa Barns."

"Don't worry, Mamá," Maria interjected. "It wouldn't surprise me if she got engaged before long."

"I second that," Sophia said.

Olivia shot her bestie a playful death stare. "Thanks a

lot." She plucked the shopping bag off the floor and set it on the sofa. "I brought your containers back."

"Gracias," Josefina said, taking hold of the twine handles. "I'll take them to the kitchen."

"You didn't have to return them, but thank you," Maria said as her mother left the foyer. "We've got plenty. You'll have to forgive Mamá. You know what she's like about marriage." She went over and set the tin on the table next to the mail. "But you will tell us the moment you get engaged?" she added with a cheeky smile.

"Please, no one hold their breath," Olivia said.

"Really?" Sophia countered.

"Really," Olivia replied with extra oomph.

"It's good not to rush relationships," Maria said. "Trust in your heart. It never lies to you."

The clinic's front door opened and A.J. stepped in, saving Olivia from any further discussion on the matter.

"Ladies, you didn't all have to come out to greet me, but I appreciate the enthusiasm."

After a round of hugs and hellos, Maria turned to Sophia and said, "Are you going to lunch now?"

"Yes. We'll be back in an hour."

"I'll talk with you then about your father's birthday party." She looked at Olivia. "Ernesto hates surprises, so I'm planning a surprise party for him next week. Bring your father. We're having it here after his ER shift ends on Wednesday. Mamá is making some of his mother's favorite recipes."

"That sounds like fun," Olivia replied. "But if he hates surprises, won't he hate a *surprise* party?"

Maria placed her hands on her hips as her lips curled into a crafty smile. "He did the same thing to me for my last birthday when I asked him not to. This is payback." She pointed at the table. "There're some Mexican wedding cookies for you, A.J. You two have a wonderful lunch."

"Fantastic, thank you," he replied.

"Congratulations, Olivia, on not getting married," Maria said with a wink as she left the foyer.

"What's this, Liv?" he asked. "Preston proposed? When? And you turned him down?"

She tilted her head back and sighed. "No. There was no proposal. I don't expect or want one. I'm not getting engaged anytime soon, or possibly ever."

He pursed his lips, puffing out his cheeks. "Just as long as you're remaining open."

"Moron."

"From you, I take that as a compliment. Are you coming to lunch with us?"

"As much as I would love to, I have some things I need to do."

"Your loss. All the cameras are up, and they're live. Having your dad assist cut the install time in half. I showed him how to adjust the settings, but I also left the instructions for you on the kitchen table, just in case."

"Thanks. I appreciate your help."

"How did your carny convos go?"

"Showmen chats. I'm not sure. I think I saw the guy you told me about from your class. A scruffy fellow with tattoos covering his arms, right? But I realize that describes probably a quarter of the men working there."

"Did you see a large skull tat on his forearm?"

"I wasn't that close to him. He just walked by someone I was speaking with. Apparently, he's a loner—a super-quiet guy."

"In school, he was very popular. He played varsity football and baseball."

"What's his name?"

"Ryan Heller, as in Heller Future Solutions. His dad owns the company."

Olivia pulled out her phone, opened a notes app, and keyed in the name.

"I know that look," A.J. said. "Do you think he's connected to the goon who came to your house, or to what happened to the carnival dude?"

"I'm not sure, yet. There are a lot of colorful characters working for the carnival. It's always the quiet ones you have to worry about."

CHAPTER 19

After exchanging goodbyes at the clinic, Olivia rushed to the inn, cutting across the town square to save time. Activity was light on the lawn, but townsfolk peppered the benches bordering the sidewalks, basking in the pleasant afternoon. A young woman wearing black joggers and a purple sweatshirt gripped the leashes of a golden retriever, a bulldog, and two dachshunds. On a mission, she was marching the motley pack toward the gazebo at the opposite end of the square. Olivia had spoken with the enterprising dog walker once before, learning that she made daily rounds of the local businesses with shop dogs. For a reasonable fee, she'd collect any pooches who needed to walk, burn excess energy, or do their business. Today, she recognized two of the lucky dogs: Duke, the bandana-wearing bulldog from the bookstore, and Honey, the golden retriever from Daisy's Feed and Saddlery.

She crossed Cider Lane in front of the newspaper suite and proceeded straight to the inn. Cassandra was probably there waiting for her by now. As she opened the lobby's door, soothing jazz music and the smell of freshly brewed coffee whisked her a world away from the carnival. A glass vase brimming with red, yellow, and white tulips sat on a plant stand beside the beverage cart near the entrance. She eyed a rattan basket of iced cinnamon rolls next to the decaf carafe. If it wasn't for her online chat, she'd swipe one and sit in the dining room with a cup of coffee to boost her energy and get her mind off things.

A party of four entered the restaurant through the open doorway, just past the tall reception desk. Zoey, the inn's five-star concierge, was recommending to an older couple the must-stop shops in town for their first visit to Apple Station. Her bubbly voice carried in the lobby, and her suggestions of Tales and Treasures, Carol's Comforts, and Jillian's Cafe would all make Olivia's list as well.

She spotted Cassandra sitting in a saddle-tan leather wingback chair at the back of the lobby. As she passed the concierge desk, Cassandra looked up from her phone and gave her a subtle smile. Olivia took a seat in a matching chair beside her, pulled her cell out, and set it on a small round walnut table between them.

Cassandra scooted forward and cut to the chase. "How did it go this morning with Nicky Klein?"

"At first, she seemed forthcoming, but later, someone

told me she'd instructed all the workers not to talk to me about Bobby."

"Intriguing. I wonder why. Sounds fishy."

"Maybe. She probably wants to prevent bad press about the family business. That makes sense, and I don't blame her. It's clear that Bobby was a tough manager to work for. He had a gopher he paid on the side to do special jobs. There's at least one disgruntled worker who feels Bobby owed him money."

Cassandra nodded. "I read a post in a forum written by a gentleman named Mad Dawg. He accused the Kleins of cheating their workers."

"I saw that too. That's the thing—everyone goes by a nickname. Aunt Bea, Cowboy, Stash, Slammer, Steady Eddie, Sparky, Angel, Lone Wolf. The police could get IDs if they needed to, but I have a feeling that few would give their real names for the record."

"Sounds like a fun bunch. Do you think any of them have motives for murder?"

"It's too early to say. Even if someone had a beef with Bobby, to suggest they'd go to that extreme is premature. There are also rumors he was a big-time womanizer. We could be looking at a jealous girlfriend or boyfriend situation. The carnival is its own culture with its own rules. It's like a dysfunctional family that handles everything in-house. Despite it all, I'm told they take care of one another."

"Cover for each other too," Cassandra added.

Olivia's cell buzzed, and they both looked down at the table. She picked it up, opened a text from her father, and silently read the message. "I knew it. Look at what the cameras caught."

Concerned, she viewed the video he'd sent of a squirrel hanging upside down on their pole-mounted birdfeeder, feasting on the sunflower seeds.

"What is that about?" Cassandra asked, looking at the screen.

"We had security cameras installed this morning at the house. Catching squirrels on the birdfeeder wasn't the intention."

She texted back, "Well done, dear Watson. We need to buy a baffle to baffle the cunning critters."

Her father's response came as a string of emojis: a laughing face, a thumbs-up, a green check mark, and a balloon. She smiled, showing Cassandra the screen.

"My mom does that," Cassandra said. "She texts me to say good morning and follows it with three lines of emojis. Any idea how the balloon fits in?"

"No. I just usually go with it and never ask. Anyway, back to the matter at hand. Despite any antipathy Bobby's crew may have had for him, none hinted at his involvement in any illegal activity."

"What about Nicky Klein?"

"She seems to be the one who handles the nuts and bolts of the carnival. Everyone likes her, or at least thinks that she's fairer than her brother. In the two photos I've seen of them together, they were all smiles—light and love. Tomorrow, I'll see if I can learn any other real names. There's a Beatrice Podder, but I'm almost certain she isn't a suspect for anything. There's a visiting priest who ministers to the crew—Father Alfonso Silva. And there's another guy, known as Lone Wolf, who might be someone A.J. went to school with—Ryan Heller."

Cassandra opened a notes app on her phone and typed as she talked. "I'll look into all of them. They could be dead ends, though there has to be a story behind someone named Lone Wolf. Any idea where the priest is from?"

"He's local, but I don't know specifics. He's a regular visitor to the Kleins' crew whenever they swing through the area. I also saw a man connected to the buyers." She left out Grasso's name for now, unsure if revealing it might jeopardize Carolyn's operation. "If Bobby had a partner, that person may still have the eggs or be trying to broker a deal for other items."

"Maybe it's one of the crew who nobody would suspect," Cassandra replied, scrolling through her notes. "A carnival would be a sly cover. They're always on the move, have means of transport, and make stops all along the East Coast. Let me give you the highlights of what I found. Like you, I researched Klein Amusements, but there wasn't much ado about them. Then I read way too much about egg smuggling. I contacted a parrot sanctuary and rescue organization nearby in The Plains and asked them about hyacinth macaws. They're known as the Great Danes of the parrot world because of their size, which makes them high maintenance. They require a large living space, and their enclosures typically need to be made of stainless steel. They have crazy powerful beaks and can be destructive if they don't have toys, or if they're deprived of social interaction with their caregiver."

"It sounds as though taking care of them is more of a commitment than some realize."

Cassandra turned the screen toward her. "Despite their adult size, this is what the eggs look like."

"Those seem about the same size as chicken eggs."

"They are very close." She swiped to the next photo. "This is one type of incubator."

The round, domed enclosure would easily fit on a countertop. "That's not what I was expecting."

"That's just an example. They can get more sophisticated. When the parrots hatch, they require a lot of care and much larger brooders."

Olivia swiped back to the picture of the incubator. "Potentially, all the supplier would need is two or three of these and a power supply. This setup could easily fit in an RV, a motorhome, or a bunkroom."

Cassandra stood up, and she followed suit.

"That's all I have for you now," Cassandra said. "I'll check into those names. I hate to say it, but things don't look good for the parrots. After they hatch, they require expert care, and I'm not confident they'll get it."

"I'm with you on that. I need to bolt for a work thing.

Afterward, I'll reach out to my contact and see if she has anything to share. I'm returning to the carnival grounds tomorrow to try again."

With their plans solidified, they agreed to keep in touch, then left the inn together. Cassandra headed toward the newspaper office as Olivia crossed the street and rushed back to her car. The dog walker was still leading her barking brood around the lawn, while landscapers were spreading mulch in the flower beds by the gazebo.

She spotted Dorothy and Floyd Peabody standing in front of the little library, close to the working crew. The older couple were often out and about town on warm, sunny days. Usually, they'd stop by Jillian's Cafe for coffee and something sweet to eat, then park themselves on a bench and chat with whoever cared to shoot the breeze. Floyd had become the caretaker of the community-lending hot spot, keeping it tidy and stocked with books from his own collection when inventory ran low. She hadn't spoken with the Peabodys for a while, and though she would've liked to say hi to them, her time crunch dictated it would have to wait until another day.

After hopping into her Expedition, she drove slowly out of town, picking up the pace as the speed limit allowed. As she hightailed it home, her thoughts drifted to the photo of the incubator. Something that small could easily be hidden and impossible to find. The parrots were in peril, and there was no telling how much time remained to locate them. Grasso's appearance on the midway and his chummy handshake with Slammer were worrisome. Bobby owing Slammer back pay seemed thin as a motive for murder, but half a million dollars could be a game changer. The potential for that payday came laced with high stakes that some may consider worth killing for.

CHAPTER 20

With ten minutes to spare, Olivia hustled into the house, welcomed by the warm scent of cinnamon wafting from the kitchen. Buddy sprung up from his cushy dog bed under the bay window and bounded over to greet her, whipping his tail to and fro as if she'd been away for days. She leaned down and patted his side while waving a hello to her father, who stood just inside the kitchen. His flour-dusted apron hinted that he'd been busy while she was away.

"I see you wasted no time in playing with your new toys," she said.

He pulled off his oven mitts. "I couldn't wait. I hope we have space in the freezer. How'd things go this morning?"

She went over to the sofa to check on Willow, who was curled up on a navy fleece blanket. The cat woke just enough to raise her head, looking up at Olivia with sleepy, dreamy eyes.

"I'm not sure," she replied, brushing Willow's cheek. "Everyone has a story, but getting people to talk is tricky. The crew is full of colorful characters. It's some of what you'd expect and some of what you wouldn't. That lifestyle isn't for me."

"Aren't you glad I didn't let you run away to join the carnival?"

"I never wanted to do that."

"Regardless, I would've stopped you if you'd tried," he said, pointing the mitts at her.

"That makes no sense, Dad. I've gotta hurry. I have an online chat super soon. It smells great in here. What did you make?"

"Come see." He waved for her to follow him. "Don't worry. I'll clean up all this mess after the last batch is out of the oven."

The kitchen was in even more disarray than when she'd left this morning. He'd moved everything she'd stacked on the counters, scattering the wares everywhere. Three wired racks sat on the table, cooling dozens of pastries that looked like two attached flattened cinnamon rolls.

"What are those? Is that puff pastry?"

"Those are cinnamon palmiers, and it's rough puff. You can still achieve good flakiness using small chunks of butter with fewer turns and less chilling time."

"You're speaking Greek to me. Whether regular or

rough puff, I'm taking one with me." She plucked a napkin from a white wicker holder attached to the wall behind the stand mixer and placed a palmier on it. Then she opened the refrigerator and grabbed a bottle of water and an apple. "There, a balanced lunch. I saw A.J. in town. He told me the install went well."

"Can you believe those squirrels?" he said, closing the door for her. "I knew that seed was emptying too fast. After I've cleaned up, I'm going online to order a baffle. I'll show them."

"Let the games begin. A.J. said he left instructions for the cameras."

He placed the oven mitts on the counter, picked up a piece of paper lying on the top of the coffee brewer, and showed it to her. "That's the name of the app. You can scan the code using your phone's camera. A.J. helped me, but I'm sure you know how to do all that."

"Okay, thanks." She set all her food on the counter, grabbed her office keys from the hook rack, and placed the ring on her pinky. Then she tucked the paper between her arm and her side, balanced the palmier and apple in one hand, and picked up the bottle of water. "Gotta go."

He quickstepped over to the door and opened it for her.

"Thank you." She hustled onto the back porch, down the steps, and across the yard. When she got to her office, she shifted the bottle into the crook of her other elbow, transferred her keys to her free hand, and unlocked the door southpaw. After rushing inside, she dumped all her carry items onto the desk and booted up her laptop. While dialing Angela's number, she removed a pair of earbuds from their charging case and inserted them for the call.

"Hello, Olivia," Angela said. "Perfect timing. How are you today?"

"Doing okay." She picked up the palmier, took a bite, and chewed while logging into the chat. "How about you? Oh, that's tasty."

"Excuse me?"

"Sorry. I was grabbing some lunch before we start. My dad made cinnamon palmiers. *Fancy.* I always called them elephant ears, but I stand corrected."

"Did he make his own puff pastry?"

"Rough puff. Are you a baker?"

"I dabble in patisseries. Rough puff is the way to go. You can still get good lamination."

"So I'm told. The nuances of puff pastry seem to be a gaping hole in my education." She scanned the camera instruction sheet, downloaded the app, and created a login while Angela went over next week's schedule.

"I'm sure you're not distraught about that," Angela said.

She looked up from her cell's screen. "Distraught about what?"

"Canceling the chat on Thursday."

"Why is it canceled?"

"Were you even listening to me?"

"Sorry. We had security cameras installed this morning, and I was trying to pull up the feed on my phone."

"Hold on," Angela said. "Something glitchy is happening here … Okay, IT wonder Ian is working on it. We'll just be delayed a few minutes. I'm going out of town, and I couldn't reel anyone in to be me for you on Thursday. Do you have any copy ready for next week?"

"Yes. I'll send it to you when we're done."

"Fabulous. That'll be one less thing to catch up on when I get back. Ian has given me a thumbs-up, so let's get the party started."

Angela welcomed everyone, then opened the chat for the Q&A. As the attendees in the chat room started to send in their questions, Olivia continued eating her lunch. While typing in her responses, Olivia kept up her usual background conversation with Angela.

"Ouch," Angela said. "That next question is a doozy. Poor girl."

Olivia read the question from a wife asking about how to handle her husband's flirtatious behavior around other women when they were out in public. She penned a line of sympathy, then continued writing as she spoke to Angela. "Do you know anyone who has sought revenge because a significant other jilted them?"

"Hold up, Olivia. Whatever you're writing, stop. That's not your answer, is it? Because legally that's a no-no."

"Of course not. Give me some credit. I'm just asking because I know you have two exes that you're not fond of." She finished the reply and posted the response.

"Things not going swimmingly with the boyfriend?" Angela asked.

"No. I mean, everything's great. Perfect. Couldn't be better."

"Uh-huh. That didn't sound defensive at all." She paused before continuing. "See, that's why you're answering these questions and not me. You handled that well. I would've been brutally honest with her. Anyway, as to your question. No. I've known a few cheaters, and I won't deny that I've fantasized about outing them by putting a bug in an influencer's ear."

"Rome should canonize you for not acting on that." Olivia read the next question, from someone who was upset about not being thanked after giving a gift to a friend.

"Jeez," Angela said. "They must have a pretty good life if this is a problem that keeps them up at night."

"People feel what they feel."

"Yes, but was that gift more about the recipient or the giver?"

"I hear you," Olivia said as she wrote her response, then posted it.

"I would've told her to get over it. That's why they pay you the big bucks."

"I don't get big bucks."

"It's just a phrase. Speaking of salary, have you thought any more about the job at *Modern Mosaic*?"

Olivia read the next question involving quarrelsome in-laws. Such issues she'd addressed many times over. She wrote her well-practiced reply, distilling advice in fewer than five sentences.

"Evelyn really wants to speak with you," Angela said.

"You're making me lose my train of thought." She posted her answer, then continued. "I'm grateful for the consideration, but my life is here now."

Angela sighed. "I understand. Do you want a cat?"

She looked up from the screen. "That's out of left field, and I wouldn't have expected you to give up so easily."

"Skip that next question," Angela said. "He needs to talk privately to his doctor about that. Just pretend like you didn't see it. In fact, pass on the one after that too. Go to Joyce's question."

She read a query about a mom's group fraught with scheduling playdates. Her fingers hovered over the keyboard as she thought of her ten-year-old self. "That's the world we live in. We have to schedule playtime. When I was a kid, I just left the house, and the only thing my parents said to me occasionally was to be home by dark."

"You're leaving Joyce hanging," Angela said.

"Right." She tapped away, responding in double time.

"I knew you wouldn't take the job. I brought it up because you'd be perfect for it. But I understand. When you decide something, you stick to it. I asked about the cat because my sister's Siamese recently had another litter."

She posted her response to Joyce's question. "That makes you a fur baby auntie once again. You must be thrilled."

"Thank you. Since you didn't take a kitten last time, and now that you have one of your own, how about a second?"

"Willow isn't mine. I'm only watching her while her owner is away."

"Do you like having her around?"

"She's adorable. I'll miss her when she goes home." Her cell buzzed with a text, and she read a message from her father asking how she liked the palmiers.

"I think you've fallen in love," Angela said. "Maybe with more than just her."

"What are you trying to say?" Olivia texted him back, "Yummy."

"Nothing," Angela replied. "Oh dear, look at Brittany's question."

"Ugh, bless her heart."

For the next twenty minutes, she continued answering questions, and at the top of the hour, Angela ended the chat.

"Another successful Q&A with the ever-fascinating, unfailingly indomitable Ms. Penn," Angela said.

"It's always a pleasure."

"Don't say it unless you mean it," Angela joked.

"I'll send you my copy for next week right now, and if

you think you need more, I can work on something tonight." She opened a folder on her hard drive, selected the file, and e-mailed it to Angela.

"I'm sure it'll be fine. Thank you. That'll be one less thing off my plate before I leave."

"Are you going on a vacation?"

Angela kept quiet for a few seconds. "Not exactly. What I'm about to say, you can't tell anyone. Nobody here at the office knows yet."

"Are you okay? Is there something wrong?"

"Oh, no. It's nothing bad. Do you remember when I told you I was thinking of leaving the paper? Well, I'm doing it and moving to Vermont. I bought a bed-and-breakfast near Rutland. I'm turning in my red pen and hour-long commutes to become an innkeeper. I'm going up there to meet with some contractors."

"What? Are you serious?"

"It's a done deal."

Olivia leaned back in her chair, feeling like she'd just been slingshot into outer space. "That's—wow. I had no idea. Congratulations. How did this come about?"

"It's always been a dream of mine. I thought I'd do it when I retired, but I have the money now. YOLO, as you kids say."

"We don't really say that anymore." Her heart swirled with mixed emotions. She was happy for Angela but also gutted that her friend and editor would be leaving. Their working relationship was one of the best parts of her job, and without it, nothing about writing the column would feel the same.

"There are some renovations that need to be done, but it's basically turnkey. The previous owners are moving to sunnier climes. I'm so excited. You'll have to come often with that boyfriend of yours. I want to meet this man. He must be special to have caught your eye."

"He is, and I love Vermont. I've been there several times."

"I wanted you to know in case it would influence your decision about the job at *Modern Mosaic*. I don't know who the paper will hire to fill my position."

"Thanks for looking out for me. I'm shocked but happy for you. I'm going to miss you. When are you leaving?"

"I'll miss you too. I'm renting out my house in Virginia starting in August. The bed-and-breakfast should be ready for guests in September, fingers crossed. My plan is to inform the honchos here next week, and I want to be up there by mid-July."

"That's right around the corner."

"I know. I'm sorry that I'm dropping this on you, but it had to come at some point. If you change your mind about *Modern Mosaic*, Evelyn and I are tight. I'm certain she'd find a place for you, even down the road. Don't forget, I have a lot of connections in publishing, and I'll go to bat for you."

"Thanks. That means everything to me. I'm happy for you. Having lunch with you at your bed-and-breakfast will feel like being in a Hallmark movie. It'll be so much better than eating pre-made, plastic-wrapped sandwiches in the cafeteria."

Angela laughed, heartily agreeing. "You've got that right, kiddo. We'll talk more about things when I return, and I'll do what I can to ease the transition with your new editor."

After a few more shared laughs, they ended the call, agreeing to touch base next week. Olivia slowly swiveled her seat, thrown for a loop by the news. Angela had been her editor at the paper from the get-go, and with her leaving, one of the few appealing aspects of her job would soon be gone.

She checked the time on her phone. At a quarter after four, she couldn't put off calling Preston for much longer. She didn't relish hashing things out with him at the moment. After Angela's bombshell, she would've liked to have thrown in the towel on the rest of the day. Sam, though, was depending on her. Lives were at stake, and that took precedence over personal business. She dialed the number Sam had given her on Monday, but the call went straight to voicemail. After leaving a message, she set the cell down and stood up to tidy the desk. As she binned her trash, the screen lit up with a text from Sam. Opening it, she read, "St. Luke's. Five."

CHAPTER 21

Olivia had last visited St. Luke's in early April, on a sunny Sunday afternoon. She and Preston had stopped by the cemetery to pay their respects to her mother, his father, and Paige before meeting Bev for brunch at the inn. While the historic church was no longer used for regular services, weddings and funerals were sometimes held there. The church cemetery occupied most of the property. The extensive acreage beyond the farthest memorial marker suggested the grounds would remain open for business for many years to come.

She pulled into the lot right at five, spotting three other cars, only one of which she recognized. The white VW Golf belonged to Mrs. Stanski, a parish administrator who oversaw special arrangements at the church. She'd helped to plan Paige's services, removing much of the burden from June during those difficult days. After parking near a silver sedan, Olivia got out, scanned the cemetery, and saw Sam standing near Paige's grave. As she made her way down the gentle slope, Sam glanced over her shoulder before focusing back on the ground by her feet.

The shamrock-green grass was lush and freshly cut, and the maintenance crew had removed all the dead bouquets that had languished without water. Potted peace lilies dominated the graveside decorations, as they always did after the Easter season. Crinkly pink and purple crape myrtles were in full bloom, and many of the dogwoods' low-hanging branches boasted their four-petal white blossoms. Small American flags marked the graves of veterans, and stuffed animals had been left behind for those who'd died much too young.

As Olivia neared, Sam half turned, then asked, "Does anyone know you came?"

"No. Are you sure it's safe for you to be here?"

"It's fine. We'll keep it short." She looked down at Paige's memorial marker. "Have you talked to June recently?"

Olivia stood beside her, eyeing a potted red geranium that June must've placed there recently. "Yes. She's leaving soon to go on an Alaskan cruise with her sister."

"That'll be nice. How's she doing?"

"She's better after visiting with her family in North Carolina. Her niece just had a baby, so I'm sure that did her heart a lot of good. With Paige's anniversary coming up, it'll be difficult for her. She'll be home by then. I thought that you, me, Soph, and Tori could spend some time with her on that day. I think she'd enjoy the company."

Sam nodded slowly. "Even though I didn't know Paige, I almost feel like I do by hearing you talk about her."

Olivia gave her a thin smile. "I tell you what—she'd be so jealous of me right now. Doing undercover work for a black-budget team would've been her dream. She loved investigative journalism."

"How did you two end up on different paths?"

"Out of graduate school, we both started with local papers. Paige stayed in Apple Station, but I worked as a staff writer for a regional Mid-Atlantic paper. She had the talent to work at any of the big national newspapers, but she didn't want to be too far from her parents. Then when her father died, and it was just her and June, she stopped looking for jobs elsewhere. Occasionally, she'd do freelance articles for magazines, and I think that gave her a sense of branching out. I was a beat reporter for several years until the opportunity came along to start the advice column. It was very different from what I had been doing, but I was ready for a change."

"Would you do the same thing now?"

"What do you mean?"

"If you had the chance to make a switch, career-wise, would you consider it?"

She thought of Evelyn's offer and Angela's imminent departure. "Yes, I would. In fact, something has come up. A great opportunity seems to be mine for the taking, but it's in New York. It goes to show you how much life can change in a year. Last May, I was on my way to New York, ready for a fresh start. Instead, I found a new beginning back home, where it all began."

A car door clunked closed, and they both looked toward the lot. The daytime running lights of a crimson SUV flicked on. Then the driver reversed out of the parking space and drove away.

"Do you think you'd be living in Apple Station right now if it wasn't for Paige?" Sam asked.

"Probably not. Her death set in motion all the changes that have happened in my life over the past year. I miss her dearly, but I feel she's still with me." She stifled a fond chuckle. "Especially since I've been watching her cat."

Sam nodded. "We honor the dead by continuing to live our lives."

"As you're doing for Aaron?"

"Something like that."

Olivia glanced back at the lot, hearing another car arrive. A vintage red pickup parked next to Mrs. Stanski's Golf just as she was leaving the church. The older man got out of his truck, holding a bouquet, and spoke with the administrator on the sidewalk for a minute before they went their separate ways. She got into her car to leave, and he walked toward a section of the cemetery behind the church.

"I take it your mother-in-law isn't lurking around here someplace."

"No."

"Are you still staying at the monastery?"

"For the time being."

"Someday I would like to hear about how you and Anne became acquainted. I told Soph a little about what's going on, but not all the details. She said you can stay at her place if you need an alternate safe house."

Sam nestled her hands in her hoodie pockets. "Thanks. I'll keep it in mind. We're working on finding the mole. The sooner we take down Grasso and the supplier, the better. I want to get back home. The workout facility at the monastery leaves much to be desired."

"No jujitsu training partners there?" Olivia joked. "That's surprising. With the way Anne can yield a shovel, maybe the sisters shade more toward the Shaolin martial arts."

"I wouldn't doubt it."

A blue compact car pulled into the lot, and they both watched for a moment as a middle-aged woman got out of the vehicle. After closing the door, she stepped onto the grounds and headed in their direction. They bowed their heads, as if in prayer, and kept quiet until she stopped at a memorial marker two rows over from them.

Sam subtly nodded toward the parking lot. "Let's go."

They gave the woman a wide berth, slowly weaving a path among the graves. Olivia stooped several times along the way to right top-heavy lilies that had toppled.

After reaching the lot, they stopped in front of the silver sedan.

"Is this yours?" Olivia asked.

"For the afternoon—which brings us to why we're here. Since you contacted me, you must have something to share."

"I saw Grasso this morning on the carnival grounds, and he seemed chummy with a crew member who goes by the nickname Slammer. In case that's not clear, he's done jail time for some sort of violent offense." She detailed the other conversations she'd had, along with what Cassandra had told her about the incubators.

"Grasso's presence makes it almost certain that Bobby had a partner or wasn't the one in charge," Sam said. "Either way, the supply network remains intact."

"There's something else. When I was on the grounds, I ran into Preston. I put him off, and I didn't tell him anything about you. But he knows I know something, and he's expecting to hear from me today with an explanation."

Sam inhaled deeply and hummed. "That was always a risk. I'm sorry you're in the middle of this."

"Don't you think it's time your team and the police got on the same page? Both of you could achieve your goals if you work together."

"I'll talk to Carolyn and see what she wants to do. Can you hold off with him until I call you later tonight?"

That wasn't what Olivia wanted to hear, but she'd cast her lot with Carolyn's cause and wouldn't stand down now, for Sam's sake. "I'm already knee-deep in quicksand with him, so the sooner you let me know, the better. If the incubators are like the pictures I saw, they could be anywhere in the camp. They'd easily fit in an RV, a motorhome, or a bunkroom."

"Do all the employees stay there on the grounds?"

"It seems so. Bobby and Nicky have—had—their own RVs. Some will stay in cheap motels, if any are available nearby. We have nothing that fits that bill around here. There's an accountant, Jeffrey Rollins, who's staying in town. Nicky says he meets them throughout the season to go over the books. There's a local priest, Father Alfonso Silva, who apparently comes to minister to the crew whenever the carnival travels through the area."

"Interesting. Do you think you can talk to the guy you saw Grasso with and dig into that connection?"

"Slammer. I was planning on returning there tomorrow, so I'll try." She shifted her focus over Sam's shoulder, hearing a car driving up the small hill that led to the church. "The camp seems quiet during the days, and if I catch some of the crew outside of Nicky's view, then— oh, no."

CHAPTER 22

Sam turned her head and looked over her shoulder as Preston drove into the lot and hemmed in her vehicle. Like a wave on the verge of breaking, there was no way now to avoid the consequences of being discovered.

"What's he doing here?" Olivia mumbled more to herself than to Sam. "I swear I didn't tell him I was meeting you."

He cut the engine, popped the door, and got out calmly, as if they'd invited him. If he was fazed by finding them together, his poker face was on point today.

"I know," Sam said. "I'll handle this."

Before he rounded the truck's hood, Olivia intercepted him by the front bumper. "Were you following me?" She knew the answer, but her shock at him being here still prodded her to level the accusation.

"You should've told me you knew where she was," he said, shifting his steely focus to Sam.

"I made her promise me she wouldn't," Sam interjected, joining Olivia by the truck.

"You were following me?" Olivia questioned again, as if her choices hadn't justified his actions. "Why?"

"Tell me what's going on," he said. When neither of them spoke up immediately, he laced his tone with more severity. "I knew your charade this morning, posing as a reporter, had something to do with Sam. Why did you keep this from me? How long have you two been in contact?"

"Don't blame her," Sam said. "I put her in the middle of this."

"The middle of what?"

Olivia glanced at her. "We have to tell him." She waited for a moment until Sam nodded, giving her the green light. "Sam's life is in danger."

His clenched jaw relaxed a bit, and his narrowed eyes softened. "Explain. And tell me why a trail camera captured pictures of Sam at Spring Hills on Sunday night."

"She had nothing to do with Bobby Klein's murder," Olivia said.

"And you know this how?"

She straightened, drawing her shoulders back, and looked him dead in the eye. "Because I was there too."

"Klein was already dead when I got there," Sam added. "Liv arrived after I did."

He pointed at Olivia. "You were at Spring Hills and

didn't think that was something you should share with me?"

"Of course, I wanted to tell you, and I was planning to, soon." She looked at Sam. "We can't wait for Carolyn's go-ahead. The police need to know what's really going on."

"Who's Carolyn?"

"Let me make the call," Sam said, removing her phone from her pocket. She turned and stepped toward the front of the sedan.

"Who are you calling?" Preston asked.

Olivia reached out and gently grabbed his hand, keeping her voice low. "Please, give her a moment. Trust me."

"Trust you?"

"I'm sorry. It's been killing me not to bring you in on what's happening, but—"

He grunted and squeezed her fingers, matching her hushed tone. "You were at Spring Hills, where Klein was killed. Why? What if the person who did it had still been there? What if they saw you? If Sam's life is in danger, *your* life is in danger."

She shook her head. "No. Nobody else knows I was there. Except for my dad and Soph, but I think they have the proper security clearances."

Sam rejoined them. "Okay. Carolyn agreed."

"That was quick," Olivia said.

"She's decisive. Do you two need a moment, or are we good?"

Preston gave Olivia's hand another squeeze, then released it. "Why don't you tell me what's going on, then I'll let you know if we're good."

For the next twenty minutes, Sam explained her team's operation and how it related to Klein's murder and the missing parrot eggs. Olivia chimed in, detailing her involvement from the time she went into Sam's house on Sunday until now. He listened as a detective, asking questions neither had considered nor had the answers to. After they finished sharing everything, his stance and demeanor had softened considerably.

"Well, what do you think?" Olivia asked him.

"You're right. This is bigger than just Klein's murder. I'll have to take this to Payne."

Olivia wanted to protest but knew he couldn't withhold the information from his boss, the chief of police. "What does this mean for Sam?"

He brushed his hand over his head. "Payne will want to know more about these people you work for."

Olivia took hold of his wrist and stepped toward him. "Excuse us for a moment, Sam." She led him around to the rear of his truck. "Can you delay telling him until tomorrow? It's probably near six, and he's got to be on his way home by now. Let Sam go do what she needs to tonight. You owe her at least that for what she did to help you in December."

"And what she did for you."

Her hand slid down into his palm. "I'm sorry this is how you found out about what's been going on, and that

I kept it from you. I'm sorry, too, about not identifying her in the pictures from the trail camera. I hope you can understand why I did it."

"Somewhat, but that doesn't mean I like it or that it was right."

He circled his thumb on the back of her hand, and she added a thin grin to the apology, sensing she'd partially won him over.

"I'll make it up to you," she said.

He seemed to consider that for a moment, then narrowed his eyes. "Even if that means helping me clean out my shed?"

"Odd penance, but I guess?"

"Where I found a snake last night?"

Lordy. She hoped he was teasing, knowing how much she hated snakes. "If I have to, I will." *In full-body armor.*

He released her hand with a quiet chuckle meant only for her. Then he got into his truck and turned over the engine. She stepped out of the way as he reversed and parked next to her Expedition.

When he came back to join them, he said to Sam, "You can leave, but I want you to be reachable."

"Liv has my number. I'll be in touch." After exchanging a knowing glance with Olivia, she settled behind the wheel, reversed, and drove out of the lot as another car entered.

"Let's go over there," Preston said, gesturing toward their vehicles. They crossed the short distance as a

Subaru parked close to the church. When they got to her Expedition, they turned and faced each other.

"Thank you for understanding," she said.

"I'm not all the way to *understanding* yet. I don't want you involved in this any further."

She'd figured this was coming, but she wasn't planning on backing down now. "There's no danger to me. I learned pertinent information this morning that we otherwise wouldn't have known."

He shook his head. "I get that, but it's still not safe for you to be near any of this. If anyone becomes suspicious of you, you'll be at risk. Let the police and Sam's team handle it."

"You didn't seem surprised to learn about what she really does."

"It doesn't shock me. A friend of mine was involved in black-budget ops for a while after he left the military. From what I know about Sam, a lot makes sense now."

She leaned with her back against the driver's door. He turned and took his place next to her.

"So, were you following me?" she asked.

He casually folded his arms. "I was."

She couldn't be angry or blame him. He was doing his job, even if that meant doubting her.

"I thought maybe you came here to visit your mother or Paige, so I waited out by the entrance. I flagged down Mrs. Stanski on the way out to say hello. She told me she saw you talking with another woman around the same age. Her description sounded a lot like Sam."

"I wasn't aware she knew me that well. I spoke with her at Paige's funeral, but the last time we'd talked prior to that was when my mom died. That was over ten years ago."

"Her quilting club meets at the inn once a month. You know how my mom likes to talk about my life, so now she likes to talk about you too."

"I get it. Why did you go to see Soph?"

"After this morning at the farm, I sensed there was a lot you weren't telling me. I wanted to see if she knew anything. I was—am—worried."

She half turned, leaning her shoulder against the door, and wrapped her hand around his bicep. "I have a good cover story."

He dipped his chin and sighed. "No, no."

"Hear me out. All I'm doing is talking to some of the crew under a legitimate guise, backed by Ellen. I'm in a position that neither you nor anyone on Sam's team can be in. There's a chance the parrot eggs are still someplace near, and if they're not, at least Grasso is. There could be another deal in the works. If we identify the supplier and the buyer, we may bring them both down together. Two birds, one stone."

His mouth curled upward as he closed his eyes for an extended blink. "We?"

"You know what I mean. Do you have any leads on the murder yet?" She'd expected his heavy sigh. "I'm going back there tomorrow with or without your help."

He turned his head to look at her, then she stepped in front of him.

"It would be helpful, if you've identified any persons of interest, for me to know who they are," she said. "Instead of wasting time, I can seek them out and speak with them directly."

"Liv, what makes you think they'll talk to you? Do you really believe you're going to get one of them to say something incriminating?"

"I found out Slammer had a beef with Bobby over money. That's a powerful motive for murder. He and Grasso seem to be buds. Did you know that before you ambushed me?" She paused long enough for his silence to answer the rhetorical question. "Didn't think so. Nobody at the carnival will talk to a cop. Each has a story to tell, but you have to gain their trust, then listen. I agree no one is going to come out and say, 'I killed Bobby' or 'Bobby was working with so-and-so selling illegal animal goods.' Time is of the essence, and right now, I'm your best option to have eyes and ears where you're not welcomed."

He shifted his weight forward, uttering a soft grunt, and lightly grasped her hand. "Promise me you'll only go there to talk. Stay out in the open where there are other people around. Don't get isolated."

"Ten-four. Is there anything you can share that would *help me help you*?"

His dimple appeared through a reluctant grin. "Are you quoting movie lines at me now?"

She playfully punched his bicep. "Mr. Wise Guy."

"Hey, you pack more of a punch than you think." He flattened his smile, narrowing his eyes a bit. "I'd be interested to hear any theories Sam's team may have. What I'm about to tell you can't find its way into the paper."

"Would it be silly to say you can trust me?"

He shook his head. "No, it wouldn't be. Of course I trust you. Truthfully, we could use some help. We didn't find much evidence at Spring Hills. The medical examiner's office should have preliminary results from the autopsy ready by tomorrow, but the full report won't be available for a while. Klein was stabbed, but I'm hoping they can narrow down the murder weapon. It would be helpful to know what we're looking for. The only thing we found near his body was a blue bracelet—the woven kind you see kids wearing."

"A friendship bracelet."

"Yeah. There's so much random garbage around that building."

"Aunt Bea makes those."

"Who?"

"Aunt Bea—Beatrice Podder. You know, kind of like Beatrix Potter, who—"

He held up his free hand to stop her. "I know who Beatrix Potter is."

"Huh. I'm impressed. Anyway, I met her this morning. She seems to have a handle on what's happening behind the scenes. She gives the bracelets out to everyone —children, the other workers, and even me."

"If that bracelet was one that she made, there's a good chance someone connected to the carnival was with Bobby at Spring Hills on Sunday night."

"Maybe his partner or the murderer. Could it have been his?"

"Klein doesn't strike me as the type to wear something like that, but I'll question his sister about it. She might know if he did."

"What about Nicky? Do you have suspicions about her?"

"We've looked into her background, but she's clean, unlike her brother. Plus, she has a solid alibi."

"What do you mean?"

"We have a priest who confirms he heard her confession about the time we think the murder occurred."

"I think I know who you're talking about. Father Silva. I saw him this morning."

"That's him," Preston said while nodding. "We believe Klein knew his attacker. There were no signs that he was dragged or dumped there. Around the back of the headquarters, there's no place to hide, and he was out in the open, so we think whoever he was meeting with killed him."

"His wallet was missing," she said.

"Please tell me you didn't search Klein's body."

"No. Sam did."

"That doesn't make me feel even remotely better."

"Was there anything else taken?"

"Just his keys and phone. It could've been an attempt

to stage the murder as a robbery gone bad, but it's an unlikely scenario given the isolation of the area."

"Can you check into Slammer's background?" she asked. "Starting with getting a real name."

His smile spanned ear to ear as he released her hand. "Are you giving me orders?"

"Of course not," she said, stepping closer.

"I'm serious, Liv. Only go there to talk."

Her heart ramped up its rhythm as he placed his hands on her waist.

"I want you to call me with whatever you learn, even if you think it's unimportant," he said. "I can stay with you and your dad until all this is over or the carnival has left town."

"As much as I would like that, we'll be okay. Grasso has no reason to suspect I'm anyone but Sam's neighbor."

His hands slid around her back, drawing her closer. "You could come to my house."

She melted into his embrace, not caring if anyone was watching. Her focus drifted from his eyes to his lips as she tilted her head. "A PJ party?"

He leaned in and softly kissed her. "The PJs," he whispered, "would be optional."

CHAPTER 23

The Expedition jounced about as Olivia drove across the rutted grass lot at Fields Farm on Wednesday morning. She eyed the console display for the umpteenth time, drumming her thumbs, quick-quick-slow, on the leather-wrapped wheel. Eleven o'clock. While eating breakfast, she'd received an e-mail from Angela requesting some additional copy for next week's columns. A trip to the office had delayed her for nearly two hours while she waited until Angela had reviewed and okayed her responses.

After parking and getting out, she locked the car and took off for the midway. Since yesterday, cardboard trash cans had been placed here and there from the lot to the carnival grounds. Festive signs on wood posts advertised the fun to come—family games, thrill rides, and tasty treats. The farm continued to operate normally, though most of the work was focused on the fields far from the midway. Workers had installed temporary orange safety fencing along the border of the closest cornfield. The young green stocks were only a foot high and could easily be trampled by folks wanting to take pictures in the field. The spring cash crop would yield the sweet white corn that Kevin's family famously sold every summer at their roadside stand. After the harvest, they would sow grain corn that would grow into the tall, thick stalks of their fall festival maze.

The five-day forecast predicted daytime temperatures in the seventies, with light sweater weather in the evenings. Clear skies boded well for strong carnival attendance and high commissions for the most salesy jointees. Her hope of enjoying the amusements was all but dashed and forgotten. If Bobby's killer was one of the crew, identifying suspects would become even more challenging after Sunday. Once the carnival jumped to the next site, the chance of bringing down the supplier and the buyer of the parrot eggs would plummet as well. Until then Preston would be working around the clock, and her focus was on doing whatever she could to gather information for Sam.

The high, bright sun warmed her skin, and an intermittent breeze wafted in with the tang of fresh fertilizer and the sweet smell of hay. Opting for simplicity this morning, she wore jeans, a navy T-shirt, and Aunt Bea's friendship bracelet. She hoped that a casual appearance might help put those she planned to speak with at ease. Slammer, Angel, and Aunt Bea had all made her wish list, preferably out of sight of Nicky.

The Ferris wheel was slowly spinning, and the carousel's lively organ music projected halfway to the lot. A small farm utility vehicle zipped by her with a load of two hay bales in its open bed. The driver stopped in front of the ticket booth, got out, and unloaded his cargo, fashioning a bench next to the stand.

She passed through the entrance, unquestioned and unbothered by a pair of crew members setting up an ATM near the tarot tent. Workers were busy around the midway, tending to their final preparations. Small teams were cleaning the rides and conducting safety checks before the grand opening at five. The game stands were stocked with unicorn, alien, and dragon inflatables, as well as panda, puppy, and porpoise stuffed animals. A few of the jointees were sitting on stools behind their counters, as if waiting for the games to begin. Cowboy was absent from his dart-toss stand. She made a note to swing back through on her way out, to see if he had any more inside information to share about his fellow showmen.

With seemingly all hands on deck, she decided to tour the campgrounds, and with a little luck, come across a loner willing to talk. Once past the Ferris wheel, she set her sights on the three bunkhouses. The units looked like the trailers from eighteen-wheelers with doors evenly spaced along their lengths. Nicky and Bobby's luxury RVs sat beyond the crew quarters, forming a rear boundary for the encampment. Motorhomes, cars, and campers were parked in a makeshift lot on the far-left side of the bunkhouses.

In just a day, the camp had taken on a more lived-in appearance. Small coolers, mini grills, and lawn chairs dotted the lanes formed between the bunkhouses. Three steps led up to each room, and based on the spacing of the doors, she estimated that the interior length of each unit couldn't be much over eight feet.

At the far end of the middle trailer, she recognized the woman Aunt Bea had glanced at yesterday while talking about how Bobby carried on with his employees. Another crew member sat on the top step of a unit closer to Olivia. He was wearing headphones and holding a can wrapped in an orange insulated sleeve. Perhaps she'd come back to him, but for now, she passed by, exchanging a head nod as a greeting. He took a drag from his cigarette, then flicked off some ashes that had fallen on his yellow T-shirt, stretched tight over his beer belly.

As she neared the end of the trailer, the woman briefly went inside her bunkroom, then reappeared cradling a cardboard box. She carefully descended the steps and placed the box on a small folding table in front of her unit. A vinyl shoe rack hung on the inside of her door, its pockets packed full of convenience foods, toiletries, and clothing accessories.

Olivia stopped a few feet shy of her, offering a friendly smile. "Hi. It looks like you're redecorating."

The woman glanced with a grin at her unit. "As much as you can change things up in a room the size of a thimble."

Olivia recognized her voice from yesterday as the one that had warned Nicky about Slammer and Stash nearly coming to blows. Today, up close, she looked different. Her brown hair hung down over her shoulders, and an oversized blue T-shirt engulfed her petite frame.

"I'm Olivia Penn from *The Apple Station Times*. I'm here this week gathering first-hand accounts of what it's like to work for a carnival."

"I've heard about you."

"If you have a few minutes, can I ask you some questions?"

The woman looked all around. "Sure, I suppose. If you don't mind, I need to sit." She lowered herself onto the middle step, resting her elbows on her thighs. "I would say have a seat, but …"

"I'm good." Olivia waved off the offer as the only other seat would be on the ground. "I've learned most everyone who works for the carnival goes by a nickname."

The woman didn't miss a beat in answering the non-question. "Yes. When you're a newcomer, it's easier to remember names that way. Most people here don't care who you *really* are. I go by Angel, but my real name is Tiffany. You can call me Tiffany. That's what I prefer."

"You don't like Angel?"

A blush of pink bloomed on her cheeks, contrasting with the purple circles under her eyes. "Aunt Bea came up with it. I saw you talking to her yesterday. It's because I like to sing. One day last season, Aunt Bea said in front of a bunch of the crew that I sing sweet as an angel. I'm not *that* good. But that's how it goes around here. I became Angel whether I liked it or not."

Olivia nodded, knowing the feeling. "I can understand that. When I was a kid, sometimes I got called Livvy, and I hated it. Aunt Bea seems very nice." Seeing that Tiffany was wearing several of Aunt Bea's bracelets, she held up her hand to show her own. "She gave me one of her creations yesterday."

Tiffany spun her bracelets on her wrist, then pointed at Olivia's. "I need a replacement. I used to have a full rainbow, but my blue one got snagged on a hook in my bunk."

Olivia's mind jumped lightning quick to an alternate TV crime-drama theory. *A late-night rendezvous with Bobby at Spring Hills?* "Do you still have it?"

"The bracelet? No. I threw it out."

"Aunt Bea seemed to have blue on her mind yesterday, so I'm sure she'll have one for you. How long have you worked for the Kleins?"

Tiffany cracked a couple of knuckles. "Are you going to quote me in your article? I really don't want my name in the paper."

"No names. I promise."

"Thanks. I joined midway through last season."

Olivia inched closer to the table and peeked into the box, then looked at Tiffany's room. "I've never seen the inside of a bunkroom. It looks quaint?"

"That's the nicest anyone has ever put it. Would you like a tour?"

"Sure."

Tiffany stood up and came down the steps. "Go right in. It'll be tight if we're in there at the same time. If I'd known company was coming, I would've spruced it up."

Olivia went up the steps and stood in the doorway of the room, which seemed no bigger than a small walk-in closet. The raised bed was within arm's reach, and a two-rung ladder provided a leg up to the thin mattress. A single flat pillow and a faded brown bedspread weren't exactly creature comforts. About three feet to her left, the wall housed a mini refrigerator, stacked organizers, and a narrow, tall shelving unit packed with personal items. A small microwave sat on the refrigerator, and a built-in shelf over it held a hotplate, paper products, and condiments. Under the bed, there was a pair of clear storage drawers filled with clothes and towels. On the top of one, she spotted a set of matching onesies and a stuffed baby giraffe. To her right, jackets and blouses hung from a mounted multi-prong hook, partially obscuring a full-length mirror. Every inch of space was wisely organized without a sense of clutter.

"I'm going to grab some water," Tiffany said, coming up the steps.

There was no place for Olivia to go but inside the unit to make way. She shuffled to the right as Tiffany came in, opened the refrigerator, and grabbed a drink.

"Would you like something?" Tiffany asked.

Even if she were as dry as the Sahara, she wouldn't take any of what little Tiffany had. "No, thanks. I'm okay."

Tiffany stepped back out and went down the steps. After another look around, Olivia followed behind with a new appreciation of her own home's abundance.

"What do you think?" Tiffany said. "I know it doesn't look like much, but it's home for now."

"I'm amazed at what you've done with the space." She glanced toward the other end of the lane, recognizing Father Silva striding toward the camp in his all-black garb. The worker who had been sitting on the top step of his unit a few doors down either had left or was inside his bunkroom. She gestured at the box on the table. "So just reorganizing?"

The energy fueling Tiffany's friendliness faded. "I'm getting rid of some stuff to lighten my load for when I have to leave."

"Oh. Why are you leaving?"

She pulled her extra-large T-shirt tight across her stomach, revealing a baby bump.

I see why the onesies. "Congratulations. When are you due?"

"In October. I want to stay on as long as I can to save up money, but ..." She clenched her lips, stifling a sigh.

"But?"

"I don't know if the Kleins will keep me on until I had planned on leaving. I'm moving in with an aunt who lives in Pennsylvania before the baby is born. It'll just be temporary until I can find another job and get back on my feet."

"Why do you think the Kleins won't keep you on until then?"

"When we arrived here on Sunday, Bobby told me this would be my last show."

"Why? Because of the baby?" Olivia's mind leapt to a cringe-worthy possibility. *Oh, jeez. Is he the father?* "They can't fire you because you're pregnant. That's illegal."

"The law doesn't apply much around here. When I told him I was pregnant, he said I was a liability. He didn't want me working for the carnival in case I got hurt and something happened to the baby. He made it clear he wouldn't be paying any medical expenses that I might *incur,* as he put it."

With the start of the carnival season in February and Tiffany's due date in October, it was within the realm of possibility that Bobby could be the father. He didn't seem like Tiffany's type, but she very much seemed like his—a young, pretty girl, perhaps down on her luck, looking for a leg up in the world. Olivia had a hard time imagining that Tiffany could unleash enough fury to kill him, even if scorned. Though dying to ask about the father, no matter how carefully she worded the question in her head, Olivia knew it was overstepping her bounds. If it were pertinent to the murder investigation, the police could dive deeper into the issue.

"Have you told Nicky?" Olivia asked. "Aunt Bea said that when anyone has issues, they talk to her because she's fair."

Tiffany's shoulders dropped a notch lower. "I had planned on talking to her, but then with what happened, it seemed like bad timing. Aunt Bea thinks I shouldn't worry. She said Nicky would understand. I mean, I run a game stand. It's not as if I'm setting up rides or sloughing. That's the dangerous work and—" She clammed up, looking toward the opposite end of the bunkhouse.

Olivia followed her focus to where Lone Wolf was walking down the lane between the trailers. He casually passed by without a word and veered across the way, rounding the corner of the next trailer over.

Fishing for information, Olivia threw out a line. "I understand he goes by Lone Wolf. Does he stay in that unit?"

"Mm-hmm." Tiffany spun and jogged up the steps. "I have to go. I'm helping Aunt Bea with some things."

That quickly nixed Olivia's follow-up question of whether he also went by the name Ryan Heller. Perhaps she'd pressed too much, or Lone Wolf's presence had spooked Tiffany into skedaddling.

"Sure, I won't keep you any longer."

Tiffany closed her door, locked it, and came down the steps.

"What about your box of stuff?"

Tiffany waved at it. "It's just junk. If anyone wants it, they can have it."

"Thanks for speaking with me."

"No problem." With that, she turned and took off, hustling toward the midway.

The odds-and-ends collection was ripe for scavenging. Plastic cups, three mugs, a hand fan, and an angel figurine. A deck of cards, a padlock, scissors, and two screwdrivers. A Boston Red Sox ball cap and a Hallmark paperback would probably be swiped soon, while a baggie of dried flower petals likely would remain at the end of the day.

Olivia glanced at the next trailer over. This may be the best chance she'd have to speak with Lone Wolf. Even if she couldn't learn anything useful from him, she could check if he had the skull tattoo of the man A.J. identified as Ryan Heller. She crossed the lane and was about to corner the bunkhouse, but she stopped short, hearing two raised voices. She crept to the edge and stole a peek around the corner. Lone Wolf and Father Silva were standing face-to-face in front of the bunkroom three doors down.

"Leave me alone," Lone Wolf whined, sounding like an exasperated teen.

"You can't back out," Father Silva said. "They know you're here."

"I'm leaving when we jump to Maryland. Nobody will find me unless you tell them."

"We had an agreement. We've already scheduled the meeting."

"I've changed my mind. The deal is off."

"They'll keep looking for you."

Silence and the sound of a door closing signaled the conversation was over. She peeked around the corner again and saw Father Silva striding back toward the midway. Her thoughts ping-ponged between the two men: *Silva, Wolf, Silva, Wolf.* It would be hard enough to get Lone Wolf to talk, but with him already heated, striking up a friendly chat would be a tall order. Now that she knew where he stayed, she could return later to find him if necessary.

She went back around the trailer to the lane in front of Tiffany's place, seeing Cowboy rummaging through the junk box. He glanced at her as she passed by, offering him a polite smile as a greeting. Even though she wanted to speak with him again, he wasn't the priority at the moment. Catching up to Father Silva, and learning more about Lone Wolf and Tiffany, was her immediate aim.

Cowboy tipped his hat in return, then called out, "Olivia Penn of *The Apple Station Times.* Can I ask you a question?"

She stopped and turned to face him with her spidey sense tingling. He seemed to be the cleanest cut of the crew, yet there was something off about him. While forthcoming yesterday, the way he'd spoken to her made her feel that he was harboring a secret or two. "That depends on what you want to know."

"I saw you talking to Angel."

Were you following me? "Yes." A polite response was all she'd offer until he played more of his cards.

He picked the angel figurine out of the box. "What are you really doing here?"

A curious question that she could mirror back at him. "What do you mean?"

"It's just that you're writing a story about carnival life, and most everyone is up there." He pointed for emphasis, as if presenting an exhibit at a trial. "Were you looking for Angel specifically?"

"How is that your concern?" She gestured at the box. "There's some good stuff in there. First come, first serve. I should be going."

He set the figurine on the table. "Nah, I don't need anything. You know, there's a reason Angel's bunk is always close to Bobby's place."

Who is this guy? His words rang true from a scan of the lot. Tiffany's room was only about fifteen yards from Bobby's RV. Olivia decided to play along as he seemed to be champing at the bit to share something. "What would that reason be?"

He contorted his face as if wrestling with feigned deep-seated reluctance to speak further on the matter. "I don't want to be spreading any rumors, and what people do on their own time is none of my business. But on Sunday night, as Bobby was growing cold at Spring Hills, Angel went into his RV at eleven o'clock." He glanced over her shoulder. "That just seems like something you'd be interested in knowing, Olivia Penn from *The Apple Station Times*." He strode past her and jogged up the steps of the neighboring unit.

She looked down the lane to see two workers coming in their direction. "Why are you telling me this?"

"Have a good one." He tipped his hat as the men neared, then went into his bunkroom and closed the door.

CHAPTER 24

Walking back to the midway, Olivia spun Cowboy's story in her head. *Why tell me about Tiffany? How do you know when Bobby died? If true, why would she have gone into Bobby's RV? She must have a key. Was she expecting to find him there? Or did she know he wouldn't be there? What's your angle, Cowboy, and for Pete's sake, why can't anybody use a real name?*

She strode by the Ferris wheel with dwindling hopes of catching up to Father Silva. Though he was easy to spot in all-black, he had a considerable lead on her and a full head of steam. Considering him as a piece in the puzzle may be reaching, but the charged conversation she'd overheard was curious. If Lone Wolf was connected to Tiffany, and she and Bobby had something going, then how did Father Silva fit into that picture? Was he linked to the Kleins in some other way than just as a local priest who blessed the workers whenever the carnival came around?

The swing ride was slowly spinning, with two of the crew sitting in chain-suspended chairs high in the air shouting at the controller to make it go faster. She'd once seen a viral video of a woman dangling from a similar attraction in Florida. Since then, she'd decided to stick to the swings on playgrounds and porches whenever she felt the urge to catch some air.

She veered toward the game side of the midway, recognizing the profile of a familiar, fine figure conversing with Slammer at the base of the fun slide. Further contact with Preston within sight of the crew could jeopardize the other workers' willingness to speak with her, so she gave him a wide berth. Cowboy was already dubious of her intentions, and she had to assume there may be others who had similar suspicions.

She passed the carousel, the duck pond, and the junior ring-toss game. There were no signs of Father Silva or Angel, but she spotted Aunt Bea in the pizza trailer, cleaning the counter with disinfectant spray.

"I'm glad we didn't scare you off yesterday," Aunt Bea called out to her.

"Good to see you again. No. Everyone has been friendly." *Sort of.* "Did Angel make it up here?"

"The last time I saw her was about an hour ago in her bunk. She wasn't feeling well, so I told her to take it easy before opening. She wanted to help here, but I've got everything covered."

Olivia stepped up to the window, spying a chance for as private of a one-on-one as she'd get on the midway. "I spoke with her, and I learned she may be leaving soon. Did you know Bobby was letting her go after this show?"

Aunt Bea spritzed the counter with the cleaner and wiped it down again. Then she balled the towel in one hand, closing her fist around it.

"This isn't for the article," Olivia added. "It's all off the record. I'm just concerned. She told me she's pregnant. Legally, Bobby couldn't have fired her because of it."

Aunt Bea's face tightened, deepening every hard-won line of wisdom and experience from her sixty-plus years. "Oh, he wouldn't have *fired* her. He would've made up some excuse to comply with labor laws, as if they even apply around here."

"Surely, you don't think Nicky would have the same stance."

Aunt Bea set her towel down, then palmed her hands on the counter. "If she does, I'll tell her exactly what I thought of that brother of hers. If she lets Angel go, I'll leave too. I can work for anyone. They need me more than I need them."

That's an interesting way of putting it. Olivia kept her voice low, betting on Aunt Bea's fancy for gossip. "Is it possible that Bobby is the father?"

Aunt Bea's eyes darted around for anyone within earshot, then she rested her forearms on the counter and leaned in toward Olivia. "I haven't asked. Lord help her if he is. It wouldn't be the first time it happened. You see some pretty young girl at the start of the season, then the next thing you know, they're no longer here. I hear rumors. Some are true. Others, I just don't know. Angel is smart. She went to one of those special music schools for her singing."

"How did she end up working for the carnival?"

"Her mom had cancer and died. Angel shared a house with her, but she had to sell it to pay off all the medical bills. She answered a help-wanted ad when we were in Richmond last year. As soon as she joined us, I noticed all the men looking at her, so I took her under my wing. If anyone tried to mess around with her, they'd have to answer to me." She folded her hands and raised her brow, looking like a take-no-prisoners grandmother.

What if Bobby was the one messing around with her?

"None of us have legal recourse," Aunt Bea said. "I know Bobby's parents. They're good people, and I'm not saying he'd ever broken any laws … that anyone can prove. I've worked for carnivals where all kinds of shady practices were happening. Half those here don't want to be found, so what are we supposed to do? Go to the police?" She shook off her own question. "Things get handled in-house."

Another worker entered the trailer, joining Aunt Bea behind the counter. Aunt Bea straightened and placed her towel off to the side, ending the discussion. "Hey there, Rainbow. Can you fill up the shakers?"

"Sure thing, Aunt Bea."

The young woman, with hair befitting her nickname, pulled out large bags of parmesan cheese and red pepper flakes from a low cabinet and set them on the counter next to a tray of small glass shakers.

"Thanks for the talk," Olivia said.

"Are you coming back when we open? Everything looks different at night."

"I think so." She scanned the midway as the carousel came to life with its colorful horses circling around, rising up, and dipping down. "Did you see Father Silva come by this way recently?"

She nodded matter-of-factly. "I did. He's a hard one to miss."

"Did you notice which way he went?"

She gestured vaguely toward the pizza oven. "I think he was leaving."

"He sort of comes and goes?"

"That's right. He's a friend of the Kleins, or maybe just more of a *special friend* of Nicky's."

Her wink and cheeky smile left Olivia befuddled, as the insinuation was clear. "Huh?"

"His kind marries."

"What do you mean, *his kind*?"

"He's one of those independent Catholics. Some denomination associated with Brazil. That's where he's from."

Could Nicky and Father Silva be a thing? "So, he's not Roman Catholic. I've heard clergy in some independent Catholic churches are allowed to get married."

"I guess. I'm spiritual, but not religious. You know, in the end, we're all the same anyway."

"Are you saying they're involved romantically?"

"*I* wouldn't want to start any rumors."

"Of course not."

Aunt Bea leaned down on the counter. "But I can tell when a man has eyes for a woman."

Olivia laughed, figuring Aunt Bea was probably a better judge of character than most people she knew. "I bet you can. Where is he based?"

She pursed her lips and shook her head. "It's around here, but I can't think of the name." She turned her shoulders, calling out toward the other end of the trailer. "Hey, Rainbow. Do you know the name of Father's church?"

She stopped mid-pour of parmesan. "I'm a Baptist."

Aunt Bea eyed Rainbow for a moment, then turned back to Olivia, speaking in a hushed voice. "I don't see how that answers the question." She sighed, looked around the midway, and yelled, "Eddie, come here."

He hurried over and exchanged hellos with Olivia. "What can I do for you, Tía Bea?"

"What's the name of Father's church?"

"Saint Anthony's."

The name didn't ring a bell. "Do you know where that is?" Olivia asked him.

"Sí. In Gore."

It must be close to the monastery. "Thank you."

"Is that all you need?" Aunt Bea asked.

"For now," Olivia replied.

"Thanks, Eddie," Aunt Bea said. "How are the kids?"

"Bueno. Mateo has one more year of school, and Camelia graduates at the end of this month. She already has a job lined up in a San Antonio hospital."

"Congratulations. You send them my love."

"Gracias." He smiled at Olivia. "Nice to meet you."

"You too," Olivia said as he turned and went back across the midway toward the game stands.

Aunt Bea straightened. "Steady Eddie is the backbone of the crew. He's the most reliable and the hardest worker here."

"I can't get these lids off, Aunt Bea," Rainbow moaned.

"You'll have to excuse me. If nothing else, my sixty-five years have given me a unique skill set that baffles the younger generations."

Olivia grinned, thinking everyone should have an Aunt Bea in their lives. "Thanks again."

Aunt Bea pointed at her. "I want to see you tonight."

"I'll be here." She offered a wave in parting, and no sooner had she passed the neighboring funnel-cake stand than her cell buzzed. After digging the phone out of her pocket, she flipped it over and saw a text from Preston. Looking around, she spotted him near the Ferris wheel, then read his message, "What are you doing?"

She replied, "Did you find out Slammer's real name?"

He kept his head bowed, looking at his phone.

After a brief pause, she read his reply, "Refer to the above question."

Harrumph. She turned her back to him, letting her fingers fly. "There's a box on a table at the far end of the middle bunkhouse. Belongs to Tiffany, aka Angel. Don't know her last name. Involved with Bobby. Pregnant, possibly his. Scissors and screwdriver in the box. Murder weapon?" She pressed send, then headed past the corn dog stand with her feet pointed toward the exit.

Quick as a whip, she received and read his reply, "Where are you going?"

She sent an emoji of a smiley face blowing a kiss, then peeked over her shoulder and saw him glance up at her, shaking his head as she walked away.

CHAPTER 25

Seated across the room from Mrs. Montgomery in the front office of St. Anthony's rectory, Olivia watched the receptionist slide yet another letter off a stack on her desk. She folded the bottom third, ironed a precise crease along its length with her thumb, and repeated the procedure with the top portion. Then she placed the letter in a business-sized envelope, peeled away the strip covering the adhesive, and sealed the contents. Over the past fifteen minutes, Olivia had observed the process dozens of times while waiting for her two o'clock meeting with Father Silva.

On a hunch that he was returning to St. Anthony's, she'd called the rectory from the farm to inquire about openings on his afternoon schedule. After Olivia spun her story about her credentials, an accommodating Mrs. Montgomery had penciled her into his only available appointment. Guided by her vehicle's GPS, Olivia drove twenty-five minutes north-west, finding her winding way to the church in Gore. Ideally, she'd love to ask Father Silva about his heated words with Lone Wolf and if he knew who was the father of Tiffany's baby. But as both fell far outside the bounds of her cover story, she aimed instead to learn more about the relationship between Bobby and Nicky. If Father Silva was as close to the Kleins as Aunt Bea had implied, perhaps he could shed light on any rifts within the family.

The tidy, cozy office was about the size of her kitchen and warmly lit by natural light and several table lamps. A broad picture window overlooked a meditation garden boasting blooming flowers, a flowing fountain, and a birdbath. The decor was a soothing mix of beige and gray: the former on the low-pile carpeting, and the latter on the plush chenille sofa and two matching velvet armchairs. A pink porcelain cross statue etched with "The Serenity Prayer" and a white vase brimming with a bouquet of yellow daisies added flair to Mrs. Montgomery's otherwise spartan desk.

At fifteen minutes past the hour, Olivia leaned forward and swiped a pamphlet from a local food bank off the glass-top table in front of her. It was that or perusing a booklet on prenuptial counseling. She was more likely to donate a bag of canned foods than to walk down the aisle anytime soon. Unfolding the brochure, she glanced at Mrs. Montgomery, hearing the crisp press of another folded letter.

"I'm sure Father will be with you shortly," she said.

On cue, the knotty honey-pine door across the room from the sofa opened. Father Silva glided into the front office, greeting Olivia with a warm smile and an extended hand.

She dropped the pamphlet onto the table, stood up, and shook his hand.

"Sorry to keep you waiting, Ms. Penn."

"Please call me Olivia."

"A beautiful name. Olivia, meaning olive tree. A symbol of peace."

His baritone and pleasant timbre were that of a late-night DJ sending out dedications on a radio station's lonely-heart line. With sparkling hazel eyes, an angular jaw, and wavy brown hair, even in his all-black and collar, he had a cover-model vibe about him. Cedar, sandal-wood, and something else spicy were the top notes of the sensual cologne he was wearing. Indeed, if he were one who'd marry, he could inspire many young women to attend church regularly.

"Very good, Father. Is that an educated guess, or do you have inside information?"

He flashed a million-dollar smile, showing off his perfectly aligned, bright-white teeth. "Guilty," he said, adding a charming chuckle. "My little sister's name is Olivia, though we call her Olive."

"Ah. I get that sometimes."

He gestured toward the door with an open palm. "We can talk in my office."

She stepped toward the doorway, following his direction.

"Mrs. Montgomery, our visitor is working on the coop. You may hear him rummaging around in the back."

"Okay, Father. I'll take him some iced tea soon. There's a fresh pitcher cooling in the refrigerator."

"Thank you. That would be kind of you."

Olivia lingered by the door, which led to a carpeted hallway with two rooms on either side. Three of the four doors were closed, but she waited for him to confirm that the open room was his. Framed photos adorned the walls, and warm-toned recessed lighting lent serenity to the short corridor. The rear exit was a stone's throw away, with a coat rack, a trash can, and an umbrella stand conveniently located for those coming or going.

"The first room on the left," he said.

She went ahead into the open office, and he followed and shut the door behind him.

"Please have a seat."

She sat in a firm burgundy armchair, facing a neatly organized cherrywood desk. Classical music played from a Bluetooth speaker positioned next to a serving tray holding a stainless-steel carafe and two glasses. Three windows with opened curtains and a banker's lamp with a green shade provided the perfect ambience for counseling. He took a seat in a high-back mesh chair opposite of her, turned off the music, and rested his hands on a black leather desk pad.

"Thank you for waiting for me," he said. "What can I help you with today?"

She pointed behind him at a framed yellow soccer jersey hanging on the wall. With the green-and-blue trim and a crest logo on the chest, the shirt was easily identifiable. "Did you play soccer for Brazil?"

"Are you a fan of the sport?"

"I'm not an avid follower, but the jersey is iconic."

He swiveled in his seat, looking up at the frame. "My cousin did. I was born in Brazil, in the city of Cuiabá. That's in the state of Mato Grosso, which is in the Central-West Region. My mother is Brazilian, my father is from New York. We moved to America when I was very young, but my brother and sister live in Brazil now, as do many of my relatives." He turned back toward her. "My youngest cousin, Diego, is one of them. That's one of his old jerseys. He's no longer on the national team, but that he was at one time remains a tremendous source of family pride."

Her eyes darted to a tall bookcase just over his left shoulder. Aligned across the top shelf were two standing framed photos, several figurines, and a stuffed-toy hyacinth macaw. "I'm sure it is. Thank you for not chastising me. I know it's more appropriately called football."

"I'm not a stickler about it. When I travel back to Brazil, I'm the one who'd get chastised if I, heaven forbid, call it soccer. I try not to let my choice of words impede our understanding of each other."

"Well said." She paused, eyeing the parrot again. *What are the odds?* She deliberated for a hot second whether it would be off-the-wall to question if he were involved in Bobby's business. "Am I right that St. Anthony's is an independent church associated with Brazil?"

"We are part of the Catholic Apostolic Church in North America. CACINA for short. Our roots are in the Brazilian Catholic Apostolic Church. We are an inclusive church where all are welcomed to receive the sacraments." He pinned his elbows on the chair armrests and folded his hands. "I'm sure you're not here to learn about our history or beliefs."

"No. But it's interesting nonetheless." A tiny wave of guilt rolled over her as she launched into her shtick. "I'm researching the ins and outs of carnival life for *The Apple Station Times*. I've seen you on the grounds, and Aunt Bea told me some about your role and relationship with the Kleins. I was hoping you'd be willing to talk about that. I've been going to carnivals since I was a child, but I never knew priests like yourself provide pastoral care for the workers."

He seemed to consider her pitch before answering. "I've noticed you too. Admittedly, I had help. Nicky told me a reporter would be around this week."

She wondered whether he'd received a warning not to talk to her about Bobby, and what threat Nicky might hold over him. "Do you visit all the carnivals that come through the area?"

"No. The Kleins are friends of mine. I've known

them for several years. I always make it a point to spend time with them whenever they're nearby."

"My condolences for your loss. Are you involved with Bobby's funeral arrangements?"

"No. His parents are handling everything with their local church in New Jersey."

"It's got to be hard on Nicky. Somehow, 'the show must go on' just doesn't seem right under the circumstances."

He leaned forward and picked up the carafe. "Would you like some water?" When she declined, he poured himself a glass. "Nicky's dedication to the family business is admirable. She has a lot of people depending on her for paychecks. Everyone deals with grief differently."

"What about the workers? How are they handling his death?"

He took a sip, then placed his tumbler on a round cork coaster.

"I've heard he wasn't the most beloved boss," she added. "Everyone speaks highly of Nicky, but opinions about him are mixed."

"You're not taking any notes," he said with an inquisitive smile. "My impression of journalists is that you madly scribble as you interview your unsuspecting targets to get them to reveal more than they should. Or maybe I've watched one too many crime dramas."

She grinned, deflecting his spot-on pinpointing of her intentions. "I have an excellent memory, and I hope that's not your impression of me."

He raised a hand in apology. "Not at all. What you say about Bobby is true. He had a strong personality that could come across as off-putting to some. I think in almost every workplace, you'll find tensions between employees and their bosses."

But they rarely lead to murder. His couched answers felt protective of the Kleins, or maybe just Nicky. She'd steer back to the family dynamics later, but diverted for a moment to maintain a reasonable facade for her cover story. "Can you tell me more about your role with the carnival?"

"It's the same outreach ministry we provide to anyone, regardless of their faith, who is in need or want of spiritual guidance. I visit with the crew, offering prayers and counseling. I'll celebrate mass at least once and hold hours for confession when schedules align."

"Yesterday, I saw you blessing the workers and the rides."

"Yes. We gather to pray for everyone's safety. Despite coming from such diverse backgrounds, many feel closer to their carnival family than their blood relatives. I've become friends with many in the crew over the years, and I consider them all a part of Saint Anthony's extended community." He took another sip of water and pointed toward her with the glass. "Is that one of Aunt Bea's bracelets?"

As she raised her arm, the bracelet slid down past her wrist. "It is. I see you don't have any."

He turned his head slightly, glancing at the bookcase.

"I have many, a whole mason jar of them. She gives them to me for the kids here at the parish and restocks my supply every year."

She spotted the collection on the shelf just under the stuffed bird. "Is that a hyacinth macaw?"

"It is. Impressive that you know your parrots." A light knock on the door cut him off, prompting him to call out. "Come in."

She swiveled in her seat as Mrs. Montgomery slipped halfway into the room.

"I'm sorry to interrupt, Father, but Meghan Mallory is here. She wants to speak with you about tomorrow's committee meeting for Saturday's potluck."

He sighed under his breath. "Please tell her I'll call her later."

Mrs. Montgomery tiptoed closer, whispering her plea. "Can you take a minute now? She'll just wait for you and talk on and on. I won't get any work done with her here."

Under other circumstances, Olivia would've politely dismissed herself. But this likely was the only chance she'd have to speak with Father Silva privately. With the carnival pulling up stakes on Sunday, time was of the essence. "I don't mind," she said. "I'll wait."

He planted his hands on the desk, then cranked himself up from the chair. "Okay. I'll be right out."

"Thank you, Father," Mrs. Montgomery said before turning and bustling out of the room.

"I'm sorry," he said to Olivia, rounding the desk. "I'll just be a few minutes."

"Take your time. I'm in no hurry."

As soon as he left, she sprung up and padded over to the bookcase for a closer view of the items along the top shelf. The pair of photos, in matching brass frames, both featured Father Silva. In the first, he was in a restaurant seated between two older people she guessed were his parents. The other was a more recent shot of him and Nicky sitting outside a pizza joint on a boardwalk by the beach. The five angel figurines were part of a collection, each with the same cherubic face but in a different action pose. The middle one, with folded hands and eyes lifted toward heaven, was identical to the figurine in Tiffany's give-away box.

"Yo, Padre," a man shouted from just outside the door.

Startled, she spun as Stash strode into the office. They both froze—she out of shock at seeing him there, and he as if puzzled, perhaps thinking he'd walked into the wrong room. Though they hadn't been that close to each other over the past two days, his handlebar moustache identified him from a mile away. If she'd sparked recognition in him, his blank face didn't show it.

"Where's Father Silva?" he asked.

"In the front office."

He backpedaled into the hallway and took off in that direction without a word or a second glance at her.

This is now officially weird. Why would he be here? She'd come wanting to learn more about the Kleins, but curiously, Nicky, Bobby, Stash, Tiffany, and Lone Wolf all had a connection to Father Silva. If Slammer and Grasso were working for the same side, could she be looking at the players on the other team?

She turned back to the bookcase, noting the volumes lining the lower shelves. Spiritual texts, science fiction novels, and guides for raising chickens made for an eclectic library.

"Do you see any books you'd like to borrow?" Father Silva said, returning to the room.

She kept her back to him for a second before turning. "I was admiring the parrot. Cute. They're native to the Pantanal and Brazil, aren't they?"

He joined her by the bookcase and straightened the crooked bird. "They are. Have you ever been?"

"To Brazil or the Pantanal?"

"Either."

"Neither."

He dialed up an amused grin. "I highly recommend both if you have the chance to visit. My niece gave me the parrot on my last trip home."

She glanced back at the shelf, allowing her eyes to wander for a moment to the photo of him and Nicky. "They're beautiful parrots. I understand their numbers are in decline. Deforestation and egg poaching being primary causes."

His expression turned neutral as he rested one hand on the other in front of him. "Unfortunately, this is true. There are many species at risk—birds, fish, and jaguars, among others."

She tilted her head, as if reading the book spines for the first time, then partially slid out a hardcover titled *The ABCs of Backyard Chicken Coops*. "Do you raise chickens here?"

"It's been a hobby of mine since I came to St. Anthony's. There was an old coop behind the rectory that had fallen into disrepair. We restored it and restocked, and now we have plenty of fresh eggs."

"Do you incubate eggs?"

"We do. Is that a pastime we share?"

Shaking her head, she pushed the book back into place. "No. I help take care of a mischievous beagle and a friend's cat. That's enough for me."

He nodded, gesturing toward the desk. "I'm sorry, but I only have a few more minutes for our meeting. If you would like to sit …"

She took the unfinished thought as an invitation and returned to her seat. "Did Stash catch up with you? He came in when you were up front. I was surprised to see him here. I would've thought with the carnival opening in a few hours, it would be all hands on deck there."

"He's on loan," Father Silva said, sitting down on the edge of his seat. "We're paying him to do some electrical work on the coop. Nicky generously gave him the time off. He came with me, and I'll drive him back when he's finished."

Reasonable. "I see. I like the quirky, but apt nickname, Stash. There's another crew member, who I haven't been able to speak with yet, and I'm interested in hearing the origin of his nickname. Lone Wolf."

Father Silva pinched his lips, dropping his gaze to the desk for a moment. "I don't know everyone, and I can't keep all the names straight."

Like heck you can't. "How about Angel, or more properly, Tiffany?"

"Ah, yes. I'm acquainted."

"She has the same figurine as you do on your bookcase. What are the odds? I talked to her earlier today. Did you know Bobby was planning to let her go after this show?"

He opened his mouth to say something, but then stopped himself. He slid back in his seat, rounding his perfect posture into the support of the chair. "I wasn't aware of that."

"Do you know she's pregnant?"

He nodded slowly. "Yes. Mrs. Montgomery collected some items for her—clothes and a few toys from a donation box we keep here for families in need. I delivered them to her yesterday."

That explained the onesies and the stuffed giraffe, but it still left unanswered how he knew she was pregnant, since Tiffany hadn't even told Nicky yet. For someone just acquainted with her, by his reaction, the news seemed like a personal blow.

"I heard that Tiffany may have been involved with Bobby," she said.

He dipped his chin for a moment, then inhaled a full

breath while making a show of checking his watch. "I'm sorry. I must be going." He rose at once. "I hope I've been helpful."

In revealing that you're hiding something. "Yes," she replied, slowly pushing up from the chair. "Thank you for your time. Maybe I'll see you around the carnival. Do you have hours set up for confessions?"

He seemed lost in his thoughts, needing a moment before answering. "I haven't scheduled any yet. Probably at the end of the week."

"Is it true you can't inform the police about a crime someone confesses?"

"Yes. That would breach the seal of confession."

"Even if the crime is murder?"

Lines creased his brow as his eyes shifted off her.

"I'm sorry," she said. "That's beyond the scope of my story. I was just curious."

Stepping around the desk, he dialed up his charm and extended his hand for a cordial parting. "No, it's okay," he said as they shook hands. "Your role as a reporter is to ask questions, and your editor demands you get answers. My role as a priest is to absolve sins, but my boss already knows the answers and has the final say."

CHAPTER 26

Olivia settled into the driver's seat, looking past the meditation garden and at the chicken coop just beyond the rectory. She'd paid little attention to it coming in, dismissing the cottage-like building as a rather large froufrou shed, considering the compact footprint of the church's property. To her, backyard coops conjured images of penned-in areas with raised henhouses. From her vantage, the coop looked spacious and country-chic, with white siding, a gray-shingled roof, and a barn-red door. Though tempted to look around, she thought the better of it, not wanting Stash or Father Silva to catch her where she had no reason to be.

Although the likelihood that Father Silva was involved in any criminal activity seemed low, she couldn't rule it out solely based on his vocation. With only a handful of random clues, some rooted in facts and others fueled by rumors, nothing was beyond consideration. Stash's presence and a convenient hiding place for incubating eggs behind the rectory made Father Silva a person of interest.

She turned over the engine and lowered the window halfway, allowing fresh air to infuse the stuffy cabin. At a little before three, she had time to kill before the carnival opened at five, though she didn't have a solid strategy for her return visit. With the jointees busy hawking their games and the ride jocks keeping thrill seekers safe, finding anyone willing to talk might be difficult.

She planned to call Sam later tonight to share everything she'd learned. If Carolyn thought she was no longer of use, that would be the end of her undercover role. Her curiosity was beyond piqued, and she wanted to stay involved. Facts weren't adding up to answers—only to more questions that painted a complex, intriguing picture.

Father Silva had seemed surprised by Tiffany's potential departure. With the carnival having just arrived on Sunday, how did he find out about her pregnancy so soon? Could the heated conversation she'd overheard between him and Lone Wolf be related to Tiffany? He'd evaded admitting even knowing Lone Wolf, yet they'd arranged a meeting with someone who wouldn't take kindly to a cancellation. Could Lone Wolf's plan to leave by the end of the weekend support the theory that a jealous boyfriend murdered Bobby? And if that was the case, they were nowhere closer to locating the parrot eggs. Unless she was staring straight at their hiding place in the coop behind the rectory.

With nothing left for her to do here, she pulled out of the parking lot and voice-dialed Cassandra's cell, wanting to touch base and see if she'd learned anything about Father Silva.

"*Apple Station Times.* Cass with the most sass speaking."

"Are you serious? Is that how you answer your phone?"

"Only for you, Penn."

"Honored."

"Where are you? It sounds like you're driving."

"I am. I'm leaving Gore and heading back to town."

"Let me guess. St. Anthony's, home of Father Silva."

"You've done your homework."

"And you, the legwork. Tell me everything."

Olivia puffed out a heavy sigh. "I'm not sure how much there is to share. I was calling to see if you'd come up with any background of note on the good Father."

"Only what you found on your own, namely, where he's based. He was a low priority target. A priest, really? I *almost* feel guilty for even having him on a potential naughty list."

Olivia felt the same way, but there was something about him she couldn't quite put her finger on. He looked the part and said all the right things. She'd certainly hang on every word of his Sunday sermons. But among all the random pieces of the puzzle, the only common connection was him.

A silver pickup zoomed past her on the four-lane divided highway. She checked her speedometer as a big rig was gaining ground in her rearview. Not realizing she'd been puttering along under the posted limit, she ramped back up to speed to avoid becoming a slow-moving road hazard.

"I think we need to look closer at him," she said. "Maybe try to find any contacts he might have in Brazil. He's from Cuiabá, in the state of Mato Grosso."

"Are you joking?" Cassandra asked. "I'm good, but that's next-level investigative prowess."

"If anyone can, it's you. I have a feeling he knows something about something he's not saying."

"*Something about something?* Could you be any less specific? Give me a direction. What would I be looking for?"

"I'm not sure, but you'll know it when you see it."

"Brilliant. Anything else, boss?"

"You're the best, Cass with the most sass." Her cell buzzed, and she glanced at her screen, seeing a text from Preston.

"Boom," Cassandra said. "That's all I needed to hear. My daily affirmation. Okay, prepared to be amazed. I'll be in touch."

They said a quick goodbye and ended the call. Olivia kept driving until reaching an area a few miles up the highway where the shoulder was wide enough for her to pull over. Once slowed to a stop, she shifted into park, opened the text, and read, "Are you around town?"

She replied, "Sorry, was on the road. Heading back there. Why?"

A biker on a low-rider motorcycle sped past her with a throaty roar. Peeking in her side mirror, she closed her window as the rest of the riding club rumbled by, sounding like thunder from a summer storm. Looking back at her cell, she saw that amid the hoo-ha, she'd received Preston's reply, "Can you meet me soon?"

She wrote, "Okay, maybe twenty-five minutes? At the station?"

He replied, "How about the inn?"

That was just as well. Whenever they got together for lunch or coffee during the week, she would try to avoid meeting him at the police station. Flashbacks to when he'd placed her in the station's holding cell in October still triggered memories of a day she would rather forget. After sending a thumbs-up emoji reply, she shifted into drive, checked her mirrors, and steered back onto the road.

Driving along the open, sunlit highway, she weighed his potential motives for the meetup. She doubted that a leisurely lunch was on his agenda. Now that she'd spent a portion of two days among the carnival workers, he would likely want her involvement in the investigation to end. He'd reluctantly agreed to the plan, surely assuming it was for the very short-term. If it were up to him, she wouldn't have been a part of it in the first place. He was the detective. His career entailed risk and danger, and she'd accepted that when they started dating. But if the roles were reversed, would he be as supportive of her as she had to be of him? Turning the thoughts over in her head, she eventually let them go until another day. Mulling a murder and missing parrot eggs seemed less complicated.

Arriving in town within her twenty-five-minute prediction, she lucked into a parking spot along the curbside of Tales and Treasures. After maneuvering between two other SUVs in front of the family-owned bookstore, she got out and locked up. She lingered on the sidewalk, gazing through the shop's wide windows at the well-stocked tables and shelves. Business was booming, and Duke the bulldog was lounging on a mosaic carpet remnant just inside the entrance.

Her last book haul had been in March, which made the window display of May's new releases a temptation she couldn't pass by without a gander. A few mysteries and a tiered rack of romances were displayed beside a collection of quilting and cross-stitching titles. A cookbook with a red velvet cake on the cover would make a delightful surprise gift for her father. She perused the cart of bargain books that sat next to a vintage wrought-iron bench, finding a thriller by one of her favorite authors she hadn't yet read. With too many choices and too little time, she'd have to put her shopping on hold and come back later to satisfy her literary cravings.

She crossed Cider Lane and, with a few brisk strides, stood in front of the inn's French doors. Upon entering the lobby, the only two people she saw were Zoey and a man she was chatting with at the concierge desk. Typically, the lobby was like a train depot with travelers coming or going, toting suitcases and shopping bags. Today, though, she easily heard the piped-in piano music and the gentle bubbling from a Zen water fountain sitting on a nearby table. Despite the lack of foot traffic, the coffee cart was at the ready, posing as a present-day miracle of loaves and fishes. The carafes were always full, and the complimentary pastries were restocked as quickly as they emptied. If Preston was delayed, she'd swipe a few of today's featured mini blueberry muffins to give herself a little pep.

Digging her phone out of her pocket to text him about her arrival, she glanced up and saw Zoey shoot her a friendly wave. She returned the greeting as the man Zoey had been speaking with bent down, picked up his briefcase, and turned to leave.

Olivia's eyes met his, sparking a simultaneous recognition between her and Jeffrey Rollins. She offered a polite smile as he approached her with a relaxed demeanor. Dressed in a crimson silk-wool polo and tapered stone-gray pants, he looked ready for a round of golf at Whispering Meadows Country Club.

He slipped his hand into his front pocket and stopped a few feet shy of her. "Hi, again." Scrunching his eyes, he appeared slightly embarrassed. "I'm so sorry and really embarrassed, but I've forgotten your name."

She waved off the sheepish apology. "Completely understandable. Our introduction was brief. Olivia Penn."

"Oh, yes. I try to use mnemonics, but you see how well that works for me. Penn. You're a writer. I should've remembered that."

"Sometimes I get asked if I became a writer because of my name."

He raised an amused eyebrow. "Did you?"

She widened her smile. "No, but it's convenient. How are you enjoying your stay here?"

"The accommodations are wonderful, and you were right about the restaurant."

"The owner will be happy to hear that. How much longer are you staying?"

"I'm not sure," he replied, shaking his head. "My flight is scheduled for Sunday, but my work here is almost done, so I may leave before the weekend."

"Where's home for you?"

"Miami, but I'm first flying up to New Jersey to see Nicky's parents. Bobby's death has been difficult for them. I'd like to visit and express my personal condolences."

She nodded, casually folding her arms. "Were you and Bobby close?"

His eyes slowly scanned from left to right, as if trying to pluck the precise words out of the air. "I think of all my clients as family. I've worked for the Kleins even before he and Nicky took over the daily operations." He removed his hand from his pocket and placed it on his chest. "My role is to help the business maintain solvency. Nicky always had more of a grasp of the actual cost of running the carnival. Bobby spent money the business didn't have and often signed bad contracts. She, like her father, is all about keeping Klein Amusements viable. For her, it's personal—her family's legacy. As a numbers guy who likes balanced books, and whose job it is to make sure companies stay afloat, I share her mindset." He lowered his hand. "Don't get me wrong, I got along with Bobby fine. He was more of a friend you have a drink with on a Friday night than someone you trust to handle your money."

Maybe a breach of trust got him killed.

"I'm going to say this to you off the record," he said. "Nicky initially didn't want you around this week. Not *you* personally. I mean any reporter. I talked her into the pros of getting good press after what happened to Bobby. When you work for a carnival, one of the first things you learn is not to talk to the police or reporters. That's just the way it is." He gestured with his hand, emphasizing his words. "Bobby left the finances in a mess, and I've been negotiating with the creditors to restructure the payments. What I'm trying to get at is that Klein Amuse-ments doesn't need bad publicity right now. With Bobby's death, stories are likely to emerge that shed a poor light on the company. The carnival travels all over, including to some very conservative areas in the South. Church festivals make up a large percentage of our bookings. If the business is portrayed negatively, we could lose some of those contracts, and we can't afford that."

Her focus shifted over his shoulder for a second, as she saw Preston step out of the dining room. Meeting her eyes, he nodded once, then turned and went back inside.

"My role there this week is to gather firsthand accounts of carnival life," she said, sounding convincing even to herself. "It's not about Bobby or anything else. The workers all have a story, and if they want to, they can share it anonymously. I've gotten a feel for the carnival culture, and I understand that interpersonal conflicts stay in-house. I respect that. I'm trying to give others who haven't been exposed to the lifestyle, beyond exaggerated portrayals in movies or TV, a better understanding of those who work the circuit. A lot of misconceptions exist, and people make judgments without knowing what working for a carnival is really like."

Jeffrey swung his briefcase in front of him, holding the handle with both hands. "Thank you for that, and I know the Kleins appreciate your intentions."

Uncrossing her arms, she punctuated the conversation with a polite smile. "I'm glad you're enjoying your stay at the inn, despite the sad circumstances of this week. You were on your way out, and I've kept you from your business."

"Not at all. It was a pleasure, Olivia Penn." He

tapped his temple with his finger. "See, I remembered. Penn—a writer."

"Very good," she replied.

After exchanging a pleasant goodbye, they parted ways. Jeffrey left the inn, and she crossed the lobby and entered the dining room, looking toward the table she and Preston often sat at by the fireplace. Preston stood up to greet her when she neared, and they shared a respectable kiss that wouldn't make either blush if his mother saw them. He pulled out a chair for her, and after she settled, he took his seat next to her.

"I didn't know you were waiting in here," she said. "I was about to text you when I ran into the Kleins' accountant in the lobby."

"My mom asked me to come by and talk to the new security company she's hired to revamp the system."

"Did something prompt that?"

He took a sip of iced tea from a glass that was half full. "No. She needs to upgrade her cameras." He picked up a pewter pitcher and filled a goblet with water for her. "Would you like coffee instead?"

She placed her hand on his thigh for a moment. "No, water is fine. Thank you."

He leaned across the table, grabbed a linen-lined basket packed with mini blueberry muffins, and set it between their glasses. "I stole these from the kitchen."

She plucked a muffin off the pile and broke it in half. "That's most unbecoming of someone sworn to uphold the law."

"Should I return them?"

"We'll let it slide." She popped the portion in her mouth. "Hmm. Delish. A.J. installed security cameras at the house yesterday."

"It's about time. How long have I been saying to do that?"

"If it makes you feel better, I'll say it was your idea." She finished the other half of the muffin before continuing. "So, what's up? Why did you want to meet? It can't be simply to implicate me in your life of crime—stealing food from your own mother's kitchen."

"Tell me about your morning."

She took a sip of water. "We could've just talked about this over the phone, instead of making me come all the way here."

"You have a harder time coloring the truth when we're face-to-face."

You're not wrong about that. "La-di-da. Did you check Tiffany's box?"

"I did, but there were no screwdrivers."

"Is that among the potential murder weapons?"

"We don't have the medical examiner's report back yet. Now, your turn."

She selected another muffin and placed it on a napkin. "I went to St. Anthony's Church in Gore and spoke with Father Silva." She recounted her conversation and the coincidence of the chicken coop, which earned a questioning brow raise from Preston.

When she finished, he was quiet for a moment before

speaking. "One or more of the crew could have a connection to Klein's murder."

She leaned in closer, lowering her voice, though nobody was around them. "I spoke with someone this morning who told me he saw Tiffany go into Bobby's RV on Sunday night around eleven o'clock."

His eyes drifted down, as that seemed to spark his interest.

"What is it?" she asked.

"Someone ransacked his place that night. There were valuables and money left behind."

"That doesn't sound like a robbery."

He shook his head. "No. Whoever did it was looking for something, but we don't know what's missing. The lock wasn't broken."

"Tiffany might have a key. Or maybe she went there and found it already opened."

"All possible."

Olivia split the muffin and ate a bite while he seemed to run through scenarios in his head.

"Have you told Payne about my involvement?" she asked.

"I did."

"And?"

"He thinks it's a good idea."

She bit back a smile, resting her hand on his thigh again. "How about that?"

He covered her hand with his. "He didn't have a choice. As soon as I arrived at the station this morning, he called me into his office and told me he'd received a call from Senator Dixon."

"As in Congresswoman Pamela Dixon?"

"That's the one. She requested our department cooperate with Carolyn Shaw's operation, offering support and avoiding interference. Then I told Payne about our conversation yesterday and what you were doing."

"Does that mean Sam is officially off the radar as a person of interest in Bobby's murder?"

"Yes."

She tilted toward him, playfully nudging his arm with her shoulder. "I guess I may be useful after all."

"I still don't like it. Call me tonight once you're home, behind locked doors." He kissed her cheek, then abruptly stood up.

"Wait, you're leaving? I drive all this way to meet you, and you just cut and run. Do you have any information to share with me?"

He flashed a sly, sexy smile. "No."

"What? How is that fair?"

He bent forward, placing his hand on her shoulder, and whispered in her ear. "It's not."

Catching her by surprise, he stole a kiss from her lips that she couldn't even enjoy or reciprocate.

"I'll be waiting for your call tonight," he added, quickly kissing her again. Then he straightened and pushed in his chair.

"Where's the quid pro quo? I offer you a cornucopia of hard-won information, and you give me muffins in exchange? You didn't even buy them. You stole them from your own mother."

He shrugged as he backed away. "Call me tonight."

She shook her head in faux frustration. "Oh, I'll call you a thing or two tonight." She grabbed the other half of the muffin, took a bite, and pointed the rest at him. "And you can just forget about that PJ party anytime soon."

CHAPTER 27

An hour after Preston's abrupt departure from the inn, Olivia sat in her Expedition in the event lot at Fields Farm, mulling over her conversation with Jeffrey Rollins. If Bobby's bad financial decisions had jeopardized his illegal activities, a partner may have used Sunday's meeting at Spring Hills as an opportunity to get rid of him. Of those she'd met thus far, only a few seemed to have the means and the forethought to co-lead a complicated criminal operation.

Nicky topped the list, but without a drop of evidence implicating her in the illicit trade or Bobby's murder, her involvement seemed dubious. She prioritized the family business, and placing it at risk by taking part in anything illegal would be out of character. Father Silva seemed an even less likely suspect. Though he was a priest, Olivia couldn't outright dismiss his suspicious connections and the odd coincidences surrounding him.

Tommy Grasso was involved somehow, but how close he was to the ringleaders was unknown. Slammer was the only crew member she knew had an inroad to him. Tiffany, Stash, Slammer, and Lone Wolf all were murder suspects, but pegging motives on each would be conjecture. None of them stuck out as likely players in Bobby's criminal activity, other than in peripheral roles. Of all the ride jocks and jointees she'd met, Cowboy stood out as the one who was the most mysterious. His suspicions of her agenda had been spot-on, and perhaps now she needed to be more wary of his intentions.

She placed her arm on the sill, allowing her hand to dangle out of the open window. The carnival had roared to life with its thrill rides whirling, much to the delight of the early comers, judging by their gleeful screams. Thumping music and lively sirens from the games previewed the fun awaiting those walking to the midway. The vibrant lights destined to color the night wouldn't take full effect until the sun set in another hour. At just five thirty, a fair number of cars were parked in the lot, arranged in random rows. On weekends during special events, a farm attendant would always direct traffic, ensuring order to maximize flow and capacity. But because opening day was a weeknight, attendance was likely to be light, and the parking already resembled a free-for-all.

She glanced at the shopping bag from Tales and Treasures sitting on the passenger seat. After leaving the inn, she'd stopped in the bookstore and bought the cookbook for her dad and a few new releases for her night-stand. Now, unsure of how long her business here would take, she texted her father to let him know she wouldn't be home for dinner. His reply, a GIF of a smiling slice of pizza, hinted he wasn't heartbroken about getting dinner delivered for a solo supper.

She unplugged her phone from its charger and swiped open her e-mail, feeling a tad guilty that she'd neglected her inbox all day. With Angela eager to clear her plate before leaving on her trip, it would be wise to check her messages to ensure she didn't need to send any additional copy. If good to go, with tomorrow's chat canceled, she'd be free over the next two days.

Sometime soon, she'd need to set aside time to research the job market, preferably for positions that would allow her to stay in the area. Angela's imminent departure had lit a fire under her to get more serious about resolving where she wanted to be at this time next year.

One thought kept coming up that she couldn't outright dismiss. If Cassandra got the job at her paper in D.C., *The Apple Station Times* would have an immediate opening for an experienced staff writer. Ellen would likely give it to her on the spot if she asked for it. She could go back to being a beat reporter with ease, though her bank account would take a hit. Until something better came along, it could be a temporary solution. The position at *Modern Mosaic* didn't seem feasible unless she and Preston tried to make a long-distance relationship work. She had friends who happily maintained such arrangements and knew a married couple who lived over five hundred miles apart. But those weren't options she'd ever considered, and she wasn't sure if she wanted to.

She took a deep breath, then exhaled all the distracting thoughts. She was supposed to be checking her e-mail, not planning the next ten years of her life. Her inbox was full of messages, most of which were staff announcements she'd look at later. Scanning and scrolling, she saw nothing terribly pressing that needed her immediate attention.

The only message that piqued her interest was one Cassandra had sent an hour ago with the subject line, "Check this out." On clicking the e-mail, she found an attached image with no text. The preview didn't load, so she opened the image in her photo app. The picture showed Father Silva standing in front of St. Anthony's during some sort of festival. A banner in the background was probably descriptive, but the writing was too small for her to read. Curious about the what and the why of the scene, she dialed Cassandra's cell and waited three rings.

"Jeez, Penn. How many times do I have to talk to you today?"

"What a lovely hello."

"Joking. What's up?"

"I just saw the e-mail you sent." Pots clanking and running water gave her pause. "Did I catch you at a bad time?"

"I'm making dinner, but it's fine. By the way, that's what normal people do. They go home after work, eat, and stream mindless TV. Where are you?"

"Fields Farm."

"Business or pleasure?"

"The former."

Cassandra lowered the volume of music playing in the background. "Who's a good girl? You are! Treat? Okay. Only because you're so cute."

"Excuse me?"

"Talking to my cat."

"Gotcha. Listen, I don't want to keep you. I was wondering about the picture. There was no context."

"I thought I'd hold off on the big reveal until we talked tomorrow, but apparently you never go off the clock. Hold on a sec." A closet squeaked open, then banged closed. "Here you are, sweetie pie. One, two, three treats for you. Okay, that'll make her happy. So, about the picture. I found a link between the Kleins and a charity drive at St. Anthony's last year to support local families in need. Fueled by the enduring truth that nothing ever completely disappears from the internet, I located a post on social media about a fancy-schmancy dinner held in Middleburg that was part of this fundraiser. You know how sometimes with these swanky events they'll list the donors in tiers according to their contributions?"

"Yeah, I'm with you."

"Well, the announcement listed sponsors who

pledged, at the top level, ten thousand dollars. Not surprisingly, there were only two donors at that tier. That's a real chunk of change."

"And the Kleins were one of them?"

"Wrong. Above the list of those high-end sponsors, there was another category. An uber-exclusive platinum circle of supporters. No dollar amounts were listed, but we all know platinum means deep pockets. This upper echelon had three members, two of which were corporate donors. Now, Nancy Drew, guess who the third member of that elite group was?"

"Klein Amusements."

"Give that girl a PI license and a dark, broody backstory."

"So, they donated over ten K."

"Probably well over."

"Huh." She placed her elbow on the window ledge and rested her chin in her hand. "That doesn't make sense. From all I've heard, the carnival is cash poor. The Kleins' accountant told me today that finances weren't Bobby's forte. So how and why would they donate that much?"

"Maybe it wasn't a contribution to the church's cause, but a payoff to Father Silva."

"You mean some kind of money laundering?"

"Who's going to accuse a priest?" Cassandra said.

"But that money would have to go to the charity and be accounted for."

"Would it? People embezzle all the time from companies and charities. If he is hands-on with the parish's finances, I'm sure there would be a way he could hide the funds."

She was right that Father Silva was smart, and as much as Olivia didn't want to believe it, the theory had merit. "That's a possibility, but we need to consider other motives for why they'd make such a generous donation. Maybe it was flat-up charity, or it could've been a huge tax write-off."

"Do you think, from what we know about Bobby Klein, he would part with that much moolah, especially with it going to a church?"

"Maybe the decision wasn't his."

"Are you thinking the sister?"

"Perhaps." Olivia spun through what she knew about Nicky in her head. Though she was more of a charitable sort than her brother, that was still a lot of money to be diverted away from the family business. "Okay, that's really great work. I owe you."

"Lunch next week at the inn should cover it."

"Deal."

"Another thing, Liv. I've kept Ellen up to speed on everything we've learned, and she wanted me to remind you to tread lightly. Whoever killed Klein is still out there. For all we know, it could be someone who works for the carnival. Just be careful. Bobby may've been murdered over a half-a-million-dollar payday. If it happened once, it could happen again. I kind of like having you around."

Olivia glanced toward the midway that promised fun

and thrills, while possibly harboring a murderer among the games and rides. "Thanks. I'll be careful." After agreeing to talk tomorrow, they said a brief goodbye and ended the call.

She leaned her head back against the seat, reconsidering the relationship between the Kleins and Father Silva. Catching up once a year when the carnival came through the area was one thing, but them giving him a mega-donation pointed to more than just a casual friendship.

A sporty bronze crossover parked in what would be the next row up in front of her, if there was any rhyme or reason to the lot. She watched as a woman about her age got out of the passenger seat, opened the door behind her, and lifted her daughter out of the car. The energetic straw-blonde cutie was wearing a pink hooded jacket with rolled up jeans and looked to be under five. She skipped to the back bumper, hopped several times, and unleashed a high-pitched, happy scream. After her father got out, he opened the rear compartment, and a Dalmatian jumped down to the ground. The girl wrapped her arms around her best friend's neck as he danced about, whipping his tail like he was swatting a swarm of flies.

Olivia smiled at the scene, thinking she must've acted just as excited whenever her parents brought her to the carnival as a kid. After the family got organized and leashed the dog, they took off for the midway. With time wasting away, she figured she'd better do the same. Just as she was about to close the window, she noticed Stash walking past the family in the opposite direction. He veered toward the white van she'd seen parked in the same spot on Tuesday. After getting behind the wheel, he started the engine, reversed, and drove across the field to the exit.

Without a second thought, she hit the push-button start, fastened her seatbelt, and took off after him. Workers leaving during operating hours couldn't be normal business procedure unless he was running a special errand. She drove across the bumpy lot, and by the time she turned onto the Snickersville Turnpike, he'd already put a substantial distance between them. Picking up her pace, she hovered a little above the speed limit, praying the police didn't have any radar traps lying in wait. At least with the large stretch between them, he probably wouldn't notice that she was following him.

Without knowing where he was going, her only play was to remain undetected, observe, and call for help if necessary. After a few turns and fifteen minutes, they were driving north on Morrow Lane, rapidly approaching Spring Hills. She took her foot off the gas to grow the gap between them, anticipating he too may soon slow down. With no one coming up from behind, she tapped the brakes, cutting her speed in half. Sure as the sun rises, about seventy-five yards ahead, he turned left onto the property. She continued for a short distance, then pulled over onto the shoulder near the entrance with a decision hanging in the balance.

Her thoughts wavered between wondering why Stash

had driven to Spring Hills and debating whether she should follow him farther. Either someone had directed him to come here, or he already knew about the unsecure, isolated location. The connections she'd been trying to piece together and the answer to the puzzle could be right down the road, driving a white cargo van. He might be making a delivery or meeting the buyers of the parrot eggs. This might be a prime opportunity to identify the players involved, one of whom might be Bobby's killer.

Feeling safe in her vehicle, she wanted to drive straight in, but her cooler head made her think twice before proceeding. Calling Preston leapt to the forefront of her mind, but he'd only tell her to stay away. Who knew how long Stash would be here, and she'd lose her shot at identifying any of the parties if they left before she could surveil them. Contacting Sam wouldn't do any good, as she was probably too far away to arrive in time.

Drumming her thumbs on the wheel, she weighed Ellen's warning against the unique opportunity now facing her. If she proceeded cautiously, following the same strategy as on Sunday, she stood an excellent chance of not being seen. She'd wind her way to the field above the parking lot and gain the high ground to observe the headquarters and lot below. If she encountered anyone along the way, a U-turn and a hasty retreat would get her back on Morrow Lane in short order.

Dusk had descended, casting its deepening shadow, but she could still see the road clearly. She switched off her daylight running lights and headlights to reduce the chances of being seen as she drove onto the property. She marked the time and allowed a few minutes to pass in case whoever Stash was meeting hadn't arrived yet. The last thing she wanted was to be driving toward the roundabout with headlights shining at her from behind. But she didn't want to wait too long and miss whatever was happening, or risk running into Stash just as she was heading in. At the ten-minute mark, she looked up and down the highway, checking that both directions were clear. With no one in sight, she figured she could reach her turnoff before anyone caught up to her from behind.

After quickly steering back onto the road, she drove to the entrance, turned, and started in. Familiar with the lay of the land, she zipped down the lane, keeping her eyes wide for approaching vehicles. In no time, she passed the posts for the auxiliary gate and continued to the roundabout. Barely tapping the brakes, she veered toward the first offshoot leading to the upper field.

Nearing the top, she slowed down to make sure no one else was there. Then, continuing onto the field, she stopped shy of where she'd parked on Sunday. Not sure whether her car was visible from that same spot, she didn't want to risk it tonight. She turned the car around, facing back toward the lane, and cut the engine.

About thirty yards separated her from where she needed to be, so she popped the door and slid down out of the seat. She scampered across the field, then slowed and lowered her profile as she neared the other side. As soon as she could see the lot, she flattened onto the ground. Stash was parked just below, back-to-back with a large black SUV. The rear doors of both vehicles stood open, and he and another man were transferring boxes into the van. She crawled a few inches forward, trying to make an ID, but the vehicles' positions obscured the stranger's face. As she was about to take out her phone to snap pictures of the scene, they finished the job, and each shut their respective doors. They exchanged a few words, shook hands, and went their separate ways.

She shimmied back, sprung up, and dashed across the field toward her car. Though doubtful they would come her way, she wasn't taking any chances. After getting to her vehicle, she hopped straight in, shut the door, and clicked the locks. She kept the engine silent and waited five minutes for them to drive off the property.

Once she committed to exiting, she switched her headlights back on and barreled down the access road toward Morrow Lane. Nearing her turn, she hit the brakes harder than needed, triggering the seatbelt to lock her in against the seat. While stopped, she looked in both directions, not seeing taillights either way. Within a count of three Mississippi, she chanced a guess that Stash was en route back to Fields Farm. The identity of the other man would have to remain a mystery, as he wasn't the priority. She steered right and gunned it down the empty highway, passing a sedan and an old-school station wagon about two miles from Spring Hills.

Once back on the Snickersville Turnpike, she spotted a white van and closed in on it in no time flat. Though not entirely sure this was the same vehicle she'd followed, she liked her chances. The driver appeared to be in no hurry, bolstering her bet that Stash was behind the wheel. He was likely proceeding cautiously to reduce the risk of being stopped by the police with his dubious cargo.

Within five minutes, Fields Farm came into view, and shortly after, the driver turned into the main entrance. She followed, watching the van continue on a road that went past the event lot. She parked, got out, and locked up, certain that Stash was heading back to the camp.

CHAPTER 28

At close to eight o'clock, the carnival's bright lights lit up the night, casting a colorful aura over the midway. Olivia strode toward the ticket booth, passing a trio of teens who were teasing each other about who would scream the loudest on Blackbeard's Revenge. She paid ten dollars for general admission, then proceeded to the carnival grounds. Mystical melodies played through a speaker outside the fringed flap-covered entrance to the tarot tent. A line of five stood waiting to hear their fortunes, or receive answers from the spirit world to the questions plaguing them. High-pitched pings, random voices, and racing music from the rides filled the air with a lively vibe.

As she passed the game stands, several jointees implored her to try her luck at winning a prize, each offering the first play for free. She smiled and waved off all the invites, including one from Cowboy, who pleaded with her to grace his humble presence. She'd come back to him later, as he was on her follow-up list, but catching up with Stash was her priority.

The sweet scent of cotton candy and the aroma of buttery, nutty, fresh-popped popcorn coated the air, enticing her taste buds with flavors from her childhood. She glanced toward the kiddie games, grouped between the funnel cake stand and the carousel with its jumpers and prancers bobbing up and down. Aunt Bea was cheerleading two hesitant children as they selected their lucky duckies from the small inflatable pool.

Animated laughter from the Ferris wheel passengers reminded her of when she and A.J. had ridden one twice the size at the state fair about ten years ago. The ride had stalled, stranding them at the top for the longest thirty minutes of her life. While waiting, somehow and for some forgotten reason, they had promised to get married to one another if they were both single at forty. Close to five years from having to commit, she secretly smiled while walking by the brightly lit wheel, wondering if pinky promises had expiration dates.

She hurried down the slight slope, passing two workers at a distance who were strolling back toward the midway. Though ready to exchange a friendly hello, she didn't even have to wave, as neither glanced in her direction. Temporary pole-mounted floodlights lit up the area, but the three bunkhouses blocked a full view of the camp. If Stash had driven back there, she figured he likely would've parked in the makeshift lot with all the other vehicles.

Upon reaching the bunkhouse closest to the lot, she slowed her stride, crept to its edge, and peeked around the corner. The floodlights illuminated the vehicles and the full length of the bunkhouse. She recoiled immediately, seeing Stash standing outside a door at the far end. After waiting a few seconds, she looked again and watched as he transferred a stack of large boxes, one by one, into the room. Once finished, he shut the door, came down the steps, and hastened toward the midway.

She scurried back around the end of the bunkhouse and hurried along the lane between the trailers, heading in the opposite direction from him. Nearing the end of the lane, she glanced over her shoulder and slowed upon seeing he wasn't following her. After rounding the corner of the bunkhouse, she now stood facing the room where he'd stashed the boxes.

Though not knowing what he'd stored inside, she would lay odds that his side trip to Spring Hills had involved the parrot eggs or something else illegal. A clandestine meeting at an isolated location where Bobby had been killed was too much of a coincidence. With lives at stake, she glanced left and right, then didn't think twice. She darted up the steps and grabbed the door handle, rolling the dice on the fifty-fifty chance. With a turn and a tug, she was stymied. Automatically, she tried again, as if all she needed to get past a locked door was a little more welly.

She turned, went down the steps, and hustled over to the white van parked next to an A-frame camper. After finding all the doors locked, she stood by the driver's window and rose onto tiptoes, craning her neck to get a view of the rear cargo bay. The angle wasn't right, and she needed more height, so she used the side-view mirror for a boost. She popped up and startled, seeing Cowboy in the window's reflection standing right behind her. She spun and put distance between them.

"Howdy, Olivia Penn from *The Apple Station Times*."

"What are you doing here?" she reflexively snapped, hyperaware of her question's irony.

He removed his hat and held it against the front of his thigh. "I think it's time we came clean with each other." His carefree, light southern drawl had morphed into the smooth, confident tone of a fine orator. "How about you go first?"

She backpedaled, channeling her best impersonation of Sam. "I'll play your dart game for a buck, Butch Cassidy, but whatever this is, no thank you."

He held up his hand. "Wait. My name is Derek Wilcox, and I'm a writer on assignment for *The Harbor Sentinel*."

That eased her retreat, but not her guard. The Boston-based paper was known for its investigative journalism, breaking national stories involving crime, corruption, and scandals. If he wasn't lying, her gut had been right in judging that he was more than he appeared. Still, she played it off with a sigh and an Oscar-worthy eye roll. "Is that supposed to mean something to me?"

He grinned, seeing through her ruse. "Okay. How about this? I think we're here for the same reason, and if we pool our resources, we can both get what we want."

She kept her face tight, not willing to give an inch. He was going to have to do more than throw out some names to earn her trust. "Cowboy—Derek—I don't know what you're getting at. Shouldn't you be on the midway, working your stand?"

He pointed his hat at her for a moment before placing it back on his head. "I wouldn't believe a smooth-talking carny either." He reached into his rear pocket, took out his wallet, and removed two cards, offering both to her.

Keeping her eyes locked on him, she stepped a little closer and plucked them from his hand. The first was his D.C. driver's license, verifying his name and likeness. The other was a press badge that backed his story and further confirmed his identity. In both photos, he looked more like an Ivy Leaguer than a carnival barker. Conceding that creating two fake IDs would be quite a ploy, she tapped the cards together and returned them to him.

"Go on," she said.

He reclaimed his IDs and placed them in his wallet, which he shoved back into his pocket. "Right now, we only have time for me to hit the highlights. I'm part of a team that has been investigating an animal trafficking ring that operates along the I-95 Corridor from Florida to Maine. About a year ago, a former Klein employee came to us with a story, claiming Bobby was one of this group's suppliers. Last August, I got a spot on the crew, and I've been trying to work my way into Bobby's inner circle of trust."

"How's that been going?"

"Not very well. Stash has been his go-to guy, but for the life of me, I don't know why. Judging by your lack of surprise, I'm taking it none of this is news to you."

She looked around, ensuring they were alone. "You're ballsy to carry your real IDs."

His lips parted in a thin grin. "I just want to make sure the police can identify my body."

She nodded, appreciating the gallows humor. "I like a man who thinks ahead. Is there any more to your story?"

"I have reason to believe Bobby was transacting a deal this week with his associates, but something went wrong, and either they or somebody on his own team killed him."

At least they'd come to the same conclusion, working the angles from different ends. "Do you have any evidence to support this?"

He shook his head. "Nothing that would hold up legally. That's why I tried to get in on the action. I've been grinding away in this job for almost eight months now. I've met a lot of great people along the way and have developed genuine friendships. But the lifestyle and work have worn me down. I want to go home. When Nicky told us that a reporter would be around this week doing research for a feel-good article, I knew there was more to it. A day after her brother dies, voilà. You show up. Quite a coincidence. It's exactly what I would've done, though. Like they say, it takes one to know one. I figured you were looking into Bobby's death, or maybe you were here for the same reason as me."

Without giving too much away, she decided the best play was to throw him a bone. "You're not wrong."

"I didn't even need to open a second browser window to learn who you really are," he said. "Then I spoke with a friendly, enthusiastic fellow on *your* staff—Cooper, I believe. He was quite helpful, telling me all about you when I called the office on Tuesday, posing as your long-lost college classmate."

She mentally groaned, noting to speak with Cooper next week about not being so trusting of what people told him. She glanced around again, then lowered her voice even more. "My source believes Bobby was off-loading half a million dollars' worth of hyacinth macaw eggs."

Derek let out a low whistle. "Egg smuggling. I thought that was mostly a European thing."

"I don't know. I'm new to these circles."

"Those are the big blue parrots, correct?"

"Yes."

"Okay, walking through this. On Sunday, Bobby went to Spring Hills and made the exchange, then someone killed him. Who? Where are the eggs? Long gone is my guess."

"Maybe not," she replied. "My source believes money

wouldn't exchange hands until the parrots hatch. Whoever took the eggs would need access to brooders to ensure the hatchlings get the early care they need. A man thought to be working for the buyers is still in the area. The guy who left the tarot tent with Slammer yesterday—that's him."

"Oof. That's not good. Slammer had a bone to pick with Bobby. He said it was about back pay, but I sensed there was more to it. His bunk is a few doors down from me. That won't make me sleep any easier tonight."

"Someone knew Bobby would be at Spring Hills on Sunday night. Maybe a business partner who wanted to become a solopreneur, or perhaps somebody who had a falling out with him. Given the collective intel, it's reasonable to assume that he went there thinking he was delivering the eggs to those who would care for them after they hatched. However, he was being set up. Whoever killed him took the eggs and will complete the transaction once they hatch. There's an alternative theory, though, that has nothing to do with trafficking. Maybe someone who was angry with him for a personal reason followed him there, then confronted him."

"If anyone other than a business partner killed him, then why take the eggs? How would they even know what they were looking at?"

"That's just it," she replied. "It could've been someone hired to do the deed."

"You mean Stash or Slammer?"

"Maybe. Or Lone Wolf. Why did you tell me about

Angel going into Bobby's RV? Do you think she's involved somehow?"

"Not directly. But as a co-carny, I can't make the same inquiries that a supposedly legitimate reporter could get away with. If my cover gets blown, they'll boot me out of here, probably with several broken bones. Asking too many questions makes people suspicious. Rumors are that she was Bobby's latest fling. I thought she might know or have heard something about his other business—pillow talk and all. She's clammed up since his death. Throwing you the tip, I was hoping to put you on her trail."

"Again, you're not wrong. Do you believe she's capable of murder?"

He winced. "After working the carnival circuit for parts of two seasons, nothing surprises me anymore. You know what they say about a woman scorned. There's someone else who has a connection to all of this that I can't pin down. Father Silva."

"Tell me more."

"I see that's not a surprise to you either. Last season, there were three stops where our informant said Bobby conducted business with his buyers. Richmond, Virginia. Frederick, Maryland. Lancaster, Pennsylvania. At each of those, Silva showed up."

She shook her head. "Back up. First, how do you know these transactions happened if you have no evidence? Second, don't you think it's a leap to say just because he was there that he had something to do with it?"

"There was someone else who paid the Kleins a visit at each of those stops. Our informant ties this guy to the trade ring. He didn't know his name, but he overheard a conversation between Bobby and this guy discussing the details of a transaction. As for Silva—"

"Hold on," she said. She dug her phone out of her pocket, opened her photos to the picture of Grasso, and turned the screen to face him. "Is this the man you're talking about?"

He studied the photo. "I don't know. I didn't see him myself. Is that the guy who was with Slammer yesterday?"

She nodded, stuffing her cell back into her pocket.

"What do you know about Silva?" he asked.

"Enough that I can't dismiss him as a suspect. I spoke with him earlier today at his church in Gore. What I am surprised about is that he showed up at those locations. He told me he sees the Kleins when they come through the area, but none of those stops are anywhere near here."

"I've checked into his background. Did he tell you he has a nephew in Brazil who's in jail for poaching?"

She took a deep breath, then exhaled quickly. "He failed to mention that, but I wouldn't have expected him to share it anyway. Still, guilt by association isn't a legal argument."

"Agreed."

"Hey, Cowboy!" a man shouted from near the other end of the bunkhouse.

Both turned as Art came toward them.

"That's my cue to leave," Derek said. Then he yelled in his southern twang, "Just coming back up, buddy."

"How long does it take to get your phone anyhow?" Art replied.

"I found it," he called out. "Thanks for watching my stand." He inched closer to her, speaking at a brisk clip. "When I saw you fly by, I figured something was up. We'll have to continue this later. There must be a reason you tried to get into Stash's bunk and the van. Silva is tight with the Kleins. You need to ask why that's the case. I don't believe in coincidences." Then he gave her a wink and made a show of tipping his hat, adding an aw-shucks chin dip for over-the-top flair. "You have a mighty fine night, ma'am. Enjoy your time at our carnival." With that, he spun and strode over to Art, greeting him with a handshake and a bro-backslap.

Both men turned, and she watched as they strolled back toward the midway, trying to wrap her head around what the heck had just happened.

CHAPTER 29

Tired from the day, Olivia drug herself up the front porch steps, carrying the shopping bag from Tales and Treasures. Her father had already drawn the curtains closed, but the living room lamps were still on, back-lighting the bay window with a warm glow. Ever since she was a teen, he'd always left the lights on for her if she was out late. She imagined he was still awake, though, as he rarely turned in until after the first segment of the eleven o'clock news.

She'd left Fields Farm following Derek's revelation, as there was nothing more for her to do there tonight. Hanging around to enjoy the atmosphere wasn't in the cards. Milling about the midway while wondering whether a murderer was running a ride or a game made for a creepy carnival outing. Lacking evidence of what Stash had stored in his bunkroom, she couldn't contact the police. Citing her gut feeling that the boxes contained illegal goods was hardly sufficient for a search warrant. Besides, she had no desire to tell Preston that she'd followed Stash to Spring Hills alone and without calling him. Derek's disclosure added a twist that may prove helpful. Unsure if Carolyn would cooperate with Derek, she'd wait to plan her next move until she'd spoken with Sam.

She opened the door and stepped inside, surprised at not finding her father half asleep in his recliner, with a black-and-white movie on the TV. Usually, Buddy would rush to greet her, regardless of the time of day. Sometimes, Willow would join in, popping her head up from wherever she was sleeping as her way of saying hello. But neither of her furry friends were in sight. There were no sounds of scratching claws or frantic scampering that suggested either of them had heard her enter.

After closing and locking the door, she tiptoed into the kitchen, set the bag of books on the table, and grabbed a diet cola from the refrigerator. Maybe her father had gone to bed early. If that were the case, she hoped he wasn't feeling ill. She popped the top off the plastic storage container of palmiers, shuffled them about, and selected the largest one. Muffins in the late afternoon and puff pastry for dinner made for an indulgent day, but desperate times called for desperate measures. She was a survivor, even if that meant sacrificing fruits and vegetables for the quick energy hit from simple carbs. Multitasking, she took a bite of the palmier and opened the can tab. With a large swig of soda and another satisfying munch, she felt a bit of life come back to her.

She set the palmier on the counter and went over to Buddy and Willow's food and water bowls, finding her father had already filled them. Thankful for one less thing on her nightly to-do list, she turned back to finish her snack. Then she heard a crack in the floorboard right above her. Having lived in her childhood home for over half of her life, she could identify the location of every creak and settling sound of the house. Her breath stilled. The noise had come from her bedroom.

Taking a few steps toward the living room, she listened, then heard water running. That, she knew, was from the sink in her father's bathroom. There was no way he could've been in her room and then made it down the hallway in the time it took her to cross the kitchen. Her heart ramped up as she heard another distinctive crack above her, knowing Buddy and Willow were too light to bend a floorboard.

She'd often been alone in the house, hearing odd noises that didn't give her pause. A squirrel scampering across the roof or a bird smacking into a window could easily fuel an overactive imagination. Admittedly, the day's events had put her on edge, and though she was safe in her home, maybe her mind was still convincing her body that danger was right around the corner. A floorboard cracking in her room normally wouldn't even register. It was the second sounding from the identical spot that poked at her frayed nerves.

If she hadn't spent the past two days immersed in cloak-and-dagger dealings, she would've dismissed the oddity and finished her palmier. Instead, she padded across the living room and grabbed the bat from the umbrella stand. Better safe than sorry when it came to self-defense.

She grumbled at herself for not checking the camera feed during the day and mentally noted that she needed to make a habit of it. After slowly climbing the stairs, she paused at the landing. The familiar glow of her nightstand lamp lit up her bedroom. Her father must've gone in and turned it on because …

Not a single reason occurred to her.

Everything's fine. It's a floorboard. You've just had a long day.

Inching closer to the room, she raised the bat and tightened her grip. Just as she leaned forward to peek inside, Buddy's favorite red ball came rolling out of the room. Startled, she jumped back as it hit the hall wall, then ricocheted toward the stairs. In a flash, Buddy scampered out of the bedroom and dashed past her in pursuit.

She stepped into the doorway and immediately lowered the bat.

"Hey there, slugger," Sam said, sitting on the bed.

"What the—you almost gave me a heart attack. What are you doing here? How did you get in?"

Buddy trotted back to the bedroom and dropped the ball by Olivia's feet.

Sam picked up the tactical pen from the nightstand and turned it around in her hand. "I came to see if you found out anything today. I didn't break in, if that's what you're thinking."

"Of course not." *Mostly.* Buddy was pawing at her legs, so she bent down and grabbed the ball. "Yes, I see you, little guy. I missed you too." She tossed his toy down the hall, watching him chase it like a hound hunting a fugitive. Then, standing tall, she stepped into her room and propped the bat by the door.

Sam rubbed her thumb over the pen's pointed tip before placing it back by the notepad on the nightstand. "Tell me when you want to graduate to something with more stopping power."

"That would be never."

Olivia saw Willow curled up on the window ledge of the reading nook. The cozy spot was one of the cat's favorite places to hang out, especially when Olivia read there at night before going to bed. She crossed the room and greeted the sleepy kitty with a few gentle pets to her cheek.

"I'm sorry I didn't give you a heads-up," Sam said. "I've been here since eight. I hung out with your dad, and we had pizza. We watched part of a baseball game until he got tired and went to bed. If you ever want to switch lives for a bit, I could get used to being a doting daughter."

Olivia came back over and sat on the end of the bed. "The job is already taken. Is it safe for you to be here? What if Grasso is watching your house?"

"That's unlikely. All was clear when I arrived."

"Does that mean you can go back home?"

Sam shook her head. "I'm still in lying-low mode. While you've been playing Jessica Fletcher, we were looking into how Grasso learned I wasn't a flunky driver-for-hire. It didn't take Carolyn long to find the mole."

"First, I'm impressed you know that reference. Second, who's the mole?"

"He's one of the computer nerds that does data analysis. Mark pulled his phone logs, and his whole call history with Grasso was practically lit up in neon. The freaking amateur used his company cell. Unbelievable. We spoofed Grasso's number, set up a fake meeting, and got him."

"What's going to happen to him?"

"Carolyn's plan is to interrogate him to see how much information he sold. She has inroads with the FBI, and I imagine they'll level cybercrime charges against him. That's all above me."

"But aren't you afraid if Grasso knows who you are and where you live, then so do the people he works for?"

"No. He'd look like a fool if his bosses found out he hired an undercover op. Not a solid bullet point for the résumé. It would make him an even bigger target for them than I am."

Buddy padded back into the room and settled on his stomach by Olivia's feet.

"Are you still staying at the monastery?"

"Yes, but it's getting old. Time isn't on our side with the carnival pulling out of town in a few days. If something is going down with the eggs, it's likely to happen soon. I should be closer to the action."

"I could've used your help tonight."

"What happened?"

"Before I go into it, you can stay here as long as you need to."

"Thanks, but I think the temptation to go back to my house would be too great."

"What about Soph's place?" Olivia asked. "She's close by and already offered the open invite. You could stay there tonight."

"That would work."

Olivia shifted to one side and pulled her phone out of her pocket. "I'll text her and let her know to expect you." She tapped out the message, pressed send, and set the cell on the bed.

"Thanks," Sam said. "I don't have too much at the monastery, just a toothbrush and some clothing. I'll ask Mark to go pick up the stuff and bring it to me later. Now tell me what happened."

Olivia related the course of her day, including her meeting with Father Silva, the exchange at Spring Hills, and Derek's revelation. After she'd finished, Sam remained quiet for a bit, as if piecing together the details in her head.

"Dang, you've been a busy bee," she said. "I don't know about the priest being involved. That just doesn't feel right, but I'll take it to Carolyn. This guy, Stash, seems to be the best lead. That was gutsy of you to follow him. It's unlikely that he was transporting the eggs in boxes, but it could well have been some other illegal goods. I need to find my way into that bunkroom. This all points to a new head of operations, maybe one on another branch of the family tree."

"You mean Nicky." Olivia watched Buddy for a moment as he closed his eyes, drifting off to sleep. "There's someone else—a worker by the name of Lone Wolf."

Sam crossed her arms and smirked. "*Lone Wolf*? Are you kidding me? It's like a reality show there."

Olivia's cell buzzed, and she tapped the screen, reading a message from Sophia.

"Soph is ready for you," she said as she texted back a word of thanks. "I'll take you over there when you're ready."

"No need. Mark dropped me off, and he's already expecting to come pick me up."

"Okay. Back to Lone Wolf. His real name is Ryan Heller, and he has local ties. I overheard him and Father Silva having a heated discussion about a meeting they'd set up with someone. Who that individual was, they didn't say. But Ryan is planning to skedaddle out of town before they jump to the next show."

"Why?"

"I don't know, but it could have something to do with Bobby's murder."

"Which could relate to the eggs," Sam said.

"Maybe."

Sam stood up, removed her cell from her jacket pocket, and sent a text. "Mark will be on his way. Do you think this reporter would speak more with you?"

Olivia rose and grabbed her phone. "Definitely, but not in front of the other workers. I would have to get him alone."

"I'd like to know what else he's learned about the buyers. Maybe we can close the net, coming in from different directions." Her cell screen lit up, and she checked the text. "Mark is five minutes out."

They left the room and went downstairs, leaving Willow and Buddy to their dreams. Sam stood by the bay window, parting the curtains to view the driveway, while Olivia sat on the sofa.

"Liv, I know you got wrangled into being a part of all this, and if you want out, it's okay. You've done more than enough. I know this has put you in a tricky situation with Preston."

"What would make you think that?" she said dryly. "No, it's fine. I want to help. My cover is intact, and Derek wants to speak further with me. I'm just not sure of how much you're comfortable with me telling him."

Sam gave her a sly grin. "I'm sure you'll figure out how to give the impression that you're sharing information without actually saying anything."

"Wonderful," she deadpanned. "I appreciate the vote of confidence in my razzle-dazzle skills."

Sam let the curtains close. "He's here."

Olivia stood, and after they exchanged goodbyes, she

shut and locked the door. Her stomach's rumble reminded her that she had unfinished business in the kitchen. Heading through the living room, she took out her phone, knowing she still owed Preston a call. She sent a text instead. She assured him that all the doors were secured and added that she'd talk to him tomorrow. Punctuating the message with a red heart, she hit send. Then she leaned against the counter, ate the rest of the palmier, and polished off the flat soda. As she binned the empty can, she received his reply, which wished her a good night and echoed her sentiments.

Though it was close to midnight, she hardly felt sleepy at all. Surely the caffeine and sugar didn't help, but her racing thoughts likely would've kept her awake anyway. Needing to quiet her mind, she picked out a book from the selection she'd bought for herself and went into the living room. Curling up on the sofa, she flipped to page one, wondering whether the facts that would come to light tomorrow would be stranger than the fiction she was about to read.

CHAPTER 30

Olivia woke up on Thursday morning to a tickle from Willow's whiskers under her nose. Last night, she'd fallen asleep on the sofa while reading, waking once at around three. Too tired to drag herself upstairs, she'd decided the couch would do for the remaining pre-dawn hours. Now Willow sat near her pillow, meowing at her to begin their daily routine. She obliged with several minutes of petting until Willow leapt down from the sofa and sauntered into the kitchen. After getting up, Olivia grabbed her cell off the coffee table and followed her in.

She flipped on the lights and opened the blinds to reveal clear skies and a thermometer reading sixty degrees. Buddy padded into the kitchen with barely a jangle from his tags and stood by the door with his tail at ease. After letting him out, she set her cell on the counter, slipped on a pair of shoes from the boot tray, and went to the pantry to grab a plastic bag in case she needed to clean up after him.

Stepping out onto the back porch, she spotted him by the tree line. He sniffed around for just the right spot, then lifted his leg by an old oak stump. Relieved that her present doggie duties were limited to opening and closing the door, her thoughts drifted to the day's agenda.

She planned to speak with Derek again, figuring out on the fly how to get more information from him than she was willing to give. She agreed with Sam that Father Silva seemed an unlikely suspect in Bobby's murder or in the trafficking ring. His connections to the Kleins, Tiffany, and Stash had logical explanations. What she had trouble parsing was the heated conversation between him and Lone Wolf. They seemed to know each other well, yet Father Silva had pretended not to recognize his name. The same question Sam posed last night bothered her as well. Why was Lone Wolf so eager to bolt by the end of the weekend when the carnival left town?

After Buddy finished, he lolloped around the yard for a minute before bounding back to the porch, now fully awake and likely hungry. She ushered him in and closed the door. He immediately went to his bowl, digging into his dry kibble as if he hadn't eaten for days. She kicked off her shoes before returning the unused plastic bag to the pantry.

Leaning against the counter, she picked up her cell and opened a browser as Willow curled through her legs. Knowing exactly what the cat wanted, she didn't even blink. "No. It's not snack time. No treats for getting me up early. We have a deal. No waking me before six thirty. You're in breach of contract."

Willow protested with a plaintive meow as Olivia typed the name Ryan Heller into a search box. She pointed over to Willow's bowl, which was still half full of dry food from last night. "Go eat your yum-yum over there." Then she added Virginia to the query and pressed enter.

Undeterred, Willow raised her voice, melting Olivia's defenses. She set the phone on the counter and leaned over for a moment as Willow headbutted her hand. "Of course you get a treat. You're too cute, and you know it."

Reaching to her side, she opened the refrigerator and grabbed one of Willow's treats from the middle shelf. After closing the door, she tore off the top of the plastic packet, went down on one knee, and squeezed out the puree as Willow devoured it. When the cat had licked up the last thick drop, Olivia stood up and binned the empty packet. Satisfied, Willow started grooming herself while Olivia viewed the results of her search.

She never would've guessed there'd be so many Ryan Hellers in the state. Narrowing her query, she added the name of A.J.'s high school to the search and tried again. Scrolling down the first page of results, she saw a promising snippet. Tapping the link took her to a social media page where someone had tagged him in a post's caption. Now knowing his username, she opened the platform's app on her phone and searched for the handle.

The account's profile picture was a fair match, though Ryan now looked very different from the posed headshot of him standing in front of a tree. He had a robust following of nearly a thousand, but he hadn't posted in over a year. Most of his photos were of food or him with friends. The only picture that caught her eye was one of him in a crowd outside an office building. There were no captions or hashtags to provide context, but a few people holding signs suggested that the gathering was a protest. She enlarged the photo, deciphering the slogan on one of the signs: "Dams Plus Mines Equals Environmental Crimes."

Not knowing much about Ryan's family business, she searched for Heller Future Solutions in a new tab. On the home page, she learned that the company was a mining cooperation with holdings in the U.S., India, Australia, Canada, Brazil, and Peru.

She crossed the company name with the term "protests," and the first page of results all referenced an accident that occurred two years ago. Opening a link, she read about a failed tailings dam in Brazil that had flooded an entire community downstream from the mining site. The controversial earthen dam was used to store waste from the mine's operation. Local authorities had repeatedly complained to Heller Future Solutions about the water level in the dam, citing the risk to the homes in the lowland below if it collapsed.

Returning to Ryan's social media page, she studied the picture of him in the crowd. With no signage on the building or other locational clues, she couldn't determine if the gathering was in the U.S., Brazil, or Timbuktu. The only vague clue that the protest was related to the accident was that a few people in the crowd were prominently wearing Brazil's national colors. Whether this meant something or nothing, she could only speculate. Furthermore, she didn't even know where to begin connecting this to Bobby's murder.

Once Buddy had finished gobbling his morning meal, he padded toward the living room, pausing for a moment to watch Willow grooming herself. Feeling peckish and in need of caffeine, Olivia decided it was time for her to start the day properly as well. She set her phone on the counter, went upstairs, and took a shower. Afterward, she changed into jeans, a black tee, and a zip-up hoodie.

Upon returning to the kitchen, she greeted her father, who was sitting at the table and reading the newspaper. While eating breakfast, she related the highlights of what had happened yesterday. She downplayed the drama of following Stash to Spring Hills to avoid upsetting him needlessly. Once more, he proposed going with her to play the role of the carefree retiree who asked nosy questions. Again, she shot the plan down, then changed the subject and gave him the baking book she'd bought him. That did the trick. He was so enamored with the recipes that he wanted to make the red velvet cake on the cover today.

After they'd finished talking and he gave her his usual speech on being careful, he started preparing the two layers for the cake. While he took over the kitchen, she addressed some household chores that needed attention. She washed a load of clothes, vacuumed, and cleaned the bathrooms. Then, after eating lunch and playing with Buddy and Willow, she left the house for Fields Farm.

At three o'clock, the carnival's attendance was light, judging by the sparse smattering of cars in the parking lot. Angling between two orange cones, she turned into the entrance and drove onto the rutted field. Space along the front row was hers for the taking, but on spotting the white van parked where she'd seen it before, she veered toward it. A four-wheel hauler that looked like an adult version of a child's red wagon sat behind its opened rear-panel doors.

Curious, she parked close by. After getting out and locking up, she walked the short distance to the van. The rugged cart held six large white cardboard boxes and two brown paper shopping bags. As she neared the van, Father Silva came around the passenger side before she could get a good look into the cargo bay.

"Hi," she said with a dialed-up smile, masking her surprise. "You've returned."

He matched her warmth as he closed the doors. "You as well. Is it business or pleasure for you today?"

"Mostly business, but it's a carnival after all. You got to have some fun."

"I agree."

Gesturing at the boxes, she asked, "What about you? This looks very official and very much like work, especially since I sense you'll be hauling your load across this bumpy lot."

He nodded as his grin grew. "Your intuition is correct."

He lifted the lid off a box, revealing that it was full of clear, gallon-sized bags stuffed with items. Grasping one, he unzipped the top, showing her the contents.

"Every year when the carnival comes around, the women's group at the church puts together these care packages for the workers. These have some basic toiletries. Toothpaste, toothbrush, hand sanitizer, band aids, sunscreen, a hairbrush. Some other odds and ends too. Whatever we can squeeze in." He laid the bag down, then selected another. "These are snack bags with cereal bars, gummies, gum, mints, and powdered drink mixes. It's not much, but we hope it brings a little kindness to a tough life on the road."

She glanced down at the wagon, then at the van's Florida license plate. "I'm sure it does. That's very generous of your church community."

"The Kleins have been good friends to St. Anthony's for a long time, so we're glad to give back."

"I've seen your van parked here over the last couple of days. I didn't realize it was yours."

"It's not. One of the crew members came and picked me up so that I could deliver the care packages."

"That makes sense." Her eyes drifted again to the specialty license plate. On the left side was a marlin, followed by a string of characters, AS1KA. She tried to memorize its number, repeating it several times in her head using the phonetic alphabet. *Alpha, Sierra, One, Kilo, Alpha.*

"I hope you don't have to hitchhike home," she joked, repeating the license to herself to test her memory. *Alpha, Sierra, One, Kilo, Alpha.*

"Thank the good Lord, no. Nicky is giving me a ride back after I deliver the packages to the crew. It's not too busy now, so I can wheel this around without being a nuisance."

"Then let me not keep you any longer. It was nice to see you again."

With an exchange of goodbyes, she turned and headed for the midway. When she passed her car, she pulled out her phone and recorded the license plate number in a notes app. Uncertain if the registration would yield useful information, she was nonetheless curious about who owned the van. Finding that out would probably require her to tell Preston that she'd followed Stash to Spring Hills. However, she'd need to do that at some point anyway.

As she made her way to the carnival grounds, her pace quickened when she saw Preston's truck and a patrol car parked just outside the entrance. Nearing the ticket booth, she spotted Tiffany sitting behind the counter. She was about to say hi when Preston and

Jayden strode past nearby, leading Slammer toward the cruiser.

Preston didn't notice her until after he'd secured Slammer in the vehicle. They caught each other's eyes, silently acknowledging that this wasn't the time to talk.

"Early bird admission is five dollars," Tiffany said. "That doesn't include rides or games."

Olivia nodded, pulling her zip wallet out of her back pocket. "That's a deal. How are you doing today?"

Tiffany swatted at a fly that landed on the counter next to her soda. "Tired. But what else is new?"

Olivia handed her the cash, then glanced over her shoulder at the two vehicles slowly driving back toward the lot.

Tiffany ripped a ticket in half and slid the stub toward her. "You can buy tokens for rides and games inside. There's an ATM by the tarot tent."

"Thanks. Do you know what happened to Slammer?"

Leaning on the counter, Tiffany blew a perfect pink bubble that she rounded to the size of a ping-pong ball. After she'd popped it and reformed the wad in her mouth, she spoke in a hushed tone. "Word came up from the camp. Aunt Bea texted me about it. Art told her, who heard it from Steady Eddie. He was down there when it all happened. The police pulled Slammer away from Blackbeard's Revenge and took him down to the bunkhouses. Eddie said they searched his room, and the next thing, Slammer was in handcuffs, screaming something about not knowing how the credit card got there. Then he went off about how he didn't kill Bobby."

"They found Bobby's credit card in Slammer's bunkroom?"

Tiffany nodded and blew a petite bubble, popping it like a thunderclap. "I mean, I'm no CSI specialist, but putting two and two together, my theory is that the police think Slammer killed Bobby."

CHAPTER 31

The midway seemed quiet as a coffin compared to last night. None of the thrill rides were running and the Ferris wheel sat idle, while most of the crew looked as if they were watching paint dry. Here and there, a few visitors strolled around the grounds. Mothers with young children or older folks were taking in the sights, stopping by the game stands without playing, no matter how loud the jointees barked. A small group of teens huddling around the snow cone stand hinted that business would soon pick up, as schools were about to dismiss for the day.

Olivia veered toward the games, aiming for Derek's stand near the tarot tent. With no one in line, she'd be willing to stop in if she believed the resident soothsayer, Madame Morgana, could tell her the location of the missing parrot eggs.

While no CSI specialist herself, she conceded

Tiffany's theory had merit. A credit card wasn't a murder weapon, but it raised a lot of questions. By Preston's account, someone had stolen Bobby's wallet and phone, possibly to stage the crime as a robbery. But why would Slammer have kept a credit card if he had a cut in the sale of half a million dollars' worth of eggs? She wondered if the police had found Bobby's other belongings in Slammer's bunkroom as well.

She spotted Derek sitting on a stool at his counter, looking bored as a sloth, in need of customers to charm. Maybe the lack of traffic would play in her favor, and she'd catch him willing to talk openly without the threat of being discovered by his co-workers. With her focus fixed, she passed Madame Morgana's tarot tent, but stopped dead in her tracks when a familiar voice called out from behind her.

"Olivia Penn. What a pleasant surprise."

It took a minute to register, but when the recognition sparked, she turned and faced a man she'd had no desire to see again. She'd crossed paths with Private Investigator John Mack in December when both were involved in a matter regarding Bev's late husband. Back then, Olivia didn't trust him one bit, but she'd since mellowed her stance. He'd been working a case, but his methods and self-interests struck a nerve with her. Now she stared him down, not wanting to make assumptions, but her intuition screamed he wasn't here to enjoy the carnival atmosphere.

He'd dressed to blend in, as a PI would do, wearing a

sea-blue camp shirt, faded jeans, and mirrored aviator sunglasses. She wouldn't have recognized him had he not called out to her, as he was adept at appearing like an everyman.

"Mack," she said, using his preferred moniker. "You're a long way from Winchester."

He tore off a tiny piece of a giant pretzel he was holding in a napkin, then popped it into his mouth. He chewed it a few times but spoke before swallowing. "I love carnivals. The rides, the games, the food. Okay, mostly the food. Did you catch the show? The police led away a carny in cuffs. I *wonder* what he did."

His over-the-top feigned interest reeked of a hidden agenda. She played along, shrugging her shoulders, and swatted at a non-existent gnat around her head. "I wonder too. Enjoy the pretzel."

He took a quick step forward before she could get on her way. "Did you know the police found the son of the owner of Klein Amusements dead at Spring Hills on Sunday night?"

She choked back a host of clever comebacks, choosing instead a vanilla reply. "I saw it on the news."

Again, he baited her, hamming it up with a shocked face that begged for a best actor trophy. "Oh. That's not why you're here?"

She wanted to fire back for him to cut the schtick and say his peace, or leave her be. But a mother was heading their way, holding her young son's hand, so she kept quiet.

The tiny tyke, wearing denim overalls, swayed from side to side, turning a short walk into a marathon. Under his arm, he clutched a stuffed tiger that was half as big as him. Mack waved to the little boy, and Olivia politely smiled at his mother as they slowly strolled toward the exit.

When they were out of earshot, she replied, "I'm here to enjoy the carnival."

He nodded, letting his smile flatline. "I guess you didn't get enough of it last night."

That hit her like a wave from behind. Never in a million years would she have been on the lookout for Mack yesterday. She hadn't even thought about him since Christmas. Now, with the playful jockeying over, she could get down to business, figuring out why he was here and what he wanted from her.

"I'm here to take in the scene," she said. "Why are you here?"

Sighing, he playacted a dramatic frown. He looked at the rest of his pretzel, then tossed it into a nearby bin. "Getting that seemed like a good idea, but it's a bit carb heavy after two tacos." He wiped his hands on his shirt like a caveman and pushed his aviators up off the tip of his nose. "Okay. It seems you don't trust me, and I understand that. I would be wary of me, too, if I were in your shoes."

"Where have I heard that before?" she blurted, recalling a roadside conversation they'd had on a chilly December afternoon.

"The past is the past. As a show of good will, I'll go first. I'm looking for someone."

She winced, slowly shaking her head. "I don't think anyone here is quite your type."

His laugh flew out, unstoppable as a sneeze. "Now that's funny. But I prefer not to mix business with pleasure, unless you're available." Reading her stone-cold face, he left the banter aside and turned serious. "I'm looking for a guy by the name of Ryan Heller."

She shrugged, hoping her eyes didn't belie her surprise. "And?"

"I believe that he's employed by Klein Amusements, but the thing is, nobody seems to have a real name around here."

"That I agree with you on. But I'm confused. Why are you asking *me* about him? You're the PI."

He inched closer, lowering his voice. "And you're an advice columnist who has been here since Tuesday talking to all the carnies. Supposedly, you're writing a story for your charming *Apple Station Journal*, according to the sweet girl manning the ticket booth. Are you looking for Ryan too?"

No, because I've found him.

Now she understood how Tiffany could have been involved with Bobby— she was way too trusting of men. Olivia had to admit that Mack was good at what he did. He could charm information out of almost anyone, and he knew that she also had a hidden agenda.

"It's *The Apple Station Times*," she said.

Placing a hand over his heart, he apologized. "Mea culpa."

"I'm not looking for Ryan ... what's his name?"

"Heller. Will you look at a picture?" As she nodded, he removed his phone from his back pocket, swiped the screen, and turned it toward her. "Have you seen him around here?"

The photo was the same headshot from his social media page, only with more of the background included. She couldn't fault Mack for not recognizing him as Lone Wolf. If it hadn't been for A.J.'s help and description, she wouldn't have either.

"What makes you think that I've seen him?" she asked.

"Because you've been talking to the carnies." He put his phone back in his pocket. "And I suspect it's not for the reasons you've stated. I don't care why you're here unless it involves Mr. Heller."

Her curiosity was beyond piqued. Why was he looking for Ryan? And how did it relate to Bobby's murder or the missing eggs? From her past with Mack, she knew he had clients with deep pockets and question-able reputations. But he also had contacts that the police didn't, as well as a knack for digging up details. She glanced around, stalling for a moment, as she weighed the cost-benefit analysis of sharing information with him.

"Why are you looking for Ryan?" she asked.

"Sorry. Client–PI privilege."

"Okay. I'll keep an eye out. Now, can I show you a picture?"

That sparked a smile from him that spread from ear to ear. "A trade of intel? Cooperation? This is intriguing. Let's see what you got."

She took out her phone, opened the photos of Grasso, and showed them to him.

Without asking, he grabbed the cell out of her hand and studied the pictures, contorting his face in obvious displeasure at what he had to work with. He tried to enhance the images using the phone's built-in editing tools, but after a minute he gave up, handing it back to her.

"If you ever want to learn how to shoot surveillance photos, I'd be willing to teach you what I know," he said. "No charge."

"Yes, I'm aware they're not the best pictures."

"I don't recognize him."

Though he'd just answered, she asked again, looking for any inconsistencies in his facial expression or tone. "You haven't seen him around here?"

"No."

She double-checked her gut on whether to trust him. "His name is Tommy Grasso, and he has some shady associates."

Mack cut her off before she could state her intention. "And you want me to find out anything I can about him? Though I know you're not implying that I have inroads to such people."

"Exactly."

"Deal." He put a hand on his stomach, grimacing as he stifled a burp. "I shouldn't have had that funnel cake. I'm feeling it now. Send me those pictures."

After they exchanged numbers and Olivia texted him the photos, they said a cordial goodbye and went their separate ways. The carousel came to life, and the Ferris wheel lights flashed as the cars spun around. Frightful screams accompanied the whoosh of the pirate ship traveling through its stomach-dropping arc. She didn't need to be on any of the thrill rides to feel disoriented. As if things weren't strange enough, now someone was going to great lengths to find Ryan Heller, and she'd placed her trust in John Mack.

CHAPTER 32

Derek's face lit up with a showman's smile as Olivia neared his game stand. He popped off his wobbly stool, swept his hat off his head, and bowed as she approached the counter.

"Howdy, ma'am. Would you do a lonely cowboy a kind favor and visit my humble home? Toss a dart and steal my heart. Your first three throws are on me."

She couldn't help but smile at the line he likely spun a hundred times a night. "I'll play your game, Butch Cassidy."

He jammed the hat back on his head and rubbed his hands together in victory. Then he turned, rummaged through a bucket, and spun back with a pink-tailed dart in his open palm.

"I want a blue one."

He closed his hand, pivoted, and switched up the

darts. Facing her again, he extended his arm and presented her with the dart as if it were a Cartier watch.

"Thank you," she said, grasping it off his fingertips.

He leaned with his backside against the counter and crossed his arms, looking at the board of under-inflated balloons. "Now take your time and aim higher than you think you need."

She adjusted her feet, slightly angling them, and raised the dart to shoulder level.

He lowered his voice but kept his slight southern drawl. "Why were you trying to get into Stash's bunkroom last night?"

Narrowing her eyes, she focused on a pink balloon directly in front of her. "Who has access to the white van?" She flung the dart, hitting her target, but it bounced off and fell to the ground. Shaking her head, she held her hands up in mock protest. "What the? Did you purposely give me the dullest dart?"

He stepped forward, retrieved the dart, and handed it back to her. "That was an excellent try, ma'am. You almost had it. Just arch it a little more."

She snatched the dart from him and examined its tip.

"I don't know who all has access to it," he said. "I've only ever seen Steady Eddie, Slammer, Sparky, and Stash drive it. Sparky uses it to pick up parts for repairs, and Eddie drives it when we jump locations. Stash takes it out the most, running Bobby's errands. Why do you ask?"

"Last night, Stash drove it to Spring Hills where he

picked up a bunch of boxes from someone he met there. A strange coincidence—meeting somebody where Bobby was murdered."

"You know how I feel about coincidences. Let me guess. You saw him stash—pardon the pun—the boxes in his bunkroom. That's why you wanted to look inside."

She adjusted her feet and stance. "Bingo."

He rubbed his chin, speaking with a volume that must've carried all the way to the food trailers. "This time I'm sure as socks and shoes that you'll pop a balloon and win yourself a prize." Then he lowered his voice, barely moving his mouth. "Are you thinking he was transporting the macaw eggs?"

"No."

"Then what?"

She raised the dart, focusing on a blue balloon slightly below her shoulder level. "I don't know."

"The police arrested Slammer shortly before you showed up," he said. "Word came up from the camp that they found Bobby's credit card in his room."

She rehearsed her arm motion a few times. "I heard, but something seems off about a missing credit card just suddenly appearing now."

"I didn't think about it before, but if he's a suspect in Bobby's murder, it makes sense now. He was always running his mouth about getting the money Bobby owed him, but I thought he was all bark. I know he's an intimidating dude, but I've never seen him get violent."

She lowered the dart, inspecting the tail. "What are you going on about?"

"Slammer left the camp in the van Sunday night around nine. When we pulled in, he unloaded some gear from it, then drove away. I assumed he was taking it to the front lot. Since our stop in Asheville, he's been really fired up, more so than usual. During slough last week, he said he was going to have it out with Bobby when we jumped to come here. I didn't take him seriously."

She resumed her ready-to-throw posture. "When did he return?"

"I don't know."

With a quick flick, she zinged the dart into the back-board, just off to the side of the balloon she was aiming for. "Son of a gun."

He launched forward, yanked the dart out, and gave her a loud carny cheer. "The third time will be as charming as you."

Grabbing the dart from him, she rethought her technique. "What can you tell me about the buyers?"

Demonstrating the proper throwing motion as a show, he continued in a hushed voice. "There's not enough time to give you the dossier, though it's riddled with holes. They operate along the East Coast, and thus far have remained anonymous. Animal trafficking can be even more profitable than gun and drug smuggling. Enforcement is scant, and those who get caught often receive only fines. They pay them, then continue with their operations. Social media has glorified owning exotic animals as pets. It has become a marketplace that authorities can't effectively monitor."

She looked around the board for a new target. "Do you have any names?"

"Not from the buyer's side. We only knew Bobby was a supplier because of the informant that approached us. That's when we switched tactics, and instead of pursuing the buyer angle, we tried to identify the players through the supply chain."

None of this was particularly helpful to her or Sam, but knowing that Slammer had taken the van out on Sunday night might be the missing link.

Adjusting her feet, she locked in on a yellow balloon that appeared properly inflated. "What do you know about Lone Wolf?"

He lifted his hat and scratched his head while glancing over his shoulder toward the midway. "Very little. He keeps to himself, but he seems like a decent guy. I've never seen him have problems with anyone."

She raised her arm, using a pencil grip to hold the barrel. "His real name is Ryan Heller, as in Heller Future Solutions—the international mining company. He's the son of the owner."

Derek covered his mouth with his hand, muting a string of colorful language. "What is he doing working for the carnival?"

Lining up her throw, she aimed, closing her left eye. "That's a good question. Do he and Tiffany have something going on?"

"I'm not sure. Of all the people here, I've seen him talking to her more than anyone else. He's always struck me as an okay, introverted guy."

"It's the quiet ones you have to worry about. I saw him and Father Silva arguing about a meeting Ryan had backed out of. He's planning on leaving the carnival this weekend."

"This is news to me. I work around him every day, and I didn't know any of this. Maybe you should head out on the road with me. We can team up undercover."

"Hard pass."

He pointed to the board as if he were giving her instructions. "Do you think the meeting involved another transaction?"

Voices approaching prompted her to glance to her side as a group of teens walked toward them.

"Uh-oh," Derek said. "Nicky is coming up hot on your six."

"I don't think it was about a deal." She looked back at her target and zipped the dart, popping the balloon.

He clapped his hands, then did a happy dance that reminded her of an inflatable Gumby tossed about by the wind. He stepped over to the side where the stuffed animal prizes lined the board. Plucking a blue bunny down, he offered it to her.

She held up a hand, waving him off. "No, thank you. Give it to the next kid who doesn't win."

He beamed a Texas-wide grin, executing a dramatic

stage bow while almost shouting, "You are as generous as you are purdy, ma'am."

She subtly shook her head, adding a playful eye roll at his showmanship. Then she turned and headed away from the teens and out of Nicky's direct path.

"Ladies and gentlemen," he exclaimed. "Gather around and stay a while to keep this lonely carny company. Your first three throws are on me."

"Hey," Nicky called out.

Unsure who that was meant for, Olivia looked at Nicky, who had changed course to intercept her.

Olivia dialed up a polite smile. "Hi. How's it going?"

Nicky was all business, marching toward her with a taut, flushed face. She clutched a walkie-talkie in one fist and a stack of papers rolled up like a tube in the other. "Pretty flipping disastrous." She stopped shy of Olivia and wiped her brow with the back of her hand.

"I'm sorry. I heard the police arrested Slammer. That's got to be awful, to think an employee may have been involved in Bobby's death."

The walkie-talkie beeped, and a voice called out to Sparky to come and cover the ground cables by the base of Blackbeard's Revenge. Nicky waited, listening until Sparky acknowledged the request and provided an ETA, as he was currently fixing an outlet issue in the taco trailer.

"Everything is friggin' falling apart," Nicky said. "Everyone's on edge. Now the police are going to be asking more questions, combing the camp. We're not harboring anyone, but everyone has a past. I've had several employees already threaten to quit. Look, it's nothing personal, but I'm receiving complaints about you being here. We're a tight-knit family, and people are getting nervous. If you don't mind, I would like for you to let my workers do their jobs unbothered."

Olivia nodded. Though phrased as an ask, her authoritative tone was anything but. "Of course. I completely understand. I appreciate the access you've given me."

Nicky loosened her choke hold on the rolled papers, allowing the tube some room to breathe. "Thank you. I have to keep the crew together. I may be without two of my best when we jump to Maryland. I just can't replace men like Slammer and Stash with walkups. They can be a pain in my side, but they have job experience that makes them worth twice as much as a rookie."

Make that three with Lone Wolf leaving. Perhaps four if Tiffany goes too.

"Thanks again," Olivia said. "If I come back, it'll only be to enjoy the show. I'm sorry this has been such a tragic week for you. If Slammer was involved in Bobby's death, maybe you'll soon see justice, and it can be the first step toward healing for your family. The police must've had solid evidence to conduct a search."

Nicky clipped her walkie-talkie to the waistband of her khaki shorts, then glanced around the midway. After folding her rolled papers in half and stuffing them into her back pocket, she let out an exasperated sigh. "I don't know if I did the right thing. The word will get out, and when it does, I'm certain I'll lose some people."

"What do you mean?"

"This morning, I found an anonymous note on the windshield of my RV. It said Slammer had something belonging to Bobby in his bunkroom." She tightened her lips for a moment. "I'm the one who called the police on him. I may have just lost the trust of my crew."

CHAPTER 33

At a quarter to five, fluffy cotton ball clouds dallied in the sky, setting the scene for a spectacular sunset in a few hours. Under the circumstances, Olivia thought it best to leave the grounds. Though Nicky's ask was a reasonable request, she took it more as a directive, one tone shy of an order. The parking lot had filled out nicely for a school night. A few visitors entered the marketplace barn as others carrying shopping bags and coffee cups exited. She'd be tempted to stop in and grab a Fields' specialty apple pie, but with a red velvet cake and palmiers at home, they had enough sweets in the house.

Needing to regroup and have a think, she settled onto the bench of an oak picnic table near the barn's entrance. Time was short, and with Nicky nixing her access to the employees, that left only Derek as a potential informant. With the carnival leaving town in a few days, and the crew skittish about police scrutiny, coming by inside information would be challenging. She glanced over her shoulder as a family of four was heading for the midway. Two tween brothers ribbed each other about who would win the biggest prize. Their parents strolled behind them, amused by their playful, competitive bantering.

The Kleins' white van hadn't moved, which likely meant that Father Silva must still be on the grounds. She took out her phone, opened her notes app, and looked at the license plate number, wondering whose name was on the van's registration. If Bobby wasn't the owner, she was curious who'd trust a company asset to Slammer and Stash, whether it be for legitimate or criminal activities.

Sam's team could access sensitive information, but she doubted that included vehicle registration. A farm-hand drove a utility ATV around the far side of the barn and slowly maneuvered along the orange fencing bordering the cornfield. He beeped the high-pitched horn to alert several people heading in the same direction that he was coming up behind them. A young couple with their arms intertwined stepped out of the barn, laughing and enjoying each other's company. She'd so much rather be doing likewise with Preston than mulling over calling him about a license plate number.

The worst he could say is no. And stay out of police business. And that I'm interfering with the investigation. But I'm not. He knows what I've been doing, and why I've been doing it. Except for last night.

Opening her recent call log, she tapped his name and waited three rings until he answered.

"Hi, Liv. I was just thinking about you."

"Oh yeah? Do tell."

"I'd rather not say here," he replied under his breath.

She smiled, imagining him looking around the station and pretending that he was discussing police business. "You'll have to share later."

"That can be arranged."

Tempted to goad him into being more specific, she shook off the flirtatious banter, as that wasn't the reason for the call. "Question for you. Say I have a license plate number for a vehicle, and I want to know who it's registered to because it could be pertinent to a murder investigation. I'm aware it would break all kinds of regulations for you to tell me who the owner is. But theoretically, would the police be interested in knowing who owns a vehicle someone may have used in the commission of a crime?"

After a healthy stretch of silence, he spoke, sounding muted. "Jayden, I'll just be outside for a minute. If the magistrate calls about the warrant, please come get me immediately."

That he felt compelled to leave the building wasn't a good sign, but she was armed and ready to remind him that his boss had sanctioned her involvement.

"Are you still there?" he asked.

"I am. I take it you're outside."

"Yeah. Theoretically, it sounds like you're asking me to run a plate."

"Is the warrant for Slammer's bunkroom? But you already looked through it. How did you do that?"

"He gave us permission."

"That's odd if he knew Bobby's credit card was there. Why would he do that? That doesn't sound right."

"Thank you, detective," he said dryly. "We're trying to get a warrant to search all the quarters."

"That must mean you didn't find Bobby's wallet or phone. If you conduct a witch hunt, some of the crew will cut and run."

"I doubt we'll get the warrant. It's a stretch to argue probable cause, but the magistrate is a friend of Payne's, so that may help."

Though Slammer seemed inclined to react before thinking, he must have realized the police would find the credit card in their search. Now she wondered whether he had been alone when he left the camp on Sunday night. Could he have been with someone who set him up by planting evidence?

"If I asked you to run a plate, would you?" she said.

"I would need to know more."

That's promising. "Okay, hear me out—"

"That's not a good start, but go ahead."

"Last night, I followed Stash, who drove a van—"

"You did what?"

She took a deep breath, giving her the steam to say

all she intended, even if he interrupted her again. "Drove a van to Spring Hills, where I saw him pick up a bunch of boxes, which he then brought back to the farm and stashed in his bunkroom." Expecting his heavy sigh and silence, she continued before he could speak. "I'm sorry I didn't call you, but there was no time. If I hadn't followed him, we'd be none the wiser. He knew about the isolation of the location, and he could've been brokering another deal. There's something else. On Sunday night, Slammer left the camp in the same vehicle—destination unknown. I also learned that Stash is planning to make himself a former employee by the end of the weekend."

"Did you even consider your safety? What would've happened if they saw you? What if they were armed? You can't just go around following people and expect nothing bad is going to happen."

Mack does it all the time. "Did you hear what I said?"

"Yes," he replied sharply. "Did you hear what *I* said?"

She took a moment, resting her forehead in her hand, probably looking as tense as she felt. "Of course, I considered my safety, and they didn't see me. You know I wouldn't put myself in danger intentionally."

His forced laugh wasn't out of amusement. "Well, then, I would like you to tell me what you consider danger."

"I can understand how you may be upset." Glancing at the barn, she saw Kevin coming down the slight slope toward her. "I just thought if the van had been involved in a crime, you would want to find out who owns it. If I need to come in and provide a statement about what I witnessed for you to get a warrant to search Stash's bunkroom, I will."

"You realize by doing so, you could be charged with trespassing on private property?"

"Maybe then use that plan as a last resort. Or preferably no resort." Kevin caught her eye, and she waved a hello as he neared. "Look, I'm still at the farm, and Kevin is coming my way. If you run the plate, will you text me the owner's name? Strictly so I can hand it over to Sam's team, as per Senator Dixon's request for your cooperation."

"I can't believe you're pulling that on me."

"Don't be angry. Are you angry?"

He sighed, acquiescing with a half-hearted grunt. "No, but leave it alone from here."

"I hear you."

"I mean it, Liv."

"I understand. Nicky kicked me off the grounds anyway. I'm all out of angles." *Unless Mack comes through.*

"When has that stopped you before? Text me the plate number. And call me tonight when you get home and have all the doors locked."

After she promised to do both, they exchanged a brief goodbye and ended the call. Kevin had pulled up short during the last bit of the conversation, but now that she'd hung up, he came over to the table.

"I'm sorry," he said. "I hope I didn't interrupt."

"Not at all," she replied as she sent Preston the license plate number. "How are things going this week with your special guests?"

"Okay, so far. I don't mean to sound insensitive. It's terrible about Bobby Klein. I'd spoken with him twice on the phone to walk through the logistics of their setup, but the first time I met him was when they all arrived on Sunday. I didn't really get any feeling about him, good or bad. Preston assured me his death was an isolated incident, and nobody here is in danger."

"That's what I hear too."

"Are you going or coming?"

"Going."

"You're welcome to join us at the farmhouse for dinner. Melissa and Mikey are here. My mom would love to have you."

She slid off the bench and pocketed her phone. "That's kind of you, but I don't want to impose. I should be on my way."

"It's no imposition. Preston was here last week for dinner, and my mom has been asking me to get both of you over here together. This will be a step toward that. She's a wonderful cook."

"And baker. I've had many of your mom's specialties that you sell at your stand during the summer."

"Dessert is included," he added, sweetening the invitation.

"I am kind of hungry, and I know whatever she has made will be one hundred percent better than carnival fare or the bowl of cereal that's waiting for me at home."

"Great, it's settled then. Are you okay walking, or do you want to bring your car around?"

"Walking is good."

They set off, going past the barn, while Kevin told her about the fun Mikey had in playing some of the kiddie games before the midway opened on Wednesday. They continued on the narrow, paved road leading to his parents' house, and within five minutes, he was holding the front door open for her.

She followed him down a hallway to the kitchen, where his parents and Melissa greeted her with smiles and hugs. Mikey was sitting on the floor by the butcher block island, too focused on petting the Fields' basset hound to acknowledge her. The food was already laid out on the rustic wooden table, arranged on platters and in bowls large enough to feed twice as many. After everyone found a spot and sat down, Nancy said grace, then they all filled their plates. Olivia sampled a little of everything: ham, scalloped potatoes, and roasted carrots, while leaving room for the pie she'd spied on the counter by the oven.

Throughout the meal, the topic du jour was the minutiae of Melissa's wedding planning. She and Kevin were getting married behind the farmhouse in front of a sprawling field of wildflowers. The ceremony was scheduled for the late afternoon to catch the golden hour's romantic light. With the sunset serving as the backdrop for their outdoor reception, the celebration promised to be a fairy-tale start to their life together. Olivia sat back, content to listen, feeling far away from the carnival camp. All the preparations sounded charming and sweet, but she'd rather find the parrot eggs than have to think about coordinating colors between a cake and table linens.

While Melissa shared a conversation she'd had with their minister, Olivia's thoughts drifted to what Slammer had said about finding religion in the pen. Though he carried on about the money Bobby owed him, stealing his credit card wasn't the best way to get even. It seemed someone wanted him to take the fall, or at least be a short-term diversion. Perhaps somebody planning to leave town, who needed to buy time for a reason. Stash, Ryan, and Tiffany may leave by the end of the weekend, most likely without providing a forwarding address. Similarly, Grasso would probably be gone once the carnival left on Sunday. Grasso had tried to set up Sam for Bobby's murder. Could he have done the same to Slammer? She thought, too, of what Aunt Bea had said about Father Silva's feelings for Nicky. In the photo in his office, had she not known the context, she would've guessed that they were a couple. He'd alibied her for Sunday, and with the seal of confession on his side, his word couldn't be legally challenged.

"What about you and Preston?" Nancy said.

Olivia looked up from her plate of triple berry pie,

realizing she'd lost track of the conversation. "I'm sorry. What about us?"

"Any marriage plans in your near future?"

She vehemently shook her head, feeling her cell buzz in her pocket. "Oh gosh, no. I mean, not never, but just not now. Or soon."

Nancy winked, cutting a bite from her pie with her fork. "If that not now ever becomes a yes, we'd be happy to host your wedding here."

Olivia's cheeks had warmed at her less-than-artful dodge of the question. Wanting to change the subject, she launched into telling them about the culinary school her father had attended. She always found her father's interest in baking a useful diversion, as others seemed enthralled by him taking up the hobby in his seventies. Almost inevitably, they'd recall memories of their grand-mothers teaching them their favorite recipes.

As the gathering wound down and Olivia got ready to leave, Nancy gave her a notecard with the recipe for the triple berry pie for her father. After thanking her hostess and saying her goodbyes, she left the farmhouse, declining Kevin's kind offer to walk with her back to her car.

The sun was low in the sky, casting the carnival in an idyllic light, but nothing was what it seemed. For the better part of two hours, she'd felt whisked away from the puzzle of Bobby's murder and the macaw eggs. Now energized by a full stomach and with rested eyes, the midway was in her sights, and so too, she believed, was the missing link.

About halfway back to the lot, she remembered the missed text she'd received during dinner. As she dug her phone out of her pocket the screen lit up, showing seven o'clock. When she opened and viewed the message from Preston, she stopped dead in her tracks, reading the name of the van's registered owner.

CHAPTER 34

Olivia leaned back against the driver's door of her vehicle and pocketed her hands in her hoodie, feeling the drop in temperature as the sun neared the horizon. The day's puffy clouds had dissipated, leaving behind wispy trails in a twilight sky brushed by pastels of pink, lavender, and blue. Thrill seekers' delighted screams and thumping music from the romping rides reached all the way to the lot. Two teenage girls wearing neon-green glow necklaces walked by her, carrying on like besties. They were chatting about a cute carnival worker who'd given them his phone number. He'd asked them both to meet up with him and some of his friends late Saturday night. Olivia had a mind to chase after them, like a mother hen, warning them not to even think about going. But after overhearing they had other plans, she figured they were safe from the potential disaster.

She reread Preston's text, curious why Jeffrey Rollins

was the registered owner of a Klein company van. He'd described the Kleins as clients, but now she wondered whether there was something more to his relationship with them. Opening a browser, she was about to search online for him when her cell buzzed with an incoming call.

Checking the caller ID, she hit accept and dispensed with a formal greeting. "Mack, I didn't expect to hear from you so soon."

His voice was low, as if he was barely moving his mouth. "I'm not sure how to take that, but I'll be an optimist and believe that you're happy to do so. I found your guy."

"Grasso?"

"The one and only. I wish I could say it was due to skilled investigation, but truthfully, I just lucked into him. I haven't revisited the inn since Christmas, and because I was so close, I stopped by to have dinner. So here I am having a scrumptious meal, minding my own business, when your mark walks in and joins someone already sitting at a table. They're across the room from me. The guy he's with has his back to me. I can't see his face, but he looks like your average Joe Blow professional type. But I'm almost certain, despite the photo I had to work with, that the other gentleman is Grasso."

She lowered her phone and checked the time on the screen. At a quarter past seven, she wouldn't hit much traffic driving back to town, but even if she left now, Grasso could take off at any minute. But Mack was there, and he could serve as her eyes, if he'd be willing. Not knowing why he was looking for Ryan remained a concern, especially since Ryan was also on her radar. With little time to debate, she went with her gut, going with the tracks on the trail in front of her.

Holding her phone back up and feeling slightly uneasy, she proceeded. "I'm still at the carnival, and it'll take me about twenty-five minutes to get there. Could you keep your eyes on him until I arrive, or if he leaves, do what you do best, and follow him?"

Mack cleared his throat, then lowered his voice even more. "Grasso? Why would I do that?"

"Because he's a known associate of a criminal organization involved in animal trafficking. There's half a million dollars' worth of hyacinth macaw eggs and potentially the lives of thirty parrots at stake. Those parrots should've hatched in the wild in Brazil—not in Virginia. If they survive, they'll be sold illegally as pets."

"Judas priest." He heavily sighed, leaving dead air between them. "I came to your charming locale simply to find a guy. Now you want me to stake out someone involved in organized crime? This isn't my deal."

She opened the car door and climbed into the seat, ready to play her ace. "Ryan Heller is here. He goes by the name Lone Wolf, but he looks much different from the photo you showed me. You probably walked right by him and didn't even realize it."

Another sigh was his reply, this one sounding more exasperated. "I'm impressed and a little peeved. You could've just told me earlier and saved us both a lot of trouble, particularly me. But I admire your deal brokering. Hold on to information until you can leverage it for your benefit. That's exactly what I would've done. Okay. In the spirit of cooperation and team building, I'll help you out. Anyone who hurts or endangers animals is forever on my bad side. I bet you didn't know that I'm a member of the National Zoo."

Why would I? "Good on you. Maybe we've crossed paths there before. The zoo is near to where I used to live."

"In Georgetown. I mean, that's where your condo was, not the zoo, of course."

Given their clash in December, she wasn't surprised he knew some about her past. Knowing the specifics of her former address, though, bordered on creepy.

"To be transparent, I ran a background check on you," he said. "Don't worry, I'm not a stalker. You'll have to trust me on that. I hope that doesn't negatively impact our professional relationship. I like to know who I may be potentially working with in the future, in case I'd have a staff opening."

"Maybe you need more clients if you have the time to check into my background. We don't have *any* type of relationship, and you couldn't afford me."

His laugh flew out quick as a blink. "For now, then, let's keep to the business at hand. You have yourself a set of eyes and a personal PI on speed dial. I'll be in touch."

With that, he ended the call without so much as a smart-aleck goodbye.

She closed the door, connected the phone to its charging cord, and turned the car on into accessory mode. Easing farther back into the seat, she returned to the browser window and entered the terms Jeffrey Rollins, accountant, and Miami into a search box. Tapping the top result took her straight to his website. His picture above the fold confirmed she had the right man. Reading through his bio revealed an impressive career marked by awards and university honors. On a personal note, he had a goal of attending a Major League baseball game in every stadium, and his hobbies included hiking, golfing, and deep-sea fishing.

Next, she turned to his social media, scanning through his posts and photos. Most of his recent written updates were tips on budgets, taxes, and retirement planning. A few were about charity events he'd attended or had a hand in chairing. True to his bio, he'd posted pictures of himself playing golf at scenic courses and posing by trailhead signs. Scrolling through several screens confirmed he was an avid fisher as well. She focused on any shots of him with other people, specifically looking for Bobby or Nicky. While neither was in any of the posts she looked through, one photo of him in a marina caught her eye. On a bright, bluebird day, he stood smiling wide as the sky in front of a boat named *The Cod Father Two.*

She set the phone down on the center console and

stared out the windshield at the marketplace barn. The warm yellow glow from the interior lights illuminated a rectangular patch of ground just outside the wide door. She recalled the photo in Nicky's RV of her and Bobby posing in front of a similar boat—*The Cod Father*. She'd assumed it belonged to the Kleins, but now she wondered whether the same person owned both.

Her cell rattled on the console, and she looked down at the screen, seeing Cassandra's name and number. She accepted the call and turned on the speaker.

"Hey, Cass. What's up?"

"Hiya yourself. Sorry I haven't been in touch today. I've been swamped. You know, I'm an actual reporter who has *real* stories to write. Kidding. I wish I had something juicy to tell you about Father Silva, but I couldn't find a single controversial thing. It's all rainbows and unicorns. Kind of disappointing."

"That makes sense. I don't think there's anything to be found on him. I don't think he's involved in any of this, except maybe in having feelings for Nicky."

"Come again, Penn?"

"Yeah, I know."

"Ooh la la. Are we talking like *The Thorn Birds*?"

"Not quite. He's part of an independent Catholic church, and some denominations allow priests to marry. But that's not important right now. I think I'm onto something."

"Do tell."

"Interesting fact: The Kleins' accountant, Jeffrey

Rollins, owns a company vehicle that travels with the carnival. I looked through his social media, and I came across a photo of him standing on a marina's dock with a boat named *The Cod Father Two* in the background."

"That's cute. What kind of boat is it?"

"It's big—looks like something you'd go deep-sea fishing in, which is one of his hobbies he listed on his website's bio. What's even cuter is that I saw a picture in Nicky's RV of her and Bobby posing near a similar boat named *The Cod Father*."

"Oh, shut the front door. That can't be a coincidence."

She nodded. "Right? Iteration of the same name, so possibly the same owner. I assumed it belonged to the Kleins, but now I'm wondering if one or both belongs to Rollins."

"Okay. So, what if he does own both? He could be uber rich. Maybe they're leased."

Olivia tapped her steering wheel, emphasizing her point. "Perhaps. *The Cod Father Two* has a Florida hull number, and Rollins lives in Miami. I'm not sure if there's any way to verify ownership of the boat. I can't look into it right now. I have something else brewing."

"I'll do it. Give it to me, and let me *fish* around."

"Touché. You don't have to. I know you're already at home."

"Just give me the bleeping number, Penn."

"Hold on." Picking up her cell, she was about to pull

the information from the photo when her screen displayed an incoming call from Mack. "Oh, shoot."

"What's wrong?" Cassandra said.

"I have another call that I need to take. Be right back." She swapped the lines. "Mack, give me a sec. I'm talking to someone else." She switched to Cassandra. "Okay, ready?"

"Pen and paper are in hand."

She enlarged the photo from Rollin's feed and recited the number. After Cassandra repeated it, they exchanged a quick goodbye, and Olivia jumped back to the call with Mack.

"Thanks for waiting," she said.

"Grasso and his friend just left the inn, walked up the street, and got into a dark-colored sedan with heavily tinted windows. I'm almost in my car. I took a picture of them, admittedly not the best, but I'm sending it to you now. I'll be back in touch."

CHAPTER 35

When Olivia saw the image in the text, she took Mack's self-deprecation as one-upmanship of her own spontaneous surveillance shots. In a front-facing photo he'd taken from across the street, she easily identified Grasso and Rollins as they walked away from the inn. Mack, being a pro, knew exactly what to do and where to be for the best angles. While taking her pictures, she'd been on guard, shooing a creepy stranger off her porch, so she cut herself some slack.

While the photo was hardly a smoking gun, the puzzle was taking shape, with Grasso and Rollins fitting together like adjoining pieces. But suspicion about two men having lunch at a tourist hot spot wasn't evidence of wrongdoing. She wanted to remain in play, which meant calling Preston was out of the question. The conversation would begin and end with him telling her to stay away from them. Another deal may be in the works, or they could be meeting with others in their criminal ring. Though she could have it all wrong, she and Mack were the only ones in a position to see where this would lead.

Mack sent a follow-up text, simply stating, "Left town, traveling north."

She set her cell on the center console, muttering that something more specific would've been helpful. After starting the engine, she fastened her seatbelt and headed for the lot's exit, mentally mapping her route. She could take several side roads, working her way east to intersect the main north-south roads out of town. Though it was a more direct course, it could delay her from joining the tail if Grasso's current route was short-lived. Instead, she decided to backtrack through town and follow Mack's trail until she received further guidance.

This might be a wild goose chase, but it was the best lead she had at the moment. She didn't think too far ahead, planning what to do if Grasso drove for hours. If the West Virginia or Maryland border came into play, she'd probably turn around. The fact, though, that he was still hanging around town heavily suggested he had unfinished business in the area.

About half a mile from her turn to head back through town, her phone alerted her to an incoming call. Glancing down and seeing Mack's number, she hit accept and switched to the speaker.

"Where are you?" she asked.

"Good question. I tailed them north to Morrow

Lane, and would you like to take a stab at where they ended up?"

Coming to a four-way stop, she diverted onto a road that would allow her to skip the drive through town by routing her to Morrow Lane directly. "Spring Hills."

"I don't think that's a random or a lucky guess on your part. I followed them in—"

"Are you sure they didn't see you?"

"Positive. But I've lost sight of them. I'm at a round-about, and I'd be lying if I told you I wasn't worried about picking the wrong door, so to speak."

"Take the first road that veers to the right. It leads to a field that overlooks the parking area and the base build-ings. The field is about thirty yards from the lot and maybe fifty yards from the old headquarters. If you stay back, it's a good vantage point. I'm about twenty minutes out. Don't take any risks."

"It's a little late for that advice."

"I mean it, Mack. If you run into any trouble, get out of there."

"I'll keep you posted."

He ended the call, and though wanting to push the pace, she proceeded cautiously. The two-lane country road was like a roller coaster, dipping up and down, with sharp curves and deep ditches an arm's length from the narrow shoulder. As a teenager, she would rev up her car while cresting the hills, trying to time it just right to make her stomach drop as she came down the other side. Now she kept below the speed limit, scanning the edges of the pavement for eyeshine from foraging deer or critters dashing across the road.

Once on Morrow Lane, she gunned the engine, passing several other drivers puttering along at a perfectly reasonable pace. She needed to give the police a reason to come, which meant gathering evidence. Grasso and Rollins together at Spring Hills spelled trouble from every angle. She and Mack were more suited for surveillance than for a takedown. They needed backup, muscle, and possibly firepower, so she voice-dialed Sam. After Olivia quickly dropped the bullet points of the plan in motion, Sam confirmed she was on her way.

Once on the access lane leading into Spring Hills, Olivia sped along until she came to the roundabout. There, she slowed before continuing to the field that overlooked the lot. At the top of the hill, she nearly collided with Mack's car, which he'd parked on the road. After pulling up next to it and seeing he wasn't inside, she shifted into park, scanned the area, and spotted him crouching on the other side of the field. She couldn't blame him for not waiting for her, as she would've done the same. After cutting the engine, she grabbed her phone, disconnected the charger, and got out. Just as she was closing the door, her cell buzzed with a call. She answered quickly to silence the noise that sounded like a drumline in the dead of night.

She whispered, though only the mockingbirds and whip-poor-wills in the nearby trees would've paid her any heed. "Cass, can't talk."

"What's going on? Are you okay?"

"Yeah-yeah. Just following up a lead."

"I'll make this quick. Identifying boat owners by hull numbers isn't impossible, but it could take some time. However, knowing that Rollins is into deep-sea fishing and that he may own two fancy-schmancy boats, I got to thinking. Big boats, bigger ego. I wondered if he was the type to enter fishing tournaments. These things are huge. Lots of press, bragging rights, and big prize money—like hundreds of thousands of dollars or more. Anyway, I searched, and boom! Found him. Last year, he won second place in a blue marlin tournament in North Carolina. Why, you ask, is this important? Because I read a write-up about the winners in which they identified Rollins as the captain of *The Cod Father*. This is the boat he caught the marlin on. Though far from definitive proof, it's highly suggestive that he owns it."

"That's great work, Cass. If you're an accountant with that kind of money, you have clients with deep pockets. Much deeper than family-owned businesses that are struggling to make ends meet like Klein Amusements."

"Or a very lucrative side hustle."

"Exactly. Okay, gotta go. Thanks."

"Where are you?"

"Spring Hills."

"Why are you there?"

"Rollins is here, and something is happening."

"I ask again, why are *you* there and not the police?"

"I'm here with someone else, and I have backup on the way. I don't have any evidence that the police would act on."

"Ah, *Preston*? He'd rather be on the sideline while you do the dirty work?"

"No. Listen, it's complicated, and I've got to go. Trust me."

"Aargh! I swear you better be careful, or I'll kill you."

"You always say the sweetest things. I will."

She ended the call with a quick goodbye, switched her phone to silent mode, and put it in her hoodie pocket. After rounding both vehicles, she hustled across the field to join Mack at his position overlooking the lot. As she neared, he glanced over his shoulder, then returned his focus toward the headquarters below. When she was next to him, she went down on one knee so that they were shoulder to shoulder.

Dispensing with pleasantries, he launched right in. "No vehicles have come or gone. There have been no signs of anyone."

"The other man is Jeffrey Rollins, the Kleins' accountant," she said. "I think he was Bobby's partner. They may be around the other side of the building or somewhere else on the property."

"Why would they come here? It seems risky."

"They could be transacting more business, or maybe there's something valuable here."

"The eggs?"

"They may never have left the area Sunday night."

He shifted his weight, shuffling the dirt under his shoes. "Should we look around?"

The uncertainty in his voice didn't ease her own apprehension. "We have backup coming. Do you remember my friend Sam?"

A nervous smile softened his jaw. He'd met Sam once before, and assumed she was Olivia's bodyguard. As things had turned out, he hadn't been far off the mark. "This is dicier than I thought if you called in the cavalry. What if they leave before she shows?"

"I'm thinking the same thing."

They glanced at each other, reading their mutual resolve.

"Are you armed?" she asked.

"No," he replied, as serious as she'd ever seen him before.

"If we can gather some evidence, we could get the police here immediately."

"I don't know about that. The cops taking the word of an advice columnist and a PI, who themselves are trespassing on private property?"

"I'll handle the police. I have an in with them. They, or at least one of them, will come. Trust me."

He let out a sharp breath, then abruptly stood up. "Let's do it."

She sprung up, grabbing his forearm. "Wait. We need a plan."

His focus shot over her shoulder. "Company."

Turning, she saw the wide glow from incoming headlights. She dropped to the ground, pulling him with her. "Get down."

He didn't hesitate as he joined her on his hands and knees near the edge of the field. They watched as a white van drove into the lot, then followed the service road that wound around to the back of the headquarters.

Now with Grasso, Rollins, and the mystery driver all here, she was certain that among them were Bobby's partner and his murderer. After waiting less than a minute, she stood up, thinking it was now or never. Mack followed a moment later. Keeping her eyes wide, she scanned for any signs of trouble.

"Let's keep the plan super simple," she said. "We'll try to see who's here, and at the first hint of trouble, we'll get out. I think someone down there killed Bobby. Maybe we'll luck out and give the police a reason to come, preferably without being spotted."

He nodded once, rubbed his hands together, and extended his fist toward her.

Six months ago, she could've happily gone her whole life without giving him a fist bump. But here they were together, trusting their backs to each other and playing on the same team. She tapped his knuckles, then zipped her hoodie pocket to ensure her phone was secure.

"Ready?" she said.

Mack's bravado returned as he cowboy-upped, giving her a wink. "I was born ready."

CHAPTER 36

Olivia scrambled down the grassy hill, quickly getting ahead of Mack. After a few steps, he uttered a choice word and slowed his stride to stop his sneakers from squeaking. At the bottom of the hill, she waited for him, keeping her focus fixed on the service road. Once side by side, they glanced at each other, nodded, and jogged through the lot toward the headquarters' front corner.

Upon reaching the building, Mack doubled over, trying to catch his breath. "I picked a bad day to wear new shoes," he said. "I thought I was going to spend a casual day at the carnival. If I'd known I'd be running like mad toward danger, I would've worn a broken-in pair. You'd think for a hundred bucks, they wouldn't squeak."

"Just step lightly or try to keep on your toes. That'll help."

The last time she'd dashed under duress, it had been

for a shorter distance while being chased onto the dock. Now her hammering heart came equally from the exertion and the suspect nature of what they were doing. Despite the pleasant early evening chill, her face felt flushed, and her core was burning like a kiln.

She placed her hand on Mack's back. "Are you okay?"

"Yeah, just give me a minute. I guess this is a sign I need to exercise more."

After patting his back twice, she glanced toward the hill. "Slow down. Extend your exhales."

Parking on the field had kept their vehicles hidden from view, but if they needed to make a quick escape, it was a long run back. Seeing him struggle to catch his breath, her concern grew, and she considered abandoning their plan. They could wait for Sam, or she could give in, stand down, and call Preston. If Grasso and the others left before help arrived, she and Mack could continue to follow them. But they'd come this far, and the answer to everything may be just behind the building.

Mack straightened, then brushed by her to peek around the corner. "What's the setup back there?"

"It's open ground between the rear of the headquarters and the old barracks on the left and the storage facility on the right. If the parrot eggs are still here, they have to be in one of these buildings. I say we go down to the end and assess."

He nodded. "You ready?"

"Yeah. But watch out—there's a lot of debris along the way."

Mack took the lead, keeping close to the building. When they were about halfway, he stopped and glanced back at her. She gave him a thumbs-up, then they proceeded. Once they were within a few feet of the rear, he slowed, waved for her to stop, and poked his head around the corner. After a few seconds, he turned around and was startled to find her right behind him.

"For the love of—" he whispered, holding his hand up to her. "Do you not know this is the universal stop sign?"

"What do you see?"

He gestured for her to move back, then did the same. "White van and the car I followed. I just got a glimpse of someone going inside. The door is about fifteen feet from the corner."

Both were quiet for a moment, then she maneuvered around him and looked for herself.

He moved behind her and spoke over her shoulder. "I could take photos of the license plates. We're close enough, and I can get clear shots from here. You could send those to your police contact."

"Good idea, but that won't be enough. We still need to find out who's inside."

All her senses were on high alert, as if fueled by back-to-back double espressos. Her eyes felt round as an owl's, and she could hear a small animal scamper over the leaves in the nearby forest. Ideally, the guilty parties would've posed under the security light's glow for a picture that she could've sent to Preston. Absent the best-case scenario, another decision had to be made. They'd risked coming this far, but they could still fall back and call the police without being seen. Now only a door stood between them and the answer they'd come seeking.

"I'm getting closer," she said, glancing back at Mack as he lowered his phone.

"That's not a good idea. I took photos of the plates. Let's send them to your contact first."

"We don't have time. They're right here. You can wait while I look."

His mouth flicked with a nervous smile, reminding her of A.J. when, as kids, she'd challenge him on a double-dog dare. "Yeah, right. And let you have all the fun? Forget that. If something goes south, you run, and I'll hold them off. Deal?"

"Let's hope it doesn't come to that. But we both run. Deal."

Without hesitation or another word, they skirted the corner and crept to the rear door. There they squatted, keeping out of view of a narrow rectangular window above the pull handle. Mack rose slowly, and after what seemed to her an excessively long look, he lowered himself just as gently.

"Dark hallway with emergency lighting at even intervals," he said. "There's an opened, lit room on the left, twenty feet from the entrance. My guess is that they brought in a few portable lights and a small generator.

Battery backup or solar cells could power the emergency system. Sometimes in buildings with communications equipment for critical services, they keep the electricity on. It could have an independent grid too."

She popped up without the slo-mo theatrics and looked through the window to confirm the layout. The red lighting made the hallway glow like a photographer's darkroom. A moment ago, the world had seemed so much safer, when they were hidden around the corner of the building. Though someone down the hall may have murdered Bobby, she didn't think it was Rollins or that he would want a homicide pinned on him. Desperate people do desperate things, yet often they still hesitate. All she needed to do was get in, see who was there, and get out—with no indecision or delay.

After squatting to be level with Mack again, she raised her arm, grasped the handle, and cracked open the door.

He muffled a grunt. "What are you doing?"

"Shh." She tilted her head, looking through the crack. "I'm going in. Stay here and hold this open. Be ready to run."

He grabbed her wrist. "No. Bad plan. Let's wait until they come out."

"We don't have time to argue. If they see us out here, we're dead in the water. Two cars versus us on foot aren't good odds. If we turn back now, we won't know who's inside. This is what we came to do."

He clamped his mouth shut for a second, then released her wrist. "I'll go in. You stay here."

"I'm quicker, and if your shoes squeak, they'll hear you." She pointed behind him at the tree line, which was about fifty yards from the door. "If we need to bolt, head for the forest and hide. Hopefully, they'll be too concerned about getting away to worry about us. I don't think either Rollins or Grasso are up for extended foot pursuits, but they may be armed."

He glanced over his shoulder, then back at her. "Make it quick."

She rose from her squat and inched the door open, listening for the slightest squeal from the retired hinges. When the gap was wide enough, she turned sideways and slipped through. Then she slowly guided the door back to Mack, who held it slightly ajar, so they kept in each other's view.

She stepped lightly but sprightly to the left side of the long, eerie hallway. Moving quickly, she glided to within a few feet of the opened room, hearing voices. Maneuvering for a better view inside, she spotted a lectern, a large folding table, and a whiteboard. Judging by the layout, it was a classroom with the door at the front, and from the volume of the conversation between Grasso and Rollins, she surmised they were in the back.

She weighed the risk of stepping past the entrance to the other side for a straight-on view. Judging the split-second move worth the gamble, she was about to dash across when Nicky's voice froze her in place.

"How much time do we have before the eggs hatch?" Nicky said.

Nicky—she was involved in the trafficking with Bobby? That doesn't make sense.

"My guy told me we have one to two days max," Rollins said.

What about the family business? Silva couldn't have been lying about how much it means to her. There's got to be more going on here.

Olivia glanced at Mack, then at the overhead exit sign at the opposite end of the hall, which seemed like a mile away.

"We agreed to the delivery on Sunday," Grasso growled.

"But we don't know what we're doing," Nicky pleaded. "If they hatch here, we don't have the proper care for them."

"Everything's going to be alright," Rollins said. "We have people who'll ensure they'll be okay after they hatch. Once they're transferred, we'll get the money, and you can pay off the loans. The business will be in good standing for the rest of the season. Think of what that'll mean to your parents."

"He's right, Nicky. Your greedy brother wasn't reinvesting his share to settle the company's debts. He was cheating my bosses just the same as his own family."

"What about you?" she shot back. "You're double-crossing them too. And you killed Bobby because of it. I should've gone to the police."

It was Grasso—and Nicky knew. How could she just go on with business as usual? The revelation that Grasso had killed Bobby didn't shock Olivia, but realizing that he must've gone straight from her house on Sunday night to Spring Hills with that intention hit her like a bolt from the blue. Grasso was playing both sides. He had tried to set up Sam to take the fall for the murder, and when that didn't work, he managed to do the same to Slammer.

"And you watched it happen, Nicky," Grasso said. "Were you planning to admit being an accessory? You know what they call that? Life in prison without parole."

"Let's all just calm down," Rollins said. "Stick to the plan. It's a good one. We have the cops looking in the wrong direction—"

"Thanks to you, Nicky."

"Shut up, Grasso," Rollins barked. "We're all on the same side."

"I'm calling our contact," Grasso said. "Maybe they'll take the delivery tonight. Once they hatch, we'll finish the deal. I don't have a driver, so you two can draw straws to see who gets to do the honors."

The room went quiet, and Olivia chanced a peek around the corner of the door. A pair of portable lights illuminated the inside, making it much brighter than the faint glow in the hallway had suggested. Grasso stood in the far rear corner with his back turned and a phone pressed to his ear. Nicky appeared to be crying while Rollins was trying to comfort her. Two rectangular units, plugged into a small generator, sat on top of a long counter that stretched across the back wall. With no doubt in her mind that they were the incubators, Olivia quickly stepped across the open doorway to get a better angle for a picture. She unzipped her pocket, and as she pulled out her phone, it slipped from her grip. Faster than a heartbeat, her hands shot down, catching it just before it hit the floor. She held her breath for a moment, trying to calm the thumping in her chest that could've woken the dead. When she was certain the near disaster hadn't alerted anyone in the room, she straightened up, opened her camera, and took a picture, the shutter clicking with a snap.

"What was that?" Grasso said.

Frak. In catching the phone, she must've accidentally switched it out of silent mode. She pressed herself against the wall and moved away from the entrance, heading toward the shadow of the neighboring room's closed door.

"What?" Rollins replied.

Olivia selected the photo and sent it in a text to Preston along with the message, "Spring Hills." Proper channels would've been to call 911, but under the circumstances, there was no chance she could speak to a dispatcher. She had to trust that Preston would understand the text and act immediately. Slipping her phone back into her pocket, she eyed Mack and her exit a short distance away.

"I swear I just heard something," Grasso said.

She prayed a thousand "pretty pleases" to whatever angels were watching over her tonight.

As heavy footsteps trudged toward the door, she looked at Mack and frantically waved at him to fall back.

Grasso burst out into the hallway, first spotting Mack, then zeroing in on her under the blood-red glow of the emergency light directly over her head. It took no longer than a second for the recognition to spark. "You!"

"Who's there?" Rollins said, stepping behind Grasso.

With her closest exit cut off, there was only one move to make. She would've never come in without a backup plan. They hesitated, but she didn't. Quick as a whip, she spun and sprinted like an Olympian down the hallway.

CHAPTER 37

"You get him, I'll grab her," Grasso growled.

Already halfway down the eerie red hall, Olivia glanced back just in time to see Grasso take off after her. Though she'd never been inside the building, the layout of the rooms reminded her of an elementary school. All hallways must lead somewhere, and places like this weren't designed as labyrinths. Knowing she was at the rear, she'd head toward the front, bail at the first exit, and dash for cover in the forest.

Her childhood and adolescence had prepared her for this, providing practice on how to run for safety, albeit when the stakes were low. From duck, duck, goose in kindergarten to stealing second base for her high school softball team, the endgame was the same—don't get tagged. If bullets weren't in play, she only had to outrun Grasso and hide until the police arrived. Faster and with at least twenty years on him, she had the advantage.

With a left-right decision looming in fifteen feet, she snapped another look back. Between the distance and the horror-house lighting wreaking havoc on her focus, she couldn't tell for sure if he was holding a weapon.

Hitting the brakes at the end of the hall, she had a split-second choice to make. To her left was a bobtailed corridor with a wall-mounted water fountain next to a closet. Staring her down was a pad-locked, chained door marked as an exit.

She immediately bolted to the right, seeing another hallway on the left about twenty feet ahead. A few yards past it, there was a door with a narrow rectangular window that looked like an exit. Barreling straight for it, she came to a shuffling stop, pushed in the long handle, and met with Fort Knox resistance.

Open, open.

Desperate, she tried again, shoving her shoulder against the door as if it was just stubbornly stuck and needed extra coaxing. When it didn't budge, she spun and spotted Grasso at the end of the hallway. She was well within target range. If he wanted to end the chase with the threat of a bullet, she was directly in his line of fire. But, with his chest heaving, he braced his hands on his hips and made no move to draw a weapon.

With her fight-or-flight instinct at full throttle, a habit she'd developed when learning how to drive kicked in. Her father had taught her to always leave space between her car and others so she could maneuver out of trouble if needed. She always applied the same principle to dealing with sketchy people. Now she just had to keep her distance from Grasso so he couldn't lay his hands on her.

Shooting forward, she veered right into the next hallway as he started after her again. Dashing past closed rooms, she locked in on a set of double doors at the end of the long corridor. If her orientation was correct, she should be close to the front of the building. After going zero for two in finding an exit, it could be her last strike if one of the doors wouldn't open.

Glancing back, she saw Grasso had slowed but still didn't seem to be holding a weapon. Flying forward, she reached the end of the hall, extended both arms, and pushed on the long door handle with all her strength.

Please, please, please.

The door swung open, and she bolted straight into the dark, cavernous lobby. The security lighting from outside the windows helped her make out the layout. Many of the furnishings remained in place, as if the base could reopen tomorrow. She'd run right past a massive reception desk that could've belonged to a Fortune 500 company. Her attention zeroed in on the only color in the room—the bright red exit sign above the front door.

Darting across the marble floor, she reached the entrance and grabbed the doorknob, giving it a turn and a sharp tug. The door shifted slightly, but a deadbolt seemed engaged. Finding the thumb turn, she rotated it ninety degrees and heard a satisfying click. But still the door refused to shift. Frustrated, she repeatedly yanked, wanting to rip it off the hinges. Gathering herself, she leaned down, ran her hand along the door, and felt a round plate with a key cylinder. She muttered a few colorful words, realizing an electronic lock controlled the door and would only open with a key.

She shuffled to the closest sash window, gripped the cam lock handle on the bottom panel, and tried to wrench it open. Tight as a vice, the hardware seemed petrified. Sliding over to the next window, she seized the lock lever and easily ripped it toward her. Grasping the lift assist on the lower pane, she pulled upward, but the sash wouldn't budge. Trying to revive the sliding mechanism, she furiously rattled the window in the casing. Then she yanked again, opening it about an inch.

She spun and scanned the lobby, making out a pitch-black open room off to her right. By the size of the double doors, it looked like a large space for special events. Just as she took a step toward it, Grasso flung open the hall door and lumbered into the lobby.

She eyed the staircase on the opposite side of the room. Without delay, she dashed for it, luring him to follow her up the two flights of stairs. If he didn't have a heart attack in making the effort, at least he'd be even more winded. Then all she'd need to do was slip around him, double back through the hallway, and exit through the rear of the building. Trusting that Mack had fled when Rollins went after him, she still may have to deal with Nicky. But she liked her chances of going mano a mano with someone her own size rather than a brute like Grasso.

The staircase led to a small landing, then turned ninety degrees before continuing to the second floor. Sprinting up the steps, she paused halfway, seeing him stagger past the reception desk. She zoomed to the top in no time, but her quads were feeling the strain. If her heart was racing like a rocket, his had to be operating at maximum capacity.

The walkway overlooked the lobby below and led to a hallway about thirty feet away. She considered running toward it, but with only the emergency lights for guidance, she couldn't see if there was an exit at the other end. He shuffled up the steps, each breath louder than the last. He might still have a weapon, but if it were a gun, she thought he would've used it to end the pursuit by now.

When he reached the top, she stood about ten feet away, centered on the walkway with four feet of space on either side. He paused for a moment, catching his breath.

"You won't get away with this," she said. "The police are on their way." *Hopefully.*

"As soon as I deal with you, I'm out of here for good. Rollins and Nicky are on their own."

"You won't have time to move the incubators."

He shrugged. "You win some, you lose some. Better to leave them behind than to risk life in jail."

"Why did you kill Bobby?"

"Money. Bobby was planning to shift all his business to a new buyer, which would've cut me out of the picture. Rollins and I have a good thing going, so we agreed he had to go. Just like you do now."

He trudged toward her. After waiting for a split second, she shifted her weight, then closed the distance between them.

She quickly juked to her left, causing him to shift clumsily. As he lunged to grab her, she dipped low and burst forward to her right. He swiped at her, but missed, and she was almost past him when her foot slipped on the tile. The slight delay allowed him to recover, and he reached out, grasping her wrist with both hands.

As he tugged, she turned sideways and dropped a bit, giving some ground with her front leg. Muscle memory kicked in for a self-defense technique she'd learned in a women's safety course she took while living in D.C. Since wrist grabs were often used during abductions, her instructor had made her practice escaping until she could consistently break his full-strength hold.

Now she reached in between Grasso's arms, grabbed her fist, and quickly tugged upwards. She broke free instantly and turned toward the stairs, but he lunged and seized the cuff of her hoodie's left sleeve. She retracted her shoulder, letting his momentum slip the sleeve off her arm. As he tried to reel her in, she spun, freeing her right arm from the jacket. The move threw him off balance, and with his weight behind him and his back to the staircase, it was too late for him to recover. With a frightful yell, he fell backward, tumbled down the steps, and came to a stop with a thud on the landing.

380

CHAPTER 38

Standing at the top of the staircase, Olivia peered down at Grasso sprawled out like a chalk outline. In the dim lighting, from half a flight up, she couldn't tell if he was conscious or even breathing. Still not feeling safe, and with her ears ringing, she glanced toward the hall then back at him, deciding which way to go. She would get help for him if needed, once there was more distance between them. Liking her chances of getting by him on the landing, she had only just hovered her foot over the first step when a bright beam blinded her. She instantly pulled back, shielding her eyes from the light.

"Liv, are you okay?" Sam called out.

Disoriented by dots spotting her vision, she grasped the railing, not wanting to reprise Grasso's tumble. "Sam?"

The light shifted away from her and illuminated Grasso as Sam jogged up the steps to the landing.

"Yeah. Are you hurt?"

"No. I'm not sure about him, though." She waited briefly until the dots disappeared, then descended one step.

"Hold up," Sam said. "Let me check him for weapons."

Just then, a heavy thump echoed through the front door, jolting Olivia. Within seconds, it flew open, and three officers quickly entered the lobby. Flashlight beams scoped out the room until they all trained on the staircase.

"Up here," Sam called out, raising her hands. "I'm Sam Steele. This is the guy you're looking for. He needs medical attention."

Two officers aimed their lights on Sam and Grasso while the third lit up Olivia.

She squinted and turned her head slightly. "I'm Olivia Penn. I'm unarmed."

"Who else is here?" Jayden yelled from the bottom of the staircase.

"No one," Olivia said as Jayden lowered the light from her face. "But Nicky Klein was in a room at the rear of the building the last that I saw her. Her accountant, Jeffrey Rollins, ran out the back. I think he went after John Mack. They may be in the woods beyond the service road." She pointed at the landing. "That's Tommy Grasso. He killed Bobby Klein."

Jayden, Deputy Lee, and Deputy Simmons jogged up the steps as Sam moved out of their way. Grasso moaned, moving just enough to verify that all four limbs were functional. One officer searched him for weapons while another cuffed his hands in front of him.

Jayden looked up at Olivia, then at Sam. "Are either of you hurt?" After they confirmed they were unharmed, she got on her radio and apprised Preston and Payne of the situation. After the chief issued his orders, she spoke to Lee and Simmons. "You two stay here and watch him. EMS is en route." Then she waved at Olivia, motioning for her to come. "Ms. Penn, this way."

Olivia descended three steps, picked up her hoodie, and checked the pocket, finding her phone secure. After turning the sleeves right side out, she slipped it on and joined the others on the landing.

Sam immediately wrapped her in a tight hug. "Are you okay?"

"Yeah," she murmured without thinking, not sounding convincing even to herself. "Thanks for coming."

As they released each other, Olivia looked at Lee and Simmons, who were guarding Grasso. The scene felt surreal, as if it weren't happening to her. She could hear the deputies speaking but wasn't processing what they were saying. Everyone's voice sounded muted, like they were behind a closed door.

Jayden waved at Olivia and Sam to follow her. "Come on. Let's go outside."

As Olivia passed Grasso, he didn't look at her, and there was nothing she wanted to say to him. Had he gotten hold of her, she might've been the one lying on the landing. She would've fought like hell, going twelve rounds to save herself if necessary. Keeping her head and emotions in check while executing her plan had kept her from becoming a victim. Now she couldn't care less if he had a broken leg, a ruptured spleen, or a Grade 3 concussion. His karma had arrived, and the payback for all the harm he'd caused was just beginning.

When they got to the base of the stairs, Jayden led them across the lobby, through the busted front door, and onto the portico. Once there, Jayden leaned down and lifted a battering ram that was lying off to the side of the entrance.

"Wait here while I get this out of the way," she said. She went down the four shallow steps and strode toward three police cruisers parked near the building.

Sam wrapped an arm around Olivia's shoulders. "Are you sure you're okay?"

"That's the third time you've asked me."

"I didn't believe you the first two times."

That provoked a thin smile from Olivia, which, judging by Sam's side-glance, seemed to be the intent. "I will be. I'm just amped up, but not in a good way. You know what I mean?"

"You should sit down. I'll join you."

They went over to the steps and settled on the top one.

"It's the adrenaline," Sam said. "You're going to

crash sometime tonight, but you'll be okay in the morning."

Olivia looked across the lot at the hill she and Mack had scurried down less than an hour ago. She shook her head, mildly amused that his squeaky shoes could've ruined everything. Between then and now, so much had happened, but all still seemed like a blur. The only thoughts coming into focus were about how Preston would react and what he'd say to her.

"Liv, I'm so sorry I put you in this position," Sam said. "You were never supposed to be in danger."

That brought her back to the scene. "This wasn't your fault. It was my decision."

Sam narrowed her eyes, looking like she didn't believe her again.

As Jayden returned, Olivia moved to get up.

"You can stay seated," Jayden said. She had removed her body armor and was holding a pocket notebook and a pen. "You're going to be here for a while."

"It was my choice," Olivia whispered to Sam. "I'm fine."

"EMS is fifteen minutes out," Jayden said. "Detective Hills would like them to see you, Ms. Penn. You too, if you feel the need."

"I don't," Sam replied. "I missed the party."

Olivia glanced at Sam, detecting a hint of disappointment. "I was at the party, and it wasn't all that. I'm okay."

"You can take it up with Detective Hills. In the meantime, let's go over what happened."

Olivia outlined how she and Mack had followed Grasso and Rollins. Then she related the sequence of events in more detail, starting with their descent of the hill. When she'd finished and answered Jayden's clarifying questions, Sam gave her side of the story. After receiving Olivia's call, she'd come straightaway. On finding the two vehicles parked on the upper field, she figured Olivia and Mack had tried to get closer to the action. She found Nicky alone and distraught in the room with the incubators. When Nicky admitted Grasso had gone after Olivia, Sam pursued them until finding both in the lobby just before the police arrived.

As Jayden made the last of her notes, Preston and a deputy rounded the corner of the building, ushering Rollins toward the squad cars. Mack was in step behind them, limping and holding a cloth over his nose. Preston locked in on Olivia for a few strides, but he was too far away for her to read his face. She wanted to smile, communicating that she was fine, but her eyes welled instead. Mack veered from the trio ahead of him and gingerly hobbled his way to the front steps.

"Stay here for now," Jayden instructed Olivia and Sam, before turning and heading toward Preston.

Olivia popped up as Mack neared, moving double-time to meet him.

"Hey there, partner," he said, managing a pained, wry smile. "There's never a dull moment with you."

"Are you okay?" she asked as Sam joined them.

"This is nothing. You should see the black eye I gave the pencil pusher." He removed the cloth from his nose and glanced at it. "See there, already clotted. It looks worse than it feels, though it doesn't feel great."

"You're limping," Olivia said.

"Son of a—he tackled me, and I tweaked my knee, but I'll live."

She winced, as he looked like he'd been in a barroom brawl. "EMS will be here soon. You should go to the hospital."

"Those are for sick people. You seem to have survived. Are you okay?"

She nodded. "Yes. I can't say the same for Grasso. He took a backward tumble down a flight of stairs."

"Did he now? If you think you'll need a lawyer, I have connections."

"He fell of his own accord."

"Well then, I believe you." He looked at Sam. "Nice to see you again. I could've used your muscle. I'm out of practice with my takedowns."

"You're a big boy, Mack. It seems like you handled yourself okay. Besides, you weren't the priority."

"Ouch. But I understand. I would've made the same call."

"Grasso killed Bobby," Olivia said to Mack. "Nicky had known the whole time."

"I'm not surprised it was Grasso, but that must mean

Bobby and Nicky were involved in the trafficking together," Mack said.

Olivia shook her head. "I don't know. It doesn't seem to fit with how she felt about the carnival and the crew. I was told her family legacy meant everything to her, but mixing the family business with trafficking contradicts that."

"Maybe the money from the trafficking was keeping the business afloat," Sam said.

"That's possible," Olivia replied. "But Grasso told me it was him and Rollins who had a good thing going, and they were the ones who decided Bobby had to go. He didn't say anything about Nicky. From what I overheard, it sounded like Nicky witnessed the murder but didn't take part."

"She'll still be charged as an accessory," Sam said.

Olivia nodded. "There are a lot of unknowns. The police investigation will untangle the web. What I do know is that Grasso felt no loyalty to Rollins or Nicky. He'd planned to leave them to fend for themselves after he'd dealt with me."

"Little did he know, you're not someone who can be easily dealt with," Mack said.

"Apparently, neither are you," Olivia said. "What happened between you and Rollins?"

"When Rollins came after me, I ran for the trees. Frankly, neither one of us is cut out for hand-to-hand combat. We tussled in the forest, and he got the worst of it. Then the police showed up, and that's the end of the story."

"What about Nicky?" Olivia said.

"The cops nabbed her. She's cooling her heels in a squad car around the back."

He continued elaborating on the police's takedown of Rollins while Olivia watched Jayden and Preston converse. When Jayden walked over to her patrol car, Preston turned and locked eyes with Olivia. As Mack kept talking, she excused herself and hurried over to him.

CHAPTER 39

Olivia hadn't wanted to make a scene, but as she neared Preston, she quickened her steps and walked straight into his arms. He held her tighter than ever, helping to ease some of her worry about how he'd respond. She felt his hands spread across her back, holding her in a tight embrace strong enough to support her entire weight.

"Are you doing alright?" he asked softly. With her cheek pressed against his chest, she could only nod. They stayed like that for a moment longer before he loosened his hold and placed his hands firmly on her shoulders. "Are you sure?"

"Uh-huh," she said, still not convincing herself.

"EMS will be here soon. I want you to see them."

"I'm not hurt. Mack is the one who needs medical attention." Feeling drained, she just wanted to go home, lie down in her room, and not think about any of this, at least for a few hours.

He ran his hands down her arms before letting go. "Why did you come here alone with Mack? Why didn't you call me?"

She swallowed hard, trying to gauge the tension in his face. She wanted to explain but lacked a simple answer for the brief moments they had. "It's complicated. I know you don't have time to talk about it now, but we will." Her focus shifted as she saw two ambulances enter the lot. "It looks like you have to go."

He glanced behind him before returning his strained gaze to her. "Jayden briefed me on what happened." He shook his head, looking troubled and flustered. "For heaven's sake, Liv, why didn't you call me?"

Her throat tightened as only a few words came to mind. "I'm sorry. Please, let's talk about this later. Okay?"

His jaw tightened as he shifted back into his official role. "Jayden will write a preliminary statement and go over it with you. We may need more information from you over the coming days. But you'll have to stay here for a while until she gets that sorted."

"I know the drill. What about Sam? Can you keep her name out of things?"

"I'll talk to Payne. If he outs someone on a black-budget team, he'll have to deal with an irate Senator Dixon, and nobody wants that kind of heat. I want you to stay close by. Why don't you wait in my truck?"

"Detective Hills!" Jayden called out from beside her cruiser, pointing toward the parked ambulances.

He glanced back and held up a hand in acknowledgment. "Coming!"

The two EMS crews got out and started removing their gear as Jayden walked over to them.

"I'll be okay hanging out here with Sam," Olivia said. "I take it you saw the setup with the generator and the incubators."

"Yeah. I don't know if they've been here this whole time. I assume so. There were no signs of forced entry into the building when we investigated on Sunday or Monday."

"Could they have picked the lock?"

He shrugged. "It's possible. We'll find out. More importantly, right now, I need to locate someone who knows what to do about those eggs. If they're due to hatch within two days, I'm guessing some could come out early."

"Cass has been in touch with a local parrot sanctuary in The Plains. Maybe they can help, or facilitate connections to arrange care for them. I'll call her and get names and numbers for you."

"That would be great. The sooner we contact them, the better." He glanced over his shoulder again as the EMS crews and Jayden approached. "I have to go." He lightly grasped her hand, about to speak, but then hesitated.

Jayden, now a few feet behind them, subtly cleared her throat. "Detective Hills?"

"I'll call Cass now," Olivia said. "We'll talk later."

After holding her gaze for a moment longer, he released her hand and turned to brief the EMS crews, while Jayden returned to her cruiser. Olivia took out her phone and called Cassandra, relating what had happened over the past hour. Though Cassandra was buzzing with questions, Olivia put her off, promising to give her the full details later. They ended the call after Cassandra offered to take the lead in contacting the sanctuary.

The EMS crews split when they got to the front steps. A pair of paramedics followed Preston inside, while the other two stayed behind to check on Mack, who was standing by the steps and speaking with Sam. Olivia pocketed her phone and joined them, not surprised by Mack's refusal to go to the ER. Reluctantly, he agreed to a quick examination and a set of vital signs.

"Let's have a seat while they're looking over him," Sam said to Olivia.

"Sounds good. I think we'll be here for a while."

After they both settled on the top step, Olivia received a text from Cassandra, informing her that the owners of the parrot rescue were on their way. She wrote a quick thank-you, then sent Preston a message, passing the news on to him.

"Help is coming for the parrots," Olivia said. "I asked Preston about keeping your name out of the official reports. He thinks it'll be possible, but I wouldn't take it as a guarantee."

Sam drew her legs up, wrapped her arms around her

knees, and interlaced her fingers. "It won't be in the reports. Carolyn will see to it."

Olivia nodded as if that made perfect sense, at least in Sam's line of work. "Are you parked on the field?"

"Mark dropped me off up there."

"You came without a means of escape?" Olivia teased, lightly bumping her shoulder. "Speaking as a pure civilian, that doesn't seem very strategic."

Sam managed a thin smile. "You didn't act like a pure civilian tonight." Her face tightened as she stared straight ahead. "This went way too far. I would've never forgiven myself if something had happened to you. I should not have gone along with it. I should have told Carolyn that involving you was a bad idea."

"I liked being involved," Olivia blurted. On Monday, she'd return to writing her column and all her daily routines. Though safe and comfortable in her cozy office, the accomplishment and the satisfaction of the work wouldn't carry the same weight. "Nothing happened to me. Everything turned out okay. It was my decision to do this."

"Maybe you're in the wrong line of work."

"Maybe," she replied, rubbing her eyes. "I'll drive you back to your house when we can leave. Finally, you get to go home."

"Thanks, but I have a ride. You're right. It wouldn't have been wise to come in without an exit strategy."

"Ah, you have a Plan B, and probably C, D, and E.

Of course, it would make sense that my backup would have backup."

Sam unlocked her fingers, placing her hands on her knees. "That's how it works. You had my back throughout this, and let's not forget that you also kept an eye on my house."

Olivia drew in a sharp breath. "Your plants. I'm sorry I haven't watered them since Sunday."

"They're African violets. They'll survive."

A paramedic came out the front door, jogged down the steps, and joined the other crew as they finished with Mack. Two of them then headed toward the ambulances, while the other EMT reentered the building.

Mack limped over to join Olivia and Sam by the steps, forcing a smile through his grimace.

"How's the knee feeling?" Olivia asked.

"Stiff. I'm supposed to rest, ice, compress, and elevate it. If it's not better in a week, I'll go see my doctor."

"Grasso, Rollins, and Nicky wouldn't have been caught without your help," Olivia said. "Thanks for doing what you did. I hope it doesn't ruin your reputation, now that you're a hero."

"Let's not spread those rumors around," he replied. "It could be bad for business. You helped me find my guy, and that means a lot to me, personally and financially. We make a good team. We should stay in touch."

She still didn't know why he was looking for Ryan, but it was no longer her concern. "Maybe we will."

The two paramedics were rolling a stretcher back toward the building as Jayden got out of her cruiser, holding a clipboard. Olivia and Sam moved off the steps and out of the crew's way. Jayden approached Mack and pulled him aside to review his statement. When she finished with him and he signed the report, he was released from the scene. After saying goodbye to everyone, he declined Jayden's offer of a ride to his car and limped across the lot toward the hill. Sam was up next, and in five minutes, Jayden was through with her. Then it was Olivia's turn, and before long, she was also free to leave.

Sam rejoined Olivia near the bottom of the steps after Jayden headed back to her cruiser.

"Are you taking off now?" Sam asked.

"I want to catch Preston for a few minutes before I go."

Sam nodded, looking toward the upper field. "What was Mack talking about—you and him as a team?"

"Nothing really. I mean—I'm not sure. He's definitely a pro at what he does. I have a new appreciation for John Mack after tonight."

"Don't grow too fond of him. Here's my ride."

She followed Sam's eyes as a white Mercedes drove into the lot.

"That doesn't seem very tactical," Olivia joked. "You have a much better ride-hail app than I do."

"Maybe you need an upgrade. Walk with me?"

They strolled the short distance to where the luxury vehicle was idling a little way from the ambulances.

"Are you sure you'll be okay here?" Sam asked. "I can wait with you."

"No, I'll be fine."

They stopped a few feet shy of the car and turned to face each other.

"If you need to talk to someone tonight, call me—no matter the time," Sam said.

"Thanks. I'll probably just crash when I get home, but I'll catch you tomorrow."

After they hugged, Sam walked around the front of the car and opened the passenger door. As she was getting in, the driver's window lowered. Olivia stepped closer, bending down slightly as Carolyn looked up at her. Dressed in an impeccable ivory pant suit, she looked ready for a seat on a private jet to Paris. It had to be nearly ten o'clock, which normally would have Olivia sporting PJs and a ponytail. She mused that if this was what sixty-plus looked like, then the future was promising.

"Ms. Penn, Olivia, I owe you a debt of gratitude. You made a good showing for yourself. I'm properly impressed."

As she spoke, not a line formed or deepened on her face. A bystander may have mistaken her for a bored British tourist. But Olivia had a feeling that Carolyn didn't dole out such compliments freely.

"Thank you," she replied. "I'd offer my help in the future, but I don't think you'll need it."

Carolyn stared at her for a moment longer as the window rose. "For now. Good night, Olivia."

As she watched the Mercedes leave the lot, a red van pulled in and parked close to the police cruisers. A scarlet macaw decal on the side of the van left no doubt that the parrot experts had arrived. Olivia planted herself on the curb and texted Preston the news. Jayden greeted the owners of the sanctuary before escorting them toward the headquarters.

Olivia sat half-turned, watching Preston leave the building and descend the steps. He scanned the area until he spotted her, then spoke with the sanctuary owners and Jayden for a few minutes. After Jayden took the owners inside, Preston walked over to her.

"Are you hanging in there?" he asked as he neared.

That made her smile as she stood up. "You know me —tough as nails."

They wrapped their arms around each other, and she melted into him.

"That's true." He leaned down and gently kissed her.

That helped ease some of the tension she felt had been building between them. "You're ready to leave, right?" she said. "The chief and the deputies can handle all the work from here while we go back to your house."

He mirrored her smile. "I wish."

"It was worth a shot," she replied as they separated.

"It's going to be a long night. The sanctuary folks prefer not to move the eggs with them being so close to hatching, but they have no choice. They'll take them to their facility. We'll be escorting them so they can drive slowly. I'll come by your house after I get back, but it may not be until after midnight."

"That's okay. Of course I want to see you, but you'll be exhausted. Tomorrow is almost here anyway." She curled her lips until her held breath forced its way out. "I know there's a lot we need to talk about."

He glanced at the upper field. "Yeah. There are some things on my mind that I can't shake, but how about we get you on your way. Jayden is taking the sanctuary owners to the incubators, and they'll be here for a while getting everything ready for the transfer. Let me walk you to your car."

Wanting to spend more time with him, she wasn't going to turn the offer down. She could only nod as the pit in her stomach grew two sizes, worrying about what he needed to get off his chest.

CHAPTER 40

From the lot to the field, Olivia and Preston didn't say a word to each other. Both seemed too lost in their thoughts to fill the silence just for the sake of it. She knew he had to be angry and was probably holding back, not wanting to make the night any more difficult for her. He would likely say she had betrayed his trust, and she couldn't argue with that. Though she had her reasons, she would understand if he felt hurt by her choosing Sam over him. Of course, it wasn't that simple. But if his trust in her had been broken, was their foundation strong enough for a repair?

She looked up at the dark, star-filled sky, feeling worlds away from all that had happened over the past few hours. On any other night, the slight chill would've been the perfect excuse for them to cuddle while taking a moonlight walk together. Now they weren't even holding hands, and the beauty of the twinkling sky felt tainted by the silence between them.

As much as she wanted to clear the air and right the relationship, it was late, and he had a job to do. He'd only come to make sure she got to her car safely, not to have a heart-to-heart about how she'd hurt him. Instead of dwelling on the damage done, she just wished to go home and curl up under the covers with Willow and Buddy lying beside her.

When they reached her car, they turned to face each other. He held her eyes for a moment, then glanced off to his side. Never had their goodnight partings been awkward. Her head felt heavy, trying to think of what to say. Thanks for walking with me, drive carefully, talk to you tomorrow—all seemed pretty lame.

He shifted his weight and shuffled his feet, looking like he was about to leave. Her heart couldn't bear it, so she let out what she hadn't planned to say.

"I know you're angry, and you have every right to be. I'm aware you don't have time to discuss anything right now, but I need you to understand at least this tonight. I came here with Mack only to gather evidence I could send to you. If the police had shown up and nothing had been happening, the chance to catch them red-handed might have been lost. I know you didn't want me involved in this, and you reluctantly went along with it. I would never have put myself in a situation that I thought I couldn't get out of. I'm sorry for not telling you about

Sam from the start, and for not calling you when I knew Grasso and Rollins were here."

When she finished, his gaze dropped to the ground between them for a moment. Though she didn't intend to start an argument or stir up further conflict, she couldn't part from him without saying some of what was weighing on her.

He stepped closer and raised his hand, cradling the side of her cheek. Drawing her in, he tilted her chin and kissed her. His tender touch sent her heart racing, and for a second, some of her concern vanished. He pulled back a bit, but she could still feel his breath on her.

"I'm not angry," he said, gently grasping her hand. "I'm relieved you're okay. From the time I left the police station until I heard you had been found safe, I was scared that you were alone and that something bad might have happened to you. So many things were going through my head." He paused, taking a breath and exhaling the world off his shoulders. "When you needed me the most, I wasn't here. I've never been upset with you. I was angry at myself for making you feel you had to do this without me. If something had happened to you …" His eyes glistened as he squeezed her hand. "I don't know what tomorrow would've been like if you weren't here. I would have to live the rest of my life with the regret that I never told you I love you."

Stunned by his words, she didn't have time to react before he leaned down and kissed her. Of all the things she'd imagined he may say, that wasn't one of them.

When they separated, she couldn't help but smile as he did the same. Her world had suddenly righted, with them being more than okay. He grabbed the driver's side handle of her car, gave it a tug, and opened the door for her.

She knew he had to go and that he didn't expect her to reciprocate. As she had needed to say her piece, so did he. Climbing into the seat, she kept her eyes on him as every cell in her body seemed to vibrate.

"Text me when you get home," he said.

"When I'm all locked up," she added.

"That's right."

After she fastened her seat belt, he closed the door and stood waiting. She knew he wouldn't leave without seeing her off, so she started the engine, shifted into drive, and made a U-turn. She slowed for a moment as they exchanged a parting wave, then drove away, keeping an eye on him in the rearview mirror. Of all the things that had happened to her since coming home a year ago, the last ten minutes she'd shared with him may have been the most meaningful.

CHAPTER 41

Sitting at the kitchen table the next morning, Olivia swirled her coffee, attempting to reinvigorate the bold dark roast that had turned tepid and humdrum tan. She'd started the day as she always did, making breakfast and tending to her furry friends, but nothing seemed quite the same. The house was quiet for the hour. Willow was napping on the bay windowsill while Buddy lay on his bed below, biding his time while waiting for his best friend to wake. Her father had left a sticky note on the refrigerator, informing her that he had gone to the store for cream of tartar, pastry flour, and vanilla beans. She envisioned many such days ahead, trying to guess what the mystery ingredients would come together to create. The red velvet cake he'd made yesterday sat on a plate under a dome on the counter. Along with her oatmeal, she had taken a sliver, both of which remained untouched in front of her.

By the time she got home last night, her father was already asleep. This afternoon, she would tell him everything that had happened before he read about it in tomorrow's paper. She'd stayed awake past midnight, relaxing in her reading nook with Willow curled up beside her and Buddy snoring on the bed. As a child, she'd often sit in the same spot, dreaming up tales of wild adventures where everything seemed larger than life. Now, in ways she'd never expected, parts of her life had become just as extraordinary. As she watched Willow's peaceful slumber into the wee hours, her thoughts kept drifting back to what Preston had said.

Over the years, she'd traveled to many places and been in several long-term relationships. Her most recent one had even been on its way toward marriage. But near its ending, she'd had a niggle of doubt, and in retrospect, the warning signs were clear. It took coming back home for her to grow and learn that what she wanted and needed weren't the same. She'd been hesitant to trust her feelings now because of how she'd been hurt in the past. After last night, she knew her feelings for Preston were true and that her heart had never once lied to her.

As her phone rattled on the counter, she swiveled in her seat, reached for it, and glanced at the caller ID. Smiling, she hit accept and switched to the speaker.

"I was just thinking about you, Detective Hills."

"I hope it was in a good way," he replied.

"Very good."

"How are you feeling this morning?"

She leaned forward on the table, pushing her bowl and plate away with her arms. "Not too bad. Surprisingly, I slept well."

"I thought you'd like to know we received word that five of the eggs hatched overnight."

She shot back up. "Are they okay?"

"Yeah. They all survived and are thriving. The sanctuary folks expect all of them to hatch between today and tomorrow. They're coordinating with two other facilities to provide care."

"Wow, just in time. I wonder what will happen to them."

"They'll keep them at the sanctuaries until they find suitable homes."

Willow brushed by her leg, then milled around and meowed for attention. She leaned down and rubbed the cat's cheek, giving her a little love, as happy-go-lucky Buddy padded in looking for his feline friend.

"Off the record, how did things go last night?"

"Grasso and Rollins kept quiet and got lawyers. In searching Grasso's car, we found an ivory-handled knife with what appears to be blood residue between the hilt and the blade. Forensics will analyze it, but the size of the blade is consistent with the medical examiner's findings. It's likely the murder weapon."

Buddy pawed at the kitchen door and whined, signaling his need to go out. She stood and let him loose, watching as he bolted across the porch and into the yard.

"It's hard to believe Nicky was involved in killing her own brother," she said, shutting the door.

"She wasn't directly. At first last night, she wouldn't talk either. But then, she asked to speak with Father Silva. We agreed to that, and after they were on the phone for about thirty minutes, she told us everything."

Olivia grabbed her mug off the table and poured the rest of the coffee down the drain. "Do you think he was lying about the alibi he provided for her?"

Preston's sigh hinted at his unofficial opinion. "Calling a priest a liar is tricky business. Charging him with obstruction for something admitted under the seal of confession is a legal pitfall."

She set her mug on the counter and looked out the window as Buddy chased a squirrel across the yard. "I think they're fond of each other—in a way that goes beyond just friendship. I bet she told him what had happened, and he used the confession to protect her. But you said Nicky wasn't directly involved in Bobby's death?"

"She claimed she hadn't known about Bobby's dealings until the day before they arrived here. Rollins told her he'd recently learned about what Bobby was doing and that he'd tried to put an end to it. But it seems Rollins had been involved all along, and he schemed with Grasso to remove Bobby from the picture. Nicky told us that Bobby had threatened to offload the eggs to another buyer, which didn't sit well with the other two."

"I heard her say that Grasso was double-crossing his

own employer. Now I see why he wanted to frame Sam. He could go back to his boss and claim his driver had stolen the eggs. Meanwhile, he and Rollins sell them and split the proceeds."

"That's an excellent theory, *Deputy Penn*."

She mentally noted to give him a good jab in the side for that later. "But Nicky witnessed Grasso kill Bobby, right?"

"She did. Rollins told her about the meeting on Sunday night. He played on her fears, warning that if she didn't stop her brother and he got caught, then Klein Amusements would go under."

"That sounds like coercion. Why bother bringing her into the fold at all?"

"I suspect we'll find that Rollins was laundering the proceeds through the carnival. The setup offers a convenient front for what they were doing. The operation is constantly on the move. They can pick up and deliver goods easily. There's plenty of shady help to take the fall."

"That makes sense. Nicky, as the manager, could keep the business afloat, which is what they needed for their trade ring to remain under the radar. I can't see her going along with that."

"By placing her at the scene, they didn't leave her much of a choice. Grasso took Bobby's wallet, phone, and keys, then gave them to her. He told her the police would think it was a robbery. But I think his motive was to hand her the evidence that would prove she was an accessory to the murder. She panicked about her finger-prints being on his possessions, so she kept them, planning to dispose of them later."

"Complicit under duress. I would almost feel sorry for her, but that means she must've been the one who planted the credit card in Slammer's bunkroom. He was a convenient patsy. Everyone knew he felt Bobby owed him money. If he didn't take the van to Spring Hills on Sunday night, I wonder where he went."

"When we arrested him, he claimed he was visiting a friend in Front Royal, and his alibi checked out."

"Did you question him about his connection to Grasso?"

"Slammer, aka Kenneth Mackenzie, said that he'd never met him before this week. Grasso approached him about handling some pickups and deliveries. He promised big money, and that's all it took for Mackenzie to agree."

"I'm sure Rollins knew he'd be an easy recruit." Buddy had abandoned his pursuit of the squirrel and was now lolloping across the yard, heading for the side of the house. She turned and went into the living room, wanting to keep an eye on him and make sure he stayed away from the road. "When I first spoke with Nicky in her RV, she received a call on a cell that was buried deep in a drawer. She didn't answer it, saying the caller was a vendor wanting their money. I bet that was Bobby's cell."

"It might've been. We did find his phone in her RV."

She stepped onto the porch, grabbed one of Buddy's

balls off a rocking chair, and went down the steps. "So, is it case closed?"

"For the time being. It'll be up to the Commonwealth's Attorney from here."

"I guess I was wrong about Stash. I still think there was something shady about what he did."

"You weren't that far off base. We searched his bunkroom, and all those boxes he'd stored contained cigarette cartons."

"That's not what I was expecting. Was he reselling them?"

"It looks that way. The cartons had the Virginia tax stamp, but you may find it hard to believe that he's not a licensed distributer. He'll face charges of possession with the intent to distribute."

She tossed the ball straight up and caught it without looking. "He doesn't strike me as the paperwork type. I've heard cigarette trafficking can be lucrative."

"Very. Cartons cost almost three times as much in New York as in Virginia. Black market cigarettes that bear the state's tax stamp are a hot commodity."

Buddy padded his way over to her and heeled by her feet. She set the ball on the ground, then gave him a chin rub as he tilted his head toward her so she could scratch all the right spots.

"You got yourself a bonus arrest," she said.

"With an honorable mention from you."

After patting Buddy's head, she picked up the ball and straightened.

"I take it you're at the station."

"I'm outside in my truck at the station. There's one loose end I have to inquire about before I head in."

"What's that?"

"I owe you a night at the carnival—that is, if you still want to go."

Smiling, she looked down at Buddy, whose eyes were fixed on the ball. "Of course I do. But no rides."

"Agreed. I'll pick you up tonight at eight. And … about last night—I meant what I said."

He didn't have to clarify, and she had things to say to him as well, but not over the phone. That conversation could wait until they were together in private. "I know," she said with a widened smile. "Eight sounds good."

After saying their goodbyes, they ended the call, and she slipped her cell into her pocket. Buddy popped up, whipping his tail into a frenzy as he anticipated her next move. She showed him the ball, slowly drew her arm back, and faked tossing it out into the yard. Taking a few false steps, he stopped when he realized her ruse. Then she spun, launched the ball toward the side of the house, and took off after it. With a bark from Buddy, the chase was on. Within a few strides he zipped by her as she laughed, feeling lighter than she had for some time.

CHAPTER 42

Preston paid the carnival admission for two, handing Tiffany a twenty. She ripped a pair of red tickets off a large roll, tore them in half, and slid the stubs across the counter. He swiped them into his palm, and as Olivia turned toward the midway, he jammed them into the back pocket of her jeans.

"Excuse you," she said, nudging his side.

He shrugged, feigning innocence. "What? I didn't know where else to put them."

Thrill seekers, gourmets, and gamblers packed the grounds. All the rides seemed to be running at once, whooshing and whirling with their bright lights flashing like a kaleidoscope against the night sky. Sweetness and burnt grease filled the air as telltales that cotton candy, funnel cakes, and French fries were on the menu. Jointees barking, delighted screams, and metallic pings created a symphony for children's ears.

"How do you want to approach this?" Preston asked, wrapping his hand around hers.

"I think we just wander around. See what grabs us."

He lifted his hand, raising her arm toward the tarot tent. "How about that?"

"Madame Morgana? Dare we divine what the future holds?"

He redirected his steps, changing her course as well. "I would like to know."

As they neared, hypnotic, haunting Middle Eastern music set a mystical mood for soothsaying. Outside the tent, a young man stood watch, wearing baggy olive-green pants, a blue-and-black checkered shirt, and a red bandana around his neck. A charcoal felt bowler hat straight out of the 1900s sat askew atop his head. He swept the heavy gold tent flap back and ushered them in with a theatrical wave of his hand.

Once they were inside he dropped the flap, sealing them off from the midway. The walk-up music immediately faded, now sounding like it belonged to a distant dream. In its place, an ethereal melody played, evoking an enchanted forest. Along the tent walls, lanterns with flameless candles hung on shepherd-hook poles, flickering as if there was a slight breeze. Straight ahead, Madame Morgana sat with her back turned toward them. A small rectangular wood table with two worn-out chairs opposite of her appeared to be the reading's venue.

"Stop," Morgana said in a deep, sultry voice. "Leave

all doubt, fear, and negativity beyond the line. Once you have freed yourself, then you may proceed."

They both looked down at a 2x4 white board lying on the ground three feet from them. Olivia glanced at Preston as he shook his head, sporting a Mona Lisa smile. She playfully jabbed him in the ribs, silently warning him to behave. Together, they stepped forward over the board and took their seats across from Morgana.

She sat in a modern swivel chair, choosing comfort over old-world charm. Her long, curly black hair reached halfway down her back, and as she spun to face them, multiple gold bangles on both wrists clinked. Wearing a red headscarf and a matching Bohemian blouse, she looked every inch a fortune teller. She was about Olivia's age, and despite the dim lighting, her flawless olive-toned skin was apparent. Her eyes were closed, and after half a minute, she opened them, staring at Olivia with a piercing, dark gaze.

Olivia and Preston sat side by side, close enough that their legs were touching. Even with the denim on denim, the contact still felt intimate. He took hold of her hand, resting her palm on his thigh. Morgana picked up a deck of cards from the beat-up table, then cut them when she appeared attuned to her spirit guides.

"Who is this reading for?" she asked.

"Her," Preston blurted.

Olivia peeked at him and mouthed, "Chicken."

"Very well. Would you like a question answered, or to know your past, present, and future?"

She hadn't prepared for either, but drawing a blank for the former, she chose the latter.

"Select a number between one and ten," Morgana instructed her.

"Four."

Morgana shuffled the cards four times, then cut them into three piles. She slid the top card off each, then gathered the rest and set them off to the side. Turning over the first card, she stared at it for a moment, then eyed Olivia as if reading her soul.

Though it was upside down to Olivia, she could discern a man dressed in blue and red with his hands behind his back and one leg crossed.

"The Hanged Man," Morgana said. "This is your past. To grow, you've had to let go of old patterns. What once was essential is no longer even in your life. You've come from a different place. Your past has charted a new direction for you. For a time, you lived suspended in the in-between. You are not as you used to be. Your course was uncertain, but now all has been set in motion."

That struck a little close to home. She hadn't been taking Morgana's schtick too seriously, as she was predisposed to think everyone got the same general readings. She glanced at Preston, who gave her a faint smile and rubbed her hand with his thumb.

Morgana turned over the second card. It was mostly yellow, with an image of a woman and a lion. She took a deep breath, nodded, and closed her eyes. "Your present has drawn the Strength card. You have come through great trials and have faced many threats. Your inner knowing has been your greatest ally, fiercely protecting you. By trusting in yourself, you have risen while others have fallen. You are ruled by your heart. When logic insists you do one thing, you close your eyes, moving toward where you feel guided."

Olivia shifted in her seat, feeling a bit exposed. Morgana's spot-on sense for what she'd been through overshadowed the fun-and-games nature of the reading.

Morgana picked up the last card and looked at it for a moment before setting it on the table. Keeping the face covered, she slid it forward. When she revealed the draw, Olivia didn't need her glasses to decipher the upside-down print. A skeleton in black armor rode on a white horse. In his hand, he held a black flag with a white rose, and underneath the image was the word "Death." Preston squeezed her hand as she tensed and slid to the edge of her seat, waiting for Morgana to say something.

"This is your future. In the beginning is the end, and in the end is the beginning. All is transformed. Nothing ever remains. What has worked will fail. With transformation comes great pain. This is the way, the nature of life. Two things cannot occupy the same space. One must leave before the new can come in. Something must die before something can live again."

Morgana dropped her palms on the table and lowered her chin to her chest as if exhausted.

Olivia stared at the Death card and leaned forward a bit. "Would that be *something* or *someone*?"

Morgana let out a deep breath. Then she lifted her head, keeping her eyes closed as pain etched across her brow. "Madame Morgana has spoken."

Olivia and Preston exchanged a quizzical look and rose slowly, supposing the reading was over.

Morgana bent down to her side for a second, then sat upright and placed a coffee can on the table. "Tips are always appreciated."

Olivia glanced at Preston as he shook his head, looking like he wasn't about to contribute to the rainy-day fund. She widened her eyes and tilted her head toward the can as a polite ask. He sighed, released her hand, and pulled his wallet out of his back pocket. He picked out two one-dollar bills and reached forward, but she grabbed his arm, shooting him a disapproving look. He exchanged them for a five, showing it to her for her approval. Smiling, she let go, allowing him to deposit the tip. Then together they crossed back over the 2x4 board of disbelief and left the tent, ushered out by an ethereal melody of dark, minor chords.

Once out in the open, jovial banter from a passing group of teens broke the moody tent's spell. She'd never put much stock in tarot readings, considering them mostly as a curiosity. Though Morgana's words seemed tailor-made, she took them with a grain of salt, opting to view the disturbing Death card akin to rain on a wedding day.

Preston wrapped his arm around her shoulder,

drawing her close to him. "You don't believe any of that, do you?"

"I was okay with the first two cards, but I'd rather she had pulled the lottery card for my future."

That earned her a chuckle. "I don't think that's part of the deck."

"It should be. And remember, it was your idea that we do that."

"Madame Morgana doesn't know more about your future than you do."

"Maybe."

As they strolled toward the game stands, she scanned the grounds, taking in the sights, and spotted A.J. standing in front of the snow cone trailer.

"Look, there's A.J.," she said. "I want to go say hi. You study up on which games you think you can win. I'll just be a second."

"Take your time."

She hurried across the midway, bobbing and weaving her way through the foot traffic that had no natural flow. As A.J. turned to leave the counter, she caught his attention, calling out, "Hey there, stranger."

"Liv, delightful surprise."

She pointed to his hand. "How did you know that's exactly what I wanted? You're the best. I haven't had a snow cone in ages."

He looked at the red snow cone in his right hand, then at the blue one in his left, offering her the latter. "Oh, okay. Sure. You can have this one."

"Kidding. I saw you over here and just came to say hello."

Lowering his arm, he looked around. "Are you here with Preston?"

She hadn't yet told him about what she'd been through, figuring it could wait a day. Tonight was only for fun, friends, and new beginnings. "Yes. And you?"

He hesitated, glancing down for a moment. "Soph."

"That's great," she said without missing a beat. She jabbed her thumb toward the far end of the midway. "Do you remember the time when we were stuck on the Ferris wheel at the state fair?"

"Of course. You practically lost your mind, worried we'd have to climb down from it."

Her jaw dropped in disbelief. "That wasn't *me*. It was *you* who thought that."

"Oh, yeah. You're right," he teased with a toothy grin. "Well, we both got down, and look at us now."

"Indeed. Do you remember the promise we made to each other?"

"Absolutely. I've been sweating it out. Almost every day since then, I've prayed, 'Please Lord, send a patient, loving soul into her life.'"

She feigned outrage and pretended like she was going to punch him in the gut.

He raised his arms in surrender. "Joking. Don't hurt me. I bruise easily." Then he stepped closer, softening his smile with sincerity. "I think someone else already has your heart, but I would've felt honored to have kept my promise to you."

They held each other's gaze for a moment as she wrapped her hand around his wrist. "I think someone has your heart too. And I would feel the same way." Releasing him, she looked around. "Where's Soph anyway?"

He gestured with the red snow cone toward the carousel. "Over there. Come say hi."

"No, I'll let you go. I just saw you and wanted to say hello. You two have fun."

"You and Preston too. Stop by the office some day this week, and we'll go to lunch."

"Yeah, that sounds good. I'll call you. I was thinking—we haven't had a picnic at Lake Crystal for a while."

"That would be wonderful—and it's about time."

They exchanged a friendly kiss on the cheek, then went their separate ways. She headed back to where she'd left Preston, but instead spotted him at Derek's game stand. As she neared, Derek caught her eye and swept his hat off his head.

"Howdy, ma'am. I was just talking with the sheriff here about how he wrangled up some nasty cowpokes."

By his twang and theatrics, she figured he was still undercover. "Cowboy, how's business tonight?"

He looked up and down the row of stands, then plopped his hat back on. With no one in earshot, he lowered his voice and slipped out of character. "Slow. I was trying to get something useful from the detective here, but he's leaving me high and dry."

She glanced at Preston. "I didn't realize you knew each other."

"We talked last night," Derek said.

"Are you staying on with the carnival?" Olivia asked.

"No need to. With the supply side of the trade ring dismantled, the buyers will be out of business for a while. Hopefully forever. With no supply, there's nothing to buy. That's the end of the story. It's on to the next assignment."

"Do you have something in mind?" she said.

"I'm working on a few things," he replied with a ten-gallon smile.

"Fair enough. Any word on what's going to happen to Klein Amusements without Bobby and Nicky?"

"We had a camp meeting this morning. Nicky's father is joining the carnival for the next show. Steady Eddie and Art are teaming up, handling everything for the rest of this week. Rumor is that could become a permanent arrangement. The old man has got to be disappointed in his kids, but the show must go on. After slough on Sunday, I'm leaving."

"Cover story intact?" she asked.

"Yes, ma'am," he replied, tipping his hat. He picked three blue darts up off the counter and handed them to Preston as a couple walked up to the stand.

Preston held his palm out toward Olivia. "Do you want to do the honors?"

"No, you go ahead."

As he lined up his first throw, she glanced around, trying to spot A.J. and Sophia, but saw Mack instead. He was escorting an older woman on one arm, with Ryan walking on her other side.

What the heck? She tapped Preston's shoulder. "I'll be right back."

She headed straight across the midway to intercept the trio as they made their way slowly through the crowd. On seeing her, Mack lit up with a wide smile, stopped, and said a few words to the woman. Ryan then took over the escort duties as Mack walked over to where she was standing.

"You're not limping as much today."

"The swelling has gone down, and I'm wearing a brace."

"I see. Did you bring your mother to the carnival?"

His laugh flew out quicker than a hiccup. "I wish. That's Grace Heller. Ryan's grandmother." He pressed his lips together for a moment before nodding. "After what we went through, and in the spirit of strengthening our new bond, I'll give you a peek behind the scenes. Ryan's parents hired me to find him. He had a falling out with his family over some business practices at his father's company."

"Is that related to the failed tailings dam in Brazil?"

"Please come work for me. How and why you know that is the only résumé you need."

"Tempting," she replied with a playful shrug. "I just

had my future predicted, and I'm not sure yet what it all means."

He thinned his smile, looking as sincere as she'd ever seen him. "I'll wait. But you're correct. Ryan has been out of touch with his family for over a year. His parents felt remorseful about the split, and they were concerned about his well-being. I tracked down some of his old friends, and I found one who was still in contact with him. That's how I'd learned he'd joined a carnival. I thought you were supposed to run away to a circus, not a carnival. Anyway, I only knew it was on the East Coast. Prior to coming here, I've been to Georgia, Florida, Maryland, and North Carolina searching for him. The only thing I'd achieved was getting permanent acid reflux from eating deep-fried fare for the past three months. I was about to give up on Klein Amusements and search elsewhere until you told me he was with this band of merry carnies."

"Showmen. Show women. What's the deal with his grandmother?"

"Grace adores Ryan. He's her only grandchild. Apparently, she's involved in a women's church group in Gore. She told a priest there about how the family was looking for him. Turns out this priest ministers to … show people, and he said he'd keep an eye out. If he found him, he'd try to put Ryan in contact with her. They had a meeting set up, but the young Mr. Heller backed out at the last minute. I thought if I brought her here tonight, maybe that would do the trick."

She glanced at Ryan and Grace as they neared the exit. Now the argument she'd overheard between him and Father Silva made perfect sense. "It seems to have worked. I better let you catch up to them."

He extended his hand, and they shook.

"Let's keep in touch," he said.

"Let's."

As they parted, she heard someone call out her name. When she turned, she spotted Aunt Bea waving at her.

She walked the short distance to the kiddie pond, where two children were deep in thought over which of the yellow duckies to pick. "Hi, Aunt Bea."

"Hey there, yourself."

"It's a beautiful night."

"It sure is. I didn't know if I'd see you again around here. Did you hear about Nicky?"

Olivia just nodded, not wanting to divulge how she knew. "Cowboy told me that Steady Eddie and Art may become co-managers. What does that mean for you?"

Aunt Bea casually placed her fists on her hips. "Those two know what they're doing. Maybe not so much with the books, but Nicky's dad can hire someone to handle that. We need bosses who understand how things work around here. I'll probably stay on. These people are family to me, and I care about them all."

"I saw Tiffany manning the ticket booth."

"Yep. It's easier on her. She shouldn't be on her feet the whole day. I'm sure going to miss her."

"She's leaving?"

"Moving in with her aunt earlier than planned. It turns out the baby's father didn't even know she was pregnant. She told him yesterday on the phone, and he proposed on the spot."

"Wow. Did she accept?"

Aunt Bea nodded, then pointed her finger, as if Tiffany was standing in front of her. "But I told her, you make him do it proper—get down on a knee and give you a ring. She deserves that."

Olivia wondered for a hot second why Tiffany had gone into Bobby's RV, but then dismissed the thought, as it was no longer a concern. Tiffany's life seemed to be turning around, and maybe her fortunes would change. She'd learned in writing her column that not everything needed an explanation. Sometimes, mysteries remain as such, leaving the curious to speculate.

"That she does," Olivia said.

"What about you and that tall drink of water who keeps looking your way? I wasn't sure if I liked him at first, but for a cop, I think he's okay."

Olivia glanced back at Preston, who was leaning against the counter of Derek's stand. "Who knows what the future will bring?"

Aunt Bea extended her arms and wrapped her in a crushing hug. "He likes you. I can tell these things."

As they separated, Olivia nodded. "I think he does."

"I want to see you next year when we come through. Stop by and say hi. You'll need a new bracelet."

"I'll look forward to it."

After they exchanged a friendly goodbye, Olivia headed back toward Preston. As she neared, he met her halfway.

"I didn't win," he said. "I think all the games are rigged anyway."

He slipped his arm across her shoulders, and she wrapped hers around his waist.

"The night is still young," she said. "You know, as I kid, I would never leave the carnival until I'd won a stuffed animal."

"Then so shall it be," he replied, pulling her in closer.

The carousel whirled, playing its organ music, and gleeful screams from those on Blackbird's Revenge added to the carnival's festive din. The Ferris wheel's colorful, bright lights flashed, and the tempting, nutty aroma of freshly popped popcorn permeated the air.

The sights, sounds, and smells of the midway took her back to her childhood. Though she was now grown, that little girl, brimming with wonder and curiosity about the world, still lived in her. The carnival was like a thread, connecting her to the past. Ever the same, the familiarity felt like spending time with an old friend.

Certain moments in her life had been etched in her memory on otherwise ordinary days. She would always remember when Angela called, offering her the job at the paper. She was on a weekend visit home, having lunch with Paige at Jillian's Cafe. When the call ended she and Paige stood and hugged, promising they would be friends forever no matter where their roads took them. She would always remember the last time her mother told her how proud she was of her. They were driving on a sunny summer day to get homemade frozen custard from a roadside stand when her mother said those precious words, just a few months before she died.

Olivia glanced at Preston, who was wearing his brown denim shirt with white pearl snaps and vintage-washed blue jeans. Then, looking up, she noticed a star near the rising moon that twinkled brilliantly, as if it were filled with glee. Most days in her life felt the same, tending to responsibilities and following routines. Now, this otherwise ordinary Friday in May would become engraved in her memory. On a perfect spring night, under the bright lights, she would always remember falling in love with Preston when the carnival came.

The End

ACKNOWLEDGMENTS

I'm deeply grateful for all those who have supported me in the writing of this book.

Thank you to my brilliant editor Serena Clarke for all your work in making this story the best it could be. Your continued encouragement, guidance, and support are appreciated beyond words.

Thank you to my wonderful proofreader LaVerne Clark for your painstaking attention to detail, instruction, and insightful feedback. You always have my back and have saved the day on countless occasions.

Thank you to Robin Vuchnich for your exquisite cover design.

Thank you to the welcoming and supportive community of Sisters in Crime.

Thank you to all my readers and to all the bloggers who share and celebrate my writing, especially to Dru Ann Love. Your support makes these stories possible.

A LETTER FROM KATHLEEN

Dear Reader,

Thank you so much for reading *When the Carnival Came*. I've always enjoyed the fun, the magic, and the little mysteries tucked into every carnival, and I wanted to share some of that same wonder with you here. I hope Olivia's latest adventure felt like stepping into that world right beside her.

If you'd like updates on new releases, a peek into my writing life, and the occasional special promotion, you can sign up for my newsletter on my website. I'll never share your e-mail address, and you can unsubscribe at any time.

If you enjoyed *When the Carnival Came*, I'd be truly grateful if you left a review on your favorite retail site or review platform. Reviews are one of the best ways to help other mystery lovers discover my books.

I always enjoy hearing from readers, so please feel free to visit my website, drop me a note, or say hello on social media. Being part of this wonderful community of mystery lovers is truly one of the joys of writing these stories.

With gratitude,
Kathleen

www.kathleenbaileyauthor.com
Instagram: @cozycrimewriter

WORKS BY KATHLEEN BAILEY

OLIVIA PENN MYSTERY SERIES

Where the Light Shines Through

Silence Says the Most

Under the Cocoon Moon

When the Carnival Came

Without a Shadow of Doubt

The Case of the Broken Heart (Prequel short story)

ABOUT THE AUTHOR

Kathleen Bailey is the award-winning author of *The Olivia Penn Mystery Series*. She writes mysteries with heart and humor that keep to the traditional and cozy sides of crime. For over twenty years, she worked as a pediatric physical therapist with children who have special needs, drawing on degrees in English, psychology, and physical therapy. She now writes in Virginia with her feline assistant, who insists on supervising every draft. When she's not writing, Kathleen can usually be found covered in cat hair, surrounded by far too many sticky notes, and plotting new twists to keep readers guessing. She is a member of Sisters in Crime. Visit her online at kathleen-baileyauthor.com.

www.ingramcontent.com/pod-product-compliance
Lightning Source LLC
Chambersburg PA
CBHW061542190726
48289CB00004B/1136